STATION K-I-L-L

The Complete

BLACK MASK®

Cases of Jerry Tracy

Volume 3: 1937–40

THEODORE A. TINSLEY

illustrations by Arthur Rodman Bowker

cover by John Drew

BLACK MASK

2024

BLACK MASK® is a registered trademark of Steeger Properties, LLC. "Jerry Tracy" is a trademark of Steeger Properties, LLC. Authorized and produced under license.

Texts and illustrations © 2024 Steeger Properties, LLC. All rights reserved.

"Murder Is News" originally appeared in the August 1937 issue of *Black Mask* magazine (Vol. 20, No. 6). Copyright © 1937 by Pro-Distributors Publishing Company, Inc. Copyright renewed © 1964 and assigned to Steeger Properties, LLC. All rights reserved.

"No More Limericks" originally appeared in the April 1938 issue of *Black Mask* magazine (Vol. 21, No. 2). Copyright © 1938 by Pro-Distributors Publishing Company, Inc. Copyright renewed © 1965 and assigned to Steeger Properties, LLC. All rights reserved.

"Make It Murder" originally appeared in the September 1938 issue of *Black Mask* magazine (Vol. 21, No. 6). Copyright © 1938 by Pro-Distributors Publishing Company, Inc. Copyright renewed © 1965 and assigned to Steeger Properties, LLC. All rights reserved.

"Station K-I-L-L" originally appeared in the November 1938 issue of *Black Mask* magazine (Vol. 21, No. 8). Copyright © 1938 by Pro-Distributors Publishing Company, Inc. Copyright renewed © 1965 and assigned to Steeger Properties, LLC. All rights reserved.

"Guide to Murder" originally appeared in the June 1939 issue of *Black Mask* magazine (Vol. 22, No. 3). Copyright © 1939 by Pro-Distributors Publishing Company, Inc. Copyright renewed © 1966 and assigned to Steeger Properties, LLC. All rights reserved.

"My Candle Burns" originally appeared in the April 1940 issue of *Black Mask* magazine (Vol. 23, No. 1). Copyright © 1940 by Pro-Distributors Publishing Company, Inc. Copyright renewed © 1967 and assigned to Steeger Properties, LLC. All rights reserved.

"About the Author" copyright © 2022, 2024 by Will Murray. All rights reserved.

No part of this book may be reproduced or utilized in any form or by any means, electronic or mechanical, without permission in writing from the publisher.

Visit STEEGERBOOKS.COM for more books like this.

Table of Contents

Murder Is News

*Jerry Tracy, Broadway columnist, has a
murder on his hands—and no corpse!*

AT PARK AVENUE and 49th the dripping taxicab slowed and began to creep patiently through rainy darkness toward the curb in front of the Waldorf. There were other cars ahead and progress was slow.

Edgar Drake leaned forward on the worn leather cushion and murmured, "Well? Well?" in a whining, unpleasant tone. He paid his driver the exact fare recorded by the meter. Then he pursed his lips, frowned, and added a dime. He was a square-chinned, square-fingered man with pouched eyelids and a middle-aged droop to his cheeks. But there was no fat on his stomach. He had the lean grayness of a timber wolf. His thick, grizzled hair, his eyebrows, even his face was gray. Cartoonists loved Edgar Drake; he was the perfect symbol of his own vast empire of industry and finance.

As he stepped under the sidewalk canopy, the hotel door-man assisted him with alacrity. The man's alacrity was born of fear. Drake was easily annoyed and a complaint might mean the loss of the doorman's job. He topped Drake's head with an umbrella and took charge of the millionaire's bulky briefcase with a deft motion.

"Yes, Mr. Drake. Horrible weather, sir."

"Mmm."

The doorman ignored hotel rules and continued across the spacious lobby to the desk. The clerk straightened like a ramrod and pasted on his glazed smile. A bellhop took the damp brief-case.

"While I was out I arranged for my reservation on the *Queen Mary*. Have the tickets arrived?"

"Yes, Mr. Drake. I surely hope it stops raining before midnight."

"Mmm."

An elevator lifted the millionaire to his tower room with no

apparent motion. Drake stared unseeingly at the operator and the bellhop. It wasn't that he ignored them; he was completely oblivious to their presence. There was mean, brooding uneasiness in his eyes. The look stayed with him all the way to his room; until the bellhop coughed gently. Then Drake pursed his lips as he had in the taxi and fished for a coin.

"Thank you, sir."

The bellhop closed himself out and hurried back across a soundless corridor rug to the waiting elevator. He said under his breath, "Nuts." He held out his palm and the operator grinned.

"Same old dime, eh?"

"I had to cough to get it."

"To think a skinflint like that is married to the most beautiful dame in the U.S. A laugh, huh?"

"She wasn't laughing the last time he had her here," the bell-hop said. "If I was Pauline Drake, I'd poison the bum. I'll bet he's got an army of dicks keeping tabs on her up in Westchester while he's in Europe making another billion."

"You think she's playing around?"

"She's a fool if she doesn't."

FOOL.... THE SAME ugly word rose in Anne Leslie's frightened mind as she peered outward at black, pouring rain through a curtained window-pane of Edgar Drake's West-chester mansion. Anne was Mrs. Drake's secretary. Blond, slim and very pretty. She shivered as she turned from the window and stared at a framed photograph of Pauline Drake. It was a calm, resolute face, one that was ageless, flawlessly lovely. Even in a photograph the dark hair and deep, lustrous eyes seemed vividly alive. Eyes that a previous marriage, a tumultuous life, a grown son and the long years had not harried.

Uneasiness tightened Anne's blue eyes. Two hours had passed since Pauline Drake had driven stealthily away through drumming rain, unobserved by servants. The little coupé was supposedly locked in Mrs. Drake's private garage. Only Anne knew where she had gone. The beat of her heart was quick, jumpy, like the gusty rattle of the rain against the window.

She remembered Edgar Drake's lean gray face and his stubby, powerful hands. She thought of David Corning, the lawyer; of his dry, unemotional voice, always a shade dryer when he talked to Pauline, perhaps to hide the flame in his hungry brown eyes. She thought of young Tony Pedley, playing a jazz trumpet in a nightclub orchestra as a bread-and-butter substitute for a career as a surgeon. Tony, who had begged his heedless mother not to marry Edgar Drake.... Who hated his stepfather so bitterly that he had given up college and career rather than accept a penny of Drake's grudging money. The whole thing was a dreadful mess. And very definitely dangerous....

IN THE CLUB Pom-Pom the orchestra men were arranging chairs and setting up music racks on the raised dais. It was not quite ten and it was raining viciously outside. A few out-of-towners were dining and drinking, unaware that the Pom-Pom before midnight was a waste of time and money. Tony Pedley was fingering the mouthpiece of his trumpet, his dark eyes bleak and unhappy. He stiffened as he heard voices behind him.

"I see where old man Drake is sailing for Europe tonight."

"Yeah? The boat should sink!"

"Nice chance to toss him a life-preserver—and make a dime!"

There was unpleasant laughter in which Tony Pedley joined. He didn't have to hide his rancor against the millionaire because none of the bandsmen was aware that he was Pauline Drake's son. Only Fred Hammer knew that, Fred was the owner of the Club Pom-Pom and a grand guy. He had kept Tony's secret and had put pressure on the band leader to make a place for Tony and his college trumpet. Fred was a stockholder in Drake Utilities. It amused him to think that part of the profits from the old skinflint's money empire should be indirectly supporting a hated stepson whom Drake had kicked into social oblivion.

Tony glanced at the clock over the band platform. He stopped smiling abruptly. He laid his shining instrument down and picked up his hat. The trap drummer glanced at him curiously.

"Hey, where you goin'?"

"I—I've got to get a breath of fresh air."

"You mean fresh rain! S'matter? You look sick."

"Stomach. I'll be right back."

He went out by the front entrance to avoid passing Fred Hammer's tiny office in the rear. But Fred was up front talking to the hat-check girl, and when Tony saw him it was too late to turn back. He told the club owner the same thing he had told the trap drummer.

Hammer nodded sympathetically. "O.K. Make it snappy, kid. Dig him up an umbrella, Evelyn."

"Never mind," Tony said faintly. "The cold rain'll feel good."

He hunched his shoulders and strode doggedly out into the downpour. Hammer glanced at the hat-check girl.

"Can you beat that for a screwy runout? Must be dame trouble."

"Not that lad," Evelyn said snappishly. There was dim resentment in her voice as she ran a smooth palm approvingly along her tight black-satin hip. "He's the only guy in the band that hasn't made a pass at me. If you ask me, he needs a tonic—or something. There's something eating at that guy and it isn't woman trouble. If he ever breaks down, I'll be the one who breaks him."

Hammer chuckled and turned away. He went back to his office.

A block away in the driving rain, Tony Pedley wiped a tremulous hand across his wet face. There was a drug-store on the opposite corner and a taxi-cab parked at the curb. Tony's eyes gleamed.

"Yes, Mr. Drake," he whispered to himself in a vicious mimicry of servility. "Yes, Mis-ter Drake!"

AT THAT PRECISE instant in a tower room at the Waldorf a waiter from the bar was repeating the same whining formula. He backed out deferentially with an empty tray and closed the door. Drake took a meager sip of his highball and then began pacing up and down the room. His quick strides seemed to release some of the suspicious rage that had been bottled up in him all evening. A spot of red came into the gray cheeks. There was a small photograph of his wife propped on the bureau and the sight of it halted him with clenched fists.

"Damn you!" he whispered.

He studied the dark, lovely eyes, the half-smiling mouth. He read a jeer into that smile. The picture was like Pauline herself—a smooth enigma. If only he could know definitely what she was thinking, planning, perhaps doing. Infidelity was something he could take care of very nicely. He'd already attended to it a dozen times—mentally—with the aid of fifty million dollars.

"If I thought," he told the picture with slow, whispered fury, "that you and that lickspittle lawyer of mine would dare to use my absence to—"

He turned and slammed down his highball glass on the polished surface of a desk. The impact slopped some of the liquor against the ivory telephone. Picking up the instrument, he called the number of his Westchester mansion.

He scowled as he heard the clear impersonal tone of Anne Leslie, his wife's secretary. He didn't like Anne. He hadn't hired her. He hadn't even been able to fire her when he had sensed a growing intimacy between the two women. Anne Leslie's continued presence in the Westchester estate was one of Pauline's few triumphs against her husband's will.

"Put my wife on. Tell her I want to talk to her."

"I'm sorry, Mr. Drake. Mrs. Drake is not in just now."

"Not in? Where is she?"

"She took her personal car and went out for a brief drive."

"Where?"

"Nowhere in particular, I believe." Anne's voice hesitated. "Mrs. Drake had a sick headache. She thought the—er—a drive would make her feel better."

"How long has she been gone?"

Again the secretary's voice seemed to hesitate. "About ten minutes, I should say. Is there any particular message I can take?"

"No. I merely wanted to chat with her. I'll be busy from now on till sailing time. You might, if you will—" his voice sneered, "—give her my love."

"Yes, sir."

He cradled the phone grimly. His eyes peered outward at the rain-swept roofs of Manhattan. He knew Pauline's fastidious distaste for any kind of personal inconvenience. She hated to be out in rain. And she never had headaches. Lies! Beginning the very moment he turned his back. By God, before he could even reach the pier!

Tortured with jealousy, he tried to decide what to do. His indecision was cut short by a ring of the telephone. For an instant he thought it might be Anne, calling back in panic to fashion a more plausible alibi for his roving wife. But the voice was that of a man. A queer, muffled voice that he had never heard before.

"Is this Mr. Drake? Mr. Edgar Drake?"

"Yes. What do you want?"

"I don't want a damned thing. I'm just telling you something I thought you'd like to know. Your wife is two-timing you with her favorite boy friend. Right here in Manhattan. Right now."

"Wait a minute! Who is this talking? Are you one of my private—"

"Shut up and listen! She's in your town house on East 56th. She arrived here half an hour ago in her own coupé. The boy friend came in a taxi. He's been in there with her ten minutes. He—"

"Wait! Are you absolutely sure about this? If you're telling me the truth, I'll be willing to pay you—"

"Save your dime, Mister."

The wire clicked and went dead. Drake jiggled the hook furiously. "I've just had an important telephone call that I want traced at once," he yelled at the operator. "I've got to know where the call came from."

"I'm sorry, sir. The party has disconnected. We cannot trace it but I'll call the Central office if—I don't think it would help, though, Mr. Drake."

"Forget it," Drake snapped.

The surge of anger left him abruptly. He didn't want any questions, alarms. Not yet. He felt suddenly as cold as ice, hard as chrome steel. He jammed on his hat and slipped into his cheap belted raincoat. With steady fingers he reached under the bed and drew out a small alligator bag. It was the only piece of baggage left in the room. All the rest was already on the Cunard pier, perhaps by this time stowed away in his Deck A suite on the *Queen Mary*. The thought of the ship and a profitable European business trip made him smile bleakly. He took a .38 automatic from the alligator bag and slipped it into his pocket.

He was starting for the door when he saw a newspaper lying neatly folded on a chair. The bold black title seemed to leer at him, damp and inky: *Daily Planet*. For an instant Drake's puckered eyes widened and went utterly expressionless. Then he spread out the paper and riffled the pages with feverish haste. He was looking for the one thing that *Planet* readers always read first. The sight of the familiar double column drew a mean, barking laugh from the millionaire:

Broadway in Person
by
Jerry Tracy

Drake stared at the most famous scandal column in the world until the print blurred under his thoughtful gaze. The gun in his pocket seemed suddenly silly. He had overlooked the one perfect revenge. To a flashy little genius of innuendo like Jerry Tracy, Pauline would be the gift of a lifetime. Only there'd be no need for innuendo. Jerry Tracy would write this story as an eyewitness reporter. The Most Beautiful Woman in America…. Drake could see the glamorous Pauline, stripped and dishonored on a million breakfast tables. A dirty laugh for anyone with two cents to buy.

He pawed through a Manhattan directory and found Tracy's number.

He thought, "I'll make her name stink from California to Maine."

The soft, faraway *burr-burr* of the signal bell was the most pleasant sound Drake had ever heard in fifty-two years of living....

JERRY TRACY GRUNTED with annoyance as he heard the loud jangle of his penthouse telephone bell. His fingers kept busily picking away at his portable typewriter. He had a weekly radio gossip spot on a national network, and that meant advance copies for the agency and the sponsor, plus a copy for the cautious studio censor.

The phone continued to ring.

Ordinarily Butch, his bodyguard-valet, whom he used for everything but guarding him, would have answered it. Or McNulty, Jerry's Chinese paragon of kitchen magic. But tonight Butch was out seconding a friend in a prelim bout at the Garden; and McNulty was down at Pell Street on some involved ceremonial business that had to do with ancestors and rice. Jerry swore, grinned a little, and got up. He could no more resist answering the call than a fireman could ignore an alarm gong. A lot of his best socko items came over the wire from disgruntled servants and amateur busybodies.

He slip-slopped in flat bedroom slippers to the ivory-inlaid phone stand, his silk dressing gown fluttering behind his hard-packed, naked body.

"Yeah?"

"I want to speak to Mr. Jerry Tracy. Jerry Tracy, of the *Daily Planet*."

"Right here."

"This is Edgar Drake speaking from the Hotel Waldorf. I've got to see you at once on a matter of the utmost importance."

"Huh? I didn't quite get that. Do you mind repeating?"

Tracy's bored eyes were suddenly bright, his face tense and alert. He had recognized the name but he wanted to listen again to make sure. Edgar Drake. Drake Utilities. A financier whose business and private life was a constant pain in the neck to newspapermen. Drake didn't even give interviews to ship newsmen. Tracy had taken it for granted that the sly old wolf was already stowed away in his suite on the *Queen Mary,* waiting for the whistle to toot at midnight. And here he was calling the town's biggest dirt-sifter, his voice an undertone of nervous, racing eagerness.

"Go ahead, Mr. Drake. Shoot!"

Incredulity came into Tracy's eyes as he listened. Then a hard exultation.

"Let me get this straight. Your town house on East 56th. Rear courtyard. Fifteen minutes."

"I promise you the biggest dirt story of your career," the financier's voice whispered chokingly. "An eye-witness story, do you understand? I'm giving you the exclusive tip. I want it dirty! And funny!"

"I'll be there," Tracy said and hung up. He added softly, "Nice guy!"

He kicked off his flat slippers and sent the dressing gown sailing like a silken parachute. He dove naked into his bedroom and began to haul on garments. In ten minutes he was fully dressed. But it took another ten minutes of whistling and phoning before he could snare an empty cab and race uptown. A downpour like this was a hack driver's paradise. Tracy left the cab at the corner of 56th and plodded east through the slant of the rain.

Drake's town house was a bleak stone relic in a park-like expanse set back from the sidewalk behind a tall grilled fence. Jerry whistled faintly as he took a look. The massive front door and every one of the windows was tightly boarded up.

There were no cars parked along the street and the soaking rain had mopped up pedestrians. Not a remote twinkle of light or life in the house. The thing had all the earmarks of a practical joke. But Tracy moved like a swift phantom past the grillwork of the fence, looking for the small gate Drake had told him he would find unlocked. There was no fake about Drake's voice, nor the venom with which he had gasped out his wife's name. Tracy knew jealous rage when he heard it.

He found the gate and tried it. It was unlocked. He moved cautiously down a broad stone driveway to a dim courtyard in the rear. The back of the mansion was no different from the front. Boarded up and black from cellar to roof. No sign of Edgar Drake anywhere.

The courtyard was walled in the rear and there was a trades-man's gate leading into 55th. This rear gate, too, was unlocked; and Tracy discovered with grim elation that there was an empty coupé parked at the curb outside. The car was Pauline's. No doubt about that at all! She'd been sap enough to use a personal car with a monogram.

Excitement quickened Tracy's pulse. With his shoulders soaked and his hat-brim spilling water, he examined swiftly the boarded windows of the basement extension. That coupé parked in the rear meant Pauline! The unlocked front gate meant the vindictive Drake! Both of them inside the house somewhere—a gray-faced front-page millionaire stalking the loveliest woman in America, a glamorous beauty whose love he had tried to buy as he would a chain of railroads. Tracy could smell dynamite in the set-up.

The first two basement windows were immovable. But the third was the pay-off. The boarded protection had been loosened on one side, so that it could be pried easily open to the space of almost a foot. Tracy squirmed between the rain-soaked boards and the window sill.

The window lifted easily. It was pitch-black inside and utterly soundless. Tracy cupped a quick match flame in his palm and lowered himself lightly to a concrete floor. The place was the laundry-room, with tubs and dryers and gaunt curtain stretchers against the wall. Beyond was a kitchen and a pantry, and a short passageway that gave access to a rear flight of stairs. Tracy ascended noiselessly and began to prowl through the house. He used matches sparingly, blowing them out after a hasty, pivoting glance.

The house was like a musty tomb. Draped furniture sent long circling shadows as Jerry's matches flared. White muslin covered pictures and mirrors. There was a pierced archway in the front hall and Tracy knew enough of architectural relics like this, to guess that beyond him was a formal reception parlor, opening from the high-stooped stone entry at the front of the mansion.

He listened but he was unable to hear the faintest sound. Then his fifth match flared—and he saw the quiet face of Edgar Drake.

The millionaire lay flat on his back. There was a knife in his chest, driven hilt-deep. Both knees were drawn stiffly up and both hands had twisted themselves behind his back-tilted head, so that he looked like a man lazily floating… on a blood-drenched Chinese rug… floating with a knife blade deep in his chest.

The match flame burned Tracy's damp fingers and he struck another, moving slowly toward a tall floor lamp, the only uncovered object in the room. A black cord on the floor connected it with a wall socket and he stepped over the cord with exaggerated care. The click of the button was the only sound in the house. Tracy glanced toward the broad, curving staircase out in the main hall and back again toward the body.

He examined Drake with grimly slitted eyes. The knife was a little off center in the dead man's chest, probably smack through the heart. The handle looked shiny and clean. No telling about tricky things like prints, but Tracy was willing to bet that gloved hands had driven that blade into the unfortunate millionaire. The rug was rumpled enough to indicate some slight evidence of struggle. There was a bruise on the back of Drake's skull.

Tracy didn't see the bruise until he had moved the tautly clasped hands. He didn't touch the flesh, just jerked gently at the cuffed sleeves. As the left hand moved, a tiny black object was exposed on the rug. Tracy stared at it a long minute before he picked it up. He crouched quietly and peered into both ears of the dead man. Neither ear was plugged.

He examined the queer object, holding it carefully in his palm. The thing had undoubtedly been dropped by the murderer, but there was scant chance of finding a print on it or of Tracy's marring the clue with a print of his own. The thing was a rubber ear stopple, the sort of contrivance worn by swimmers to keep out water. Black rubber, with a red dot on the outside surface. Tracy made reasonably sure that Drake hadn't dropped it by searching the pockets of the corpse with swift efficiency for a duplicate.

He started to put the rubber disc into his own wallet, then changed his mind. Instead, he slipped it inside the tight leather sweatband of his soaked gray fedora. He didn't stop to analyze his reason for this extraordinary precaution. When a hunch came to Tracy he always followed it. He kept his eyes and his ears centered on the pierced doorway and the broad staircase in the soundless corridor.

The killing must have been done damned recently. The body was warm and Jerry had lost no time. The murderer must be still in the house. Into Tracy's mind came a quick picture of David Corning, the millionaire's good-looking, athletically built lawyer. Drake's venomous voice on the wire had hinted at his attorney without actually naming him. Tracy knew he was no physical match for Corning, but he felt no fear. Pauline and Corning—upstairs—wondering who had turned on the lamp in the reception room, rigid with guilt. The biggest, most sensational murder story in Tracy's whole career! He felt able to cope with twenty Cornings.

He was close to the foot of the broad staircase when he saw the footprint.

It was on a white, fleecy rug, so vaguely defined that he dropped to one knee to make sure. The mark of the heel was clearest; a tiny circlet of faint crimson. The rest of the sole had left a sliding smudge on the strands of white fleece; but Tracy was able to reconstruct the fragile outline of a woman's slipper. The toe pointed directly toward the staircase.

JERRY TRACY WAS still examining the faint toe-mark when he heard a barely audible sound. The noise came from the floor above. A faint squeak, followed by a louder echo—one that instantly brought Tracy racing up the stairs. Someone was ripping the boarding away from a covered window!

It was dark at the top of the stairs. The upper hall was a tunnel of blackness. But there was a narrow line of horizontal light at the far end. Beyond a closed door was a lighted room, its brilliance visible under the crack of the door. Tracy sprinted, caught at the knob, whirled it. He spilled into the room, throwing himself prudently sidewise on hands and knees.

The room was empty.

It was a bedroom, its furniture covered with decorous muslin like the rest of the house. Rain slanted inward through a wide open window. The window's wooden protection had been pried loose. It lay wet side uppermost on the rug like a flat gray shield.

Tracy darted for the opened window. Rain slashed at his outthrust face, dripped from his nose and chin. He saw a dark figure rolling headlong on the wet concrete of the rear courtyard. A woman! She had leaped desperately from the sloping roof of the laundry extension. Tracy had a blurred glimpse of exposed silken legs and slim, pointed slippers, Then the woman was up and racing for the courtyard's rear gate.

It was impossible to catch a glimpse of the vanishing woman's face. She was shrouded by a long raincoat, its rubber hood drawn over the back of her head. An upflung arm and elbow had concealed her features, and she was out the gate and gone before Tracy could straddle the sill. The explosive roar of an automobile engine was followed almost instantly by a shrill accelerating whine.

Tracy started to drop to the shed roof, then suddenly changed his mind. He knew he had no chance whatever to stop that fleeing car. He had seen no sign of Corning. The murderous lover of Drake's wife must be still somewhere in the house! Tracy's identification of the fleeing woman as Pauline was pure guess, based on an indefinable sense of grace and loveliness as she fled, and on her car.

He drew back into the bedroom. There was a woman's handbag on the covered dresser; a comb, a lipstick. A faint odor of perfume was rapidly vanishing in the damp smell of rain on the rug.

Tracy didn't touch the handbag or the smaller articles. He had only one tense thought in his mind. He had seen down below in the reception room the unmistakable outline of a sheeted telephone desk. He thought hotly: *"Murder is news!"*

The *Daily Planet* first! Then the police. McCurdy, the night chief of the city room would have a chance to rip out an extra almost before the *Queen Mary* sailed. The opposition would print the usual stereotyped story stating that Edgar Drake had sailed at midnight, maintaining his usual policy of granting no press interviews. The *Daily Planet* would rip the town wide open with the sensational truth, under the famous by-line of Jerry Tracy himself! Front page socko!

He sneaked swiftly down the broad staircase. Drake's body still lay stark and motionless on the blood-soaked Chinese rug. Tracy's lean fingers trembled as he uncovered the telephone. The chances were a hundred to one that the line was disconnected. But as he lifted the instrument he was overjoyed to hear the strong steady hum of the dial tone. His finger began to twirl *The Planet's* exchange letters.

Without warning the room went pitch-black.

Feet came thudding across the rug, straight toward the star-tled columnist. He threw up a defensive arm as a man's plung-ing body crashed into him. The impact bent Tracy backward across the sharp desk edge.

He rolled sidewise and slid to the floor. His twined fingers caught behind the hinged hollow of a bent knee and slid upward to thigh and crotch. Tracy was no fool in a rough and tumble fight. He was small-boned but as active as a flea. He used both hands and a quickly thrust foot in an effort to trip his unseen assailant and get him on the floor. In a savage gutter roll Tracy was as tall as anybody else.

But this foe was too strong to upset. And Tracy's blind thrust had left him unprotected. He felt a hand clutch his throat and tighten like a vise. Both men went down in a thrashing huddle with Tracy underneath. A knee dug into Tracy's groin. His mouth flew open with a gasp of agony. He knew the fingers had left his throat but he was powerless to move. Then he heard a grunt, saw the dark silhouette of an upraised arm whizzing downward at his skull.

There was no sense of impact. A spasm of brilliant flame, vivid and edged like a buzz-saw, was the last thing Jerry Tracy remembered. He could see the flame whirl, throwing off fiery chunks like molten baseballs. Then, nothing....

THE SOUND OF feeble groaning roused him. It was a long time before he realized that the groans came from himself. The back of his head hurt horribly. It was sticky, oozy with blood and his fingertips grated against it like sandpaper. But the pain brought him back to reality. He remembered the murderous attack, the downward whizzing arm. He got one knee under him, bracing himself in the darkness with both palms flat against the floor.

He felt drunker than he had ever been in his life. But once he was up on his feet, with the hard edge of the telephone desk behind him, he was able to orient himself and to recall the layout of the room. The electric light cord on the floor led him to the lamp.

He missed the Chinese rug before he missed the body.

The floor where the bloody rug had lain was now completely bare. Both the rug and the dead millionaire were gone. A sudden wondering thought jerked Tracy's muddled eyes toward the foot of the stairs. The white fleecy rug was gone, too—the rug on which the bloody imprint of a woman's slipper had been faintly traced.

Jerry said slowly, "Whoa! Wait a minute!" with the drowsy gravity of a drunken man.

He caught hold of the balustrade of the stairs and climbed upward with grim persistence, knowing damned well what he'd find in that upstairs bedroom.

Nothing!

The light was out, and he guessed that the window was boarded up before he found and clicked the switch. The woman's handbag was gone. So were the comb and lipstick. The boarded covering over the window looked as if it had never been moved. Jerry plodded thoughtfully back downstairs.

Except for a splitting headache and a raw lump at the base of his skull Jerry Tracy had nothing to show for his big sensational murder triangle. The story had slid away from him with the deft speed of the fleeing Pauline Drake. That she was Pauline,

Tracy still didn't doubt for an instant. It was possible that someone else might have been using her car with the monogram. But Drake would not have risked dragging a tabloid columnist in on such a scandalous mess unless he was sure of his evidence.

The wily David Corning had killed both Drake and the story! Murder *wasn't* news—not without a body! Drake in death was still as stubbornly anonymous as if he were already locked in his cabin on the *Queen Mary,* waiting for the long-drawn hoot of the vessel's midnight Coronation departure.

A sudden exclamation came from the *Daily Planet's* columnist. He jerked out his watch and glanced at the dial. The hands showed ten minutes past midnight. There was only one thing he could do now: Call police headquarters and get hold of Inspector Fitzgerald. Fitz would look funny when he heard the screwy yarn. The only understandable thing that had happened all evening was the sticky lump on the back of Tracy's own noggin. No fantasy about that, he thought grimly.

For the first time in his life Jerry Tracy was in the ridiculous position of a professional wrecker with a stick of Grade A dynamite and no fuse. To allow the slightest hint of what he knew to leak into newsprint would involve more than ridicule at a wild story; it would mean a damned nasty libel suit. The principals in the case were too prominent in society and finance to fool with in the absence of a *corpus delicti.*

"O.K.," Jerry breathed softly. "We'll get Fitz and we'll *find* the body."

He reached for the telephone that should have been disconnected, but wasn't. At this exact moment a cold voice said:

"Stick 'em up!"

Tracy whirled—and gasped. So did a lean old man with a blue-barreled gun. He was tall, gray-thatched under a shapeless felt hat, with a florid, ruddy-veined face and eyes like blue mica. Tracy dropped his half-lifted hands.

"Fitz! Where in hell did you come from?"

Inspector Fitzgerald growled a vicious reply. His voice was like the rasp of a file; but the rasp came from incredulous amazement, not anger. There was deep-rooted friendship between the pint-sized columnist and this arrow-straight police veteran.

"I might have known it, you little punk. Killan bet me a buck you'd beat us here somehow. How do you do it—tune in on the corpse?"

A man, shorter and a lot heavier than Fitzgerald, emerged from the shadow of a velvet drape. He had a square, cobblestone head and a neck like a letter-box. This was Sergeant Killan, Fitz's right hand and fist on a murder case. Killan looked puzzled but pleased. He held out a pudgy palm to his superior and said, "Give." Fitz paid him the dollar.

Killan grinned. "O.K., Jerry. Where's the body?"

"There isn't any. Somebody swiped it."

"Huh?" Fitzgerald said.

"Wait a minute, Fitz. Let's get this thing straight. How did you know there was a corpse here."

"Got a phone call from a west side pay station. The guy that phoned the tip did his talking through a handkerchief. He talked damned fast, too. He was gone before I could rush a squad car to the drug-store. He said if I hopped up fast to Edgar Drake's town house I'd find a board loose on a rear courtyard window and the old guy dead in his own parlor. Did the lad with the handkerchief phone you first?"

"It was Drake himself who called me. I was supposed to meet him here."

"So what? Didn't he show up?"

"He sure did," Tracy snapped. "The last I saw of him, he was flat on his back on a Chinese rug over there."

"What Chinese rug?"

Tracy told him the whole amazing story with swift, incisive phrases, beginning with the phone call he had from Drake and ending with the arrival of Fitz and Killan.

"It doesn't make sense," Killan growled. "A guy slugs you to get rid of the body and the evidence, then he calls up headquarters and says come and get it. Let's see that clue you found."

Tracy showed it. The sergeant and the inspector examined the object with blank faces. Like Tracy's story it didn't make sense.

"Mind if I keep it?" Jerry asked.

"Why? Got some kind of an idea about it?"

"Nope. Not even a hunch. I'd like to sort of hold on to it a while and think about it. It's no good for prints—no good unless there's a corpse to make a murder case. I give you my word I'm not trying to hold a thing back. You can have the clue—if it is a clue—whenever you want it."

INSPECTOR FITZGERALD HAD worked with Tracy too often to suspect his motives. Tracy had his own intuitive methods that sometimes brought home the bacon. And when the bacon arrived it always meant one hundred per cent police credit for the long horse-faced inspector. He let Jerry have the ear stopper.

Then Fitz said abruptly, "Stick around a minute. I want to give this whole dump the once-over. Come on, Killan."

The two vanished upstairs after a careful inspection of the spotless reception room. After a while they returned and went down to the basement. Jerry knew they were giving the deserted old mansion a thorough search, but he didn't have much hope they'd find anything. He improved his time by staring at the telephone and pondering a few interesting questions. He was smiling faintly when the pair drifted back with a gruff, unhappy: "Nuts!" from Killan.

Fitz stood on stiffly planted legs, chewing morosely at his lip.

"I'm accepting as gospel everything you've said, Jerry. That gives us Drake, his wife and probably David Corning. Corning's a hell of a smart corporation lawyer. He'd have to be, or Drake wouldn't hire him. The whole set-up suggests a love triangle with a jealous husband getting the works. But if Corning did it, why should he first cover it up and then call the cops?"

"I don't know," Tracy admitted. "But I can think of three questions for a starter."

He told them and Fitz said, "Right," with sparkling emphasis. He yanked up the phone. He identified himself to the operator and got the exchange manager in a hurry.

"Has this phone been in continuous operation since the Drake home was closed two months ago?"

"No. It was disconnected up to three days ago. Then we had a request to resume service."

"From whom?"

"From Mrs. Drake. Is—is anything wrong?"

"No. Forget I called you."

Fitz's second number got him the Cunard pier. From the night superintendent he learned that Edgar Drake had changed his mind and had not sailed on the *Queen Mary*. A last minute cancellation had come through and Mr. Drake's baggage had been taken off the liner and left on the pier. He understood that the millionaire had been obliged to leave hurriedly for an unexpectedly important business conference in the Middle West.

"Did Drake himself cancel his passage?"

"No, sir. His attorney called up for him. A Mr. David Corning."

"Thanks."

Fitzgerald glanced approvingly at the impassive face of Tracy. He got back to the operator. After an uneasy wait, he located the number of Corning's New Jersey home and asked for the lawyer. All he could get was a very dry and very fishy-voiced butler. Mr. Corning was not at home. He was staying overnight in New York on some urgent business connected with Drake Utilities.

"I'll say it was urgent," Fitzgerald muttered. His heavy paw cradled the receiver. "Jerry, are you damned sure that the dame who dived out that upstairs window was Pauline Drake?"

"I told you I don't know. But my guess is yes."

"All right. Here goes for a Westchester call. Boy, this is going to be ticklish."

He held the receiver partly away from his ear, so that the voice on the wire was clearly distinct to Killan and Tracy. Both leaned forward so as not to miss a word.

"Mrs. Pauline Drake?"

"Yes. Who is this, please?"

"I'm sorry to have to bother you at this hour of the night. This is Inspector Fitzgerald of the New York police. We have reason to believe that something serious may have happened to your husband. He seems to have disappeared."

"That's ridiculous. My husband is away on a business trip. He sailed at midnight on the *Queen Mary*."

Fitz's head half turned. His lips framed a noiseless question: "Is it her?"

Tracy nodded. He had seen Pauline Drake at too many social functions to miss the calm throatiness of her voice, even on a telephone wire. He was not surprised at her prompt answering of the Westchester phone. Tracy's long lapse into unconsciousness, plus the time used up since the arrival of Fitz and Killan had given the wife of the dead millionaire ample time to drive back to Westchester.

"Your husband didn't sail," Fitzgerald said deferentially. "He canceled at the last moment."

There was soft, indulgent laughter. "That doesn't mean anything. My husband often does things like that."

"The information I have would indicate your husband may have been murdered."

Fitz shot it bluntly to her, but all he got was a brief sigh that could have been polite annoyance—anything.

"There must be some mistake, Inspector. Edgar called me a little after ten tonight. He seemed in excellent spirits over some business deal—a merger out West—something of that sort. Really, Inspector, I—"

"Did he talk to you personally?"

Pauline Drake's voice hesitated for a perceptible instant. The pause was neatly covered, but not quite well enough to deceive the three rigid listeners.

"As a matter of fact, he talked with Anne Leslie, my secretary. I was out driving in an effort to get rid of a bad headache."

She sounded almost conversational. No excitement. No sign of grief or worry. Suddenly the well poised voice hardened.

"Do I understand you to say that you merely *suspect* my husband is dead?"

"We haven't found his body yet," Fitz admitted.

"Then I'd be very careful if I were you," Pauline Drake replied coolly, "not to start any police wheels turning or to make any fuss in the newspapers. You may be interfering with well meaning zeal in a confidential business trip that doesn't concern you or the public. My husband is a prominent man and might be angry enough to interfere with your police advancement when he returns."

Fitzgerald's ruddy face flushed a deeper crimson at the threat.

"I have an eye-witness, madam, who will swear he saw your husband on a bloody Chinese rug, with a knife jammed up to the hilt in his chest. You can take my word, Mr. Drake's dead—corpse or no corpse."

"Oh!" There was a long pause. Fitz let it continue. "Very well. I intend to be in New York tomorrow morning. At the Waldorf. If you care to see me, I shall be at your disposal. Will ten o'clock be convenient?"

"It will," Fitz said. "Thank you for your cooperation."

He hung up with a slow lingering gesture and turned toward Tracy.

"No publicity, Jerry. We're both walking on eggs—expensive ones, too! You're stuck as much as I am. Not a single word about Drake except that he missed the boat."

"You're maligning the *Daily Planet,* Fitz. The ship newsman will have that item already. I'll be as mum as an oyster provided I get an exclusive when the case breaks. And provided I'm in on that interview tomorrow morning at the Waldorf."

"Did I say no? You're my star witness, you little punk."

"Witness to what?" Killan murmured sourly.

The three left the empty house via the loosened board over the window of the rear extension. Fitz's car was out at the curb but Jerry refused a lift in spite of the pouring rain.

"It's too much out of your way. I'll grab a cab over at the avenue and buzz home to bed. My head feels like a hardboiled egg and I ache all over. See you in the Waldorf lobby at ten tomorrow."

TRACY HEELED RAPIDLY westward through the rain, head bent, his raincoat flapping. The thought of a double Scotch and a tired dive between cool sheets was a pleasant picture to contemplate. If he was lucky enough to spot an empty cab.

He was. A taxi was rolling sedately down the deserted avenue, and it swerved in toward the curb at Jerry's whistle. The driver hooked the door open and Jerry sighed and ducked in. But only for an instant. With one foot on the running-board and the other in the cab, he uttered a startled yelp and threw himself backward. There was a figure crouched on the floor of the cab, hidden up to his eyes by a concealing lap-robe. The eyes and the glint of a pistol barrel spelt stick-up to the startled columnist. He bounced backward to the sidewalk as though he'd been shot from a gun.

He had no chance to run or even to duck. The taxi chauffeur

had piled out of the front seat. He swung a wet fist to Tracy's jaw and the columnist went down.

Instantly Tracy was in the midst of a mad, squirming tussle. A heavy body jammed down on his back, shoving his face against the puddled sidewalk. Tracy spat out water and yelled at the top of his lungs. He continued to yell, squirming and kicking as he felt hands probing through his pockets, searching him thoroughly from head to foot. The man on Tracy's back kept him from turning. A palm cut short Jerry's shrill cries, but he bit grimly and freed his throat.

He managed to swing up an arm and clutch blindly at one of the crooks, but the rip of cloth lost him his grip, and the next instant a gun butt against his skull drove his nose flat against the pavement.

Dazed, he tried to turn over. The crooks were no longer on top of him, but he was too paralyzed to move. He heard the quick slam of the taxi's door and the roar of its engine. The cab skidded around the corner in a drunken slither. It was gone before Tracy could sit up and unglue his eyes. He was puzzled at the holdup men's swift flight until he heard the faint blatting of a police whistle far up the avenue. A cop, thank God! The onrushing thud of his slopping brogans made Jerry grin with relief.

But the grin was only momentary. It was replaced by a hard watchfulness. The whole attack had been too pat, too completely managed to be an ordinary stick-up. He had had merely a vague glimpse of the taxi driver's face and none whatever of the man who had searched his pockets with such desperate, panting haste. Jerry remembered, with a catch of his breath, the clue he had picked up from the body of Edgar

Drake. His hat was lying upside down in a puddle and he stuck an anxious finger inside the sweat band. The black-and-red rubber ear gadget was still safely stowed away.

Tracy was on his feet by this time, steadying himself on the sleek, rubber-clad arm of a panting young patrolman. He told a vague story of a crooked cab driver and omitted all mention of the man under the lap-robe. He said he was Harry W. Messer of Harrisburg, Pa. In town for a week's vacation. Had a few drinks in a little place up in Harlem and, like a fool, had shown a well filled wallet at the bar. The cop wrote this all down in his notebook shielded from the rain by the flap of his raincoat.

"Ain't hurt much, are you? Want an ambulance?"

"I'm all right. A cab is all I want."

His eyes had been watching the sidewalk and curb as he talked. There was a sopping wet match-pad lying near the curbstone, green pasteboard with bold yellow lettering. It hadn't been there when Tracy had hailed the phoney cab. The cop at his elbow was staring up the avenue. Tracy scooped up the match-pad with an innocent bend of his body and slipped it into his pocket. He knew it wasn't his. It must have fallen from the pocket of his assailant. He remembered his quick clutch and the rip of tearing cloth as the fellow had fled.

He didn't look at his find until he was on his way again behind a law-abiding hackman. Then he cupped the thing in his palm and changed his mind about going home. The name of a man he hadn't thought about all evening popped into his mind. Tony Pedley! Pauline Drake's son by a former marriage. The son Drake hated so!

The printing on the match-pad helped to concentrate his thinking on Tony:

CLUB POM-POM
Entertainment and Dancing
In the Modern Manner
Moderate Cover Charge.

Sure! Tony Pedley played a trumpet in the Club orchestra. Tracy was familiar with his lean, youthful face, his dark, sullen eyes. He had looked the kid over several times after he had wormed out of Fred Hammer, the Pom-Pom's genial owner, just who Tony really was, and that the kid hated Drake's guts enough to quit college and take a lousy trumpet job rather than accept a penny of the millionaire's support. But there might be more to the feud than that—a hell of a lot more.

Tracy leaned forward suddenly and slid back the front glass panel.

"Do you know a good clean place where I can wash up and get some of this mud off my face? Somewhere in the neighborhood?"

"Sure."

He swung around a corner and braked in front of a small all-night Grill and Bar. "Cleanest washroom around here. I use it myself."

"Wait here. I'll be out in a minute."

There was nobody inside but a sleepy counterman. He looked mildly startled as the bedraggled columnist walked in.

"S'matter, pal? Take a nose-dive somewhere?"

"Yeah. I almost got it on the tail from a hit-run down at the corner. Where's the washroom?"

"Straight back. To your left."

Ten minutes later Tracy was in his taxi, clean as a whistle, heading for the Club Pom-Pom. The bump at the base of the skull was still messy, but his upturned coat collar took care of that. He kept thinking about Pauline Drake's son. The kid was young but plenty hefty in the shoulders. He could easily have been the guy who'd knocked him cold in the mansion on 56th and the guy in the taxi, too.

The Club Pom-Pom was still going strong. A hot swing number had the customers doing epileptic things on a packed dance floor. Everybody was half-canned and noisy. Tracy shot a quick glance toward the orchestra and then slid unobtrusively along the rear wall toward his favorite table near the curtained angle of Fred Hammer's office. The waiter grinned and brought Jerry's usual. Hammer drifted through the curtains before the columnist was half through his double Scotch.

"Hi, Jerry! I thought you hated rain."

"I do. That's why I'm mixing it with Scotch. How's biz?"

"Not bad." He eyed the noisy bedlam and his face crinkled pleasantly. "When they yell, they spend. You like?"

Tracy made a wry face. "All except the trumpet player. He's lousy."

Hammer chuckled delightedly. "Trust you to notice that! The punk is a substitute; we had to hire him on short notice. Tony took a run-out tonight. Left us short a trumpet."

"Uh-huh?" Tracy sipped. "Nice guy!"

"Not the way you say it. The kid really is nice. He has a bum stomach. Sat around looking sick and unhappy. I didn't have the heart to stop him when he slipped out to grab some fresh air. He phoned in from a drug-store, saying he was sicker than a pair of pups. Sent for that punk to play out the night for him. Listen to that corny blast! The band leader's sore as hell and you can't blame him.....'Nother drink?"

"Nope. Nice Scotch, but I want bed. So long, Fred."

He took one of the club's gyp cabs home. He paid the exact legal fare plus a quarter, and the driver grinned at his famous little fare.

"Night, Mr. Tracy."

JERRY WISHED BY now that he had taken that second drink. The lump under his turned up raincoat collar felt like hot roast beef. And his thinking was just as painful. One more question mark to play with. His cock-sure suspicion of Drake's clever lawyer looked anemic in the light of Tony Pedey's midnight ramblings. Maybe Corning wasn't in the mess at all, except maybe to cover a murder for Tony's sake, or rather Pauline's. It was Tracy's business to know the town's rumors, and he was aware of divorce trouble between Pauline Drake and her husband. Pauline wanted to be free and Drake had said no—with gestures, if Tracy's info was correct. Her son, Tony, had made threats that if Drake didn't step out of the picture and allow Pauline an uncontested suit, he'd find a way to force him, millions or no millions.

Tracy took his unsolved questions into his penthouse suite—and Butch handed him still another.

The big, pug-nosed valet was sprawled in a deep leather chair in the living-room, with his bare feet propped up on a hassock. He was glaring at the telephone desk with an expression of deep animosity. Except for peppermint-striped pajama pants, Butch was as solidly naked as an ox and looked something like one. So intent was his baleful scrutiny of the phone that he failed to notice the soft-footed arrival of his employer until Tracy murmured, "How were the prelims tonight at the Garden? Did your boy win?"

Ordinarily Butch would have grunted, grinned, scratched his matted chest with a slow fingernail. But tonight even Butch was screwy!

"Where the hell have you been?" he growled.

"Huh?"

"You been sleepin' with anybody?"

For the first time in his wise-cracking life Tracy stared at Butch without a comeback. The infernal impudence of the question made his jaw sag. But before he could spark into anger, Butch was gabbling confused talk. The big fellow wasn't impudent; he was scared.

"Honest, Jerry, I been on pins and needles. The phone's been ringin' every five minutes. Every damn columnist in town is on your tail tonight. A lot of 'em that hate your guts. Nick White called up twice from the *Chronicle*."

"That guy?" Tracy looked suddenly as if he had bitten into a mouse. "What did he want?"

"I'm trying to tell yuh. Jeez, Jerry, if you been playin' around, I hope you didn't leave yourself wide open for a punch. Somebody tipped those wolves. They all want to know about a date you had tonight. Were you sleepin' with some dame? That's the idea I got from the dirty laughs."

Tracy's hand moved unconsciously toward the lump under the collar of his raincoat.

"I slept alone," he said grimly. "And I'd like to know just how in the name of Hades—"

The phone began to ring. He pivoted and grabbed it.

"Yeah?"

It was Nick White. Tracy tightened as he heard the oily chuckle of the *Chronicle's* columnist.

"Hello, Casanova. I've been hearing a little dirt."

"You should. You've always got your ear in a spittoon."

Nick's voice cracked back:

"I got a tip that I'd get a grand story if I could find out from you where and under what circumstances you took an hour's sleep tonight."

Jerry thought fast. He knew exactly what had happened. The mysterious lad who had telephoned Inspector Fitzgerald that Drake's murdered body was lying in his boarded-up town house had pulled the same little stunt on Tracy himself. Somebody seemed deliberately anxious that Drake's body be found—and found in a blaze of newspaper publicity. Otherwise why drag Jerry into it with a provocatively phrased tip to every one of his columnist rivals?

Tracy's prompt laugh on the wire was twice as nasty as Nick White's.

"I knew you'd fall for it. You're the sixth sap that's called up. Thanks for an easy grand."

"What do you mean I'm the sixth? What's the gag?"

"Did the fellow who phoned you that tip sound as if he was gargling through a handkerchief?"

"Maybe he did. So what?"

"A thousand bucks, sap! I always get bright ideas when it rains. I bet a friend of mine that I could get six of my worst enemies out of bed to inquire after my health. It's been a real pleasure to hear from you. Good night, Stinker."

"Why you dirty little ——"

Jerry banged the phone. He was feeling better again. But

as he squirmed out of his raincoat he grimaced. Butch's eyes rounded as he saw the blood-matted lump that had been concealed by Tracy's coat collar.

"Jerry! For the luva Joe Louis! Where did you—"

"Forget it. G'wan to bed. I'm all right."

"C'mere, you!" When Butch got gruffly paternal like that, there was no arguing with him. He shoved Jerry into the bathroom and snapped on the light. "Stay there, Scrapper, till I get me kit."

His kit was a ratty little leather bag that contained all the implements and unguents that Butch used when he seconded friends of his at the ringside. Jerry winced at the realistic treatment.

"Shuddup! You ain't hoit bad. That bum I seconded tonight was worse off than you before the foist round was over. Hold still till I clip the hair away."

It hurt like the dickens and then felt magically better.

Butch spun Jerry around.

"Jeez, your chin is bruised, too. How'd you get it?"

"A guy hit me and I hit the sidewalk."

"Bigger than you, huh?"

"Yeah."

"Tch, Tch. Look, Jerry, you're a pretty good little featherweight, but you ain't in condition, and even if you was, gutter fightin' is the bunk." He tightened the adhesive straps and patted the neat bandage with a brief, loving pressure. "O.K. Now if you'll just tell me the name of the big lug who—"

"Go to bed," Jerry grinned. He poured himself a stiff peg of Scotch and downed it. "Turn out the lights like a good guy. Call me first thing in the morning. I've got four people to dream about and I don't want to over-sleep."

Four people was right! Pauline Drake and two men who loved her: her son, Tony Pedley, and her dead husband's lawyer, David Corning. The guy on the phone made the fourth. Jerry knew it was silly to think of him as the murderer—Jerry had never yet heard of a murderer who wanted the body *found*—but a queer hunch continued. He fell asleep wondering about it.

AT TEN O'CLOCK sharp the next morning Jerry Tracy met Inspector Fitzgerald and Sergeant Killan in the lobby of the Waldorf. He had already read all the morning papers for the news concerning Edgar Drake. There wasn't much but it hit the front page. The thing that had made Tracy frown, as he read, was the emphasis. It was all about Drake Utilities. The vast railroad and industrial empire of the *missing* millionaire appeared to be on a bullish upward movement. Wall Street was apparently not disturbed by the sudden cancellation of Drake's European trip. The news account ended with a reassuring statement from David Corning pointing out that Drake's sudden departure for the West was to sign papers for a vast new merger with a competing rival. Tracy had looked at yesterday's closing prices on the stock market page. Drake Utilities was up two points and a half.

Tracy rode up in the elevator with Fitz and Killan to the spacious tower suite Mrs. Drake had reserved from Westchester by telephone. It was exactly four times bigger than the miserly one-room apartment her husband had occupied the preceding day.

The door was opened by a very pretty blonde who nodded and ushered the three men in. Behind her, Killan caught

Tracy's eye and his lips formed a noiseless and approving: "Not bad." To Tracy the girl looked definitely tired, perhaps frightened. He wasn't sure of the latter. He got it from the stiffness of her shoulders, the rigid way she walked as she preceded them to a gorgeous, sun-drenched living-room.

A tall dark-haired woman had risen from a couch, her glance serenely questioning. Tracy had seen her a dozen times before on opening nights and at swanky receptions, but the effect was just the same as ever. He gulped as he knew Fitz was doing. Killan's mouth hung open.

It was as though the blond secretary had disappeared from the room, although she was standing almost at Pauline Drake's elbow. The older woman's beauty made the fresh prettiness of her secretary fade to something pert and silly. It wasn't Pauline's face or her faultless figure; it was something deeper in the dark eyes that made men bend attentively at sight of her. The charm and poise of maturity. The blonde was the bud; Pauline Drake was the breathlessly perfect flowering.

"Inspector Fitzgerald, I presume?"

"Yes, ma'am." Fitz mumbled.

"And these other gentlemen?"

Tracy said nasally, "And Mr. Jerry Tracy of the *Daily Planet*."

She ignored him. "Do you think, Inspector, that it was quite fair to bring a newspaper reporter?"

"Not a reporter, Mrs. Drake," Tracy corrected swiftly. "An eye-witness to a murder."

He snapped it out brutally, his eyes watching both women narrowly. They took the challenge like thoroughbreds. The flick of terror in the blond secretary's eyes was instantly covered; Pauline Drake showed nothing but a well-bred incredulity.

The pause was broken by a sardonic masculine voice from a far corner of the room. A man had risen from a deep armchair whose tall back had concealed him from view.

"Are you bringing us a sensational news item, Mr. Tracy, or an accusation of some sort? I find it hard to decide from your tone."

He came forward, smiling courteously; a medium-sized man with a large handsome head and pleasant brown eyes.

"Mr. David Corning," Pauline said with a faint intake of relieved breath. "My husband's legal adviser, and—mine. Naturally I consulted him after your peculiar phone message last night, Inspector. Anne and I thought—pardon me, this is Anne Leslie, my secretary."

There were awkward how-de-does, cut through by Corning's amused voice. There was a whiplash at the tip of his polite drawl. "Would it be too much to ask you to repeat your eye-witness story of Mr. Drake's alleged death?"

"That's what I came here for." Tracy said.

He repeated carefully everything that had happened the night before, beginning with the moment Edgar Drake had telephoned him his angry suspicion of his wife's fidelity. When he described the flight of the woman from the upstairs bedroom window Corning chuckled dryly.

"Do you attend many motion pictures, Mr. Tracy?"

Tracy didn't answer. Pauline's face was dead white, but she kept her head high, her gaze directly at the *Daily Planet's* columnist. Tracy suppressed only his finding of the rubber ear-stopple and the subsequent attack on him in the rain.

"It's utterly ridiculous," Pauline gasped. "My husband never—"

Corning stopped her with a light touch of his hand on hers. Her face flushed at the brief contact; she seemed to sway toward him, then checked herself. Corning's face, too, was pinker. The friendliness was gone from his calm voice. His words were like the clink of ice.

"I don't, of course, believe this wild yarn for one moment. The whole preposterous story rests on the unsupported word of a man who—pardon—who makes his living on hints, winks and gutter innuendo. You choose to ignore my own reasonable explanation for Mr. Drake's departure. Instead, you invent a body, conveniently missing. You frame an imaginary—"

Tracy kept his temper. His finger touched the neat little bandage Butch had taped on the back of his skull.

"You think this lump is imaginary?"

"I'm not interested in the mementos of your barroom brawls, Mr. Tracy. In fact, I'm not interested in you at all. I merely want to point out to Inspector—"

He reached a sinewy hand to swing the columnist out of his path, but Tracy beat the angry lawyer to it. Corning went abruptly back on his heels from the straight-arm shove and Jerry rasped a point-blank question at Pauline Drake.

"Where was your son last night?"

The shot was a bull's-eye. The woman quivered as if she had been struck. Her mouth flew open and her rigid control left her. She began to stammer.

"My—my son has nothing to do with this. I haven't seen him lately. Don't you dare attempt to—"

Corning stopped her frightened babble. This time he cupped her shoulder protectively, held her close to him. Tracy was aware of the possessive tenderness of the man's gesture, the answering flaring from the woman. These two were in love!

"You've had divorce trouble with your husband, Mrs. Drake?" he said quickly.

"Perhaps. What of it?"

"Don't answer him," Corning snapped.

"You don't have to," Tracy told her. "It's my business to know things like that. For the past six months your life with Drake had been a living hell. You asked him for a divorce and he laughed at you. He told you that if you tried to get one in his absence, he'd use his millions to smirch you and ruin you. Your son knew that. He went to Westchester three weeks ago and threatened Drake. He told Drake that unless he agreed to a quiet divorce—he'd kill him. He even gave him a deadline. The deadline was midnight last night, when the *Queen Mary* sailed.... I'm not asking you any of this; I'm telling you."

"Are you accusing Mrs. Drake's son of murder?" Corning cried.

"Not at all," Tracy said evenly. "I'm accusing *you* of that, Mr. Corning. Mrs. Drake's son got to the town house too late. He merely stole the body and removed the clues after you and Mrs. Drake fled from that boarded-up mansion on East 56th Street."

Anne Leslie screamed as Corning sprang. But Sergeant Killan had been watching the lawyer shrewdly and he caught the upraised fist in a grip of steel. The two men wrestled fiercely for an instant and then Corning's violent rage evaporated. He became perfectly quiet. Killan let go his arm. "Easy, mister. No rough stuff!"

"You're quite right, Sergeant," Corning said calmly. "I lost my head for a moment. I'm sorry."

He smiled evenly at Inspector Fitzgerald.

"If you'll look at this telegram you'll realize that all this sensational talk about murder and corpses is rather idiotic."

Fitz took the sheet of yellow flimsy and Tracy read it over the old man's shoulder. It was a telegram from Edgar Drake to Corning, ordering him to cancel the millionaire's reservation on the *Queen Mary* and stating that he was obliged to leave suddenly and secretly for an important conference in the Middle West.

Jerry Tracy said coldly, "So what? It wouldn't be the first time a man sent himself a telegram as an alibi. You naturally have to have something tangible to clear yourself if Drake's body is found—or is never found, as you hope."

Corning ignored the columnist's deliberate baiting with a perceptible effort. He continued to stare challengingly at Fitzgerald.

"As an experienced police official, I need not tell you that without a body there can be no murder. I advise you to find your corpse before you intrude on Mrs. Drake again. If the smallest hint of scandal or accusation appears in the *Daily Planet,* I shall sue both the newspaper and the police department for malicious libel. You're not dealing with cheap underworld characters. You're threatening the good name of prominent personages."

His voice kept getting quieter and quieter. He went on:

"You're attacking, whether you mean to or not, the financial integrity of Drake Utilities. A false report of Edgar Drake's death might wreck his whole enterprise and bring ruin to millions of innocent stockholders."

"You mean the company is shaky, eh? Is that what you

mean?" Tracy said. "In that case, how about a man who deliberately issues a falsely optimistic statement to lure more investors to buy?"

"Get out, all of you!"

"You're not selling short, by any chance, are you, Mr. Corning?"

"Get out!"

He watched the three move toward the door. His eyes were smoldering. His finger pointed wrathfully at Inspector Fitzgerald.

"One last warning. I know your thick-skulled police methods. If I find that you're attempting to shadow me or Mrs. Drake or Anne Leslie, her secretary, I'll go straight to the mayor's office! We'll see who has more influence in this town, Inspector Fitzgerald or Drake Utilities."

Sergeant Killan said, "Yeah?" in a belligerent growl, but Fitz silenced him.

"The police department has no intention of persecuting anyone in the absence of proof, Mr. Corning," Fitz said very blandly. "As you say, there's still a body to be found. Good day."

FITZGERALD LOOKED HAGGARD and worried on the sidewalk downstairs. The strong sunlight made him blink. He asked, "What about this son of hers, Jerry? Were you bluffing his mother about him?"

"No. That stuff about her divorce quarrel and the son's murder threat is true. I had it from a confidential source."

"Do you know where he is?"

Tracy said truthfully, "No, I don't.

What are you going to do now?"

"Damned if I know," Fitz admitted. "I'll probably have another look at the house. I've got a plainclothes man watching the rear in case anyone tries to sneak in. If Drake's body has been really hidden there—"

"My guess is that it was taken away. It could've been dragged through that window when I was out cold."

"I've covered that, too," Fitz murmured grimly. "I've sent out a quiet alarm to comb every vacant lot in the five boroughs. Across the river they're searching the Jersey meadows."

"Let me know if anything turns up."

"Where are you going?"

Tracy chuckled. The last trace of puzzlement vanished from his lean face. The same strong sunlight that had emphasized the wrinkles in Fitz's countenance made Tracy look eager and boyish.

"Believe it or not, I work for a living. I've got a column to write, keed. I'll give you a buzz later on…. Hey, taxi!"

He got downtown to his Times Square office in jig time. But he didn't get promptly to work. Instead, he stared meditatively at the typewriter and the dictograph machine. He was thinking of something he had said on the impulse of the moment back there in Mrs. Drake's hotel suite. It had made Corning damned sore. In fact, it had broken up the interview. Maybe….

He grabbed his telephone and called a number in the financial district.

"Hello, Andy? Jerry Tracy. Got a job for you. Look, Andy, see if you can do a little fast nosing around and find out if anyone is selling short on Drake Utilities. C as in confidential."

"What's the idea? Do you think—"

"Call me back if you dig anything."

He pronged the instrument and got to work. The minute hand of the clock went round and round but he was oblivious to the passing of time. The secret of Jerry Tracy's journalistic success was that he'd rather play with words than eat. Every wise-crack he fed into the dictograph brought a pleased grin of self-approval. He played the record back, changing a phrase or a word here and there with a brief nasal toned postscript at the end of the record. In his own words, "he always finished his act with a script-tease."

The wrapped cylinder was on its way to the *Daily Planet* office when the phone rang. It was Andy.

"You're a good guesser, Jerry. I got the info but it's gonna cost you dough. You sounded eager enough to spend a grand."

"Right. I'll send you a check. Who's selling short on Drake Utilities?"

"Some guy named Amos Brandt."

"Who is he?"

"I don't know. It's all I could get. I had to turn the heat on just to get the name."

"You did perfectly well. Thanks a lot."

Tracy picked up a Manhattan phone book and slapped it open. There was a whole column of Brandts but no Amos. The name was obviously a phoney; the whole deal a smart under-cover transaction.

Tracy called up again and got a quotation on Drake Utilities. The stock was up two more points. Evidently Corning's reassuring explanation of the financier's trip was bearing fruit. But if Corning was really the mysterious short seller, why was he boosting the stock's price? For a public alibi? A damned expensive one!

The afternoon sun was getting thin outside. Time for a cocktail. Tracy decided to get it at the Club Pom-Pom. He had told Inspector Fitzgerald grim truth when he had said he didn't know the present whereabouts of Mrs. Drake's son. It was high time he hunted up this Tony Pedley. Tony might be on the lam by this time, his pockets lined with his mother's dough; but Fred Hammer would have his last address.

Hammer looked puzzled when Jerry finished his cocktail and made his casual request.

"What's the idea, Jerry? This makes twice you've been in here asking about the kid. Now you want his address. Is he in a jam?"

"I just want to ask him a couple of questions."

"He's a good kid, Jerry. If you knew who he really was—Say!" Over the noisy bleat of the cocktail music, Fred Hammer's good-natured voice became louder. "Come to think of it, I did tell you once who the kid really is. You promised not to print it."

"Well, did I?"

The nightclub owner hesitated. He leaned closer.

"I've been reading the papers. You think Tony's sick stomach last night had something to do with Drake not sailing for Europe?"

"I want to find out if Tony's still in town, that's all."

"He is," Hammer admitted slowly. "He called up at noon, said he was still sick and couldn't make it this afternoon. I'll give you his address if you insist, but I'm telling you, you're hunting trouble. The kid has a quick temper."

"So what?" Tracy's tone was playful but he remembered suddenly the two vicious attacks on him the night before. A picture of the dark, sullen eyes and the strong, muscular hands of Tony Pedley became unpleasantly vivid in his mind.

He said, "Fred, I've never asked you before to do me a favor. You can do me one right now. Come on along with me. If Tony trusts you, you may save me a little wear and tear."

"You got him tabbed for something?"

"Maybe."

Hammer stared, then went back of the office curtain for his hat. In the taxi on the way across town he made only one remark. "I'll lay you an even grand that the kid's nose is clean."

"No bet. I've already spent a grand today."

Pedley's address proved to be in a cheap red-brick apartment house on the west fringe of the theatrical and restaurant district. There was a dingy-looking gray coupé parked at the curb, and Hammer said in a tone of surprise, "Hello! What's that doing here, I wonder?"

"Tony's heap?"

"Yeah."

Tracy looked it over. The rumble seat was locked. He had a queer tingling in his fingers as he tried vainly to lift it. A glance at the instruments on the dash made him frown. The locked rumble made him suspect a filled gas tank and plenty of oil for a long drive. But the indicator showed a little more than a gallon of gas.

"Has the kid been flush or broke the last few days, Fred?"

"Broke," Hammer said. "He got into me for five bucks day before yesterday. Why?"

Tracy shrugged, located Pedley's name over a vestibule bell, led the way up one flight to a door at the rear. When the door opened Pedley had his hat on. He had evidently been just about to leave. He took one look at Tracy and promptly tried to slam the door. Fred Hammer stopped that with a quick shove of his foot.

He said, "Easy, Tony. Don't be silly. What's the hell wrong with you, anyway?"

"What are you bringing that cheap tabloid hound here for?"

Tracy said quietly, "I asked him to. If you're sensible, you'll uncurl that fist. I'm an easy guy to talk to. Cops might be tougher."

"What do you mean, cops?"

"They wear blue uniforms. They arrest people for murder.... By the way, exactly where were you last night between about ten-thirty and midnight?"

"None of your damned business."

"Maybe I'd better save time."

He saved it by shooting crisp, direct sentences at Tony Pedley. Hammer's amazed mouth opened wider and wider as he listened to the columnist. But Pedley's lips got so tight there were white ridges along his jaw. By the time Tracy got to the talk of divorce and Tony's murder threat against his stepfather, the kid was like a carving in ice. The expression in his dark eyes made him look for an instant like a vivid good-looking counterpart of his mother.

He laughed shudderingly.

"For gosh sake, Fred, don't look so solemn. I didn't kill Drake. I should have, because if ever there was a mean-tempered, dirty-minded skunk, he was it. Yes, I knew all about those lies he was whispering about my mother and Corning. That's why I faked a stomach-ache and went to his hotel last night. But I didn't kill the old devil; I didn't even see him."

He elaborated, his dark eyes vengeful. He had taken his gray coupé from the garage and driven over to the Waldorf to have it out with his stepfather. But Drake had already left his suite. He'd left no word at the desk. Tony parked across from the hotel entrance and waited grimly in the rain. Waited until a quarter of midnight. Then he raced across town to the Cunard pier, only to find that Drake had suddenly changed his plans and the ship was sailing without him.

"Did anyone see you while you were waiting outside the hotel?"

"No."

"Do you remember exactly who told you that Drake had canceled his trip?"

Tony Pedley flushed. "I saw his baggage piled on the pier. That was enough for me. I talked to nobody."

"No alibi, eh? I didn't really expect you to have one, and I'll tell you why. Drake did come out of the hotel while you were waiting outside. You followed him to his deserted town house. It scared you because you knew your mother and Corning were inside for a secret conference regarding the feasibility of an absentee divorce action. While you were nerving yourself to follow Drake through the basement window, I came along, and you realized the scandalous nature of the trap Drake had laid. You sneaked in while I was upstairs and found Drake dead. You had to do something damned quick to protect your mother and her lover. You did it by socking me unconscious and hiding the evidence. Where's the body now? Downstairs in the locked rumble of your car?"

Tony Pedley's laughter was jeering. He said nothing.

Tracy hesitated. Then his hand whipped out of his pocket with the black-and-red rubber ear-stopple he had found on Drake's body. He held it palm-upward for an instant.

The effect on Pedley was immediate and frightening. He shrank back with a shrill cry.

"My God, where did you get that?"

Tracy's eyes never left the suspect's. Pedley was making a tremendous effort to control himself. An expressionless mask seemed to slide like a steel plate over his face. When he spoke his voice was barely audible.

"You found that on the body?"

"Of course. You're playing tag with the electric chair, son. Don't you think you've been a fall guy long enough? You hid Drake's body, didn't you?"

There was a long breathless pause.

"Yes. I—I took it. I hid it. My God, what a sap I've been!"

"Where is it—down in the car?"

Pedley shook his head. Fred Hammer stared wordlessly at him. Tracy didn't try to press the kid with questions.

"I—I meant to drive it away today and dump it. I didn't kill Drake. But I did steal his body. The corpse is right here. In this apartment."

"Where?"

"Come on!"

His face was twitching. He was sobbing with relief. He led the way to a tiny bathroom and flung open the door.

"In the bathtub, gentlemen. Behind the shower curtain. And thank God, you came. You've saved me from—"

Hammer's tremulous hand reached out to slide back the green waterproofed curtain. Tracy, who was nearest the door, swerved suddenly around. He had heard the grating sound of a stealthily withdrawn key. Pedley leaped back out of the tiled bathroom entrance and slammed the door. Tracy clutched wildly for the knob but he was too late. The key clicked in the outside of the lock.

Pedley's muffled laughter was freezingly triumphant.

"Stay there and sweat, damn you!"

FRED HAMMER WAS still holding the parted shower curtain with a paralyzed hand. The bathtub was empty. The nightclub owner snapped out of his trance and hurled himself at the locked door. It was solid, well fitted timber. No give to it. He tried three times and then Tracy grabbed his hunched shoulder, spinning him.

"It can't be done. You're wasting time. Gimme a hand up to that window."

The bathroom window was ground-glass and very tiny. Braced by Hammer, Tracy got his head out and peered eagerly.

He said in a clipped whisper, "Oke. It's small but I think I can squeeze through. There's a narrow stone ledge out here. Quick—twist me around! Get my feet up!"

His legs pivoted upward. He slid feet-first through the tiny opening. It was so small that he had trouble working his shoulders through. Hammer, looking upward, saw one hand vanish from the sill, then the other. He waited for what seemed like hours. Then there were quick, racing foot-steps outside the bathroom door and the lock clicked open.

Tracy was grinning haggardly, his forehead damp with sweat.

"That was a hell of a ledge to inch across. Got in again through the living-room window. If I hadn't worked the trick fast, I'd have broken my neck. A blank brick wall in the rear, or somebody would be blowing a police whistle right now.... Let's go!"

There was no sign of Pedley's gray coupé at the curb downstairs.

"You'd better get the cops," Hammer whispered uneasily.

"Cops, hell. There's no time. You say the kid is flat broke? He'll have to borrow dough in a hurry for his getaway. Only one place to go. His mother!"

They had hurried up toward the corner while they talked. Tracy's brisk yelp halted a rolling cab.

"Come on! We'll have to move fast to nail him."

Fred Hammer shook his head. His grin quivered.

"Where do you get that 'we' stuff?" he said faintly. "Count me out. I've had all I want. I'm going home."

"O.K., but keep your mouth shut till you hear from me."

The cab whirled away and Jerry stepped up its speed with an advance payment that made the hacker's eyes glisten. He entered the Waldorf from the Lexington Avenue side and whizzed upward in the tower elevator. A brisk knock at the door brought the pale face of Anne Leslie. Tracy slid through the closing aperture like a well tailored eel and darted into the living-room.

Pauline Drake screamed faintly as she saw his blazing eyes.

"What do you want? How dare you force your way into my— If you don't leave at once—"

Tracy sprang past her, searching every room of the suite with grim speed. There was no sign of Tony Pedley. He hurried back to the living-room—and stopped short. Anne Leslie was holding a wicked looking little automatic pistol and its muzzle was trained steadily on the vest button that covered the columnist's navel.

Tracy stood prudently still. He knew that a frightened girl

with a gun was more dangerous than a cornered criminal.

"What's David Corning's Manhattan address? Where does he live when he's in town?" he asked.

Pauline Drake said slowly, "Keep that gun pointed, Anne. I'm going to telephone the police."

"If you've got any sense, you'll telephone Corning. You might save his life."

"What do you mean?"

"I mean your son, Tony Pedley. He didn't come here, so it's a cinch he headed straight for Corning. He needs money and he needs it bad. He admitted he stole Drake's body. He's wild with rage because he's found out Corning double-crossed him."

"That's—that's ridiculous."

But Pauline's dark eyes had suddenly become pinched—like her son's when Tracy had shown him the rubber ear-stopple. She sprang toward the phone and whispered a hasty number. There was a long silence, then:

"David! Is that you? David, I can't hear you! What are you saying? Are you in danger?"

Tracy's ears were straining to hear the unintelligible mumble on the wire. A voice seemed to be gasping something with a dreadful, sticky slowness. Pauline swayed.

"No, no! David, that's not true! He didn't—he couldn't—"

The dropped instrument made a dull bump as it fell against the polished table. Pauline Drake flung out a weak, wavering hand and pitched forward to the rug in a faint.

Anne Leslie was holding the unnoticed pistol as though it were a block of wood. Tracy snatched it out of her hand. He pitched the weapon to the sofa and yelled an insistent question into the ear of the dazed secretary.

"What's Corning's address? Quick!"

She gave it to him automatically in a dead voice. He shoved her toward the unconscious woman on the floor.

"Take care of her. Don't let her out of here. And don't do any foolish yelling for help until I can find out just what the hell is going on."

The elevator dropped him in a hurry to Lexington Avenue. He picked the first of a long line of taxis and spent more money for speed. His route took him across town and south. His goal was the tremendous beehive of a modern apartment development in the lower Twenties west of the Ninth Avenue Elevated. The sort of place a man like Corning would pick as a Manhattan oasis for overnight stays when he was in town. Kitchenettes and dressing-rooms and folding beds. Smart, comfortable living in the midst of an ancient slum section.

The first thing Tracy saw at the curb was Pedley's gray coupé. The rumble was still locked.

David Corning's apartment was one flight up. Tracy didn't bother with the elevator. He rapped a brass knocker against polished wood and waited. Nothing happened. He tried again and again. He was about to slip downstairs and try for a fire-escape route to the rear windows, when he heard inside the apartment the sound of slow, shuffling steps. Fingers fumbled awkwardly at the catch, then the door opened.

It was Corning, his eyes dazed and out of focus. His face was paper white except for the thin, thread-like tracery of blood on his left cheek and jaw. A bullet had creased his temple. There was a gun in one of his dangling hands but he made no objection when Tracy disarmed him and pushed briskly into the apartment.

TONY PEDLEY WAS flat on his face on the floor. Tracy turned him over. One look was plenty. The kid had taken a slug straight through the heart. His mouth and eyes were wide open and would stay that way until somebody did the kind thing and closed them.

Tracy didn't. His own eyes were too busy sucking in his surroundings. The rear window was open. A chair was overturned. There were blood spatterings in a thin trail from the chair to the rigid body of Pedley. Two shots had been fired from Corning's gun. There was a fire-escape outside the opened window and beyond that was a framed courtyard glimpse of the Ninth Avenue Elevated.

Tracy picked up the swift, helter-skelter facts without any coherent system. But the facts made him eye the dazed lawyer grimly. Jerry's mind worked with the sensitive speed of a woman. He knew that Corning had been badly dazed when he had opened the door. He wasn't so dopy now by a long shot; he was only pretending to be.

"Come on! Snap out of it. What happened?"

The lawyer talked hesitantly in a blurred voice.

A murderous attack had been made on himself and Pedley by some unknown assailant on the fire-escape. The first shot had killed Pedley in his tracks. The second had creased Corning, knocking him silly and robbing him of his wits. But he had managed to fire two shots through the window before he passed out. He had seen nothing of the killer except a gloved hand and a smoking gun muzzle. He had staggered across to the window, fallen over a chair and fainted.

"That makes four shots," Jerry suggested. "Two from your gun. Two from his. Funny nobody heard anything."

"There was a Ninth Avenue El train going past at the time. It made a terrible racket. That's the last thing I remember."

"You don't remember hearing the phone ring and answering it?"

"Eh?" He looked fixedly into space as if he were trying hard to think. "By jove, I believe the phone did ring. I have a vague, dreamy recollection of talking to Pauline—Mrs. Drake. I must have roused when the bell rang—Look, my receiver is off the hook."

"Yeah. So I see. You haven't told me why Pedley came here."

"I don't know."

"You mean he was killed before he could open his mouth to talk to you?"

"Yes."

Corning answered so swiftly and so emphatically that Jerry knew he was lying. The columnist's jaw tightened. He walked over to the dangling phone and jiggled the hook.

"Police headquarters, please."

"You—you want the police? I mean I—"

"Sure I want 'em. Any objections?"

Corning looked as if he could think of plenty, but he shook his head without reply. Jerry paid no further attention to him. His own eyes were shining with suppressed eagerness. Something that had been bothering him for a long time seemed a heck of a lot clearer now. If his idea was true—and it had nothing to do with the room or the state of the furniture—it explained why Pedley had made such a quick rush to see Corning, and why he had been so promptly killed.

"Inspector Fitzgerald? Tracy! Look, Fitz, get this address down. I'm up at Corning's apartment. There's been a murder

here.... No, not Corning—Tony Pedley. Huh? The son—
Pauline Drake's son—No! No! Don't report it yet. Get up
here fast. I think I may have this damn thing figured!"

The last sentence must have lit a fuse under the Inspector's tail. He hung up with an exultant yell. In ten minutes he
walked swiftly into the apartment living-room. Sergeant Killan
was with the old man. Tracy choked off their prompt questions.

"Wait a minute!"

He sprang eagerly toward the dead Tony Pedley and began
swiftly to search his pockets. Before either cop could yell a
protest, Jerry had found what he was after—a bunch of keys.
He thrust them grimly toward Sergeant Killan.

"Pedley's car is down at the curb. It's a small gray coupé. The
rumble is locked. Pick out the right key and get that rumble
open in a hurry!"

"What's the idea?"

"I want to find out if there's a corpse in it. But if I'm right,
there won't be any corpse in that blasted rumble. Scram!"

Fitz nodded and Killan took it on the run. He was back in a
few minutes, his beefy face respectful.

"You were right, Jerry. The damned thing is empty. Just a
blanket and an old inner tube. No sign of blood anywhere."

Corning was still sitting dejectedly in a chair, his eyes on the
rug where his feet rested. The feet were trembling. So were the
hands and knees.

"Ever hear of a man named Amos Brandt?" Jerry asked him.
"No."

"Ever see this before?"

Corning's head lifted slowly. He stared at the rubber
ear-stopple that Tracy held grimly before his eyes.

"No. I never saw it before."

Tracy's gaze held him for a long minute. Then he turned away.

"Fitz, Killan, both of you stick here. I'll be back in fifteen minutes."

"Whoa! Where are you going?"

"I'm going to see if I can dig up another ear-stopple exactly like this. If I do, I'll give you your killer, and Drake's corpse, too."

He vanished from the apartment with an eager stride. He was gone nearer twenty than fifteen minutes. But when he returned his face was grimly wrinkled. Fitz halted his uneasy pacing up and down the room.

"Well?"

"How's this?" Tracy's palm shot out. There was a tiny pasteboard box in his hand and he opened it and showed a replica of the ear plug he had found on Drake's body. He laid the two tiny objects side by side. They were identical in shape, size and coloring.

"Where did you get it?" Fitz rapped.

"They belong to a guy named Amos Brandt, who's been selling Drake Utilities short. He's the same guy who tipped you to the murder and then called half the columnists in town to ring me in. In short, he wanted that body found—for profit. Go ahead and ring up Homicide. Then grab your hats and we're off to grab our man!"

"But—" Fitzgerald shut up suddenly as he saw Jerry's averted eye drop in a sly wink.

Corning was still staring at the floor, his whole attitude one of lax inattention. He sat stolidly as Fitz barked a brief official alarm over the wire. He didn't even raise his dazed head when Fitz said sharply, "You wait here, Corning, until the police and the medical examiner get here. Don't touch anything in the room. Understand? Hey, wake up and listen!"

"I—I understand."

KILLAN, FITZ AND the *Daily Planet's* perspiring little columnist hurried downstairs and out to the street.

Killan growled, "What's the idea of a dumb run out like this? You guys gone nuts?"

"Where's your car, Fitz?" Tracy said.

"Around the corner."

"Swell. Come on! Duck across to that grocery doorway."

They squeezed in out of sight behind crates of vegetables and fruit. Tracy kept his eye anxiously on the entrance of the apartment house diagonally opposite and the gray coupé of Tony Pedley's that was still parked at the curb. For three long minutes nothing happened. Then David Corning came out of the building entrance. He walked quietly toward Pedley's car. He had washed the blood from his cheek and chin and his hat was drawn low over the shallow bullet furrow at his temple. He sprang into the gray coupé and sent it whizzing around the corner. The car vanished rapidly north.

Killan muttered, "For gosh sake! Where's *he* going?"

"To Drake's boarded-up mansion on East 56th," Tracy said. "Where the corpse has undoubtedly been hidden all the time. Come on, Sarge! Let's see you show a little speed."

Killan obliged grimly. He was an excellent driver and he sent the car humming through the gathering dusk. But he slowed whenever traffic cops loomed in front and he skipped no lights.

Tracy didn't want any publicity—not yet. They made excellent time to East 56th and slowed at the rear of the Drake mansion.

Fitzgerald swore suddenly. The familiar gray coupé was parked at the curb. Corning had more than matched their speed and held his desperate lead.

The grilled gate to the rear courtyard was slightly ajar. There was no sign of the plainclothes man Fitzgerald had left on guard. They found him in a limp huddle in a dark angle of the private garage's wall. Someone had slugged him on the skull before he could yank his gun. The butt of his half-drawn weapon lay impotently under his unconscious hand.

They tiptoed to the rear basement window of the house and Killan pried the wood gently away. The lower floor was in complete darkness. But as they climbed the rear staircase and crept noiselessly toward the front reception room, Fitz's hand closed tautly on Tracy's arm. Light was visible through the pierced doorway of the high-ceilinged old room.

The next instant Fitz and Killan were diving headlong at a man who had whirled with a frightened squeal.

"Take him, Sarge!"

"I got him!"

Handcuffs clicked. The wrestling match ended as suddenly as it had begun. David Corning stood sullenly, head downcast, staring at the grisly figure that lay on the floor at his feet. The hilt of the knife still protruded from the chest of Edgar Drake. *Rigor mortis* had frozen the corpse forever into the ugly knee-drawn posture that Tracy had witnessed twenty-four hours earlier.

Fitz gave only a scant glance at the body and the captured prisoner. He was staring at the wall where a square opening disclosed a closeted recess from which all the shelves had been removed. The tapestry that had hidden the opening had been slid aside into a slitted groove in the wall. The inside of the ghastly little crypt was smeared with the brownish stain of dried blood. The soiled Chinese rug was in there. So was the white fleeced one from the foot of the stairs.

"Looks like we've found the body," Fitz said dryly. "That's what you asked us to do, wasn't it, Mr. Corning?"

"I didn't kill him. I didn't!"

"Shut up!" Killan snapped.

Tracy was about to say something when there came a sudden rush of feet in the hallway outside. Killan's gun snapped level—and lowered again. A woman was swaying in the doorway, her lovely face twisted by terror out of all semblance of beauty. She was holding tightly to the arm of Anne Leslie, holding it with a grip that made the trembling girl wince.

Corning raised his muscled hands in a gesture of despair. "It's no use, Pauline. They've got me."

"No!" she gasped. "No!"

She came slowly toward Fitz. The yellow light from the floor lamp made her look tall and ungainly like the sheeted furniture.

"David is lying. He's trying to protect me. He hid the body and meant to take it away. I—I killed Edgar!"

She drowned out Corning's shrill cry of protest.

"Edgar found us both here and threatened a scandal to ruin David and me. I killed him. Then Tracy came and I fled upstairs. David's only crime is that he attacked Tracy and hid the corpse. You see, I had already told him about the Bible closet and he—"

"Bible closet?" Fitz grunted.

Her smile was ghastly.

"That empty recess behind the tapestry. This house is very old. The original owner used to hold divine services in this room. The hymnals and Bibles were kept in that wall cupboard. It—it pleased my husband to cover the closet with a wooden-backed tapestry and use the space to keep business records. He thought the idea was—amusing."

Corning had found his voice.

"It's no use, Pauline. You can't get away with it, darling. They've caught me and I'm tired of pretending. Drake was a damned dirty louse. I love Pauline and I couldn't stand his treatment of her. So I—"

"So you're willing to shoulder the blame for a murder you never committed," Anne Leslie said suddenly in a queerly choked tone.

She faced Inspector Fitzgerald defiantly. "Corning thinks Pauline did it. Pauline thinks he did it. The simple truth is that I killed Drake and I had plenty of provocation. He made my life a hell with his slimy back-door attentions. He maneuvered me into a position where I had either to leave Pauline or give him what he—wanted."

Sergeant Killan wheeled toward the blond secretary. "Say, what the hell is this? A game?"

"No game," Anne replied steadily.

She gave Pauline a misty look that was redolent of loyalty and devotion. Tracy, watching silently, realized anew the power of Pauline Drake. Her charm was like something palpable, hoops that bound closely to her everyone with whom she came in contact, men and women alike. Except her husband....

Tracy moved back a step. Another. His toes turned sidewise

but he was still facing the group, smiling a little. The pale light from the floor lamp in the corner threw his lean profile into strong relief. He was staring at a silk embroidered Chinese screen that stood in a dark corner of the room. There were two things about that screen that made Tracy's heart beat quicken. The screen had been moved fully ten feet from the spot where it had stood the night before. And it was now upside down! The embroidered stork on the front panel was standing on his head. Someone had jerked that screen in such guilty haste toward the dark corner that he had dropped it and replaced it in an inverted position without noticing his error.

Corning and the two women were glaring with tragic fixity at Inspector Fitzgerald. Tracy said slowly over his shoulder:

"All three of them are lying, Fitz. The killer we really want is two other guys. A sort of smart Siamese twin. Gentlemen and ladies, allow me to present to you Mr. Amos Brandt—alias Fred Hammer of the Club Pom-Pom!"

TRACY WHIRLED LIKE a flash and threw himself at the inverted Chinese screen. He was clutching grimly for it when it was thrown violently aside, knocking the charging little columnist off balance. Fred Hammer was on his knees, gripping two flat automatics. Flame streaked toward Fitz and Killan, sending them leaping apart. Before they could swing into action, Hammer was on his feet with Tracy a helpless shield in front of him, a gun muzzle digging viciously into the columnist's spine.

The second weapon peeped over Tracy's shoulder, menacing Killan and the inspector. Their hands jerked unwillingly upward.

"O.K.," Hammer gasped. "Now move together, all of you! Make a nice tight bunch."

His low laughter rasped behind Tracy's ear.

"And keep away from that telephone, friends. I don't want any emergency trucks tossing tear gas at me. I'm going out of here without—"

His gun roared without warning. Killan's hand had dropped like lightning toward his hip as he doubled sidewise, but Hammer's bullet broke his arm before he could clutch and draw.

"Any more like to try?"

"Easy, Fitz," Tracy gasped. "I'm in a spot."

He didn't have to put any deliberate waver into his voice. He was sick at heart. But his damned flair for theatricalism had given Hammer the play, when he could just as easily have whispered a warning to Fitz about the screen. Time.... He had to play for time....

His eyes glanced briefly downward at his feet and lifted again. The murderer crouched behind him didn't see that glance. But Fitz did.

Tracy let his upraised arms sag deliberately until the savage whisper behind him snarled: "Keep 'em high or I'll split your spine open!" Tracy wanted Fred Hammer to keep thinking about his hands—not his feet. He had stepped on the trailing edge of his shoelace and had drawn one foot gently sidewise, pulling the loose bow of the lace open.

He felt the crafty shove of Hammer behind him. He stopped the killer's shielded progress across the room with a jeering whisper that held a touch of his nasal Broadway arrogance:

"Well, I gummed it at the end, Fred. But you've got to admit that I pick winners."

The pistol muzzle hurt Tracy's spine. But the slow double-shuffle halted.

Fitz was like carved granite across the room. He kept his hands high, his eyes away from Tracy's feet.

"How did you know it was me, wise guy?" Hammer snarled.

"Easy." Tracy crammed complacency into his brief chuckle. "You're the guy that tipped Drake to the presence of Pauline and Corning in this house. You're also the guy who called up the police and the columnists of a half-dozen newspapers. You planned it to look like a love triangle. When I butted in, you tried to ring me in, too. But the trouble was you dropped that rubber ear-stopple. You didn't discover it until you had tipped the cops. Then you came racing back here, but it was too late. By that time I'd been cracked on the skull by Corning and he'd hidden the corpse. You see, Corning and Pauline both thought Tony Pedley had done the job. Tony was the only one who knew about the secret appointment—until you innocently wormed it out of him. Tony was never near this house last night. He was trying to cover Corning and his mother—until I showed him the clue left by the real murderer. And Corning was trying to protect Tony."

"I still don't get it," Fitz insisted stubbornly from across the room.

Tracy heard Hammer chuckling behind him. The columnist had managed to twist his left foot free from the loosened laces. Very gently he slid his stocking heel, then his toes out of the low-cut shoe.

"You tell him, Hammer. Pedley got wise to you, just before he locked us in that bathroom. He recognized the ear-stopple. Right?"

"Right. I guessed the kid would make a bee-line to Corning to tell him what he'd found out. I got rid of you and trailed him. Shot him through the rear window just as an El train went by—but not till Corning had admitted to him where the body was hidden. The kid died before he could tell Corning who I was."

Pauline Drake uttered a faint, choked, dreadful sound. Her face drained dead as ashes. Then she said—and the quietness of her voice was more violent than hysterics, more dreadful than a scream: "You killed Tony? You killed my son?"

Corning raised his manacled arms in a futile gesture to comfort her—to catch her. She had fallen headlong on the floor.

Hammer's crooked exultation vanished. He said in a hard undertone: "Get going, Tracy. Take it slow ahead of me to that hall doorway. If anybody breathes, I'll start a slaughter!"

Tracy's stocking foot felt gently for the lamp cord on the floor. He hadn't looked at it since that first downward glance. Now he felt the ridge of it under his foot and his toes curled around in a taut grip.

The stiffening of his muscles warned Hammer. He saw the extended foot, yelled.

Tracy flung himself flat as his toes jerked the cord.

The lamp toppled and crashed, plunging the room into pitch darkness. Streaks of flame from Hammer's guns pierced the blackness. But Tracy had twisted against the killer's knees and his furious clutch brought the man down.

A bullet blasted past Tracy's ear, deafening him. His fumbling grasp caught at the hot barrel, shoving it convulsively away. Hammer had lost one of his guns in that mad tangle of arms and legs. His free hand closed on Tracy's throat. Gasping, Tracy fought to keep the jerking muzzle of the gun averted.

Then there was a quick thud of approaching feet, a desperate squirm of Hammer—and the roar of a police positive. Tracy felt the killer's body bounce under the bullet's impact. His limp weight pinned Jerry's chest and shoulder to the floor.

The silence that followed was broken by the faint, thoroughly scared whisper of the *Daily Planet's* columnist.

"I—I think you'd better light a match, Fitz."

The beam of a pocket torch played through the darkness like a bright tunnel. Fitz was crouched alertly about six feet away. He had knocked Pauline Drake and Anne Leslie headlong as he sprang to the aid of Tracy, but he hadn't had time to shoot the killer. Sergeant Killan had attended to that.

Killan was on one knee next to Hammer's faintly squirming body. The sergeant's broken arm still hung limply at his side, the fingers dripping blood. But there was nothing wrong with Killan's left hand—or the gun either.

Tracy got up, swayed, fell down again. Fitz steadied him. "You hurt?"

"I'm all right. I just—" He didn't get sick, but the successful throttling down of his heaving stomach brought cold beads of sweat out on his forehead. "I just can't take it, I guess."

Killan grinned. "The hell you can't, Jerry. That trick with the lamp cord was a darb. I was bettin' a thousand to one against your spine being a target."

He glanced at Hammer with a bleak, professional brevity.

"Not bad for a blind target—with a pal of mine all wrapped around him. He'll last about twenty minutes. With luck."

He added, in puzzled tones, "Why did the dope sneak back here anyway? Was he after Corning?"

Tracy shook his head.

"Hammer was after the body. He heard Corning tell Pedley where it was concealed before he shot the kid through the window. He had to get Drake's body discovered in a hurry in order to cash in on his short-selling coup in Wall Street. So he dragged the body out, but before he could call the police and scram, Corning arrived here, desperate to sneak the corpse away from the house to protect Tony, and Pauline's fortune from a market crash. Hammer heard him coming and ducked behind the Chinese screen."

Across the room Inspector Fitzgerald was already hanging up the phone. Corning's hands were no longer cuffed in narrow steel bands. They were spread wide and tightly, and Pauline Drake was inside the lawyer's arms. They were both shaking with emotion. Tears poured down her white cheeks but Corning, curiously, was making most of the noise.

"Darling, oh, darling, darling!" she said.

She reached up and touched his lips fumblingly with her finger-tips. Tracy got a straight look at her eyes and at Corning's. They couldn't see him but he turned away. He had a funny feeling that for the first time in his irreligious life he'd been in church.

Fitz's low voice was at his ear.

"How in the hell did you tie up those rubber ear-stopples to Hammer?"

"The guy that slugged me to get 'em back dropped a match-pad from the Pom-Pom Club. When Pedley was killed, I suddenly thought of Hammer. He'd been willing to go with me to Pedley's apartment, but the minute Pedley recognized the clue and locked us up, Hammer was twice as eager to get away from me. I beat it down to the Pom-Pom, showed the clue to the hat-check girl, and she spilled the answer. You remember how noisy it is at the Pom-Pom? Fred always wore them in his ears when he figured up accounts in his rear cubby. Couldn't concentrate on business with the noise of that swing band slashing through the velvet drapes. I slid into his office and found the duplicate tucked away in a pasteboard box in one of the desk cubby-holes. As simple as that."

"How about this Amos Brandt business? Did you find a broker's memo there?"

Tracy shook his head.

"That was pure luck, Fitz. Before I could scram the phone rang. It was Hammer's broker, calling him up to tell him that Drake Utilities was still climbing. He wanted fifty thousand additional cash to cover the margin on Amos Brandt's short-selling speculation. No wonder Hammer was so nuts to find Drake's hidden body. He had to bring it to public notice and drop the stock or be wiped out."

"There's more to it than greed," Fitz said. "Hammer must have hated Drake's guts. I've got a hunch you'll dig up a hell of a big scandal before you're finished with the Drake family."

"I've got a hunch I won't!" Tracy snapped. "What kind of a louse do you think I am!"

There was nastiness in his tone, challenge in every line of his shrewd little face. But he was smiling, too. He kept staring at Fitz, and after a moment the big horse-faced inspector flushed and nodded.

"You're going to forget for once in your life that you're a

dirt columnist, eh? Give a couple of people a break, eh?" His glance swung toward Pauline and Corning, then back to Tracy. "Damned if I don't think you're decent."

"If you think so, sue me!" Jerry Tracy said harshly, but there was pleasure in his eyes.

No More Limericks

Jerry Tracy strikes at labor killings

JERRY TRACY SCOWLED at the elevator man who was dropping him from Jack Davy's apartment to the street level. Jerry's stomach was pleasantly distended with beer and cheese sandwiches. His annoyance had nothing to do with the food or the elevator man. He was sore at Jack Davy.

Jack had just had the gall to ask if there was anything serious back of that silly limerick Tracy had printed in last Tuesday's column of the *Daily Planet*. And Jack was the nitwit who had started the whole mess!

Tracy had told him savagely, "Ssh! Don't expose me, pal, but it's true. I'm really a heel! I run half the rackets in this town."

He had said the same thing, bitterly, to a dozen other friends in the past three days—including Inspector Fitzgerald, who should have had more sense. Funny how a feeble little joke could turn so damned sour!

Tracy was a victim of his own disinclination to kick out friends who dropped into his office on rainy days. Like a sap, he had listened to Jack Davy and his blasted string of limericks. Worse, he had fiddled idly with his typewriter after Jack had gone. It had been a dull day for snappy items and Tracy had needed an amusing filler. So he'd typed a few lines batting out what he thought was a mild joke for the customers, and boxed the whole thing at the head of his column.

After that, the deluge!

The lines of the idiotic jingle stuck in Tracy's mind. He could stare at the wall of the descending elevator and see the cold

black type that had given the town's gossips a chance to lift
smart eyebrows and exchange wise whispers:

POPULAR IDEA OF A BROADWAY COLUMNIST
When the last scandal item is in,
I can still earn a living from sin—
    I'm a pal to the mugg,
    And the lug and the thug—
And, my Gawd, how the money rolls in!

The elevator man yawned and headed for a chair at the rear
of the lobby. Tracy walked grumpily to the street.

His annoyance increased as he stepped into the stinging
impact of sleet cutting through the black night. Hail bounced
off Tracy's hat-brim, crunched like frozen sand under his

feet. He slipped and fell awkwardly to one knee as he started toward the curb.

His darkened car was parked across the street behind two or three others.

The sight of it made Tracy forget his grouch. Even under the milky blur of the storm, that car was a double-barreled honey! It was a brand-new sport sedan, sleek as a bubble, with all the gadgets, from the stainless steel nude on its radiator cap to the streamlined trunk in the rear.

Tracy didn't quite like the idea of driving his brand-new boat along streets like glass. He could easily call up the garage and have somebody drive the car back while he took a taxi. Or he could put on chains and take a chance on a skid.

Unlocking the trunk, he fumbled irresolutely in the interior. The chains were there. They jingled at his touch. Sleet beat against his bent shoulder and pelted him in the ear.

He had no warning of the girl's presence until a sudden clutch at his arm spun him on the slippery pavement and almost upset him.

The girl was panting. Quick puffs of vapor came from her throat. She cried, "Hide me! Hurry up!"

"Huh?" Tracy's defensive arm lowered.

He saw the fur coat first, then her legs below the coat. The girl had no shoes on. There was nothing between her feet and the frozen pavement except the cobweb thinness of silk stockings. Her fur coat was only partly buttoned. Tracy caught a glimpse of the wreck of a white evening gown. It had been ripped from one shoulder. There was a jagged scratch of blood on the bared flesh running partly downward toward the swell of the girl's breast under the white cobweb of her bandeau.

"Please!" she begged. "Help me hide!"

She had evidently been running fast and hard. Her hair was disheveled, but she was easy to look at. Tracy's quick glance at her stockinged feet and her scratched shoulder didn't blind him to the fact that the girl was a stunning beauty. Dark-eyed, dark-haired, she swayed under the lash of sleet like a long-stemmed orchid. Her high cheekbones and the slight slant to her eyes registered automatically in Tracy's observant mind. Russian? Polish?

Her fingers were still vise-like on Tracy's arm. She shoved him aside with a strength that surprised the columnist. With a lithe bend of her body, she crawled hastily inside the opened trunk at the rear of his sedan.

"Lock it!"

Tracy was turning the key before he realized he was obeying. He stared up and down the street, wondering if anyone had witnessed the girl's swift appearance and disappearance. There was no one in sight.

The girl couldn't have rushed from the front entrance of the near-by apartment house; the hallman would have noticed her frantic appearance and barged out after her. She had probably raced from the rear service alley where a dim light glowed above a wide-open gate.

Something about her Slavic beauty teased Tracy's memory. He was certain he had never seen her before in his life. Yet the formation of her face reminded Jerry of somebody she resembled. He couldn't focus his memory. It annoyed him.

So did the bouncing fury of the sleet. The icy little pellets stung like buckshot. Tracy hunched his chin into his coat collar and unlocked the door of his sedan. He slid behind the wheel and sat there, feeling a little foolish, listening to the click of hail against his windshield. He didn't switch on his lights.

He thought, uneasily: "Now what?"

Then he saw the man.

The fellow came running so fast from the service alley that his feet slid out from under him on the turn, and he went skating along the glassy sidewalk on the back of his neck. He was up in an instant, glaring through the blur of the sleet.

There were three or four darkened cars parked closer to the man than Tracy's. He approached them swiftly, peering into each. One hand remained stiffly in a pocket of his coat.

"Gun," Tracy thought. His heart expanded with a quick lift of excitement.

He had no idea whether the girl curled up inside his locked trunk was a sneak thief or a pet-and-run virgin. He didn't much care now. He could smell the unpleasant stink of trouble blowing his way unless he pulled a quick sneak. He stepped on his starter.

As it whirred, the man with one hand in his pocket straightened. He hauled around from his inspection of the other cars and darted toward Tracy's. He caught at the door handle, wrenched it open. His face was distorted with fury.

"Wait a minute, you!"

The sedan's engine was already roaring. Tracy cut it to a murmur which died almost instantly in the freezing weather. He turned around, pretending anger, but making sure his hands were in plain sight on the rim of his wheel.

"What the hell's the idea yanking my door open like that? What do you want?"

The man had been peering watchfully over Tracy's shoulder into the rear of the sedan. Suddenly he blinked and shrugged. His lips twisted in a sheepish grimace. But Tracy sensed a deadly tension behind the grin.

"Sorry, Mac, I wasn't trying to get tough. I—I guess I'm a little excited. Did you see a girl run out of that apartment alley a minute ago?"

He had a square, fleshy face with rather full lips. There was liquor on his breath, but no haze of drunkenness in his eyes. They were hard, clear, watchful; like wet, gray stones. As he leaned closer, Tracy saw a trickle of blood on his forehead near the hollow of his left temple. Something circular and solid had banged the man with bruising effect. The spiked heel of a woman's slipper could have done the trick nicely.

"A girl?" Tracy said. He let his gaze and the tone of his voice prod the man into awkward explanation.

"My wife. She just ran out on me. We had an argument. She's pretty tight. Ran out in her stocking feet. I'm afraid she'll—"

"I didn't see her," Tracy said.

He knew it was a mistake the moment he said it. He could see the man's forehead wrinkle, estimating time. Barely a minute had elapsed between the girl's disappearance and the man's arrival. Tracy should have told him that the girl had rushed down the street and had darted into a doorway somewhere. But it was too late now!

"You didn't see her?"

"No."

"You're a dirty little liar!"

His clenched hand jerked from his pocket. The gun was a small one, but the muzzle was not more than three inches from Tracy's ribs.

"Reach back and snap on your dome light. Unlock the rear door."

Tracy obeyed. The man took a quick look at the lap-robe that hung in bunched folds from a chromium bar. He made sure that no one was crouched on the floor under the bulky material of the robe.

"Satisfied?" Tracy said, trying to start the car again.

"Like hell! She wasn't in any of those other cars. She's *got* to be in yours. Get out and open that trunk!"

"I might have a minute ago," Tracy said evenly. "A minute ago you were excited enough to pump lead. Now you've had time to think things over. The gun's a bluff."

"Yeah?"

"You live in that apartment house, mister. Or the girl does. One bang from that gun and out comes your doorman and identifies one of his tenants with a corpse."

The drawl went out of Tracy's voice. It crackled. "What's your racket?"

All Tracy got was profanity.

He laughed and dropped his palm on the horn button. He kept it there in a long sustained blast. A uniformed figure came hurrying out from the ornate front entrance of the near-by apartment house. The doorman paid no attention to Tracy, He was goggling at the gunman. The weapon was no longer in sight, but the heel dent on the man's forehead was still trickling blood.

The doorman's frightened ejaculation sounded like the bleat of a goat. "Mr. Spane! What's—what's happened? Is anything wrong?"

The man didn't say anything. He had walked quietly to the front of Tracy's sedan and was staring intently at the license plate. Tracy started the car again and the motor caught. The man jumped sideways.

"Mr. Spane has had a little accident," Tracy murmured to the doorman. "He was reaching for something and fell out the window."

Spane laughed briefly. It sounded nasty. "I'll be reaching for something else damned soon and next time I won't flop!"

He turned and walked with swift, slippery strides toward the apartment entrance. The doorman gave Tracy a frightened look and then followed Spane.

Tracy meshed gears and eased his sedan away from the curb.

He drove slowly on the slick pavement. He tried to keep his mind on the tires as he jockeyed the new sedan safely around the corner and headed down the avenue at a sluggish pace. He didn't want a ten-thousand-dollar custom job wrapped around a light pole a week after he'd bought it!

That was what Jerry Tracy pretended to think, but it wasn't the truth. The apartment-house doorman had given him something more sinister to think about. A guy chasing a frightened girl in a torn white evening gown didn't mean much in Manhattan. But when the guy's name was Ed Spane....

Ed Spane had been very much in the news lately. Labor news. He was executive vice-president of the Textile Worker's local in New York. For the past month Spane had taken over the leadership of the union, acting in the place of the union's president, Nicola Durensky. Durensky had been slugged over the head and badly beaten by unidentified thugs.

An unauthorized sit-in strike had brought violence and death to the huge, sprawling factories of the Chanler Knitting Mills. Durensky had tried to settle the strike—and now he was lying in a hospital in a coma from concussion of the brain.

The trouble had flared up after years of peace between the union and the Chanler Mills. Spane charged that Roy Chanler had fomented the mysterious violence with paid spies, that his plan was to smash the union and break his labor contract. Spane ascribed the brutal slugging of Durensky to professional gorillas hired by Roy Chanler's plant superintendent. Chanler denied it.

The girl locked in Tracy's trunk was no longer a mystery to the dapper little columnist of the *Daily Planet*. Tracy had realized her identity the moment he had heard the doorman call the man with the gun Mr. Spane. She was Vera Durensky!

Her resemblance to her father was the thing that had nudged Tracy's memory. She had his same high cheekbones, his slanting brown eyes. Tracy had met Nicola Durensky several times and had liked him. The old man had a reputation for brains, courage, and honesty. He had come to New York from Poland many years ago and had become one of the best loved labor leaders in the country. He was one of the original organizers of the Textile Union.

Tracy wondered if the attack on Durensky was linked with the frightened flight of his daughter from the apartment of Ed Spane. Spane was a relative newcomer in the union. Tracy made a mental note to get in touch with Leo Pelman and find out more about this ugly labor trouble. Pelman would know plenty about it. He was the *Daily Planet's* labor expert. He ran a department called "News Along the Labor Front."

Meanwhile there remained the awkward problem of Vera. Tracy glanced uneasily over his shoulder. Unless he got her out of that damned trunk the girl would smother to death. He started to pull in toward the curb, then changed his mind.

There were plenty of cabs on the avenue and enough pedestrians to make things a nuisance. So many people knew Tracy there was a chance he'd be spotted and recognized if he tried to release a sketchily clad brunette beauty on a public street. And Tracy didn't want any more publicity. Spane's threat when he had memorized Tracy's license number, was proof enough to the *Daily Planet's* columnist that he had already stuck his neck out.

The only improving situation was the weather. The sleet was changing to snow, and driving was a bit easier. Tracy stepped up his speed, keeping his eyes alert for an all-night garage.

He spied one presently and drove in. The only person in sight was a Negro car washer. Tracy got out of his sedan and the Negro shambled sleepily toward him. Tracy told him he needed an extra headlight bulb.

"Don't reckon we got one that'll do you, suh."

"How about taking a look in the stock room?"

"Yassuh."

The minute the Negro disappeared, Tracy worked fast. The girl's teeth were chattering. She was so stiff she couldn't move. Jerry hauled her out with a grunt. He shoved her in the rear of the sedan and dropped the lap-robe over her. He pulled a pocket flask from a compartment in the dash and thrust it into the cold clutch of the girl's fingers. She gave him a glassy smile of thanks.

"Ain't got no light bulb like you need, boss," the Negro reported presently, "We don't carry them big—"

"O.K. Never mind."

He gave the man a dime and backed the heavy sedan to the street. He headed toward his penthouse. The girl was now hunched forward on the rear seat, the lap-robe tucked across her knees. Her teeth had stopped clicking. There was a flush on her lovely cheeks as she handed Jerry back his flask.

"Thank you. You have good liquor."

"Good?" He grinned. "It's perfect, Miss Schmalz! By the way, what's your name?"

"Smith."

"Not Mrs. John Smith?" Tracy asked dryly.

"No. Miss Johanna Smith." He liked the way she laughed. Sleigh bells. Silver ones.

"Who was the guy that chased you? I had a time getting rid of him."

He could almost hear the click of Vera Durensky's brain as she hesitated. Locked in the air-tight trunk, she probably hadn't heard a thing.

"Was he ugly about it?"

"No. I told him you had ducked into another doorway. When he chased after you, I scrammed. What was it all about?"

"I was silly enough to go look at his etchings. We had a couple of drinks and he got fresh. I'm afraid I said 'No' with the heel of one of my slippers. I lost the other one racing down the backstairs. I'm sorry I dragged you into it."

Again Tracy was conscious of a pause, an indefinable hardening of the girl's voice. "Or *did* I drag you in?"

"What do you mean?" Tracy asked her, his gaze flicking swiftly across his shoulder. Her brown eyes were steady.

"I thought I recognized you, but I wasn't sure until I saw your initials on the flask. You're Jerry Tracy of the *Daily Planet*. I'm wondering how you happened to be waiting so providentially outside that apartment house. It doesn't make sense. I mean, *your* saving me from *him*."

Tracy could sense cold, cautious antagonism. "What the hell are you talking about?" he asked.

"You write a Broadway column every day, don't you?"

"Sure. So what?"

"Skip it," she said. "Do you mind turning this car around? I live uptown."

"You can't go home in stocking feet and the wreck of an evening gown. You need a hot bath and some new clothes. I can let you have both. And there isn't a single etching in my whole penthouse."

To his surprise Vera didn't protest. He had a queer feeling that she had expected his suggestion, was glad that he had made it.

TRACY PULLED INTO the curb in front of the canopied entrance of the smooth granite cliff on whose pinnacle his penthouse was perched. The doorman's discreet smile ignored the fact that Tracy was accompanied by a very lovely and very rumpled looking girl.

"Good evening, Mr. Tracy."

"Go upstairs, Eddie, and tell Butch to give you the smallest pair of slippers in the house. Scram."

"Yes, sir." He hurried away.

"Do they all have that sublime lack of curiosity?" the girl asked.

"They do when they're on your personal payroll," Tracy grinned. "I could bring home a white elephant in lace panties and Eddie would act just the same." His grin widened as he gazed at Vera's slim figure. "No offense meant, of course."

Tracy slid the borrowed slippers on Vera's feet while Eddie held the sedan's door open. The girl held out her stocking feet indifferently. They were really lovely legs. Eddie kept his head up and his eyes down. It must have hurt his neck. Tracy locked the car and he and Vera went upstairs.

Butch was listening to a radio program. He gawped but didn't say anything when Tracy and the girl walked in. Butch was Tracy's valet, bodyguard, messenger boy and pest-chaser. He had the body of a behemoth and the mind of a child. A career in the ring as a second-rate pugilist hadn't added anything to his intellect any. But he was as tough as a squad of marines and just as handy.

A swing band was pouring hot rhythm from the radio. Butch rubbed his bad ear and leaned closer to listen, a blurred smile on his thick lips.

"Look, lemme hear this number, will you? Boy, listen to it! Hatch Talbot's sure playin' with his pants down tonight—'scuse me, lady."

"Scram!" Tracy said. "I'm busy. Take the funny paper to bed with you."

Butch didn't argue. He departed with his underlip hanging sadly.

Vera Durensky was calmly watching Tracy. Dance music filled the silence between them.

"There's a key in the bedroom door," Tracy told her. "You'll find a selection of evening gowns and anything else you may need in my man-about-town closet. Second door to the left. The bathroom is private. You'll like it."

"Thank you." Her glance as she left him was half mockery, half challenge.

Alone in the living room, Tracy wasn't quite sure what he ought to do next. He paced up and down, listening to the dance music. Vera's story about her visit to Spane was phoney. Spane might have made a lustful pass at her, but it didn't explain why he had chased her to the street with a gun. There was no lust in his eyes when he had argued with Tracy; there was despair and fear. Vera had swiped something from Ed Spane! That was the only sensible answer.

Whatever Vera had stolen, it was probably in the pocket of her coat, Tracy decided to try and get hold of it. He grinned as he figured out a pleasant way to frisk the girl.

While Tracy waited, he had a good chance to call up Leo Pelman, the *Daily Planet's* labor reporter. He wanted to fill out his sketchy knowledge of the trouble between Durensky's union and the Chanler Knitting Mills.

He was leafing through the phone book for Pelman's home address when a series of staccato sounds from the radio whirled him around with instant tension. *Bap-bap-bap....* It cut through the rhythm of Hatch Talbot's swing music like the echo of rapping knuckles.

Tracy knew what it meant. It was the click of a phone dial, picked up as electrical interference by the radio and magnified in the loud speaker. He tried to fix the number of sounds in his memory by rapping his own knuckles against his palm. He knew that for every hole in the phone dial there was an additional click from zero to A. But he was too late to get the exchange combination or the four numbers of the call. He caught only the last two.

The numbers were a seven and a three. Tracy was certain of that. He was also grimly certain of the sound origin. Vera Durensky was telephoning somebody from the phone in Tracy's own bedroom.

He had no way of listening in. Every phone in his penthouse—and there was one in each room, including the bathroom—was a private instrument. People who called up with scandal items were entitled to protection from eavesdroppers, and some of Tracy's pals were not above curiosity.

Frowning, Tracy picked up his living-room phone to call Leo Pelman. But he slammed it down before the operator could complete the call. His radio was rapping again!

This time Tracy got it. Seven series of bangs like the pop of a tiny firecracker. The first three was the exchange. The last four was the number. Tracy's right hand transferred the sounds to paper as his left repeated the raps.

He glanced at the dial of his own phone and translated sound into sight. The exchange letters were grouped in threes. But the only letter combination that made sense was CH. And the next number was 9. CHester-9.... The whole thing added up to CHester 9-3248.

Tracy knew the neighborhood of the Chester exchange. Grabbing the phone book, his fingers raced tremulously along the S's. Spane, Edward, Arlington Street, CHester 9-3248.

Tracy was afraid to turn off his radio for fear the sudden silence might warn the girl in his bedroom. He laid his ear against the door but the music ruined any chance to listen. Grimly, he decided to take advantage of the music himself. He called Leo Pelman.

Pelman sounded sleepy and puzzled.

He kept asking Tracy to talk louder. Finally, he made sense of the low urgent whispers that Tracy spat at him.

"You mean Ed Spane? Gosh, no! Where did you ever get a screwy idea like that? He's rough and he's tough, but he's on the level. As honest as they come.... What? Speak up, Jerry! I can't hear you."

"Wait a second!"

Tracy tiptoed to the bedroom door. He thought he could hear the splash of water from his bathroom. He raced back to the phone.

Rapidly he told Pelman about his unexpected adventure with

Spane and Vera Durensky. The *Daily Planet's* labor reporter gasped.

"Durensky's daughter, eh? And Spane had a gun? It doesn't sound like him. He usually swings a fist, a tough one, too. Did you see any signs of Chanler when Vera came tearing out the alley?"

"Chanler?"

"Roy Chanler. The head of the Chanler Knitting Mills."

"What's he got to do with it?"

"Durensky's daughter is in love with him," Pelman sputtered over the wire. "She's nuts about him! She's living in his home right now as a guest of Nell Chanler, Roy's sister. The two gals were roommates at college. When Vera's old man was slugged on the skull, she went to live with Nell."

"So what?"

"Vera's gone high-hat in a big way ever since she tangled with the Chanlers, My hunch is that she'd do anything Roy asked her to. Sell out her old man and bust up his union, to take an altar-walk with a guy who has a cute dimple in his chin and eight million dollars." All the sleepiness had whipped away from Pelman's voice. "You don't believe that?"

"I'm listening," Tracy said. He kept watching the closed door of his bedroom, ready to snap down the phone at the first click of a key in the inside of the lock.

Pelman's voice shot him labor dope over the wire. Roy Chanler was a union baiter, he said. There had been no trouble while his old man had run the mills. Durensky and old man Chanler liked and trusted each other. But after Chanler died and Roy took over, trouble had started. Mysterious violence that had sent Durensky to the hospital and had baffled Ed Spane in his efforts to make peace. Roy Chanler didn't want peace! He wanted to smash the union and cancel his labor contracts. And Vera Durensky was hand-in-glove with him—against her own father.

"I'll look over my files and records and call you back," Pelman promised. "In fifteen or twenty minutes."

"Yeah. Do that, Leo."

A moment later the lock of Tracy's bedroom door clicked.

Vera emerged smilingly. She looked demure and well groomed. The fact that her borrowed evening gown was a little small for her, didn't hurt her figure any. Tracy noted that she was carrying her heavy coat. She put it on, although the temperature in the penthouse was quite warm.

"You've been very kind."

"Not at all." Tracy smiled and moved closer. "I like to accommodate my lady friends."

Vera made no effort to withdraw from him. She had smooth, warm hands. Her dark eyes were sultry, dimly encouraging.

"Do you have many—lady friends?"

"None as gorgeous as you, my dear."

Tracy drew her closer. She made no effort to withdraw from his tightening embrace. He kissed her experimentally, then with more ardor. He was disgusted with her easy compliance. But it made the task of frisking her coat pockets a cinch. As she swayed against him with eyes closed, Tracy's left hand explored both pockets of her coat.

He found nothing.

"I—I think I had better go," Vera whispered.

"I'll drive you home," Tracy said.

"Please don't. If you'll lend me a dollar for a taxi...."

But Tracy insisted on escorting her downstairs to his sedan. Vera seemed uneasy. Tracy knew why! She was hurrying back to see Spane for some urgent reason—the same man who had ripped her dress half off and had chased her with a gun. Was it to return whatever it was she had stolen from Spane? And what in *hell* had she taken?

On the sidewalk Vera refused definitely to ride in Tracy's sedan. He shrugged and handed her a five-dollar bill. She hurried through the blur of falling snow toward the corner where a taxicab was parked. The door slammed. The cab circled into the avenue.

Tracy turned toward his own car, reaching for his key ring.

It was gone!

For an instant he stood like a fool, his fingers vainly probing his pocket. Then he realized how cleverly Vera had worked on him. Her love play upstairs had been as phoney as his! She had lifted his key ring while Tracy had probed vainly in the empty pockets of her coat.

It explained Vera's reluctance to have him accompany her downstairs. She had wanted a chance to unlock the trunk at the rear of his sedan. That was where she had hidden whatever object she had stolen from Spane!

Whirling, Tracy ran back into the apartment house. To the startled hallman he shot a quick order.

"Eddie! Get outside and watch my car. Don't let anyone go near it until I come back!"

He dashed for the elevator and ran it upstairs himself. He kept a finger on his bell button until Butch came stumbling to let him in. Butch was in his underwear, fuzzy-eyed, half asleep.

"Hey, Jeeze, what the—"

Tracy raced to a desk and grabbed duplicate auto keys. He was darting toward the foyer when he suddenly stopped. The sight of his phone gave him an idea. He was still eager for a check-up on that first mysterious phone call Vera had made. The last two numbers might mean something to Leo Pelman. He grabbed the phone.

But Pelman didn't answer. After listening to three long rings, Tracy banged down the receiver.

Butch grabbed him by the arm. "What's wrong, boss? Wait'll I pull on me pants and I'll—"

"Go to bed! I don't need you."

They were still arguing about it when the phone bell rang. It was Leo Pelman. The reporter sounded elated, excited.

"I promised to call you back, Jerry."

"I just tried to get you."

Pelman chuckled. "Keep your shirt on. I heard the bell, but I was knee-deep in stuff about the Chanler strike."

"Do you know anyone whose phone number ends in 7-3?"

"No. Why?"

Tracy didn't waste time trying to explain. "Listen, Leo! Get dressed as fast as you can. Grab a cab and go up to Ed Spane's apartment. Wait outside for me. And, listen, bring a gun!"

He could hear the startled gasp of the *Daily Planet's* labor expert. "What's the idea, Jerry?"

Tracy told him about Vera, her theft of Tracy's keys, her unsuccessful effort to recover whatever she had hidden in the trunk of his sedan.

"She's heading back to Spane's. I'm going to cover that conference if it kills me. I want you to back me up."

Pelman hesitated. Then he said in a strange tone: "Jerry, I hate to get personal. Is your angle on this thing clean?"

"What the hell do you mean?"

"There's been some funny talk about you all over town. You ran a limerick in your column—"

"Are you going to bring *that* up? It was a joke, a gag. It was supposed to be funny.... Will you meet me or not?"

"I'll meet you," Pelman said slowly.

Tracy banged down the receiver. "Go to bed, Butch! I'll explain later."

He raced to the elevator and dropped himself downward to the street. The hallman was still watching Tracy's parked car.

"Anything happen while I was gone?"

"Yeah. That dame who took that taxi drove back. She must a just circled the block. She stopped right next to your sedan and started to hop out. Then I came running from the doorway and she changed her mind. She went away fast in the cab."

"Thanks."

Tracy bent swiftly in the whirl of snowflakes and unlocked the sedan's trunk. He searched the interior with quick thoroughness. He found something tucked under one of his tire chains. It was part of a page torn from a newspaper.

Staring at it, Tracy had a sudden sick feeling. He was staring at one of his own columns, torn from the *Daily Planet*.

It was idiotic, a mad coincidence, but there it was! The thing that Vera had stolen from Spane was something that pointed at Tracy himself. His eyes ran down it mechanically, looking for an answer to the riddle. A bunch of social gossip that didn't mean a thing. No marks on it, no paragraph underlined.

Tracy placed it in his wallet with fingers that were not quite steady. Why should Spane pull a gun to get back one of Tracy's columns? And what did Vera mean by that sullen remark of hers when Tracy had first questioned her? "I'm sorry I dragged you into this. Or *did* I drag you in?"

He slid behind his wheel and drove hard and fast through the storm toward Ed Spane's apartment.

THERE WAS NO sign of Vera's taxi outside. Tracy parked at the curb and waited for Pelman. He had a gun with him, and the feel of the weapon sparked his impatience. He got out and locked the car. The wind whipped at his coattails and sifted snow down his collar. The street was like a sheeted tomb. And still no sight of the leisurely Pelman.

Tracy was afraid to wait downstairs too long. He entered the apartment's dimly lit lobby. It was after midnight and the doorman had gone off duty. The house was one of those self-service elevator places. Tracy located Spane's apartment by inspecting the names tucked below the letter boxes. He rode the elevator to the fifth floor.

Listening outside Spane's door, he could hear the subdued mumble of voices. A man and a woman. He waited until the woman's voice lifted, then his jaw hardened. Vera! She sounded shrill with fright. She was arguing about something. Tracy caught the quick syllables of his own name.

Drawing his gun, he rang the bell. The voices ceased inside. There was silence for a moment. Then heavy feet approached the door.

"Who is it?"

"Jerry Tracy. Open up, Spane! I want to talk to you."

"I told you he'd come back," Vera's voice sobbed.

"Shut up!" Spane growled. "Oke, Tracy. Wait a minute!"

The bolt on the door slid back. Tracy lifted his gun and set himself for trouble.

But the face that peered at him from the open doorway startled him so that he recoiled with instinctive amazement. It wasn't Ed Spane! It was a younger man with a hard, frightened face and blazing eyes. Tracy had barely time to see the deep cleft of a dimple in the man's chin when a hand clutched at the columnist and yanked him headlong into the darkened room.

Tracy tried to jerk up his gun. He was no match for the strength of his foe. The weapon was wrenched from his hand. A rap on the skull dropped him, stunned, to his knees. Another blow filled his brain with blazing pinwheels.

He went down on his face, and a knee jammed into his limp backbone.

He could hear Vera scream in a fading faraway echo: "For God's sake, don't hurt him! Don't, don't!"

The weight lifted from his body. Footsteps raced away. Somewhere—thousands of miles from Tracy's blurred consciousness—a door slammed. Then silence....

Tracy fought against the blackness that was blotting out his senses. Gritting his teeth, he pushed himself up from the floor. He took a blind, dizzy step and fell over an unseen chair. That was all he remembered.

The sound of his own groaning brought him back to reality. The chair he had fallen over helped him. He leaned on it till the blackness of the room stopped rolling like a ship at sea. His probing hand touched the cool surface of a wall. He found a light switch and clicked the room into yellow brilliance.

It was empty, of course. Vera and Roy Chanler had taken it on the lam down the back stairs. Tracy knew his assailant was

Chanler. That dimpled cleft in his chin recalled Leo Pelman's sardonic description of the mill owner. "A guy with a cute dimple in his chin and eight million dollars!"

Tracy thought suddenly of Ed Spane. With a sinking feeling of horror, he began to move from room to room, searching for Spane's body. But tonight his hunches weren't working. Dead or alive, Spane was nowhere to be found. Having peered hastily into a bedroom, a bathroom and a small kitchen, Tracy returned to the living-room.

His watch was still running. He was surprised to discover that barely five minutes had elapsed since he had noted the time in the ascending elevator. Chanler's blows had been hastily delivered. Tracy had been stunned rather than knocked cold.

There was still a faint chance of picking up the trail of the fugitives.

However, glancing toward the desk of the missing Ed Spane, Tracy saw something that brought a startled exclamation from him. There was a pile of tabloid newspapers on the union official's desk. They had all been folded open to an inner page. Every one of them was a *Daily Planet*.

A familiar double column of newsprint met Tracy's incredulous gaze:

BROADWAY IN PERSON

by

Jerry Tracy

Unlike the specimen that Vera had hidden in the trunk of Tracy's sedan these columns were marked. In each of them a single paragraph had been circled with a blue pencil!

They were routine paragraphs that Tracy himself had composed. Not one had come from an outside source. The thought that someone might have used his column to send private code messages to Spane vanished from Tracy's mind. It was ridiculous—unless Jerry himself had a split personality and was in cahoots with a crooked labor leader without being aware of it.

But there were the marked paragraphs!

Tracy shivered as he thought of the frosty blue eyes of Inspector Fitzgerald. Fitz had already called him down to Center Street to question him about that silly limerick Jerry had printed, boasting about his underworld connections. If Fitz ever saw these marked columns....

He took one for a sample and placed it in his wallet with the one he had taken from his sedan trunk. Then, drawing a deep, unhappy breath, he tiptoed through the kitchen to the rear service door. He'd had all he wanted of trouble for tonight! He'd been threatened by Ed Spane, hoodwinked by Vera Durensky, slugged by Roy Chanler. But the thing that frightened him most was the grim feeling that he was being framed.

He threw open Spane's kitchen door.

He took one step across the sill—then he stopped.

A TALL, GRAY-HAIRED man in a derby and a black overcoat was standing in the hall. He had eyes the color of a blue lake under moonlight. There was a gun in his hand and it was pointed menacingly at the startled columnist.

The cops had guns, too. There were two of them, standing on either side of the man in the derby. Tracy said weakly, "Hello,

Fitz." Amazement remained only a second in Inspector Fitzgerald's eyes. They were cold and hard.

"Get back inside! Take his gun, Devlin! Kennedy, go through to the front and let the others in."

"Listen, Fitz," Tracy said. "Don't be a damn fool."

"Shut up!"

It was his way of telling Tracy that friendship was out. Two more cops came in from the front door. Sergeant Killan, Fitz's Homicide assistant, was with them. Killan gave Tracy a crisp scrutiny and then hurried out of sight. Tracy could hear him searching the other rooms of the apartment.

"Where's Spane?" Fitz barked.

"I don't know."

"What are you doing here?" Tracy didn't answer. He was thinking swiftly. It was obvious that someone had phoned the police to pin him tight in a frame-up. That the situation was serious, he could tell from Fitzgerald's grim scrutiny. He decided to say nothing about Vera Durensky or Roy Chanler. He had no idea what he was involved in, or how deeply. His only refuge was to keep his mouth shut about what he knew, until he could investigate personally.

"What are you doing here?" Fitz repeated.

"I came to see Ed Spane on a personal matter."

"Alone?"

"Yeah."

"Who gave you that lump on the skull? Spane?"

"Yeah. We had an argument. He socked me and I swung a couple myself. Then Spane ran out."

"Out where?" Sergeant Killan interrupted. He had returned from his search of the apartment in time to hear Tracy's statement.

"Out the front door."

"Yeah?" Killan grasped Tracy by the arm. His tightening fingers hurt. "I wanna show you something."

What he showed Tracy was in the bathroom. Killan pulled back the rubber shower curtain with a gloved hand. Tracy had missed it in his hasty search but there was Spane—in the tub. His legs were doubled up, his hands clasped over his belly. There was blood all over his hands and a lot more of it in the tub. The knife that had killed Spane was gone.

"You socked him and he ran out," Fitzgerald suggested. He was standing alongside Killan. "Is that your story?"

"I'm sorry. I was lying."

"Did you kill him?"

For a second Jerry pulled out of his daze with a trace of his nasal Broadway insolence.

"Don't be a sap! When I kill a guy, I don't use a knife. I use a typewriter." He grinned but nobody else did.

"Do you know who *did* kill him?"

"No."

"How did you get in?"

"Duplicate key. Spane and I were pretty friendly."

"Your friendship have anything to do with that underworld limerick you printed in your column recently?"

Tracy's pale cheeks mottled with impotent rage.

"Damn it, Fitz! I've told you that limerick was a joke."

"So you let yourself in with a key," Fitz grunted. "And Spane wasn't home, or you thought he wasn't.... Let's get back to the living room."

He walked to Spane's desk and picked up the pile of folded *Daily Planets.*

Sergeant Killan said softly: "What did you come to see Spane about, Jerry?"

"I happened to be in the neighborhood. Across the street, as a matter of fact. I was visiting a friend of mine named Jack Davy. When I left him, I walked across here."

"This Davy, he's a great guy for limericks, ain't he?"

"Go to hell!" Tracy rasped.

Fitz was still staring at the newspapers. His grizzled head lifted and he nodded to one of the uniformed cops.

"Get hold of this Jack Davy. Bring him over here."

The cop saluted and vanished. He had barely left when there was a sudden commotion at the door. The policeman on guard growled: "Wait a minute! Where the hell are you going?"

A man came barging in excitedly. It was Leo Pelman. Tracy gave a cry of relief.

"Leo! You're just the guy I want to see. Will you tell these dumb Sherlocks that we—" He stopped short. He was going to add impulsively: "—that we had an appointment to meet here?" He choked it off. It would mean mentioning Vera and the column she had stolen from Spane. He finished, weakly: "That I'm on the level and I'm not a crook or a killer?"

His eyes flashed a warning to Pelman, but the labor reporter didn't get it.

"Killer?" Pelman echoed. "You mean Spane is dead?"

Inspector Fitzgerald eyed him coldly. "If you didn't know it, what are you doing here? You a mind reader?"

Pelman laughed scornfully. "You're nuts, Fitz, if you think that Tracy is mixed up in a kill. I knew all about him coming to see Spane. We had an appointment to meet here."

To Tracy's despair, Pelman told about Jerry's telephone call.

Fitz listened with a granite face to the story of Vera's flight from Spane's apartment, Tracy's rescue of her and their subsequent visit to Tracy's penthouse. Pelman mentioned Tracy's request to meet him at Spane's and back him up in case of gun-play.

"You didn't think there was anything queer about all that?" Fitzgerald asked grimly.

"Well, there's been some silly gossip in the underworld. Jerry ran a joking limerick in his column about his hook-up with crooks and the dough it brought him. I mean—hell, I don't mean anything! Tracy's O.K."

Fitz didn't reply to the rattled labor reporter. He showed Tracy one of the folded *Planets*.

"What's the idea of the marked paragraph in that column?"

"How the hell do I know? I didn't mark it."

"You and Spane wouldn't be using that Broadway column of yours for a secret code?"

"No!"

"All right. Don't yell at me." Fitz laid down the paper. "Why did you lie about being alone here tonight? Are you trying to hide something about that crooked strike set-up at the Chanler Knitting Mills?"

Tracy didn't answer.

"Durensky's daughter didn't stab Spane. No woman could have jammed a heavy knife home that way. A man did the job, and he had five strong fingers around Spane's throat while he did it. Who was it—Roy Chanler?"

"I wouldn't know."

"Any idea where Chanler and the girl are now?"

"No."

Fitz swung irritably toward Sergeant Killan. "Get on the phone and call Headquarters. Have a general alarm sent out right away for Vera Durensky. Pick up Chanler at his home— or wherever he is."

While Killan was at the phone there was another scuffle at the doorway of the apartment. Patrolman Kennedy strode in, dragging a meek, inoffensive looking man by the collar. It was Jack Davy. He had a quizzical, friendly face, but there was no friendliness in his voice. He was yelling indignantly at the top of his lungs.

"What's the idea, you—you Cossack!"

Tracy said tonelessly: "Skip it, Jack. I'm in a spot. They want to know why I was in this particular neighborhood tonight. Tell 'em."

Davy grinned. "That's easy. We had some beer together. I told Jerry a few new limericks. I'm a great guy for limericks."

"Did you tell him that one he printed in *The Daily Planet?*" Fitz snapped.

"Not me. Jerry is still kinda touchy about that one. In fact, he got sore tonight when I—"

"When you asked him if there was any truth behind it?"

"That's right."

"What did he say?"

Davy blinked. "He said: 'Sssh! Don't expose me, pal, but it's true. I'm really a heel! I run half the rackets in this town.' You know—kidding."

"Yeah, I know."

The irony in Fitzgerald's snarl didn't disturb Davy. He had recovered his good nature. He stared at Fitzgerald with a reminiscent air.

"Do you know the one about Mrs. Logan?"

"Nuts. Don't bother me."

"It's a pip. Listen:

"Have you heard about poor Mrs. Logan?

"She had dandruff all—"

Fitzgerald's voice roared. "Kennedy, shove this nitwit over in the corner!"

Tracy tapped the inspector's angry shoulder. "I'm walking out of here, Fitz. Right now! If you don't like it, arrest me! Or you can have some fool trail my sedan."

"What sedan?"

"The one I left downstairs at the curb."

"What are you trying to do, kid me? If you mean that big new boat you bought, it ain't downstairs."

Tracy darted to the window. There were two police cars parked below like white-blanketed bugs. But no sedan.

Tracy had left the car locked. There was only one person in New York besides Tracy who could have unlocked it. That wise little floozie who had stolen his keys. Vera!

He took a deep breath as he turned from the window. He walked over to Spane's telephone. Killan looked at Fitz, but Fitz shook his head slightly.

"Hello. Gimme police headquarters.... Who's this? McDougal? This is Jerry Tracy. I want to report a stolen car."

McDougal's voice chuckled across the wire. "You're having your troubles with that new boat, ain't you? What's the matter? Somebody got a grudge against you?"

"What do you mean?"

"Somebody called up an hour ago. Gave us your license number. Wanted to know who owned it."

Excitement made Tracy's voice crackle. To a newspaper man the inference about a license call made directly to police headquarters was obvious.

"Did the guy say who he was?"

"Yeah. Some fella named Springer. He's a reporter on the *Daily Chronicle.*"

"O.K. Thanks a lot."

Fitzgerald had leaned close enough to hear both ends of the conversation. He didn't say anything. Nor did Killan. In the silence only the voice of Jack Davy was audible. He was backed in a far corner of the room, talking smilingly to Patrolman Kennedy.

"You think that last one was a honey? Listen to this:

"A Bolivian princess named Paca
Liked to float nude on Lake Titicaca.
But the trouble with that,
Was the gal got so fat—"

Fitzgerald's outraged bellow drowned the last line of the limerick.

"Kennedy! Throw that damned fool out of here! Kick him downstairs!"

Jerry Tracy had picked up his hat from the floor. He jammed it on his head and started for the door. Fitzgerald stepped in front of him, blocking his exit.

"Take it easy, Jerry."

"I'm walking out of this dump. You know where I live. Or

you can arrest me right now and I'll crucify you and the whole damn police force in my column, after I blow your case apart!"

Fitzgerald's expression was not a happy one. He said harshly, "Listen, Jerry, I don't like that kind of talk."

"I'll talk any damn way I please!"

"Mmm, big, huh?"

"Damn right—if you force me to act that way. I don't want to use my publicity connections to make a monkey out of you, Fitz. But I'll do it if you shove me in a corner. I don't have to tell you that I swing a lot of weight in this town and in plenty of others, too, for that matter. If you think I'm kidding, try me."

Fitzgerald had never seen Tracy in such a quiet, tight-lipped fury. He made an awkward gesture of conciliation.

"How about talking this thing over privately, Jerry? You going straight home?"

"Yeah." Tracy wasn't, but it gave him a chance for an easy exit. He let his stiff lips relax into a blurred smile. "How long do you expect to be here, Fitz?"

"Probably another hour. Why?"

"When you're through, come to my penthouse. I may have something to tell you that will save you from making a complete ass of yourself."

His heels clicked calmly down the hall. He took the service elevator to the street.

IT WAS SNOWING harder than ever. The sky was a dirty orange-gray. Tracy trudged a block or two before the cold gale blew the rage out of his system. Blinking through clogged eyelashes, he tried to locate a taxicab.

To his delight he saw one presently. He ploughed into the

middle of the street with arms waving. It slowed at his yell, its chains clotted with white. It was empty, but the hackman shoved an arm back and held the door shut.

"Sorry, but I've had enough snow plowin' for one night. I'm headin' for the garage."

Tracy changed that with a crisp ten-dollar bill. "You can take care of all I want in a half hour. Ten more bucks when you're finished."

He piled into the cab and slammed the door.

"Stop first at an all night drug-store."

In the drug-store Tracy opened a Manhattan phone book and leafed rapidly through the C's. He wrote down the address of Roy Chanler on a scrap torn from the margin of the phone page. But as he came out of the store, he halted for a quick instant.

A block behind his taxi, at the invisible curb on the other side of the avenue, was a parked police coupé. Tracy swore. Fitzgerald wasn't as trusting as he had seemed. He had put a prompt police tail on the *Daily Planet's* suspicious gag-and-humor man.

The scrap of paper in Tracy's hand fluttered behind his overcoat into the snow. There'd be no use going there. He got back into his cab with a wry grin.

He had himself driven back to his penthouse. His head ached from the crack Chanler had given him. He felt worn out, mussed up, weary. Fitz could go to hell when he showed up! He'd tell the hallman no dice on visitors and Fitz would need a warrant to get past Eddie on that basis, inspector or no inspector. All Tracy wanted now was some hot liquor and bed. The hell with everything else till morning!

He gave his hackman another ten and watched the cab depart. Then he waved his arm toward the slowly approaching police car. Sergeant Killan was driving it. What Tracy said to Killan made him squirm a little.

"No use getting sore, Jerry. Maybe you're a swell guy, but we'd like to be sure about it. If it's all the same to you, I could do with a drink before I start back."

"You can stick your head in the East River," Tracy rasped. "And tell Fitz for me—Oh, skip it!"

He strode into the apartment lobby, stamping the snow from his feet. The elevator door was open but Eddie wasn't in his chair back of the switchboard enclosure. Tracy knew where to find him, however. He'd be curled up in one of the soft chairs in the swanky imitation cathedral vestry at the rear of the lobby.

Eddie wasn't there, but somebody else was. A tall, thin man with a flat spongy nose and eyes as glazed and as hard as a blue China doorknob. He was waiting there patiently with an expensive overcoat folded over his left arm. He rose languidly and said:

"Hello, Jerry."

Tracy felt himself get very quiet from head to foot. He could feel the rug under his soles, the soft hammer of blood in his eardrums.

He knew this thin, lazy-looking man. He didn't like him, but the two had always been fairly friendly. The guy's name was Joe Wilkie. He was not exactly a gunman, not exactly a businessman. His specialty was labor, although he had never done a tap of physical work in his life. He had been in and out of several unions, each time escaping a Grand Jury indictment. Wilkie knew when to get in and when to get out.

Five years ago, you couldn't have bought a chicken or any other kind of poultry without dropping a small tax into Joe Wilkie's pocket. After that it was building materials. But the police never bothered Wilkie. He had money and plenty of guts—more guts than anyone on earth, according to underworld gossip. Brains, too; although Tracy had always suspected that Wilkie was a front man for somebody a hell of a lot smoother than he was.

"Hell, Joe. Where'd you drop from?"

"I didn't drop," Wilkie said. He was on his feet, the coat still hanging loosely over his left arm. "The hallman dropped, not me. He's down in the cellar, in case you're worried about him."

"I'm worried about myself," Tracy said.

He noted that Wilkie's right hand was under the coat that was draped across his left arm. The coat lifted slightly and the motionless black O of a pistol muzzle pointed at Tracy.

"Get going, Jerry. Straight ahead of me to the rear stairs."

"You sore at me, Joe?"

"Why get sore? I'm doing all right."

"What have you got against me? Can't it be squared?"

"You stuck your neck out, that's all. Too far out to pull it in again." The gun muzzle hurt Tracy's spine. "Get moving!"

The pistol pressure shoved Tracy through the warm, dimly lit cellar of the apartment house and out the rear to the white blur of flying snow. Emerging from a long alley to a back street, Tracy saw a car at the curb.

The appearance of that car frightened Jerry more than the hurtful jam of Wilkie's gun in his back. It was an ancient and decrepit Chevrolet coach, five or six years old. For the dapper Wilkie to be riding a bone-yard heap like that—It meant a torch job, or the river....

"Open the door," Wilkie said. "Bend the seat forward and get in the back."

Tracy obeyed. He knew what was coming, but he didn't utter a sound. He saved that until he felt the numbing smash of the gun butt. He fell with a groan that he tried to taper off artistically into fake unconsciousness. He had twisted his head slightly at the instant the blow was delivered. Part of the impact landed on his hunched shoulder. He clamped his lips tight as Wilkie tested him with a vicious kick in the ribs.

A mouldy lap-robe was dropped over his sprawled figure. The coach got into motion. Tracy lay perfectly still under his covering, although the smell of the robe made him sick. It smelled like rancid cheese.

Tracy, had fallen purposely so that one arm stretched under the robe toward the hinged seat in front. He tried to picture in his mind the outline of the coach's door and the exact location of the rusted door-handle.

He knew now that he was going to have to force that door open under water!

The hoarse toot of a river tug sounded very close. It was followed by the rumbling mumble of wooden planks under the slowly rolling car.

The Chevrolet halted. The mournful hooting of the tug boat gradually faded. Then suddenly the automobile began to roll forward. Tracy's throat ached with the tension of his locked jaws. There was nothing he could do. To make a move now would merely add a cracked skull or a knife in his ribs before he went overboard.

He felt the quick swerve of the car as Wilkie's hand left the wheel. There was a squeak from the open door, a slam, a duller thump as Wilkie's feet struck the planks of the pier.

Then the speeding car rammed against a low string piece and bounced outward into space.

Tracy felt a sickening emptiness in the pit of his stomach as his fist sent the hinged coach seat crashing forward. The lap-robe whipped away, clawed desperately loose by his left hand. His right darted for the door-handle and gripped it. Then… "*Whosh!*"

He was under the surface of the river, cradling downward in utter blackness. Water jetted into the car through every crack and cranny. Tracy could feel its coldness burning his blinded face as he wrenched fiercely at the door-handle. It was hard to force the door outward against the pressure of the river. He got it partly open, and the spout of roaring water almost tore him loose from his grip. He held rigidly, lips clamped, feet braced. A convulsive kick shot him away as the sinking car settled with a quiver in the soft mud of the river bed. Tracy's chest was still expanded with every ounce of air his lungs could hold. He shot upward, trying desperately to slant shoreward as his body rose.

The freezing bite of the water wrenched his mouth open. Bubbles raced from his lips. Then his head broke the surface of the river. His numb fingers slid wildly across the slippery surface of an upright timber. He was under a pier.

He missed his grip and went down again. But he had taken a quick gulp of air and he fought back to the surface. This time he caught at one of the pier's horizontal stringers. Tracy got an arm over, then a leg. His weight, rather than his strength, rolled him across the squared beam.

He wriggled along it, inch by inch, his buttocks humped high like a crawling baby. The wind sucking under the pier, brought snowflakes sifting against his face. It slashed knifelike against his soaked body. Twice he slipped and hung breathlessly. But he kept on.

How he did it, he never knew. But he found himself, presently, hanging partway over the combing at the edge of the pier. There was a vertical ladder under his feet that led to a kind of floating boom in the river. Somehow, he had managed to swing to the ladder and climb it. He squirmed over the pier edge and fell headlong, his cheek aching from the feel of soft snow.

Wilkie was no longer in sight on the pier. Tracy, reeling on his feet, staggered over to the marks where the coach had toppled into the river. He saw where Wilkie had leaped to safety. He followed the prints of the killer's feet down the pier toward the street. Tracy began to run, swinging his arms awkwardly, slapping at his face and ears and chest. There was a sharp pain in his lungs.

Front Street was like a white desert when Tracy reached it. There was no trail to show where Wilkie had fled after committing what he had conceived to be a perfect murder job. The driving snow had filled in his prints.

But a block up a side street was something a lot more important than Wilkie. Tracy saw a neon sign on the corner: *Coffee Pot.*

As Tracy hurried toward it, he saw that there was a taxicab parked outside. The thought of hot coffee and a quick dash homeward in a cab restored his courage.

He peered through the steamy window of the restaurant and gasped with dismay. Joe Wilkie was sitting at the counter with a half dozen other men. He was calmly swilling hot coffee.

Tracy backed away hastily, opened the taxi door and crawled in. The cab was heated. Tracy would have stolen it, if he'd been in any condition to drive; but he wasn't. He leaned through the open glass panel in front and pushed the horn.

A fat man in a dirty sheepskin coat came shambling out of the restaurant. "What's the big hurry, guy? Can'tcha wait till—"

He saw the soaked, and shivering columnist and his jaw dropped. Tracy held out his wallet to him.

"Take it! Everything in it is yours. But hurry up! Drive!"

The hackman opened the wallet, fingered the damp wad of currency, gave a quick grunt and slid behind his wheel.

"Where you wanna go?"

Tracy told him.

"What the hell happened to you? Fall overboard?"

"Yeah. I got drunk and woke up floating. Make it fast!"

"Pal, I'll make it faster than that!"

But he slowed as he approached Tracy's ornate apartment entrance. There was sly curiosity on his beefy face. He went thoroughly through Tracy's wallet with the fingers of one hand. And he found something that Jerry had forgotten. Tracy's column from the *Daily Planet!*

"I'll take that wallet," Tracy said faintly. "The money's yours. The rest is mine."

"You're Jerry Tracy, ain't you?"

"Yeah. Keep your mouth shut about all this. I don't want any trouble."

"What kinda trouble?"

Tracy knew he had said too much as he watched the hackman's eyes.

"Never mind. Keep quiet about my dive in the river. Garage

your cab and go on home and I'll double that dough of yours in the morning. O.K.?"

"You bet," the driver said.

But Tracy knew he was lying. The guy was eager to race back to the Coffee Pot and tell all about his pick-up of the famous Jerry Tracy. The only hope was that Joe Wilkie had already left the Coffee Pot.

Tracy cursed as the cab raced away through the storm. He thought of Roy Chanler and Vera. He'd protected them and they had hired Wilkie to rub him out! They'd had plenty of time, after they fled from Spane's, to make telephone arrangements with Wilkie....

HE SAW NO sign of the slugged doorman, Eddie, inside the apartment lobby. Tracy operated the elevator himself and let himself, shivering, into his warm penthouse. The light in the living-room was still burning the way he had left it. He walked to a bottle on a side table and poured himself a long slug of Scotch. The liquor made him choke, but it burned like a welcome flame in his belly.

"Butch! Hey, Butch!"

He flung open the door of Butch's room and stared. Butch wasn't there. The bed was rumpled, his clothes were flopped across a chair, but there was no sign of the big lop-eared valet.

Tracy had no time to worry about that. He hurried to his own bedroom. He wanted a hot bath more than anything he had ever wanted in his life. He darted across the bedroom, toward the door of his bath. But before he could reach the inner door, it opened. A gun pointed steadily at the startled columnist.

"Hold it, Tracy!"

Roy Chanler was staring grimly over the barrel of a gun. He moved cautiously from the bathroom and a girl followed him. She had a gun, too. Like Roy, she looked pale. But like Roy, there was a lot more anger in her eyes than fright. It was, of course, Vera Durensky.

The sight of her sleek, lovely face whipped Tracy into blind rage. He sprang bare-handed, clutching at Chanler's gun. He got his fingers on the barrel and tried to wrench it loose. But Vera shoved him and he fell over Chanler's outthrust leg.

He was too exhausted to make much of a fight of it. Chanler's gun whacked him over the ear, cutting his temple and making the room rock before Tracy's vision.

Vera had eight swaying faces, all of them beautiful. They bent in a dazzling semi-circle over Tracy.

"Good Lord, Roy! Look at him! He's soaking wet, half-frozen!"

Tracy felt his outstretched heels drag across the rug. Chanler had him by the shoulders, pulling him into the bathroom. The noise of roaring water filled Tracy's tub. He felt his shoes come off and his socks. Hands unbuckled his belt and ripped at his trousers.

Vera's voice came in an embarrassed whisper from a long way off. "I guess I'd better get out of here, Roy."

"Find his bathrobe and slippers. Dig out some wool underwear. Take these wet duds out and fix him a drink."

The next thing Tracy knew he was naked in the tub. It was hot and getting steadily hotter. Through bleared eyes he could see Chanler staring at him, one hand poised on the faucet.

"Want it any hotter?"

"Go ahead. Let it run," Tracy gasped.

He could feel the grateful heat stealing into all his aching joints. Steam rose from his reddened arm as he lifted a weak hand from the water.

"That's—that's fine."

He lay there, soaking, getting sleepier and sleepier. Chanler's supporting arm kept his head from wobbling under the water. Chanler, who had socked him, was now trying to help him.... Tracy wondered dimly about that. He let his brain drift and his eyelids close....

Chanler roused him, finally. He helped Tracy out of the tub. He rubbed him vigorously with a bath towel. Tracy couldn't understand Chanler's solicitude after the crack on the head, and said so.

"I'm just a big, friendly guy," Chanler grinned. "And maybe I want you to have a clear head to answer a few questions."

With his help Tracy climbed into heavy, woolen underwear and belted a flannel robe over that. Vera came in with slippers and a hot, tall drink. It was potent enough to make Tracy's legs wobble as the pair walked him back to the living-room.

Something glazed and watchful in Vera's smile put Tracy back on his guard. He noticed something he hadn't realized when he had first rushed into his apartment. The place had been thoroughly searched. Drawers were opened in desks and cabinets. Chairs had been moved. The rug looked rumpled.

Tracy spied Vera's gun lying on the liquor cabinet where she had laid it down when she had mixed his drink. He made a sudden dash for it, but Chanler beat him to the gun, whipping his own out as he sprang forward. His face was menacing.

"Back up! And hands high, you dirty little crook!"

"Where's Butch?" Tracy growled. "What have you done with him?"

Vera took her gun back from Chanler. The feel of it seemed to do hard, sneering things to her brown eyes.

"Is Butch the big fellow with the twisted ear? I had to tap him on the skull, I'm afraid."

"You mean Chanler did."

"I mean I did," Vera snapped.

"How did you get so cold and wet?" Chanler asked harshly. "Did you fall overboard somewhere?"

"You know damned well what happened," Tracy said. "You hired Joe Wilkie to do your second murder job, but he bungled it. That's going to make it tough for you."

"Second murder?" Vera said in a strange voice. "What are you talking about?"

"Skip it," Tracy said. "What were you searching my apartment for?"

Chanler's gun tightened grimly in his grasp.

"I'm after that code book of yours. The one you've been using to send crooked messages to Ed Spane through your column."

"You must have been reading a joke book," Tracy growled.

"Not jokes. Limericks. You were dumb enough to tip your hand, Tracy. I looked through your file of *Planet* columns while I was waiting here for you to show up. For instance:

"When the last scandal item is in,
I can still make a living from Sin—"

Tracy kept his temper. "I'd much rather discuss a guy named Ed Spane. The guy you stabbed in the gut. The guy you shoved in the bathtub behind the shower curtain."

Chanler gasped. His face turned suddenly pale. "You're a liar! Spane wasn't in his apartment."

"Then why did you phone for the cops to frame me for his murder?" Tracy's cold chuckle was like the clink of an ice cube. "Luckily, I'm in the clear. I was able to tell Inspector Fitzgerald a few pertinent facts. The result is a general police alarm for one Roy Chanler and one Vera Durensky. Incidentally the cops have traced that phone call Chanler made after he fled from Spane's apartment."

The lie was smoothly uttered and it brought a frightened answer.

"I made no phone call," Chanler protested thickly. "And I didn't kill Spane."

"What were you doing in his apartment?"

"Quit bluffing, Tracy! You can't stall me off with guff. Hand over that crooked code book of yours! Or I'll use a very painful method to—"

"Wait a minute!" Vera cried.

She had been staring keenly at Tracy. There was fear in her shining eyes.

"I don't think this man is bluffing. If Spane is dead, you and I are in a spot, Roy. We've got to tell Tracy the truth. Let me talk to him, Roy! Please!"

She began to speak in a low voice that carried candid conviction. Or else she was doing a beautiful acting job. Tracy couldn't be sure which.

She explained why she had first gone to Spane's apartment. She suspected Spane of fomenting the wildcat strike at Chanler's plant in order to discredit the union and force out her father. She was sure that Spane had slugged her father, Nicola Durensky. But she didn't think that he was smart enough to be the head of the racket. Someone was behind Spane, she suspected, directing the whole criminal set-up. So, knowing Ed Spane was a fool for women, she wangled an invitation to his apartment, hoping to find some clue to the truth.

She had seen the Tracy clipping on Spane's desk. She had noticed him awkwardly cover it with something else when she first came in. She waited until Spane turned away to mix a drink, then she stole it. Spane was watching in a mirror and he saw her.

He leaped at her and they fought.

Vera's gown was ripped and she was hurled to the floor. But she managed to jerk off one of her slippers and club Spane with its spiked heel. The blow dazed him and Vera fled downstairs to Tracy's car. She lost the other slipper on her mad race down the backstairs.

"Okey so far," Tracy said dryly. "Why did you go back to a guy who had just tried to kill you? And who else did you telephone to from my penthouse bedroom?"

"I called Nell, Roy's sister. Nell knew I had gone to Spane's and I was afraid she'd tell Roy. She had! She said Roy had left the house in a rage. I knew he'd rush straight to Spane's to protect me. So I called Spane's apartment and got no answer. I was terrified. That was why I—"

"How about you, Chanler?" Tracy said swiftly. "What happened to you?"

He had both of them frightened, on the defensive. He pressed his psychological advantage. If they were lying, they'd make some slip in the manufactured alibi.

"Spane slugged me in the dark the moment I walked in," Chanler said. "Or I thought it was Spane. Anyhow, I went out cold. I was still unconscious when Vera came in. Spane had left the door ajar when he scrammed. Vera said—"

"Go ahead, Vera," Tracy suggested.

"I found Roy unconscious. I roused him. We figured that Spane had slugged Roy and had fled. We looked through the apartment and found no sign of him."

"You didn't go near the shower curtain in his bathroom?"

Vera's face was ghastly. She shook her head.

"We searched Spane's desk and found his file of *Daily Planets*. All of them were opened at your column and marked with blue pencil. Then you arrived and—"

"I took it on the skull," Tracy said, without inflection. "A nice plausible story."

"It's better than yours," Vera flashed. "If you try to turn us over to the police, you'll have a heap of explaining to do about those marked columns that passed between you and Spane. What's your story, mister?"

"I don't give a damn what it is," Chanler grated. "All I want is the proof that Tracy and Spane were behind that fake labor war at my plant. Tracy, I'm giving you two minutes to hand over that code book of yours—or else!"

He wasn't fooling. His face was twisted in ugly determination. But Tracy ignored Chanler's gun and watched Vera. He noted exactly where she stood and where Roy stood. Vera, too, had a gun, but Tracy's desperate intent was to make her forget about the weapon.

He began to jeer at her in a low, sneering voice. He implied that her visit to Spane had been made for personal and physical reasons. Laughing unpleasantly, he looked straight at her. He used a brief Anglo-Saxon word.

Chanler yelled with fury. But Vera was quicker than he. With blazing eyes, she sprang straight at the columnist. She forgot about her gun. Her open palm slapped Tracy hard across the mouth.

For an instant her body was directly between Tracy and Chanler's impotent gun. With a quick clutch, Tracy twisted Vera's weapon from her grasp. His other hand shoved brutally, hurling her forward against the onrushing Chanler. They collided and went down in a heap.

Before Chanler could pull his pinned arm free, Tracy slugged him with the butt of Vera's gun. An instant later the columnist had both weapons and had sprung clear of the tangle on the floor.

"Get up, stupid!" he told Chanler.

Chanler swayed to his feet. His mouth hung vacantly open. Vera was laughing in the shrill pitch of hysteria. She reeled feebly toward a chair and fell into it. Her laughter filled the living-room with ugly echoes.

BEFORE THE SOUND of her laughter died, a voice said very calmly: "How about letting me in on the joke?"

Tracy whirled. Inspector Fitzgerald was standing on the threshold, very quiet and self-possessed behind the mask of his pent-up fury. Roy Chanler started forward, then relaxed. Fitz's police gun looked as big as a house. Vera continued to laugh helplessly.

"I'm glad you came, Fitz," Tracy said breathlessly.

"Shut up, you little rat!" Fitz's cold rage broke through his self-control. "You're glad I came! You told me you didn't know where this crooked pair was. You lied to me! And like a fool, I listened to you. I've got detectives searching all New York for two killers and where do I find them? Right in your own penthouse, under your protection. Laughing like hell at the way you kid the dumb police!"

"But, Fitz—"

"You double-crossing skunk! You and your crooked limericks! Stand still, Tracy, or, by the Lord, I'll plug you!"

Tracy didn't halt. Moving slowly toward where his damp clothes lay, he said over his shoulder: "Shoot me if you want to, Fitz. You can't stop me from trying to prove my innocence."

He bent over his sodden clothing and took his wallet from an inner pocket. Standing erect in his bathrobe and heavy underwear, he fished out the wet newspaper clipping that Vera had tried vainly to hide in the trunk of his locked sedan.

"What's that?" Fitz growled. "Another gag?"

"I don't know what it is. All I know is that I've been framed for something I don't know a damned thing about. I'm going to find out right now or break Roy Chanler's neck."

His voice was the only steady thing about him. His fingers trembled. The damp clipping fell to the floor and he bent to recover it. Fitz watched him like a hawk. So did Chanler.

Suddenly Tracy uttered a strangled cry. He hadn't touched the fallen clipping. He was down on hands and knees, staring at it. He got up shakily, holding the moist paper flat in the palm of his hand. His eyes never left it as he spoke.

"Fitz, I think I've got it! The only answer that makes sense! What a blind, conceited, egotistical fool I've been!"

They stared at him. Fitz remained wary. Chanler was shrunk

a little alongside the wall, his face impassive. Vera's teeth were tautly together behind quivering lips.

"The thing that fooled me," Tracy began slowly, "was the very thing a smart murderer counted on. Conceit! Jerry Tracy, the famous columnist, with his stuff syndicated in a thousand newspapers—"

He stopped short. He had half turned and his eyes faced for an instant the living-room window that gave access to his penthouse terrace. He caught a glimpse of the haze of falling snowflakes and, pressed close to the window-pane, the white smear of a thin, peering face.

Joe Wilkie! The killer who had dumped Tracy into the icy swirl of the East River! With hate in his eyes and a lifting gun barrel....

"Look out!"

Tracy's yell came a scant second before he flung himself at Fitz and knocked him staggering. From the terrace window came a crashing roar. The bullet missed Fitzgerald's neck by an inch and drilled through the open flap of Tracy's bathrobe.

Tracy whirled and darted toward the window. He dived through it with lowered head in a jangle of shattered glass. He hit the open terrace on his belly and skidded through the soft snow. Flame jetted at him from the retreating gunman. Tracy rolled over and over, with snow spurting at him like white spray from the impact of Wilkie's hasty slugs.

The flame streaks veered away from Tracy as Fitzgerald sprang into view through the shattered window. Unlike Tracy, the inspector landed upright, solidly on his feet. He crouched slightly forward, his gun hand steadied on his left wrist. He fired so fast that there was no stutter to the roar of his shots.

Wilkie turned, took two sliding steps toward the penthouse wall, then his blind clutch slipped and he went down on his face in the snow.

"He must've come up the fire stairs and swung through the tower window to my terrace," Tracy gasped.

Fitz nodded. With a face like granite, the police inspector carried the dead gunman through the smashed window and threw him to the living-room floor. Wilkie's body landed with a thump like a sack of potatoes. Crimson oozed sluggishly from him.

"Maybe I'm wrong about you, Jerry," Fitz said, pantingly. His stolid face was pale. "He'd have plugged me if you hadn't yelled and shoved me out of range. If you want to talk, I'm willing to listen."

Tracy hesitated perceptibly. He started to speak, then stopped. His glance swerved oddly from Fitz toward Roy Chanler and Vera. The knitting mill owner and Durensky's daughter were staring with frozen terror at the corpse of Joe Wilkie. Tracy, however, seemed to be more interested in Fitzgerald.

He said slowly, "I've got almost enough to settle this thing right now. All I need is a little labor information to clear up a couple of weak points. Is Leo Pelman still covering the news story over at Spane's apartment?"

"He was there when I left."

"Call him up. Tell him to hurry over here. I can settle this Chanler-Durensky conspiracy with about three more facts."

Fitzgerald leaped to the phone.

"I didn't kill Spane," Chanler gasped.

"Shut up!" Tracy snarled.

GUN ON CHANLER, Tracy waited until Leo Pelman came hurrying in. The *Daily Planet's* labor expert gave a quick cry of enlightenment as he saw the crumpled figure of Joe Wilkie.

"So that's who was behind them!" he breathed. "Joe Wilkie! I wondered who did the muscle work. Three of 'em in it, eh?"

Tracy nodded. "There were three crooks right from the start. But not these three. I'm still after the master mind."

"I don't get it," Pelman said, puzzled. "Do you mean Ed Spane?"

"No," Tracy said softly. "I mean—you."

"What!" Pelman stared stupidly at the business end of Tracy's gun. It was lined accurately at his heart. Tracy's finger was taut against the trigger.

"Cuff him, Fitz!" Tracy said.

Pelman made no effort to elude the shining steel bracelets that Fitzgerald snapped on his upraised wrists from the rear. He seemed dumbfounded.

"That winds up the racket 'trio,'" Tracy said. "Ed Spane and Joe Wilkie—and Leo Pelman. Two of 'em dead. But the smartest one, the real boss of the labor racket, is Mr. Leo Pelman."

Pelman asked quietly, "Jerry, have you gone silly in the head?"

"Nope. I was silly for most of this mad evening, but now I know exactly what I'm talking about.

"You killed Spane to shut his mouth and protect yourself. When I was foolish enough to phone you, you realized it was only a question of time before I tumbled to the truth about that newspaper clipping. That would mean the police would crack down on Spane and Spane would come clean to save his own skin. So you got rid of him.... Take a look at this, Fitz."

He showed Fitzgerald the sheet torn from the *Daily Planet.* "I was too conceited to remember that a paper has *two sides.* All I could see was my own famous column. When I was foolish enough to call up Pelman on the phone and involve myself, he saw a chance to play up my mistake and pin the whole business on me. He's the guy who blue-penciled those columns of mine in Spane's apartment—after he had killed Spane!"

Fitzgerald said, "I don't understand, Jerry. What was on the other side of the paper?"

"The real column that was being used to carry code messages between Pelman and Spane. It's usually headed: *"News Along the Labor Front."* But when the sheet was clipped from the *Planet,* Pelman's by-line wasn't clipped with it. Naturally, I saw only plain newsprint and paid no attention to it. I didn't realize the truth until I dropped the clipping a little while ago and it landed wrong side up. When your own stuff is syndicated to every city in the country, you...."

Pelman's face was gray. "You forget I've got an alibi. I was talking to you on the phone, Tracy. You asked me for information and I called you back fifteen minutes later. I didn't have time to leave my apartment and kill Spane."

"Spane was already dead when you called me back," Tracy said. "You called from his apartment! You weren't home when I tried to get you the second time. You only pretended you were. Actually, you had already killed Spane to shut his mouth, and you slugged Chanler a moment later and scrammed. You also called the police."

"You'll have one hell of a job proving that in court," Pelman sneered. "Any more wild guesses?"

"Sure. You made a mistake when you telephoned police

headquarters after Spane gave you the license number of my sedan. Nobody but a newspaperman would know that a car license can be verified in a hurry at police headquarters. Nor would the police give that information to anyone but a reporter. You covered yourself by saying you worked for the *Chronicle*."

Pelman laughed jeeringly.

"If you think you can indict me for murder on a few lousy guesses like that, you're only kidding yourself. You'll need proof, boy friend."

Tracy said, "I was saving that for the last. I've got the best proof in the world that you were using Spane and Wilkie to smash an honest union and turn it into a racket under your hidden leadership. You see, Pelman, *I've cracked your newspaper code!*"

Pelman cringed at Tracy's triumphant shout.

Then, suddenly, he was plunging forward. His manacled hands closed on Tracy's gun. The attack was made so swiftly that Tracy had no chance to defend himself. The gun was wrenched from his startled grasp. A knee-cap in his groin sent him reeling backward. Pelman swung the gun in both hands and fired point-blank at Inspector Fitzgerald.

Fitz's hinging knees dropped him under the rip of the bullet. He sat squatting on his thighs for an instant like a Russian dancer. He fired only once from that strained pose. His bullet hit just below Pelman's navel and tunneled outward near the top of his spine. Pelman hit the floor. He was stone dead.

"That's that," Tracy said in a tired voice. "I didn't really have an ounce of proof to convict Pelman. All I had was the knowledge that he was guilty. You'd have one hell of a time getting a grand jury to indict him, Fitz."

"What about that code he used? I thought you said—"

"Pure bluff. That's why I didn't tell you Pelman was guilty until he got here. I was afraid you'd lose your head and order Sergeant Killan to arrest him before he left Spane's. He'd have time to think things over and to make you prove your case. Even with the code, it would have been a toss-up to nail him for Spane's murder."

Tracy drew a deep breath.

"However, I think that if you turn Pelman's labor columns for the past six months over to the police cryptography division, you'll be able to crack the code and find out what he was doing. He probably used it in conjunction with Spane to get in touch with gunmen to do specific jobs. In that way he could get in touch with lots of gunnies and strike breakers who were lying low to avoid the police. He wouldn't be caught meeting any of them. It was a clever business. No doubt he ordered Durensky's slugging that way, too. And fomented all that strike trouble."

Vera sobbed faintly. Tracy flushed as he turned toward her.

"I hope you'll forgive me for that word I called you a little while ago. It was done only to force a break for myself. You had a gun on me. You were sure I was a crook, like Fitz here and everybody else in town."

Fitzgerald grinned sheepishly. "Could you blame me, Jerry? You were giving me such an infernal run-around! Even at that, I never really thought...."

Tracy's smile was rueful. "You're a liar, but I can't blame you, old-timer. For a while tonight I was beginning to believe, myself, that I was a crook with a dual personality or something. Vera will tell you that I—"

Vera didn't say anything. She was folded tightly in Roy Chanler's straining arms, her lips crushed against his.

"No more limericks," Tracy said.

Fitz nodded approvingly. "That limerick that Jack Davy recited was the craziest junk I ever heard:

> "A Bolivian princess named Paca,
> Liked to float nude on Lake Titicaca.
> But the trouble with that
> Was the gal got so fat—

"How do you s'pose the damn thing really ends?" he asked wistfully.

Make It Murder

Jerry Tracy sleuths at an Amateur Hour kill

THE JEWELER'S CLOCK on the corner said twenty after ten as Jerry Tracy walked eastward toward the bright sunlit glitter of the elevated. He blinked and thought wistfully of his dim penthouse bedroom. If he had any sense he'd still be asleep, relaxed in naked comfort between silken sheets, taking the morning sunlight on hearsay.

Trouble was, Jerry couldn't sleep. He kept thinking uneasily of a cute little blonde with an awful soprano voice. The kid called herself Vivian La Grange. Her stage name was a fair measure of her intelligence. She came from Altoona, or maybe it was Bridgeport. She had everything but talent and brains.

Tracy had never heard of Vivian until the night he had dropped in at the leased theater where the Paragon Broadcasting Corporation put on its big audience programs. Ned Carlisle had pestered Jerry for weeks to give the Sparkling Soapsud Amateurs some publicity in his Broadway column. If you own a radio you know the Soapsud Hour—the man with the zither, the fellow who imitates roosters and railroad trains, the over-eager soloists. A warning bell to choke off the worst; twenty-five bucks and a chance at a vaudeville job for the winner.

This Vivian La Grange had won. Ned Carlisle's kindliness had made the radio audience forget her squeaky voice. The real winner should have been the zither man. But Carlisle's mike conversation with the tremulous Vivian had dramatized her personality, had built up her ambitious hopes; and his word

picture of her shy beauty sold the girl to the unseen listeners.

Honesty made Jerry Tracy tell the truth in his famous tabloid column. He went a bit further than he actually intended. The pompous commercial announcements of the Soapsud Hour had always irritated Tracy, and this time he allowed his sharp wit to run away with his judgment. He shot a brilliantly amusing broadside at the soap company, but his barbed attack brought down Vivian. She played two nightmarish days in a New Carlisle vaudeville unit and was laughed off the stage.

She took it pretty hard. A reporter on a rival sheet wrote up the girl's two-bit tragedy in a way that made Tracy look like a heel. He didn't mind the unpleasant kickback from people who hated his guts and were glad of an excuse to boot his reputation. Jerry Tracy could take that. But he was afraid little Vivian La Grange couldn't. He couldn't put the memory of her pale, frightened face out of his mind. He'd feel a lot better if she were on a train bound for Altoona—or wherever the hell she really belonged.

That was why Jerry Tracy had crawled out into raw sunlight at the filthy hour of ten A.M. Ten was when the bank opened.

He cashed a check for a hundred and took it in five twenties. He had found out where Vivian lived, and he walked hesitantly up the grimy front stoop of the rooming house. He wasn't sure whether he'd run into tears, stony silence, or a poke in the jaw. He felt guilty enough to hope that the girl would sock him.

You could stand in that dim ground-floor hallway and know that you were in a cheap theatrical rooming house west of Broadway. A front door never locked; a coin box telephone; numbers scrawled in pencil on the flowered wallpaper; a cabbage smell from the basement; ugly green carpet on a staircase that squeaked at every step.

A list of names in the hallway showed that Vivian lived at the top floor rear. Tracy rapped on her door and got no answer. The continued silence made him suddenly scared. He didn't realize he was sniffing until he caught himself staring at the gas bracket in the hall. There was no smell of gas, however; the bracket was capped and useless, a relic from an earlier era. Nor were the cracks of Vivian's door stopped up with paper, as Tracy for an instant had feared. It was his conscience that was sniffing, not his nose.

He rattled the loose knob, and to his surprise the door yielded. It was not locked as he had supposed.

Vivian La Grange was in bed. She was staring at Tracy, but she didn't say anything. There was a gun clenched in her right hand and a gaping wound at her temple. Her cheek, her throat and one smooth breast were sticky with blood. Her body was nude.

Tracy said, "Jees!"

It took guts to move forward. Vivian's left hand lay stiffly open at the edge of the counterpane. Two pieces of paper had fallen to the floor. One was a clipping of Tracy's column from the *Daily Planet*—the one in which he had made brilliant mockery of the Soapsud Hour. The other was a note written in pencil.

Tracy didn't attempt to pick up either of them. He felt packed in ice from his lips to the pit of his belly. His toe pushed the note tremulously apart from the column clipping. Bending, he read it where it lay on the floor.

"Tell Mr. Tracy I can take it. You get courage in the dark. I'm passing out like Tracy predicted—stripped and broke. But it's a lot more fun than living in Altoona."

Tracy had hurt plenty of people in his long career on Broadway. Killed a few, too, if you counted the ones who had gone to the electric chair as a result of Tracy's unofficial hook-up with Inspector Fitzgerald of the Homicide Division. But this was the first time in his life Jerry Tracy had consciously hurt someone who couldn't strike back. Nausea crawled at the back of his throat.

This poor little blond jackanapes on the bed had pulled the trigger that killed her; but it was Tracy's merciless wisecracks that had cocked the gun.

He was almost grateful when the scream came from the doorway behind him. It wrenched him out of horror. He had left the door wide open. A fat, untidy looking woman was standing there. Tracy guessed she was the landlady.

She fled, still screaming. Roomers were stirring behind closed doors as Tracy darted for the stairs. He remembered the telephone in the lower hall. By the time he reached it, the landlady was out on the sidewalk, making shrill echoes like a dog that had been run over.

Tracy dropped a fumbling nickel in the phone slot and called police headquarters. The rasp in his voice got him Inspector Fitzgerald in a hurry. He said things that left him out of breath. He added, gaspingly: "Do me a favor, Fitz. I'm in a stinking mess. Keep reporters out of this for a while."

A second nickel connected him with Ned Carlisle's suite of offices in the Wickersham Building. The kindly, booming-voiced impresario of the Sparkling Soapsud Hour wasn't in. Like Tracy, he seldom stirred before noon.

"Quick, sister! Get me Hal Bruce! Tell him it's Jerry Tracy!"

The noise outside the vestibule quieted suddenly. The swift slap-slap of a policeman's brogans became audible. Bruce was Ned Carlisle's executive assistant. He did all the routine work on the Amateur Hour and supervised the show.

"Hello, Jerry. What's the matter?"

Tracy told him in four words.

"What!" Bruce sounded stunned. "No!"

"Keep it under the hat, will you, Hal? And get over here!"

The vestibule door crashed open. The cop had a gun in his white-gloved hand. He dove at Tracy like a four-ton truck.

"That's him!" the landlady shrieked. "That's the guy!" She had a mouthful of gold teeth.

The cop's hand thumped Tracy's pockets and probed his armpits with bruising emphasis. He was a young cop, pretty excited.

"Who were you trying to phone?"

"Police headquarters," Tracy said. "Inspector Fitzgerald is on the way here now." He added, a bit more evenly: "Take it easy, officer. This is a suicide, not a kill. Reach into my inside pocket and you'll find my press card. I'm Jerry Tracy."

The cop hesitated. Tracy's imported suit and his custom-shod feet impressed the policeman. And there was something about the nasal voice of this well dressed little guy that made the cop recognize the crisp-toned Broadway and Hollywood radio gossip to which he and his wife listened every Saturday night.

Another patrolman arrived in the vestibule. Faces peered behind him. He swung about and slammed the door. "Keep those dopes outside," Tracy's captor said. "There's a dead girl upstairs, but this guy claims it's suicide. Says he's Jerry Tracy and he phoned Inspector Fitzgerald about it. Better give Homicide a quick buzz."

The second cop was flabby around the jaw-line, but there was nothing flabby about his voice in the transmitter. He seemed disappointed when he hung up. "Inspector Fitzgerald is on the way over here. Switchboard says Jerry Tracy made the call."

The hefty landlady tried to follow them upstairs. She was still yelling vindictively at the columnist.

"Keep that noisy cow down here," Tracy snapped.

"Cow, is it?" she shrieked. "Why, you little rat, if I'd given you the eye ten years ago you'd have eaten outa my hand. You killed that poor girl upstairs, and if you think I'm afraid to—"

Her mouthings faded below him. There were people peering from room doors, but they withdrew at sight of Tracy's stony face and the gun in the cop's hand. Doors closed discreetly all the way up as if it were a game. Mind your own business! If they grab you as a witness, give 'em a fake name! The jungle creed of Manhattan....

The cop took one look at Vivian La Grange and whistled. He

shut the door. Tracy walked stiffly over to the bed and lifted the loose edge of the coverlet from the foot of the mattress.

"Don't touch anything!" the cop growled. "Let her stay the way she is."

The girl's nudity was like cold wax. Tracy let the coverlet fall gently across her. The cop didn't remove it.

INSPECTOR FITZGERALD BROUGHT Sergeant Killan with him. Two more cops came in. Fitz read the suicide note and the clipping from Tracy's column. Sergeant Killan whispered, and one of the cops took a post in the hallway outside the door.

Tracy didn't pay any attention. He was sitting hunched forward in a chair, his jaws knuckled between his clenched fists. Except for a small scatter rug near the bed, the floor was bare. The boards were painted a dark brown that was almost black.

Fitzgerald showed the suicide note and the column clipping to Sergeant Killan. Both men stared briefly at each other. They were old friends of Tracy's. Fitz touched the hunched columnist on the shoulder.

"It's tough, Jerry. Suicides always are."

"Did you read the note?"

"Yeah. I wouldn't worry about that, if I were you." Fitzgerald's voice was soothing. He was a tall man with a thick mop of gray hair and broad shoulders that stooped a little. His deep blue eyes looked ten years younger than the rest of him.

"G'wan home and get yourself a drink, Jerry," Killan said gruffly.

He was shorter and heavier than Fitz. He had a head like a cobblestone and a mouth like a slit in a mailbox.

There were footsteps in the hallway outside, followed by the murmur of voices. Then the door opened and two men came in.

The paunchy, middle-aged man with the gold watch chain was Hal Bruce whom Tracy had summoned from Ned Carlisle's office to help identify the dead girl.

Bruce's eyes glanced toward the sheeted corpse on the bed and then veered quickly toward Tracy. The horror in Bruce's face changed to sympathetic awareness of the plight Tracy was in. Hal was a man who could sense things like that. A nice guy.

He crossed the room toward the columnist, his left foot dragging with a perceptible limp. He and Tracy shook hands. Ten years ago Hal Bruce's name meant far more than a production understudy for Ned Carlisle. Hal had been the greatest tap dancer on the stage. Arthritis had stiffened that left leg of his, ended his career as a dancer. He was as cheerful now in the minor role fate had handed him, as he had been when two nimble feet had made the name Hal Bruce a synonym for "Tops" on stage and screen. And "Tops" had meant twenty-five hundred a week. Now he was getting two fifty—and no one had ever heard him complain.

Tracy didn't recall the other man who'd come in with Hal until he smiled. Then he recognized the even white teeth. He was Freddie Colling, the announcer who read the commercial for the Soap Hour. Like most big air shows, Ned Carlisle used his own announcer.

Colling's twisted smile was a nervous grimace. He strode across the room and bent over the pathetic, partly draped body on the bed. He made a small nasty sound in the back of his throat, but he didn't say anything.

"Tracy's identified her," Fitz said. "All we want is your confirmation."

Colling whirled suddenly. There were tears in his eyes and his face was like flint. With a single leap he was over Tracy's chair.

"You dirty rat! You and your —— column!"

His fist crashed into Tracy's face, driving his head against the back of the chair. Tracy made no effort to retaliate. Blood dripped from his nose. Somebody yanked the enraged announcer back on his heels. Somebody else smothered his wildly flailing fists. Sergeant Killan shoved him into a corner none too gently. The trembling announcer stopped struggling suddenly.

"O.K. I'll quit. I'm sorry." Tracy watched the announcer over the stained handkerchief he held bunched against his nose. Colling's rage seemed overdone. He had snapped out of it too easily. The thing smacked of ham acting. Tracy had never exchanged two words with the guy, but he knew his type. There wasn't an ounce of real emotion in him. He was too conscious of his white teeth and his dimples.

Tracy transferred his doubt of Colling to the suicide set-up itself. Things Jerry hadn't thought about before began to bother him. Except for the ghastly pun in the note Vivian had left, there was no sane reason why she should have stripped herself before she crashed a bullet through her brain. The strip act wasn't in character. And the note was too patly ironic to fit a desperate little dumb-bell from Altoona.

Murder? The word swept through Tracy's mind like a cleansing gust of cold wind. He eyed the wall over the bed. There was an electric fixture above the ledge of an imitation mantelpiece. The fixture contained two light sockets. Both sockets were empty. The unscrewed bulbs lay underneath it on the mantelpiece.

"Why do you suppose she did that?" Tracy asked Fitzgerald.

"She wrote: 'You get courage in the dark'," Fitz reminded Tracy somberly. "Women are like that. She was probably scared to death. The feel of the gun in her hand, the cold muzzle up against—" Fitz shut up. Sergeant Killan said softly, "Look, Jerry—why don't you go on home?"

"Why didn't Vivian just *turn off* those lights? Don't you think that's a hell of a funny way to make a room dark—unscrew two bulbs and lay 'em on the mantel-piece?"

"It's suicide, Jerry. You're only kidding yourself."

"Have you done anything about fingerprints?"

"What's the use?" Killan said. "We'll get a sackful when the photographer arrives. Prints of the kid, prints of the landlady and the window-washer, prints of the kid's latest boy friend." He flushed and added hastily: "I don't mean anything nasty by that."

Fitzgerald laid a friendly hand on the columnist's shoulder.

"A murder would suit me as much as you, Jerry. I know exactly how you feel."

"I'll stick around a while," Tracy said. Hal Bruce was over at the window, looking down into the back yard. Colling stayed in the corner where Killan had shoved him after his outburst. Tracy teetered on his chair, lifting and dropping the front legs with a mechanical rocking motion of his hips. His downward side gaze flicked suddenly toward one of the chair's raised legs.

There was a small scrap of black paper adhering to the bottom of the left leg. It became invisible when Tracy let the tilted chair drop flat. The paper was almost the same color as the dark-painted floor boards. That was why it hadn't been noticed.

Tracy scratched his left ankle lazily. His cupped palm passed under his gaze on the way to his pocket. He took out a package of cigarettes and lit one as he saw that Colling was watching him. Colling's mouth twitched, but Tracy didn't know whether that meant he had seen the pick-up or not. The fellow's lips were always moving like that. It was an habitual gesture. Most of the time he turned it into a meaningless smile.

Tracy knew little about photography, but that tiny scrap of paper in his pocket made him think of a camera. It was like the black stuff that came wrapped around camera film.

Tracy was grimly certain that someone other than the girl had unscrewed those two bulbs. The blood from Vivian's wound and the rigidity of her body made the time of her death fairly certain. She must have died hours earlier, long before dawn. A photograph under those conditions would certainly require strong light. If a killer with a camera had used a couple of photoflood bulbs....

Tracy got up from his chair, puffing deeply on his cigarette. He dropped ash in a tray on a low table, and continued to move about the room, scanning the floor for faint powdery traces of pulverized glass.

"Sit down," Fitz growled. "You're making me nervous."

"Funny the girl should lie there without being discovered until I walked in. A .38 caliber gun makes a noise, doesn't it?"

Hal Bruce turned from the window. "That's right. Why didn't someone hear the shot?"

"Were any of the tenants questioned?" Colling asked.

Sergeant Killan's neck turned a brick red.

"It doesn't mean a thing. The elevated is only a block away. And there's a big trucking garage near the corner. The bang of a .38 would sound a lot like the backfire of a heavy-duty truck. I've already questioned the tenants and nobody heard nothing. My guess is that they'd lie if they *had* heard the shot."

"You're not being smart, Jerry," Fitzgerald murmured. "You're just being anxious."

Tracy went back to the ashtray. A camera at the scene of a girl's fake suicide could mean only one thing. Blackmail! Two men and a dead girl! A wise guy and a sucker. Without the sucker angle, a camera didn't make sense. And for bait to hook the sucker, what better than a desperate little blonde from the sticks who had made a hopeful try for fame and had flopped?

Tracy's logic was partly an excuse for his own conscience, and he knew it. The ashtray on the table, however, made him catch his breath. There was a cigar butt lying among the gray litter of cigarette stubs and ashes. It was long enough for Tracy to identify it by its shape and smell. He smoked Corona Coronas himself. A cheap cigar butt usually smelled like an outdoor cesspool, but not this brand!

The cigarettes in the tray were Camels. There were five of them, and all had lipstick smear on the tip. The set-up still didn't show two men. But Tracy now was all eagerness inside, like a bloodhound on the scent. He could feel the beat of his heart against his ribs as he gave Fitzgerald a thin smile.

"Mind if I poke around a bit, Fitz?"

"Go ahead, if it makes you feel any better."

There was a closet with one very good dress and a couple of cheap ones hanging beside it. A pair of shoes. One hat. A nest of silk stockings, most of them ruined by runs.

Behind the bedroom was a smaller room that contained a washbowl and a toilet. The faded linoleum on the floor left a narrow crack along the wall. Tracy fingered the crack and found a flattened cigarette stub where someone's shoe had crushed it. It was a Lucky Strike. There was no lipstick smear on it. Tracy found another, shoved under the warped edge of the linoleum.

"Two men!" his brain whispered.

It was still guesswork. Vivian could have smoked the Luckies. Or the Corona Corona guy. But Tracy knew darned few cigar smokers who liked cigarettes. And he knew what happened when you tried to give a Camel addict a Lucky—or vice versa.

Tracy sounded tired when he came back to the bedroom. "I think I'll beat it, Fitz."

Hal Bruce came over from the window and touched Tracy's arm hesitantly.

"We're putting on the Amateur Hour tonight at the Paragon Theater. I—I'd appreciate it if you could drop around and perhaps—"

"If I do, I'll continue to tell the truth," Tracy growled.

"That's all I ask," Bruce said quietly. "This time we've got someone whose act I'd like you to watch. She's—"

"Her name is Thelma Wood," Colling cut in. The announcer was smiling eagerly, apparently forgetful that Tracy's nostrils were still pink from the punch he had landed. "This Thelma Wood girl is the best natural blues singer since Ethel Merman broke in."

Tracy wondered if Colling had seen him pick up the scrap of black paper. "I'll try to make the show," he told Hal Bruce.

He went quietly downstairs, but not out to the street. Turning, he tiptoed along a dark hall and descended wooden steps to the back yard. He glanced upward and located Vivian's window on the top floor. He estimated the drop and the distance from that window to the angle of a brick wall on the other side of the rear fence.

He climbed the fence, after making sure that the yard didn't contain what he was seeking. He found it at the foot of the brick wall. Two threaded metal sockets. There was a faint powdering on the stone pavement where thin glass had shattered.

"Photoflood bulbs," Tracy breathed, "or I've never had a hunch in my life!"

He hurried downtown to the *Daily Planet* office and saw Dave Brennan. Dave was a news cameraman.

"Paper from a film pack," Brennan said when Tracy showed him the bit of black paper he'd picked up.

Brennan explained to Tracy how film packs worked. After you shot a picture you pulled a tab and tore out a paper sheet. This turned the exposed film and drew a new one into position for the next picture.

"What do you do with the paper?" Jerry asked.

"Nothing. It's no good. You throw it away."

You threw it away! And if you were careless and had allowed a chair leg to rest on the discarded paper, you left a hunk torn off when you grabbed at it in a guilty hurry.

Tracy's eyes wrinkled tight. "Thanks," he told Brennan.

THE *DAILY PLANET'S* famous little columnist had no trouble that evening getting backstage at the Paragon Theater. The Amateur Hour was already under way on the stage. Ned

Carlisle's soothing voice was exchanging bland comments with a bumptious little fat man, who held a fiddle under his chin in front of a microphone. The fat man was trying to be funny with Ned. The audience roared with laughter as the suave Carlisle topped the amateur's feeble wisecrack and made him look silly.

To Tracy, the fiddler looked like a phoney, planted for laughs. He was not surprised when the gong clanged and the performer shuffled from the stage with exaggerated despair. Crude stuff. But the audience ate it up.

Hal Bruce was standing guard over a trio of jittery looking people beyond the wings. He grinned as he caught Tracy's eye and motioned him over.

"Spares," he whispered, indicating the nervous trio. "In case the show runs short. Have you seen Thelma Wood yet?"

"No. Which one is she?"

"You can spot her better from the other wing. Next to the last chair on the right. Hurry it up. The kid's due next."

Thelma was already singing by the time Tracy crossed behind the back-drop to the right wing. He heard her before he saw her. He liked her voice. It was rich, throaty, honeyed with sex.

Her song faltered for a moment as Tracy squirmed noise-lessly past a man who was watching the stage. Tracy wasn't sure whether the girl was staring at him or the man into whom he had bumped. Her face jerked back toward the audience. She recovered her poise.

The man growled under his breath: "Take it easy, stupid. Who the hell are you pushing?"

Tracy was conscious of swift, instinctive antagonism. He didn't like any part of this sleek, hard-panned guy. Dark, solid face with a barbershop flush under the tight skin. Black eyes and blacker eyebrows. Like a Hunkie from a mining town—except for his expensive clothes and the glitter of an expensive stickpin diamond.

"Sorry," Tracy snapped, and let his glance shoot back to the stage.

The girl was Thelma, all right. The second chair on the stage was empty. She was facing the audience now, singing raw jazz with a gorgeous, throaty depth that made the orchestra accompaniment sound thin and tinny. Tracy felt the hair stir along his scalp. It was that kind of singing.

She was a honey blonde. Her face was a little too long to be beautiful. She was wearing a pale green dance dress with capped sleeves, cut modestly high at the throat. She stood stiffly angular, without sway or motion, like a singer at a church social. That stance of hers did the trick. It killed the hot suggestiveness of words and rhythm. Once or twice she sliced a high note or slurred a phrase with the wrong impact. If it hadn't been for that, Tracy would have tabbed her for a ringer, a professional.

Tracy's eyes glowed. He forgot to be cynical. This kid had everything but training.

She finished in a tornado of applause. Even the dopes out front sensed talent when it hit them smacko like that!

The girl took a breathless bow and started toward the wings. Tracy inched quietly forward along the shadowy canvas. He wanted to get hold of this Thelma Wood and pump her for a column. She was worth it!

A hand spun Tracy, suddenly shoved him backward. The dark-eyed man with the stickpin strode contemptuously to where the columnist had stood.

Thelma Wood saw the sleek guy grinning coaxingly at her. She halted on the lighted stage and backed away, fright in her blue eyes. The audience thought she was returning for, another bow and they rocked the house with applause.

Ned Carlisle was smiling. He took the spotlight with the girl, but not the bows. He was a born showman and he knew how to build excitement.

His bushy gray eyebrows seemed to quiver with delight. His wide-lipped mouth was stretched in an expansive grin. Thick, stubby fingers tousled his unruly gray hair in the famous gesture of artistic abandonment that always told a delighted audience this was really the time to let go—to whistle, stamp feet, raise the roof with yells.

The audience took the cue. Ned Carlisle beamed paternally at the uproar. He didn't wait for the applause to subside. It would continue as long as he willed it. Tracy knew Ned enjoyed a din like this as much as anyone in the crowded playhouse. But presently the stubby fingers waved a sweeping farewell that was a subtle tribute to the crowd as well as the performer.

"The guy should have been in opera," Tracy thought with a grin, as Carlisle escorted Thelma Wood triumphantly from the stage. But to the opposite wing.

Tracy heard the dark-eyed man swear. He tried to block the fellow's path as he whirled. But sinewy fingers tightened on Tracy's windpipe and flung him backward. Applause from the theater drowned the crack Tracy's head made against the floor. He swayed to his feet after a dazed instant, but there was no sign of his foe.

Instead, he saw the pale, peering face of Freddie Colling.

The commercial announcer had evidently witnessed the

swift attack on Tracy. His eyes looked scared. He started to melt away in the backstage gloom. Tracy nabbed him before he could pull his quick sneak.

"Who was that guy? Do you know him?"

"No." The lie was apparent in Colling's nervous tone.

Anger made Tracy's word spurt like hard pellets. "Give me the lowdown or I'll bat your ears off. You know him! You saw what he did to me. What's his name?"

"I—I think his name is Visco."

"What's he doing back here?"

"I think he's a friend of—Thelma's," Colling gasped.

A friend? Tracy's jaw hardened as he thought of the fear he had seen in the girl's face when she had made her quick retreat across the stage.

"Don't drag me into this," Colling muttered. "I don't know a thing about it."

Tracy left him abruptly. He ducked behind the backdrop and hurried to the other side of the stage. Thelma Wood was surrounded by a group of people, congratulating her. Her face was deadly pale.

There was no sign of Visco. He had evidently hurried down the long exit corridor and vanished into the street through the rear stage entrance.

Hal Bruce came over to Tracy. His face was aglow with delight. "What did you think of Thelma's singing? Is she good or not?"

"Good enough for a full length splash in my column," Tracy said slowly. "Bring her over. I'd like to talk to her."

"Why don't you wait for the sign-off? You can't talk much here. Thelma's a cinch to win tonight, and Ned Carlisle always blows the winner to a victory supper at the Terrace Club in Radio City. There'll be oodles of big shots there. Why not come along?"

Tracy said, "Thanks, Hal. I'd like to. By the way, do you happen to know a man named Visco?"

"Visco? Who's he?" Tracy described him. "Oh, yeah. I've seen him around, backstage somewhere. Somebody told me he had an in with our sponsor. They clutter up the place, but there's nothing we can do. Remember, this is an advertising racket, not show business. What about this Visco?"

"I just wondered, that's all," Tracy said.

He continued to wonder after Hal Bruce buzzed away. He remembered the look in Thelma's eyes. Those staring blue eyes of hers made him think grimly of a dead girl named Vivian La Grange.

Tracy had no illusions about the nattily dressed Visco. He could smell a dangerous crook six blocks against the wind. Was Visco the finger man in a brand-new radio racket? One that involved the pretty and inexperienced girls who won amateur contests? Tracy also wondered whether the dark faced Mr. Visco smoked Luckies.

RADIO'S TERRACE CLUB was not a place, but a celebration party. The party was held twice a week, immediately after the Soapsud Hour went off the air. The winner of the amateur contest was feted and publicized at one of the two swank restaurants that abutted on the sunken terrace in the heart of Radio City.

Ned Carlisle's kindly personality attracted a host of important figures from the city's night life. Ned threw these noisy jamborees with a friendly eye to the interests of his amateur winners. Once or twice a girl had been picked by one of the big Broadway impresarios who liked to drop in on Ned Carlisle's blow-outs. No one in town was more pleased about that than Ned himself.

Tracy checked his hat and coat in the lobby, but he didn't go at once into the restaurant. He waited patiently until he caught sight of a very pretty girl. She was a brunette with perfect legs, practically no clothes, and she carried a cigarette tray suspended by silver cords that circled her bare neck.

"Hello, Alyce."

"Oh, hel-lo, Mr. Tracy!" Her voice was like creamed sugar. "Cigars, cigarettes?"

She turned sideways as she offered her tray. The movement placed her face and her bust in profile. Both were good. Being a smart girl, Alyce didn't ask Tracy for a boost in his famous Broadway column. She let her figure ask him for the favor.

"How about a Corona Corona?" Jerry asked her.

She made a pretty frown. Her laughter tinkled like a small, silver bell. "I only carry one brand of cigars, Jerry. You wouldn't smoke it. Confidentially, it stinks!"

"What do the expensive cigar smokers like me do? Go without?"

"People like that always carry their own with them."

"Do many smoke Corona Coronas?" Jerry's tone was playful.

"Oh, lots of them."

"Name three," Jerry said promptly. He said it with a careless grin. His palm caressed her fleetingly, just short of the edge of insult.

Alyce giggled. People crossing the swanky lobby glanced

curiously at the pair. Tracy waved a greeting or two and then leaned close to Alyce's ear.

"Would you like a nice build-up in tomorrow's column?"

"Damn right!" Alyce said. She stopped smiling.

"Then find out for me the name of every guy at the Ned Carlisle radio party who smokes nothing but Corona Coronas. Phone me the list at my penthouse tomorrow. Is it a bet?"

"What's a bet?" a smooth male voice interrupted.

Freddie Colling had emerged from the inner door of the lobby. He grinned fleetingly at the cigarette girl, more steadily at Tracy. Hal Bruce was with the announcer.

"Ned Carlisle was wondering if you had come over," Bruce said. "He's saving a place for you. Better come on in. Thelma is doing a couple of blues songs for the party. Without accompaniment, that's how good we think she is."

Alyce moved off with her glittering tray. As she did so, she turned for an instant toward the *Daily Planet's* columnist. Her voice dripped with sweet conspiracy.

"Don't forget, Mr. Tracy. It's a bet! Corona Corona!"

Watching the quick twitch of Colling's mouth, Tracy could cheerfully have kicked the shapely Alyce in her rounded rear. But his face was impassive as he walked into the club. If Tracy's feeling was correct, there was some sort of hook-up between this white-toothed Colling guy and the dark-faced Visco. And Colling was now doubly aware of Jerry Tracy's interest in cigar butts. He had watched Tracy at the dead Vivian's apartment. He was watching him here.

For the rest of the evening the *Daily Planet's* columnist circulated deftly through the noise and joviality of Ned Carlisle's big party. In a spot of this sort Tracy was always like an agreeable little flea in patent-leather shoes. He knew everybody and talked with everybody—theatrical men, sporting figures, big spenders who wanted to be seen and heard.

He was puzzled by the absence of Visco. He had expected to see Visco's natty, overdressed figure somewhere on the fringe of the celebration. Thelma, he noticed, kept glancing unobtrusively about, too. There was still a flick of worry in her blue eyes. She flushed and averted her gaze as she saw Tracy studying her.

Tracy was the only one who saw the waiter hand her the note. He followed her when she excused herself and left the table.

It took a little time to make his pursuit look casual. When Tracy reached the side corridor that led to the sunken terrace outside, he discovered that Colling was ahead of him. The announcer was crouched just inside the door that Thelma had left partly open behind her.

Colling was so intent on listening to what went on outside that he failed to notice Tracy step noiselessly behind a velvet drape in the corridor.

The two figures on the terrace were shrouded in darkness. Their voices were low. But the words were distinctly uttered.

"I'm not angry at you," Thelma cried tensely. "I'm just—"

"Afraid? Is that it, babe?"

She didn't reply.

"Afraid of what?" Visco's voice growled. "Is there any harm in my seeing you home? I'm not a bad looking guy. Anyone would think I had warts and a hair-lip! Be nice, babe. What do you say?"

Thelma's reply was too low to be audible. But Visco's was curt with rage.

"O.K.! Thanks for the insult. But remember this, sister! If you won't go for me, maybe I'll go for you! Think it over."

His stocky figure swung away from the girl. He crossed the sunken black terrace to the opposite side, ran lightly up a flight of stone steps and vanished.

Thelma returned slowly to the corridor door. She seemed surprised when she saw Colling. The announcer murmured something but the girl was too frightened to notice his embarrassment. There was eagerness in her quick murmur.

"Mr. Colling, will you do me a very great favor? Will you take me home tonight?"

Colling hesitated. In the light from the door lamp, his good-looking face was muddy.

"Sorry," he said huskily. "I happened to hear what Visco said. I'm not sticking my neck out. I don't want any part of that guy."

He turned on his heel and left her. Thelma remained stiffly where she was. Tracy could hear the hysterical catch in her throat as she leaned against the wall, staring out at the black terrace. He stepped noiselessly from behind the drape.

"Is something the matter?"

She whirled at the quiet sound of his voice. He liked her blue eyes at close range. The longness of her face gave her a lean boyish look. But there was nothing masculine about the tremble of her lower lip. He saw the lip stiffen as she made up her mind. "Mr. Tracy, do you have a car nearby?"

"Parked right around the corner."

"Would you—will you drive me home now?"

"Sure. Why not?" There was a lot he wanted to ask her, but he didn't. "Make a quiet getaway as soon as you can. I'll be out front on Fifth Avenue near the corner."

He had to wait a little over ten minutes. It gave him time to mooch around, with an eye cocked for Visco. But if the sleek lad with the nasty voice was anywhere in the neighborhood, he was under cover.

Tracy drove Thelma away without any fuss. Her address was not very far away. Tracy choked down the powerful engine of his sedan and took his time driving.

"Has this Visco guy been bothering you much?"

Thelma gave him a quick, probing glance. She could have evaded his question, but she didn't.

"Off and on," she said. "He's quite a nuisance."

"What's he after?"

"The usual thing, I suppose."

"Who is he? Where's he from?"

"I don't know."

"Did he ever bother Vivian La Grange?"

Thelma's composure fled. It was difficult to understand her blurred voice. Tracy patted her trembling shoulder.

"O.K., keed. Don't think about it."

Thelma lived on Sixth Avenue in a forlorn brick building that looked ready for wreckers. There was an empty store on the ground floor alongside a narrow vestibule. Subway construction had turned Sixth Avenue into a planked-over morass of sand-piles, concrete, and red lanterns. Night laborers flitted in and out of holes like gnomes. The planked street quivered with the dull boom of a subterranean explosion. The elevated structure overhead seemed to sag wearily on gaunt steel pillars.

"Do people like to live in a spot like this?" Tracy said faintly. He said it to himself, rather than to Thelma.

"I like the glamour of it," Thelma said with a wan smile.

Workmen on a swinging scaffold were riveting under the grilled belly of the el. There was a noisy *tat-tat-tat-tat* and a stream of golden sparks spilled downward like the spreading petals of a flower. To Jerry Tracy there wasn't any garden flower on earth that could compare with that sudden hot gush of beauty.

Thelma's crack had been intended as a brave little joke; but to Tracy it was truth. Glamour? Tracy lifted his eyes, sensing the things no outlander to Manhattan ever realized.

The el, outlined starkly against the black night sky, was lovelier than a temple. This was the real New York, the kind that milkmen knew, and cops, and night-hawk columnists.

Tracy sighed and took the girl's tired arm. He climbed narrow bare stairs to her room on the top floor. Thelma unlocked the door and opened it.

A man with a black, stubby automatic stood just inside the threshold.

"Skip the yells," he said grimly. "Just walk in."

THE GUNMAN'S LEFT hand bolted the door behind them. He was swarthy and sullen, with a hint of foreign accent in his husky voice. One of his eyes looked faintly milky, as if a cataract were beginning to form over it.

A second man stepped out of the bathroom. He grinned over his gun, showing a tooth-gap in the left of his mouth. He had a spreading nose and one of his ears seemed larger than the other.

"Nice handling, Sammy," he said to the first gunman.

They didn't look like brothers, but they might have been cousins. Short, chunky, heavy in the hip. Foreign in everything but speech. No sign of coal dust on them; but coal dust was what Tracy thought about, in spite of their expensively cut suits.

"Over against the wall, suckers!" Sammy said. "Spread apart."

"Bohunks!" Tracy thought.

He felt ice in his upraised fingertips. These gun guys were carbon copies of Visco. Hard guys from the hard coal district of Pennsylvania. Tough enough to get ideas. Smart enough to graduate to the mobs of Pittsburgh. Riding eastward in a Pullman to hunt in the richer jungles of Manhattan.

Thelma's face was so pale it looked bluish.

"Let's hurry this thing up, Lefty," Sammy said. "I want to collect."

A hollow boom from the tunnel under Sixth Avenue made the floor jar. The sound of riveting from the el made intermittent echoes like the snarl of a machine-gun.

"We better wait for an el train to go by," Lefty grinned. "Make things a little neater for the blowoff."

"You boys sore about something?" Tracy whispered. His tongue felt like blotting paper.

"What's there to be sore about?" Sammy said. "This is just a business deal."

"You're dough on the hoof, Mister," Lefty said. "A five-hundred-dollar bill, waiting to be folded up with a slug and split two ways."

Thelma's mouth opened. She tried to say something and couldn't.

"I'll take Tracy," Lefty said. "Listen for that damned el train, Sammy."

His finger cuddled around the trigger. Thelma was making queer, mouthing noises. Suddenly she was able to break the paralysis of her pale lips.

"For God's sake, wait! There's something wrong! You're not

supposed to *kill him*. He's here just to get a good beating. Visco said so!"

Both killers laughed.

Tracy's face swung unbelievingly toward the girl. He was dazed. He didn't believe the thing he had just heard. But he had to when he saw Thelma's face. She had deliberately put the finger on him. Visco's pugnacious encounter with Tracy backstage at the theater was a phoney build-up. So was the scene on the dark restaurant terrace at Radio City. Visco and a girl with clear blue eyes! And two hunkie gunmen who needed five hundred bucks!

The faint hum of an approaching el train made a thread of far-away sound. The riveters had stopped again.

"I'll give you one thing, Thelma," Tracy said with bitter slowness. "You're the smoothest little tart in Manhattan. You did a nice job."

She didn't hear him. She kept crying hoarsely: "A beating! Just a good going-over, not a murder. Visco said so! Can't you understand?"

"Better shoot him through the belly," Sammy said. "It'll look better to the cops. More like a woman done it."

"That's how I figure, too," Lefty said.

He darted toward Thelma and whirled her suddenly on her heels. His stubby fingers caught the neck of her gown and ripped it. The material split in a ragged tatter from one shoulder, uncovering the swell of her left breast.

"You shouldn't have tried to rape her, Tracy," Lefty jeered. "She's a nice girl. That's why she shot you in the gut. No jury would blame her."

"Only she lost her nerve after the kill," Sammy said. "Maybe she figured juries are tougher these days. So she bumped herself, right through the temple. Eh, Lefty?"

Tracy couldn't breathe. There was an acrid taste in his throat. The train was getting closer. *Tat-tat-tat-tat* went the riveters on Sixth Avenue.

Blood trickled from Thelma's lower lip. She was moaning through tightly clenched teeth.

"No, no! Don't, please. For God's sake, don't!"

She twisted hysterically to face the gunman behind her. The blind terror of her motion loosened the rest of the torn gown from her covered shoulder. It dropped in a green shimmering puddle about her feet. She tripped on it and fell against the startled Sammy. Terror wound her groping fingers around his gun. Instinct brought her leg upward, the knee bent. Its impact caught Sammy in the groin and he went down, with the clawing, fighting girl on top of him.

Lefty fired almost point-blank at Tracy.

The slug singed Tracy's hair as it blew plaster from the wall. He had dropped under it, landing on knees and chest and chin. For an instant he lay motionless, his rump tilted upward like a cow in a stall. Then the soles of his feet kicked at wall. He dove forward below the flame of the jerking gun muzzle and struck Lefty head-on. His skull pushed between Lefty's legs, toppling him backward.

The two rolled over and over, fighting for the gun. Jerry's sweat-slippery palm clutched and missed. Lefty brought the barrel around with a grunt. He lined it pitilessly and his finger tightened. But the weapon swerved at the last second. The bullet pumped wide of Tracy's ear. The explosion deafened him.

Lefty's head sagged.

There was a crimson smear on his forehead and a spill of blood down his nose. Thelma had grabbed the weapon from the man her knee had disabled. She had swung the butt against Lefty's skull with desperate haste. But her aim was bad. The blow had skidded, merely ripping the skin. Lefty's glazed eyes cleared.

Thelma reeled and dropped her weapon. Tracy's fingers darted for it like a scrabbling spider. He whirled the muzzle, jammed it against the elastic pressure of flesh, fired.

Nobody stopped him as he swayed to his feet.

He was unaware that Lefty was dead or that Thelma had fainted. He was glaring at the bent figure poised on the sill of the rear window. The thug who had been kicked in the groin had crawled with agonized effort to the sill and had lifted the sash. He hung forward, like a top-heavy snowball.

Before Tracy's dazed brain could telegraph an upward lift to the gun in his hand, Sammy tumbled groaning to the fire-escape platform outside the window. He fell down the first slanting ladder and ran down the second. Tracy didn't shoot Sammy as the gunman weakly straddled a low back fence. He didn't want to kill anybody. He just wanted to be let alone. He was shaking like a leaf. So scared that it hurt.

He shut the window and made incredulously sure that Lefty was dead. Tracy's single bullet had made a ghastly mess of Lefty's jawbone and throat. The girl had fainted almost on top of him. Tracy pulled the unconscious Thelma away from the edge of spreading crimson.

After a while he got his nerve back.

He worked on Thelma roughly, slapping her face, rocking her

head briskly with his fingers twisted in her thick, honey-colored hair. She came out of silence with a dull moan. Tracy shoved her torn gown at her.

"Come on! Get it on! You're damn near naked, dope! Got any pins?"

He was so close to hysteria himself that he was able to get tough with her. He knew now that she wasn't a cheap tart, but a sucker like himself. Like Vivian La Grange!

"Do you live here? You don't, do you? This was just a spot that Visco arranged?"

"I didn't realize what he—I swear I—"

"Come on! I've got both the guns and I don't think we left any prints." He smiled thinly as he helped her tie her dress on. The riveters on Sixth Avenue were still stuttering noisily. "Listen to that! That's exit music!"

They slid like ghosts down the creaky staircases of the quiet house. Tracy knew why it was so quiet when he saw there were no names in any of the rusted name-plates downstairs. He'd been too careless to notice that on the way in.

The pair drove eastward through a dim, soundless street flanked by drowsy warehouses and loft buildings. Tracy blessed his luck in parking that big showy sedan of his out of sight of the subway workmen around the corner on Sixth Avenue. Nobody'd remember it. His knuckles stayed taut on the wheel.

"What made you think I needed a good beating up, Thelma?"

He heard her quick breathing. There was no vibration in her words now. She sounded lifeless.

"Vivian was my best friend. We starved together in cheap rooming houses, hoping for a break. She got one. You ruined that with your column. You hounded her to suicide."

Tracy looked sideways at Thelma's pale face, at her mouth and her square little chin.

"You've got a nice voice for singing. Suppose I got sore about what happened tonight? Suppose I put the heat on you in my column to even up things? Think you could take it?"

She said in the same expressionless tone: "You could kill me, Mister, and I'd sing on a slab in the morgue."

"You've answered yourself, sweetheart," Tracy said huskily. "No human being on earth can down a girl with guts and talent. Vivian was licked by herself. Not by me. And she didn't commit suicide."

He spun the sedan swiftly around a corner into Fifth Avenue. "She was murdered!"

He felt the quick pressure of Thelma's cold fingers on his wrist. She didn't speak.

"What was Visco's line to you about Vivian?"

"He said he was Vivian's boy friend from Altoona. He asked me to—to help him get even with you for her death."

"I know. Forget that. We were both dumb."

"But why would he want to kill you—or me?"

"A little matter of a scrap of black camera paper and an expensive cigar butt," Tracy said grimly. "I think somebody saw me pick them up." He added: "I can see Visco as the trigger boss behind all this, but not the brains. Somebody who's very smart has been using desperate little kids like Vivian in some water-tight racket. Green-as-grass kids with pretty faces and fresh, cushy figures. Vivian is the fourth girl like that who has 'committed suicide' in the last six weeks.... Where do you live?"

She told him and he shook his head.

"Too dangerous now. Our fugitive friend Sammy will unknot

his bruised belly and report to Visco. I'm going to tuck you away in a spot where gunmen and chiselers will need a hell of a genteel alibi to get at you. We'll make it Fifth Avenue. Hotel Plaza."

Thelma gasped. "The Plaza! But look at me! And I have no baggage or—"

"And while I think of it," Tracy interrupted, "I want you to concentrate about Vivian's boy friends. I mean the elderly kind, the lads with dough. Try and remember if any of them smoked cigars. Men that Vivian might giggle about as middle-aged suckers."

Thelma was silent for a while. Then she mentioned haltingly three or four names. Tracy slipped her a notebook and pencil stub and made her write them down.

He kept watching her for a moment, a faint frown creasing his forehead.

"Are you particularly friendly with Colling?"

"No," Thelma said, "I hardly know him."

"Then why," Tracy said, "did you ask him to see you home tonight?"

Thelma flushed. "That was a build-up," she admitted. "I knew you'd have no suspicions of my motive if I asked someone else first instead of going directly to you."

"Suppose Colling had agreed to see you home?" Tracy murmured, his glance still steadily on hers. "Your whole scheme would have gone haywire, wouldn't it? I can't figure why you took so big a gamble."

Thelma's flush deepened. "I knew Colling would refuse. Visco told me he had thrown a scare into the announcer. He told Colling he'd blow him apart if he ever caught him playing around with me."

"Visco must be a lovely character," Tracy said dryly. He skimmed the sedan circlewise from Fifth Avenue and halted before the dimly decorous front of the Hotel Plaza.

"You're in damned serious danger of death, sweetheart. Don't stir an inch without orders from me. Find out what room service means and use it. Understand?"

She nodded tremulously and Tracy grinned at her.

"Now we'll see how much attention a little guy from Broadway rates along Central Park South!"

JERRY TRACY DIDN'T sleep much the rest of that night. Most of the time he spent lying awake, thinking hard, in the privacy of his sound proofed penthouse bedroom.

In the morning Butch, his combination servant and bodyguard, brought him the papers and he read all about the death of Lefty in a crumbly old Sixth Avenue house. Only the papers didn't call the guy Lefty. He figured in all the stories as "the victim." The police ascribed his death to a gang quarrel. There was no record of his fingerprints in Center Street. Copies of the prints had been sent to the Federal Bureau in Washington. Opinion was that the guy was an ambitious out-of-town hoodlum who had tried to cut in on a Manhattan gang, and been neatly cut out.

Naturally, there was no newspaper mention of a gun mugg named Sammy or a sleek, dark-eyed chiseler named Visco.

Tracy had no real hope of locating Visco. He and Sammy were probably holed up somewhere, figuring their next move. The puzzle of Vivian's death would have to be cracked at the middle angle of the triangle—the sucker who smoked Corona Coronas.

Jerry waited until almost eleven, hoping to get a phone call from Alyce, the cigarette gal at the Terrace Club. But there was no call; and Tracy didn't want to start possible gossip by phoning the restaurant to find out where she lived.

He didn't even like to phone Thelma, but he did. She said everything was all right, in a small, far-away voice. She sounded scared.

Tracy reassured her, grabbed a cab and hustled down to his dusty Broadway coop. He locked the door, disconnected his phone and got busy. He was neither a cop nor a dick. He was a columnist, working under an iron-clad contract. He was only two columns ahead, and they snarled down at the *Planet* office when he didn't have four under his belt.

He tailored some new ones and when he finally quit, the afternoon had faded to dusk. He had a swim, a rub-down and a shower at the Midtown Athletic Club. Dinner in a side-street eatery where they cooked the best pork chops in town and he could eat in peace. Then a dash to a first-night performance where he had to review a dull drama with a single set, a dress-suit adultery problem, and five characters who spoke with a British accent and seemed vaguely sorry they had ever left England.

Tracy was sorry, too. He sneaked out during the last act, wrote two hundred words in the men's room downstairs and phoned it to the *Planet* to save time hunting for a messenger boy.

Then he was off to Billy Rose's new spot, and that was a lot better. He went to bed mildly cockeyed and very tired. He thought dully about staying in bed for a week, but fell asleep before he could decide about it.

His phone buzzed him awake in mid-morning. The easiest

way to stop it was to unhook the thing, yell, "Go to hell" and hang up. But the sweet strawberry syrup voice on the wire snapped him wide awake.

It was Alyce and she wanted to talk about cigars.

"Why the hell didn't you call me yesterday morning?"

"I din' wanna disturb you," Alyce cooed. "They say you never get up before noon. Then in the aft'noon, I called your Broadway office and I can't get no answer, and what's the idea anyway, Mr. Tracy? Are you handing me a horse's tail on that build-up you promised me in your colyum?"

"Don't be silly," Tracy said. "What did you find out?"

"Well, I mooched around and got a line on the big spenders and heavy tippers. I tested each of 'em with a little eye work and hip wriggle and, believe me, they're all gal conscious. All of 'em are on the fat side and middle-aged. I—"

"Let's have their names."

"Wait a minute," Alyce said. "There's a catch in the thing."

Her voice dropped to a hushed whisper. She sounded like Special Agent F-38 in a spy melodrama.

"Not *one* of them smokes *cigars*. I ask 'em if they'd like a Corona Corona, and three of them laughed and one pinched my leg. Look, Jerry, about that write-up of me in the colyum, you could say I was born in the South—"

"Sure, sure," Tracy said. He thought fast. "These big spenders come pretty regularly to those radio parties, don't they?"

"Yeah."

"Did you notice whether any of them were missing? Take your time and think hard. It's important."

There was a long silence at the other end of the wire. Tracy waited tensely.

"Come to think of it—" Alyce said.

"What's his name?"

"Phil, they call him. I'm not sure of his last name. I think he's an Irishman. Ryan or Regan, somethin' like that. I don't think he lives in New York; I've seen him fussing with timetables when it gets late."

"You're a sweetheart! Thanks."

"Look, if you made me a Southern gal in that colyum write-up—"

"I'll build you six white pillars and a big moon over a cotton field, and—"

"Put in somepin' about mint juleps and a sweet old mammy who's been with the fambly for years," Alyce said dreamily.

Tracy clicked down the receiver and bounced to his feet. He darted to his wardrobe closet and found the suit he had worn the night he had driven Thelma to the Plaza. A guy named Ryan or Regan.... The name Regan seemed to hit a fuzzy chord in his memory. He looked at the list Thelma had scribbled for him in his speeding sedan that night.

The third name on the list was Phil Riggam.

Tracy rubbed his head and took a drink. Then he grabbed a taxi and went down to the *Planet* building. He had a private office there but he seldom used it, preferring to work in the untidy rat nest he had leased in Times Square. He went downtown because he needed the expert help of nosy Al Decker who covered the hotel news.

Jerry's arrival created a sensation among the *Planet* copy boys. All of them nourished the hope of some day being assigned to Tracy, of darting in and out of hot spots on the twinkling coat-tails of the town's most famous columnist.

Tracy jabbed a forefinger at a smart-eyed kid named Tony and drew him into the private cubby. He liked the way Tony nodded silently and listened. He sent him out to the city room to look up Phil Riggam in all the suburban telephone books.

Then he got busy on his own stuff. He had a radio news spiel to assemble for his weekly air program. Hot, crackling items about Hollywood and Manhattan. *Flash, flash!* in a voice like pelting pebbles. But there was nothing *flash, flash!* in the slow sifting and verification of the stuff.

Tony came back presently. No luck. There wasn't any Phil Riggam listed in Westchester County, Long Island or northern New Jersey.

Tracy closed his eyes and tried to think coherently. If Riggam had been photographed with the dead Vivian before she had been posed to look like a suicide, it meant blackmail. That meant dough to be handed over to Visco, or some smart guy behind Visco. They'd never let the sucker leave town till he paid! It would take time to raise any sizeable wad of cash. And the sucker would have to move slowly for fear of arousing suspicion on the part of his wife or his business associates back home.

Riggam had probably already overstayed his New York visit and was sweating with worry in some Manhattan hotel.

"Look, Tony," Tracy said. "Has Al Becker come in yet from his hotel tour?"

"No, sir."

"Stick around until he does. Here's what I want you to find out. I'm interested in a middle-aged chump from out of town. He has plenty of dough and a job that brings him to New York regularly. He likes night clubs, excitement and the fun of meeting Broadway big shots. He's a push-over for women, especially when the gal is young, blond, and a little on the dumb side."

"I getcha," Tony said.

"Here's the question you ask Al Decker. What hotels would a sap like that be apt to go to? Ask Decker to make up a list. You'll have to tell him the info is for Jerry Tracy and he'll be curious as hell. So how will you shut his trap?"

Tony grinned. "The managing editor canned a switchboard girl to get Margie Graham her job. The M.E. is nuts about this Margie. Decker's been dating her on the quiet. Okey?"

Tracy chuckled. "Swell! Keep away from journalism schools—and some day you'll be batting out a neat column. Scram!"

Tony didn't come back until long after lunch time. He brought with him a list of fourteen hotels. Tracy handed him a dollar bill and a bigger one that made the kid's eyes pop.

"The big one's yours. Change the buck at a subway booth and get nickels. Call each of these hotels and ask for Mr. Phil Riggam. If Riggam answers, hang up. Now tell me why you're going *outside* to make those calls."

"Because Al Decker will have Margie all primed at the switchboard to find out what's going on."

"I think you're going to work for me regularly," Tracy said.

It took eleven of the fourteen calls to locate Phil Riggam. He was at the Hotel Nagler, but Tony hadn't actually talked to him. Riggam had left orders at the Nagler desk that he was ill and didn't wish to be disturbed.

Jerry Tracy decided that it was time to disturb him.

DARKNESS WAS SETTING over Manhattan when

Tracy drove up to the Nagler. He picked up a house phone. The operator gave him a prompt nix on Riggam's room number. Tracy buttonholed the clerk and said a few crisp words. The clerk hesitated. Tracy had done plenty of favors for him and this was the first time he had ever tried to collect.

"Will this jam me in any way, Jerry?"

"No."

"Miss Weaver, let him have 924."

Phil Riggam sounded high-pitched and nasty. He yelled a profane oath at being disturbed and hung up. Tracy buzzed him again.

"The name is Jerry Tracy. Of the *Daily Planet*. I want to talk about a photograph. Or would you rather I'd just go ahead and print the yarn?"

He could hear all the air in Room 924 rush into Riggam's gasping mouth.

"Oh! I—you better come up."

Riggam was a heavy man. He had bulging, sleepless eyes and a grayish face. He was so frightened he looked ready to collapse. The moment he closed the door his hand wrenched into view from behind his back. He was clutching a gun. He swung the warning muzzle in line with Tracy's stomach. His face was green with fright.

Tracy took one look at the shaking gun and the spasmodic finger on the trigger. He didn't want gun-play or a fight, but he didn't want to be killed by a sucker almost out of his wits with terror. He kicked Riggam in his fat shins and sighed as he saw the gun drop. Then he hit Riggam in the jaw.

He put the captured gun in his pocket. He talked briefly and to the point.

"I didn't kill her," Riggam whispered. "I swear I didn't! You've got to believe me. You—"

He went completely to pieces under Tracy's fish-cold eye. He was softer than a ripe banana.

"Spill it," Tracy rasped. "How was Vivian killed?"

It was about what Tracy had figured. Riggam had gone to Vivian's apartment for a couple of drinks. He made a play for her and Vivian seemed complaisant. Then, suddenly, she turned nasty. She shoved him away from her and grabbed a gun. Riggam froze with his hands up. Then two guys came in, one of them with a camera.

"What did they look like?" Tracy asked.

The man with the camera was obviously Lefty, the mugg Tracy had killed on Sixth Avenue. The other fellow was Visco. Visco grinned at Vivian and said. "You done swell." He asked her for the gun and she handed it to him. Then, still grinning, he leaned coolly close and blew out her brains.

Riggam witnessed this with sick horror. But he wasn't too sick to ignore Visco's purring whisper. He was forced to kneel close to the bed, with the murder weapon in his hand, pointed waveringly at the girl's shattered temple. Visco unscrewed the bulbs over the mantelpiece and substituted photoflood bulbs. He took the pictures and tossed the bulbs out the window, crashing them against a brick wall in the next yard. Then he wiped the weapon clean, adjusted it carefully in the girl's dead hand and waited with grim patience for *rigor mortis*.

"How much was the shakedown to let it stay suicide?" Tracy asked.

"Fifty thousand dollars. Even if I could prove the conspiracy,

I didn't dare try. I'm a member of a conservative firm. I've got a wife and children who—"

"But you did try to make Vivian, didn't you?" Tracy said in a hard, bitter undertone. "I mean, *make* her."

Riggam's lips quivered. "I'm human," he whispered.

"Human! That's what every one of you lice yelp when you're caught. Out-of-town hypocrites on the loose in Manhattan! Yelling to your small town friends about New York's dirt, and then sneaking here to find it! Sure you're human! That's why Manhattan's overrun with pimps and gamblers and gun muggs—to take buzzards like you who roll in on Pullmans from the sticks.... Well, how much of the bite did they collect from you?"

"Half. I promised Visco I'd raise the other twenty-five grand if he'd give me a little time."

"Where do you meet Visco?"

"He phones and sets the spot."

"How can he? You told the desk downstairs to stop all incoming calls?"

"I have two phones here. One of them is a private wire."

Tracy walked across and took a note of the private number. Standing there, eying the phone, he felt a sudden queer chill along his spine. A girl's face popped into his mind, her lips scared, her blue eyes pleading. He hadn't phoned Thelma in two days!

He scooped up the receiver and called the Hotel Plaza.

The desk clerk's reply made Tracy go empty inside. Thelma was gone! She had left the Plaza about an hour earlier. She had gone away with a man. The clerk couldn't remember the man, but the house dick did. Thelma's companion was a big, broad-shouldered, good-looking guy with white teeth and a kind of a twitchy smile.

Colling, of course! The announcer who read the commercials on the Soapsud Amateur Hour!

Tracy remembered with a gasp that the air show was a twice a week program. That was where Colling was taking Thelma! Tracy had felt right from the start that the whole criminal racket stemmed from the Paragon Theater where the air show was held. Was Colling the brain behind Visco? If so, Thelma was done for! She knew too much.

But so, Tracy thought grimly, did he!

He decided to beat it quickly over to the Paragon Theater and force a blow-off with himself as bait. Riggam looked scared as the *Daily Planet's* lean little columnist darted for the door.

"Where are you going? What about me? What shall I do?"

"I hope you fry in hell," Tracy grated.

But he calmed down in the elevator. By the time he reached the ground level he knew what he was going to do. He got five nickels at the cigar counter and closed himself inside a public phone booth. He called the Paragon Theater and tried to get Ned Carlisle. But Ned was up to his ears, too busy even for Jerry Tracy. Jerry asked for his assistant and finally Hal Bruce came on the wire. Tracy made his request quickly.

He asked for two seats in the sponsor's row. That was the first row in the theater and it was never disposed of to the public. Most of the time it was half empty, and it was so now. Bruce sounded puzzled; but he agreed to hold two seats at the box office for the two gentlemen who would ask for them in the next few minutes.

Tracy's second nickel got him Phil Riggam over the private telephone in Room 924. He made his voice gruff, like Visco's, and he filtered it through a bunched handkerchief over the transmitter.

"I haven't got the money yet," Riggam gasped.

"The hell with that. I want to see *you!* Hustle right away to the Paragon Theater. Tell the guy at the box office you want one of those seats in the sponsor's row. A tall guy with blue eyes and a mop of gray hair will sit next to you. Don't talk to him unless he talks to you. Got that straight?"

"Y—yes."

"Okey. Now scram!"

The tall guy with blue eyes and a mop of gray hair was, of course, Inspector Fitzgerald of Manhattan Homicide. Tracy was sweating freely in the hot booth by the time his third nickel bounced his call through police headquarters to Fitz's divisional office.

Fitz said with quick awareness of Tracy's tension: "What's the matter? Something wrong?"

Tracy bounced Fitz out of his chair with the flat announcement that he'd found out the truth about Vivian's death and could prove her suicide was murder. He told Fitz the same thing he had told Riggam about the sponsor's row tickets.

"The blow-off is coming tonight, Fitz! Right in that theater, or I'm crazy! You'll be sitting next to a fat, paunchy guy who'll look sick and worried. Don't say anything to him unless he says something to you. Just sit."

"You're a little guy, Jerry," Fitz said slowly, "but you have the damnedest habit of raising a big stink. Are you sure this stink is on the level?"

"Don't go then!" Tracy snapped and hung up. Boy, that ought to get Fitz down there in a hurry.

Tracy grabbed a cab and hustled over to the theater.

APPLAUSE ROCKED THE darkened auditorium. The show was already on the air. Colling, smiling and debonair, had just left the commercial mike and was deftly fading offstage. The applause was for Ned Carlisle and a radiant honey blonde whom the producer was leading to the center stage mike.

The show always opened with the winner of the preceding contest, Ned explained unctuously, and this time he had particular pleasure in reintroducing a talented little lady whose gorgeous, God-given voice....

Jerry Tracy watched Thelma's nervousness add an electric tension to her loveliness. Her voice steadied after the first faltering note, then it was like rich, velvet warmth in every nook and cranny of the darkened playhouse. Tracy listened, relaxed and dream-like in spite of himself.

A moving light in the rear of the center aisle roused him. He saw the bulky figure of Phil Riggam following a soft-footed girl usher. Riggam's ticket to the sponsor's row had admitted him to a show where customarily no one entered after the on-the-air signal was flashed to the door.

Tracy ducked quietly out the lobby and hurried around to the stage. Almost the first man he saw was Colling. The announcer gave him a quick, startled look. "Hello, Jerry," he whispered, then he was gone with an apologetic smile.

Thelma had already left the stage. But no one to whom Tracy spoke seemed to know where she was. The watchman at the stage door said she hadn't left the theater.

Hal Bruce appeared in the dimness behind the backdrop. He grinned and shook hands hastily with Jerry.

"Thelma? I don't know. Maybe she's in one of the dressing rooms."

He trotted off to confer with a lanky electrician in soiled overalls. Tracy swore anxiously under his breath. Uneasiness for Thelma's safety pricked him to speed. He found where the dressing rooms were located and hurried along, opening doors. Thelma was sitting quietly in the last room along a dim corridor. She seemed to be relaxed and comfortable.

Her smile of recognition faded at sight of Tracy's blazing eyes.

"I told you not to leave the Plaza! Why did you permit Colling to bring you back to the theater?"

"I was afraid that if I didn't I'd lose my chance for a stage career. The winner has to appear on the next program for an encore. I've fought and starved and waited too long to risk failure now. I'd rather be dead like Vivian, than a flop!"

Tracy loved her for the courage in her clear eyes. But it didn't make him forget her danger.

"How did Colling discover you were hidden at the Plaza?"

"I don't know. I just—"

"O.K. Hold that pose, suckers!" a voice growled.

Visco had stepped from a closet in the end wall of the room. The man with him was Sammy, the thug to whom Thelma had given the knee in the murder spot back on Sixth Avenue. But there was no agonized crouch to Sammy now. He was erect with catlike vigilance. There was murder in his pinched eyes.

Visco said curtly: "We're leaving this theater, folks. Don't spoil a pleasant trip by making us sling lead. Sammy, go get rid of that old duck on the rear door."

"Wait a minute," Tracy said quickly. There was sweat on his

pale forehead. He forced calm, sneery complaisance into his smile.

"Do you guys actually think I walked into here tonight with my head in a bag? Take a look out that stage door and get a load of the plain-clothes arrangements. Or better still, duck backstage and take a quick slant through the curtain peep-hole. Figure out why those two guys are sitting together in the front row."

"It's a bluff," Sammy snarled.

"It's a blow-off," Tracy corrected.

"Watch these muggs!" Visco said harshly.

He vanished down the dressing-room corridor like a dark streak. When he came back, there was rage in his eyes, but no worry.

"You've been smart enough to make it hard," he admitted. "But you're still a sucker. Lock that door, Sammy! We're going out the closet, same as we came in."

The rear of the closet was thin partition board. A newly cut panel came away without fuss or trouble. Visco went first and Tracy and the girl followed. There was nothing else to do. Sammy replaced the panel.

They were in a dimly lit dressing-room corridor. Narrow steps led downward. Two flights. Dusty and utterly silent except for the faint echo of amateur hill-billy music from the distant stage.

The cellar of the theater was a quiet white-washed cavern. A man in overalls saw the stiffly moving group and came closer with a puzzled look. Sammy's gun-butt against his skull sounded like a home run in a ball park. The thug lugged the victim's trailing heels back of a pile of empty wooden cases.

"What do we do with Tracy and the dame?" Sammy whispered eagerly.

What he'd like to do was clear and pitiless in his eyes. But Visco shook his head.

"Nix on the gun stuff. When these dopes are missed after the show, there'll be a police search. We've got to bunk 'em until we can figure how to get 'em out. We're still in one hell of a spot, Sammy."

"Hey, maybe you better ask—"

"Shut up!"

"I always figured you weren't the brains in this racket," Tracy told Visco softly.

Visco hit Tracy back of the ear. Sammy kicked him in the ribs until he groaned and swayed upright again. A black muzzle kept Thelma's shriek dammed up in her throat.

The cellar was a maze of pipes and machinery. But Visco seemed to know exactly where to go. Jerry and Thelma were forced to walk forward under a line of asbestos-covered pipe supported by metal brackets from the low ceiling. The rear end of the basement was partitioned off from the rest. Visco opened an unlocked door with a quick twist of his hairy hand. Then Tracy saw the huge radio cabinets massed against the wall.

That's what they looked like. Enormous steel radio cabinets, built side by side, taking up most of the space from floor to ceiling. A rhythmic hum made a pleasant murmur. Ducts led away from the smooth cleanliness of the massive equipment.

Tracy knew what it was before Visco opened a metal panel that pivoted vertically downward on a bottom hinge. An air-conditioning unit. Fans and blowers and compressors that sucked in air, filtered and tempered it, and then forced it through ducts to the theater auditorium upstairs.

"How the hell you gonna shove 'em in there?" Sammy growled.

The whole space was packed with an intricate pattern of machinery. Visco had opened the compressor unit. He swore and closed the tilted panel. He had better luck on his next try.

"Okey," he said curtly. "Tracy first. Then the girl."

Sammy tied them with some heavy cord he had found on a work bench outside. Then they were shoved into a shelflike space to the left of what looked like a big dynamo. It was silver-gray and Tracy saw that it was an aluminum housing for an enormous fan that whirled and hummed out of sight.

Over the bent heads of the jammed-in prisoners were two tilted screens that made an inverted B. The screens were honey-combed like the radiator of an automobile and behind the grill work was spun-glass filter material, flecked with crimson spots that looked like mashed cherries.

"Nobody can squeal if they're dead," Sammy growled. "Why not lemme blast 'em right now?"

"Go ahead," Tracy said coolly. "If you want gun echoes to be heard all over the theater through those air ducts. This spot is a perfect mike pick-up."

He knew it wasn't, but the lie worked. It postponed the kill, but it got hasty gags jammed into the prisoner's mouths. Tracy's frown warned Thelma not to struggle. He didn't want either of them to be slugged unconscious.

The tilted, metal door slammed upward. Tracy began to chew fiercely at his hastily applied gag. He got it loosened enough to gasp a low-toned order into Thelma's ear.

They were lying back to back, but he twisted painfully until the girl's bound hands touched his coat front. Thelma managed to unbutton the coat, and to feel with numb fingertips in the pockets of his vest. She got hold of Tracy's miniature cigarette lighter. She lifted it slowly, inch by inch, rigid with the fear that she might drop it. Her thumb clicked it tremulously and the tiny blue-tipped flame glowed.

Tracy told her what to do. She didn't protest. She knew as well as Jerry did, the desperate urgency of their predicament. A wriggle of the columnist brought his back around to face the bound hands of Thelma. She held the flame of the lighter below Tracy's tied hands, at the edge of his coat.

The cloth charred. Then suddenly Tracy felt the agony of flame. Thelma gasped. Her joined hands beat the fire out.

"The hell with me!" Tracy cried. "Let it burn! They've got to smell it in the theater—the stench of it coming out through the air ducts!"

Again pain licked at his body. He writhed, gritting his teeth. He could smell the acrid stench of the cloth. He knew every duct from the mixing chamber was carrying the stink upward through the air conditioning system. Noses would sniff. People would blink and dart questioning glances at one another in the darkness of the auditorium. Fitz, too, sitting stolidly in the first row, waiting for a blow-off that Tracy had promised....

Again Thelma pounded Tracy's back and the flaming coat smouldered. The odor made his eyes brim with tears. He told himself fiercely that it *was* the odor, not the agony in his flesh. He could take it! Fitz had told him he was a little guy who was always raising a big stink. His lips twisted into an ironic grimace at the thought.

His ears were listening with every atom of his will. Suddenly he heard the muffled tread of footsteps racing toward the closed panel of the air-mixing chamber. A hand swung the panel downward.

The dark peering eyes of Visco were opaque as black frosted glass. A gun muzzle thrust itself at Tracy's face.

But before Visco's finger could explode shattering thunder into Tracy's skull there was a warning yell from the basement beyond the line of Tracy's vision. Sammy was shouting harshly.

Visco whirled and ran. Tracy, kicking with all his strength at the soft pressure of Thelma's body, fell headlong outward. He landed with a jarrying thump on the basement floor. Rolling over, he saw two men racing toward the killers. Colling was sprinting forward, his mouth wide open. Behind him was Hal Bruce. Bruce saw the armed gangsters and gave a startled cry. A gun leaped from his hip pocket.

But as he levelled it, Colling stumbled. The two men collided and fell. Visco stood stock-still for an instant, watching their writhing figures. Then Bruce's arm jerked and a bullet drilled into Visco's stomach, dropping him as if he'd been chopped by an ax.

Sammy had leaped sideways toward the concrete wall. He was firing like a maniac. Bullets ripped between Colling and Bruce as they rolled apart. Two more men were racing from the gloom of the distant stairway. Tracy's heart pumped as he recognized the gray mop of hair and the big police gun. The gun was in Fitz's right hand, and his left was firmly gripped on the arm of Phil Riggam. He forced Riggam to run with him like a jerking, terrified dummy.

Fitz fired in mid-stride. Three bullets criss-crossed the path of Sammy's blind fusillade of lead. One of them missed. The other two didn't.

It was Fitz who untied Tracy and released Thelma. Hal Bruce was shaking like a leaf. Colling looked like a man who had been in and out the seven gates of hell.

"I'm sorry I tripped you," he told Bruce dully. "I didn't mean to. I couldn't help it."

"That's all right," Bruce said.

Fitz had re-hooked his fingers on Riggam's quivering arm. "Was this guy one of them, Jerry?"

Tracy was still staring at the inert figures of Sammy and Visco. Both were stone dead. Tracy turned stiffly, shook his head.

"Let him alone, Fitz. He was the sucker, the come-on. Visco was trying to take him for fifty grand."

"Just those two rats on the floor, eh?"

"No," Tracy said. "Three rats. There was one more—the brain behind the whole dirty racket."

He looked grimly at Colling.

"How did you know Thelma was at the Plaza Hotel when you went there tonight to get her?"

Colling hesitated. His mouth twitched. "Why, Hal Bruce said—"

"I said nothing," Bruce barked. "Don't try to shift any trouble on me, you damned liar!"

"Somebody is lying," Tracy agreed in a mild voice.

He had turned slightly, his tone belying the tension of his tightening muscles. When he leaped he took Ned Carlisle's assistant entirely by surprise. Hal Bruce's hand jammed half-way out of his pocket. The two men rocked desperately together, then Fitz clipped Bruce and wrenched his gun away.

Bruce shuddered. He recovered his calmness with an effort. "I didn't mean to start any fuss. You scared me with that dive of yours, Jerry. I'm sorry."

"I'm sorry too, Hal," Tracy said. "I hate to turn in someone I always thought was on the level. But you're guilty as hell. Colling told the truth about his visit to the Plaza. You told him to go there! If he were guilty, Colling would never have appeared openly and tipped his hand. He'd know, as you were afraid, that I'd find out."

Tracy's lips tightened.

"You knew Thelma was at the Plaza because you trailed me there the night I slipped out of your trap on Sixth Avenue. You couldn't have found out any other way. The girl wasn't even registered."

"Jerry, you're being ridiculous," Bruce said quietly.

"I also noticed how you killed Visco. That was a miracle of luck for you—if you were innocent. Visco had the drop on you, but he backed up and didn't fire. He didn't, because you were his boss! He left the play to you, and you killed him to shut his mouth. In other words, I'm old enough to vote and I don't believe in miracles."

"You'll need a better case than that to take me into court," Bruce said. "You can't blast a man's reputation with surmises."

"You can with proof," Tracy said. "The photographs that Visco snapped to put the bite on Phil Riggam went straight to you. You'd be a sucker to trust Visco with them—and you didn't."

Jerry Tracy was a good poker player. He was bluffing to the limit of his wits. But it was sound bluffing, based on the psychology of a desperate and shaken antagonist who could see only the backs of the cards. Tracy kept his glance on Hal Bruce's necktie, but he was watching the man's eyes from under lowered lids. His voice was soothing, almost hypnotic.

"Those photographs are dynamite, Hal. You'd have to hide 'em in a spot easily accessible to you, yet safe from discovery. You picked this theater cellar because you know every inch of it. Those blackmail photos have your prints all over them, Hal. I know—because I've already examined them!"

"Rot!" Bruce cried hoarsely.

His hunted glance swept circlewise toward the air conditioning chamber where Tracy had been hidden. It was beautifully done, a bit of desperate artifice by a man whose crooked brain had transformed guile into habit.

But Tracy, watching hawk-like, saw Bruce's chin lift slightly, saw the terrified eyes pause overhead for the whiplash fraction of a second. The milky cylinder of an asbestos-lined pipe hung low from the ceiling. A small segment of the asbestos covering looked smoother than the rest. Its smoothness had not been quite camouflaged by the paint brush or the cleverly smudged dirt.

Tracy's upflung hand clawed at it.

The covering was thin cardboard. It ripped away, disclosing a space around the pipe. Curved papers fluttered downward to the floor. Tracy pounced on them like a bright-eyed ferret.

Bruce must have expected doom. His swift glance toward the air-conditioning apparatus had been meant merely to turn Inspector Fitzgerald. His fist crashed against Fitz's profile. As the inspector staggered under the blow, Bruce snatched the gun from his loosened grasp.

Thelma screamed. Tracy darted forward. The gun barrel made a glittering arc. Fitz, recovering instantly, tried to grab it, but he was a shade too late. Bruce's ghastly grin quivered as he pulled the trigger. His head bounced with the impact of the bullet he sent ripping through his own brain.

He slid inertly through the instinctive circle of Fitz's outflung arms.

Tracy said faintly: "Let go of him, Fitz. You'll get yourself messed up."

The little columnist's face was pale. One of his arms had slid around Thelma, just how he didn't remember. He patted her quivering shoulder as he talked.

"Bruce did what I hoped he'd do. He's made this thing a D.A.'s report instead of a Grand Jury and a court-room trial. Ned Carlisle is one hell of a fine human being and a trial would have smirched Ned and forced him off the air. You can choke off a lot of the publicity, Fitz. I'll talk to the D.A. myself."

Fitz nodded mechanically. He was still dazed by the suicide.

"I don't think Hal Bruce was quite sane," Jerry Tracy said. "You remember what he was on the stage ten years ago, the greatest tap dancer in the world. Then arthritis hit him and dropped the curtain. I don't think he ever reconciled himself to an anonymous career as Ned Carlisle's assistant. And he was used to big dough—you know how much, Fitz.

"Those poor little amateur girls gave Bruce a perfect set-up for crime. He picked the desperate ones and sold 'em on easy money. It was a cruel and water-tight variation of the old badger game—because on each job Bruce killed the deluded girl and protected Visco and himself. The suckers paid up and kept quiet to save their own reputations."

Thelma shuddered. "I'll always be seeing Vivian's face. I'll never sing again." There was a blurred smile on the columnist's lips. It made Fitzgerald think of all the talented kids who were famous now because Jerry Tracy believed in them and liked them. "Oh, yes you will!" Jerry growled. "You'll sing, baby! A year from now it'll probably cost me a week's salary to get inside to hear you. For further details see tomorrow's column!"

Colling was staring at the little guy, his lips twisting. Tracy realized suddenly that the announcer's white-toothed grimace was purely physical.

He said sharply: "Why the hell do you do that? You've been doing that guilty mugging so much, I was all set to collar you instead of Hal Bruce for murder. Don't you like yourself?"

Colling flushed. "My teeth are artificial. I had to have a lot of bad ones yanked out and—well, a radio announcer lives on his voice and appearance. The new plate bothers the life out of me."

Tracy grinned. In a columnist's life a feeble gag was better than no gag at all.

"You better get yourself another dentist, son," he drawled. "That tooth carpenter of yours damned near put the bite on you for murder."

Behind the Black Mask

LAST WEEK WE CALLED up Theodore Tinsley and said to him, said we, "Ted, how about opening your soul to us? Frank Gruber did it last month, and now it's your turn. How do you write those Jerry Tracy stories?"

Ted said, "What's that? The baby's crying and I can't hear you."

So we raised our voice and shouted, which resulted in the following.

Before you turn over the page and begin Theodore Tinsley's new story, "Station K-I-L-L," perhaps you'd like to share with us this look behind the scenes:

Ted Tinsley now broadcasting:

The editor of Black Mask wants to know (a) how I think up Jerry Tracy stories, (b) how I write 'em.

I've picked up Jerry Tracy ideas from all kinds of places—but this is the first time I ever found one in an ashcan. The ashcan was on 50th Street in the short block between Broadway and Seventh Avenue. Some one had thrown away an old peaked cap. I took one look at it and thought about Jerry Tracy. (Naturally, when you're a writer of detective stories on a Broadway prowl for ideas, you're not thinking about the price of potatoes in Ireland.) So the junked cap instantly became a brand-new, imported snapbrim fedora.

That seemed queer! Why should Jerry Tracy toss his brand-new hat in a 50th Street ashcan? It wasn't so damned queer when I took a mental look at the Little Guy's hat and found a bullet hole through the crown! That was all the start I needed, particularly after I glanced east past the Sixth Avenue elevated and caught a glimpse of the dizzy stone pinnacle of Radio City. *Flash!* Someone must have taken a potshot at Tracy while he was on his way to a broadcast! And that, believe it or not, is how I got the idea.

Writing the yarn is a bit more complicated. It usually happens like this: I rise as late as possible, enjoy a leisurely breakfast, smoke two cigarettes, wait to see what the postman has brought, play with my thirteen-months-old daughter a while, sharpen three pencils, rearrange my Royal portable, look out the window, think wistfully how nice it would be if I were a plumber, an aviator or a subway motorman....

At this point my wife comes in very quietly, pulls down the shade, removes all books, papers and magazines, then goes away, locking the door behind her.

After that I write the story.

Station K-I-L-L

*It was a network of greed over which Jerry
Tracy broadcast a sentence of death*

THE BULLET WHIZZED through the crown of Jerry Tracy's fedora, tilting the hat crookedly over his left temple. He heard the thwack of the leaden slug against the brick theater wall that paralleled the sidewalk. Whirling, he stared with dazed incredulity at the wall. There was a powdery gouge on the surface of the brick. A flattened chunk of lead lay on the sidewalk.

The explosive banging from the motor of a truck up near the corner had drowned out the crack of the pistol shot.

Butch flung his massive body in front of Tracy. He had a pugilist's instinctive reaction to peril in spite of the fact that it was ten years since Butch had been in a ring. His loyalty to the dapper little columnist of the *Daily Planet* went beyond his duties as body-guard and made him risk his own life without hesitation.

But no more bullets came from the dingy row of rooming houses across the street.

"Are you hoit, Jerry?" Butch growled.

"I'm O.K. Where'd it come from? That middle doorway?"

"I t'ink so."

That doorway, in the middle of a row of rooming houses, was slightly ajar. The street was a narrow one, and someone with a lousy aim had gummed up a perfect ambush.

"Stay here!" Tracy snapped.

"Nuts to you," Butch said. His beefy palm shoved hard. Tracy spilled awkwardly to one knee and his tilted hat fell off. "What the hell do you t'ink you got me for?" he growled at Tracy.

He faded across the dark street—not too fast, because a couple

of pedestrians were approaching. Butch's big hand scratched at what might have been an annoying itch under his armpit. He leaned for an instant against the casing of the rooming-house entry. A quick glance inward and he vanished without hesitation.

Tracy guessed sourly: "The gunner must've made a backyard sneak."

He remembered suddenly that he was down on one knee, alongside a bullet-drilled hat and a flattened slug. The slug was still warm as Tracy palmed it and dropped it into his pocket. He got up, kicking petulantly at a crack in the sidewalk for the benefit of the two staring pedestrians.

One of them kept going. The other—the dopier of the two—said solemnly: "S'matter, Mister? Didja fall?"

"Yeah."

"Ain'tcha gonna pick up your hat?"

Tracy looked at it. The two holes in the soft crown were hidden by the flare of the upturned brim.

"You saw me fall!" Tracy said in a brisk, lawsuit tone. He flipped out a notebook and a pencil. "What's your name? Where do you live?"

"Who, me?" The dope reared like a pony. "I didn't see nothing."

He went rapidly away. Tracy picked up the drilled hat. He ripped out the monogrammed sweatband and dropped the hat in a near-by ashcan. That changed it from a front-page news item to a hunk of junk.

Butch's big lop-eared face was peering from the doorway across the street. Tracy joined him.

"Did the guy get away?"

"Yeah. But I wanna show you something he lost."

They tiptoed quietly across the dim floor so as not to attract any attention from curious lodgers. They descended steps to the yard. It was paved except for a strip of earth alongside the rear fence where tall weeds grew. Butch's big feet had smudged the smaller prints of the escaped fugitive. Butch had gone over the fence in a hurry but the other fellow had enjoyed too big a start.

There was a cellar on the other side, Butch reported glumly, and a whitewashed alley that led to the rear street. The guy must have had a car parked, one with a nice, speedy pick-up.

"This here is what I meant," Butch said, pointing downward at the weeds. "The guy musta tore it off on the same nail that almost ruined my—"

"Let's not go into biology," Tracy said dryly.

He picked up the white carnation that had fallen by the fence. There are all kinds of carnations, beginning with the ones you can buy for a nickel from sad-looking street peddlers. This was the expensive kind, the sort Bert Lord always wore.

There was no surprise in Jerry Tracy's mind. He had suspected Lord the moment the bullet had ripped through his hat. The sleek, good-looking Englishman must have found out what Tracy was going to spill on the air tonight in his cigarette broadcast. It was hard to keep juicy items like that under cover.

Scandal tipsters, particularly women, had a vengeful habit of phoning the victim beforehand, to make sure that the barb hurt.

Tracy wanted it to hurt. He never used poison arrows except on crooks. And Bert Lord was the dirtiest kind of crook. The sort who go after easy dough by the marriage route. It was so fatally easy, too, when the girl was twenty-three, pretty as a rotogravure special, and too decent to smell a rat hidden under a layer of barber-shop culture and British tweeds.

Tracy could have gone directly to Bruce Hilliard, or perhaps to Hilliard's young and socially ambitious wife; but the radio method was better. When you told the world— and that included the ships at sea—that the adopted daughter of Tracy's own cigarette sponsor, Bruce Hilliard, was in love with a sleek graduate of a British jail, it didn't leave Alice Hilliard much chance to do anything foolish.

It didn't leave Lord much chance either, except for a quick try at murder along Tracy's usual route to Radio City.

The *Daily Planet's* dapper columnist dropped the carnation into the pocket that contained the flattened bullet. Butch gave his employer a low-lidded glance.

"Would this thing have somepin to do wit' tonight's broadcast, boss?"

Tracy had recovered his composure. His voice sounded as thin as a dime. "I'll give you the air instead of putting you on if you don't mind your own business, Butch."

Tracy stopped at an avenue shop and bought a new hat. To appear bareheaded was not in the well dressed Tracy manner; it might excite curious comment.

"Wind blow it away, sir?" the clerk asked politely.

"I threw it away. It had a rat hole in it."

"You mean a moth hole, sir?"

"I mean a rat hole."

It was a foolish thing to say, but he couldn't resist the quip. He took a cab over to Radio City. He always came and went by the rear elevator used by bandsmen with their bulky instruments. It was insurance against nuts and cranks. Tracy's broadcast was done from a private studio. The public never saw him at the mike; and if they hung around the rear corridor, Butch's shoulder took care of that.

But Butch didn't try to shove away the girl in the furred wrap. She stepped quickly in front of Tracy.

"Please! I've got to talk to you."

It was Alice Hilliard. Slim and lovely, with blue eyes and hair the color of strained honey. Butch and Tracy got the same look at her, but saw different things. Butch noticed the slender line of thigh and hip candidly molded by the evening gown, the soft cleft of her bosom as she swayed appealingly toward Tracy. Tracy saw only her eyes. They were filled with tears.

"Jerry, don't do it! I realize you're trying to protect me. But, Jerry, you're not God! You can't judge a man and condemn him and punish him in one—"

So she knew! That made it tougher.

"Who told you?"

"The woman who phoned you the scandal tip was vicious enough to telephone me, too. Jerry, you're so wrong about Bert. He's a straight shooter."

Tracy's nostrils whitened. "Not so damned straight at that," he said. "Almost six inches too high."

"Wait until next week before you—"

"A week and you'll marry the louse." He stared at her. *"Won't you?"*

Before she could answer, a suave, perfectly modulated voice sounded behind them. "Mr. Jerry Tracy, I believe? The scandal-monger?"

The man had stepped noiselessly into the corridor from the street. The first thing Tracy saw was the fresh white carnation in his lapel. He was a tall, strongly built man in his middle thirties, with a dark smudge of mustache and a scrubbed, pink skin. His clipped voice was insultingly polite. He was wearing dinner clothes under a Chesterfield. His expression was cool and remote, like a British gentlemen in an ad for Scotch whiskey.

Alice Hilliard gave him a quick, frightened look. "Bert, you mustn't—"

"I'm afraid I must," Lord said. He took her gently by the arm and turned her toward the street exit. "A blackmailer can always be reasoned with—that's the heart of his trade. Wait for me in the public lounge, darling. I think I can promise you there'll be no dirt concerning you and me on the wireless this evening."

Alice hesitated, then she obeyed. It irked Tracy to witness her childlike submission. After she had left, Butch stared grimly at the fresh white carnation in Lord's lapel.

"He must a just bought himself a new one. Jerry, is this guy the louse?"

Lord's gloved hand tightened on his Malacca stick. But he kept his hard, smiling gaze on Tracy.

"I'm not used to haggling. What's your lowest price?"

"Take him. Butch," Tracy snapped. "I want his gun."

Butch dove with a low growl of pleasure. Lord's cane struck like a whiplash at Butch's skull, be he swerved and took the blow on his hunched shoulder. There was a quick, panting tussle, followed by a shrill squeal. Lord's stick was wrenched from his grasp and fell clattering to the floor.

One of Lord's arms was twisted behind his back. The painful angle at which it was bent drained Lord's face of color. Butch's big knee was poised for an upward thrust at the belly of his antagonist.

"Stand still, pal, or I'll rupture you. Go ahead, Jerry."

Tracy frisked the man. There was no gun.

"What did you do with it?" Jerry asked him tonelessly. "Park it somewhere after you went over the backyard fence?"

Lord didn't say anything until Butch released him. Then profanity bubbled from him in a husky whisper. Nasty stuff. Gutter talk from the slums of London. All of his culture forgotten.

"You bloody fool! I'll 'ave your 'eart for this!"

"I'm skipping that gunplay of yours a while ago," Tracy told him steadily. "But I have no intention of skipping the broadcast. If you have any sense, you'll hop the nearest garbage scow and take a quick sneak to England."

Lord's narrowed eyes were bits of mica. He kept watching Tracy with a bloodless smile as he adjusted the damage to his clothing. He picked up his cane. When he finally spoke he had regained both his self-control and his faultless accent.

"I'm int'rested in your remark about gunplay and a backyard fence. Are you suggesting—"

"I'm suggesting that you get the hell out of New York and let Alice Hilliard alone."

"Cards on the table, eh? Right-o. I think I can play any style of game that suits you, Mr. Tracy. If you slander me on the wireless tonight, I'll see that you stop living. Good evening."

He left the building with a quick stride. Butch growled "Nuts!" as Tracy grabbed him. The columnist swung him around and punched the elevator button.

"It's eight o'clock sap! I'm on the air in thirty seconds."

THEY ASCENDED SWIFTLY. In the upper corridor a man's head was jutting anxiously from a doorway. At sight of the *Daily Planet's* columnist his worried forehead smoothed and he patted the tip of his nose as a signal to someone inside the broadcasting room.

Tracy was arriving exactly on time. Even a bullet couldn't spoil his record of never being late for his weekly gossip show.

The announcer was reading the commercial at the floor mike. Tracy slipped into his familiar wooden chair, grabbed his table mike, placed the neat pile of script pages under his eyes. The announcer's voice crackled with the familiar introduction that once a week turned a million listening ears toward loud speakers:

"And now the Hilliard Tobacco Company reminds you that 'Where there's smoke there's fire.' Light up and let America's greatest gossip columnist tell you the news you like to tell your neighbors! Presenting—Jerry Tracy!"

Jerry came in as he always did, like sleet bouncing off a tin roof. He ripped competently through his assignment, tossing each script sheet to the floor as he finished it. The squib about Bert Lord was not in the script. Tracy would be deliberately breaking studio rules by inserting it. He watched the clock and killed his last item to make room for it. He was conscious of the gasp of the announcer as he spoke his piece with hard, nasal clarity:

"What British crook has come to the U.S.A. under forged passports on a suave hunt for cigarette money? According to your correspondent's information this gentleman's specialty has led him close to the adopted daughter of a well known tobacco tycoon. 'Where there's smoke there's fire' is a swell warning for a crook to remember. It may save him a bad burn when the girl's father realizes what's going on. Will the crook be smart and scram? *Lord only knows!*"

Tracy's jaw was tight at the sign-off. Dabney, the announcer, stared curiously at him. Dabney was a veteran on the hour and a good friend of Tracy's.

"It's none of my business, Jerry, but did Bruce Hilliard O.K. that last item?"

"Why?"

"I just wondered. Do you think it's a good idea to dump a load of dirt in the front yard of your own sponsor?"

"If you got the point," Tracy said slowly, "Hilliard will, too. That's what I wanted. If I have to, I'll take the rap for it," he added grimly.

"Looks like you may have to," Dabney said.

A light began to flash inside a glassed booth. It was Tracy's private phone to enable him to take last minute news flashes from his secretary. Dabney answered the call, said very gently. "Yes. Mr. Hilliard."

The voice on the phone was thick with anger. Tracy had to listen hard to make out the slurred words.

"What the hell do you mean by publicly humiliating my

daughter? If you had information that this Bert Lord is a crook why didn't you come privately to me?"

"Because your daughter is a headstrong girl, Mr. Hilliard. I don't think you could have stopped her. Or your wife, either. You might have made it tough, but I wanted to make it impossible. That's why I went on the air and told the world."

"Damned kind of you! I'll expect to see you in fifteen minutes. If you're not—"

"I'll be there," Tracy said quietly.

He glanced wryly at his watch. Eight thirty-two. He'd expected a quick reaction and he'd got it—two minutes after the sign-off.

He scribbled the name and address of Bert Lord on a card and handed it to Butch.

"I want you to watch this guy's apartment. It's a swanky penthouse, with a private entrance and a private elevator. If Alice Hilliard shows there, stop her. Make a scene, grab her purse, do anything that will get the two of you picked up by cops. Phone me at Hilliard's home from the police station. I'll take care of everything. Scram!"

Butch nodded. If Tracy had asked him to disrobe in Times Square and bark like a dog the order would have been cheerfully obeyed. In Butch's simple philosophy there was always a sensible reason for everything Tracy did. His big feet went rapidly away.

A few minutes later Jerry Tracy descended in the rear elevator and emerged on the sidewalk. There was a row of taxis parked along the curb. He slammed himself into the first in line.

Before he could talk to the driver, the door on the street

side of the cab opened and slammed. Alice Hilliard dropped panting into the seat beside Jerry. She had come racing from a doorway across the street. Tracy, who had just sent Butch to head her off from Bert Lord's penthouse, was completely discomfited. Alice's sob didn't help him much, either.

In a stony voice he gave the driver Hilliard's address.

"I'm going with you," Alice said.

"You're foolish. You're only making it tougher. Why not let me drop you off at your own apartment?"

"Sorry. I want to be there when you tell Father that I'm in love with a louse."

"Oke by me." His shrug stung her to anger.

"If you're wrong about this, I'll never let up on you, Jerry! Not until I've driven you from New York,"

"And if I'm right?"

She didn't reply.

HILLIARD'S HOME WAS an ornate old-fashioned dwelling on a west side street that rammed into a quiet dead end above the twinkling darkness of Riverside Drive. The house was set back from the sidewalk and there were green, park-like grounds. Tracy rang the bell and waited. There was no answer.

"That's funny. Aren't there any servants in this joint?"

"It's their night out, except the butler, and father's a little deaf," Alice suggested. "Perhaps he can't hear the bell."

"Does he have to? He's got a butler and a secretary and a wife."

"A very pretty wife, too," Alice said.

Her soft words made Tracy glance sharply at Hilliard's

adopted daughter. Alice and Betty were almost the same age. Tracy had never thought of friction between them, but he did now. He had supposed that Alice's switch to a small apartment downtown had been her tactful withdrawal from an oldish foster father with a young wife.

"You don't like Betty very much, do you?" Tracy said, his columnist's mind instinctively probing this new angle.

"I admire her." Alice said.

Tracy seemed to remember vaguely a young man named Kenneth Dunlap. Betty Hilliard had seen a lot of him before her marriage to the tobacco king. Tracy could tell nothing from Alice's blue eyes as she opened her evening bag. She didn't find what she was searching for.

"This is ridiculous. I seem to have lost my key to the house. I distinctly remember putting it in the bag with my own apartment key."

"Did you have dinner tonight with Bert Lord?"

Alice didn't answer. But one look at her face told Tracy his suspicious guess had scored a bull's-eye.

"Wait here," he said curtly. "Maybe I can find an unlatched window."

He darted around the side of the house, flitting swiftly through the darkness. His face was wrinkled with sudden apprehension. Why should Bert Lord want to steal Alice's key? Was it because Alice had warned him what Tracy intended to do on the radio tonight? Lord might take any steps to keep Hilliard from hearing that broadcast.

There was sweat on Tracy's forehead as he lifted an unfastened window on the ground floor.

The main hallway was quiet under the glow of shaded lamps.

Tracy unlocked the front door and admitted Alice. There was a dim light burning in the reception room to the left of the hallway. The room was empty. Tracy crossed to an inner door and knocked. When there was no answer, he opened the door.

Tracy took one look and stiffened. The rustle of Alice's evening gown seemed enormously loud in the room's stillness. She swayed and Tracy caught her as she fainted, lowered her down gently.

He lowered her gently to the floor and walked toward the dead man. Bruce Hilliard was lying on the study rug where he had fallen from a wide-armed chair. He had been shot twice; through the head and through the chest.

Evidently death had come to him without warning. His blood-smeared face was placid. He was lying close to a console radio cabinet which stood alongside his desk.

Tracy had seen enough gunshot wounds in his career to recognize lethal bullet holes when he saw them. The slug through Hilliard's skull had pierced his brain; the hole in his chest was directly over his heart. The body was faintly warm to Tracy's touch.

No doctor on earth, Tracy thought grimly, could ever decide which of those two shots had actually killed Hilliard. It puzzled him why the murderer should have risked firing twice. The shots must have raised thunderous echoes in the house. Did the killer know the house was empty? Where was Hilliard's pretty young wife—and his secretary, and his butler?

All this and more zipped through Tracy's mind in the few seconds he stared at the corpse. There was no gun near the body and he made no effort to search for it. He wrapped a handkerchief around his hand and picked up the phone. He called police headquarters and recognized the voice at the switchboard.

"Jerry Tracy speaking! Is Inspector Fitzgerald around?"

Inspector Fitzgerald was one of Tracy's oldest friends. Out of their mutual trust had come Tracy's unofficial tie-up with the police department. Fitz was an honest and fearless cop. Tracy had his finger on many pulses. The combination had solved many a baffling case in the past.

Luckily Fitz was still at headquarters, Tracy told him the news and Fitz said quietly, "O.K. Stay where you are. I'll be up there in a hurry."

Fitzgerald hung up at the other end, but Jerry continued to talk. In picking up the phone he had turned about, so that his back was toward the unconscious figure of Alice Hilliard. He caught a sudden glimpse of her pale face in the square, gilt-framed mirror on the wall behind Hilliard's desk.

It was the sight of Alice's eyelids that made Jerry continue to talk calmly into a dead wire. He crowded close to the desk, so that his left hand that depressed the phone's cross-bar was invisible to the girl lying on the floor in front of the sofa.

Alice was faking that swoon of hers! Her eyelids were quivering. She was so intent on watching the back of Tracy's head that she failed to notice the mirror.

She was lying closer to the sofa's edge than she had been when Tracy had left her. One of her arms was under the sofa, moving slowly. She became rigid as Tracy cradled the phone and walked casually toward her.

He was still holding his handkerchief. He stood staring down at her limp body, aware of a quick feeling of pity. A loyal girl in love with a rogue could learn trickery swiftly!

She screamed as Tracy clutched suddenly at her gloved hand and jerked it into view. She was still holding the gun she had tried to push out of sight.

There was a quick, sharp struggle, then Tracy's handkerchief-swathed hand closed on the barrel and he wrenched the revolver from Alice's grasp.

The gun was an English model, a Webley. Two of the chambers had been exploded. There was a strong acid reek of burned powder at the muzzle.

Tracy said gently to the sobbing girl: "Do you love Bert Lord that much?"

"He didn't do it! He couldn't have!" Her face lifted and it was white with horror. She stared at Tracy numbly.

"Better sit up and take it easy," Tracy said tonelessly. "We'll just forget about this little episode. Inspector Fitzgerald will be here in a few minutes. I'll tell him I found the gun."

She sank down on the sofa. Tracy stared grimly at the gun he had laid on Hilliard's desk.

He was turning away to examine the rest of the study when he heard a sudden faint squeak. Someone was lifting a window in the adjoining reception room!

Before Tracy could move there was a quick thud of feet beyond the curtained doorway. A man's hand thrust fiercely past the edge of the curtain and jabbed at the light switch. The study was plunged into darkness.

The murder gun was the first thing Tracy thought of. He snatched it up by the barrel, throwing out a blindly defensive arm as the unseen figure of his assailant raced through the blackness toward Hilliard's desk.

A fist crashed against Tracy's arm, numbing it from shoulder to elbow. The blow toppled him against a high-backed chair. He managed to reel aside and to overturn the chair between himself and his foe. It gave him only a second's respite, but that was all the time he needed. He remembered a high-topped cabinet in a corner of the room. He threw the Webley revolver upward, hoping it would land out of sight.

The clatter of the overturned chair drowned out the thud of the gun is it landed among piled books and papers on the top of the cabinet. Somewhere in the dark Alice Hilliard was screaming with terror.

Tracy dived to the floor, clutching at the legs of his foe. A knee banged against his forehead, filling his brain with dancing stars. Then he was knocked flat. Fingers clutched swiftly at him in a search for the murder gun. His pockets were probed, his coat was ripped open.

He heard a fiercely muttered oath in a voice he thought he recognized as Bert Lord's.

Then the front doorbell began to ring. The sound of it revived Tracy's waning strength. Clawing wildly, he managed to trip his antagonist. The two rolled over and over on the floor.

Dimly, Tracy realized that Inspector Fitzgerald was waiting patiently outside the street entry, unaware that a trapped murderer was fighting desperately to get away. He tried to yell at the top of his lungs, but a fist smashed at his stomach and drove the wind out of him.

His feeble hold on his enemy was broken. He heard a rush of feet toward the outer room. The overturned chair helped him to pull himself drunkenly to his feet. He staggered headlong through the darkness toward the doorway. The velvet curtain steadied him while his blurred eyes swung toward the open window.

He could see vaguely a tall, racing figure outside the house, vanishing swiftly toward the rear of the grounds. Tracy was trying to swing a leg over the windowsill, when a man's voice yelled harshly behind him. He was dragged violently backward.

Someone began savagely pummeling him. Blood trickled from Tracy's nose. A blow on the chin almost snapped his head off. His knees bent and he would have pitched to the floor except for the quick clutch of the fool who seemed to have unwittingly helped Lord to make a clean getaway.

"The window!" Jerry gasped through waves of pain. "Get him—window!"

Fitzgerald didn't seem to understand. He dragged Tracy toward the wall where the light switch was located. There was a click and a sudden flare of brilliance.

Tracy said thickly: "Fitz, you damned fool, you've—"

Then his voice trailed into silence. It wasn't Fitz at all! He was a good-looking young man with a straight, slim back and a crown of dark, glossy hair.

The young man cried fiercely: "You dirty little sneak-thief! How did you get in here—and what were you up to?"

A moment later both men recognized each other. The excited young man was Walter Furman, Hilliard's missing secretary.

"Right now I'm not up to—much of—anything," Tracy gasped, and proved it by slumping into unconsciousness.

WHEN JERRY RECOVERED his senses the first thing he heard was the angry snarl of Inspector Fitzgerald. "I don't care what you thought! What the hell did you have to beat him up like that for?"

"I didn't. The fellow who went out the window did most

of it. I thought Tracy was a burglar. I didn't realize what had happened until I turned on the lights."

Tracy's eyes opened. He was on the same sofa where, centuries earlier, he had told Alice Hilliard to lie quietly. She was slumped nearby in a chair, her dulled eyes staring tragically at the floor.

The room was full of people. There were a couple of uniformed cops. A fingerprint expert and a police photographer were standing stolidly in a corner, watching a bald-headed man who was crouched on his knees beside Bruce Hilliard's corpse. That was Grady, the medical examiner.

Hilliard's secretary was still trying to explain to Fitzgerald what had happened.

"As I told you, no one answered the bell and I let myself in with my key. Naturally I was suspicious of trouble. When I found the lights turned out, and caught a man racing toward an opened window, I didn't pull punches."

The medical examiner got to his feet, "Impossible to tell which shot killed him, though I suspect he took the one through the skull first. When you're mad enough to kill a guy twice, you don't aim at the heart. That was probably done to make sure. Hard to set the time. Could have been a half hour, could have been an hour and a half."

"He was alive at 8:32," Tracy said slowly. "That's when he phoned me at the broadcasting studio. I'd just finished my program."

"That might fit," Grady said. "Body's still fairly warm. No time for *rigor mortis*. He probably took it while you were on the way over here. The killer was either mad with rage or a blasted psychopath. I may have more dope after the autopsy. Good night, Fitz."

He went out with a brisk tread.

"I heard your broadcast tonight, Jerry," Fitz said abruptly. "Did that crack you made about Hilliard's adopted daughter have anything to do with this kill?"

Tracy glanced at Alice. Her pale face seemed drained of everything but an overpowering exhaustion.

"Tell him, Jerry."

Tracy shrugged. He told of the scandal tip he had received over the phone from some unknown woman. He told of his check-up on it, and recounted the attempt on his life on the way to the broadcast. He showed Fitz the flattened slug and the white carnation which the escaping gunman had dropped.

"I'm certain it was Bert Lord. Having failed to wipe me out before I could ruin him on the radio, he rushed over here, let himself in with a key he had stolen from Alice's bag, and bumped Hilliard. He must have figured some stunt to get every one else out of the house.... By the way, where were you, Furman?"

Fitzgerald answered for the secretary.

"His alibi is O.K. Jerry. Hilliard sent him over to the Delton Hotel to see Nick White about a show Hilliard was thinking of backing. I checked on that and Nick verified Furman's story. He was in Nick's suite from eight o'clock until a quarter of nine. We know Hilliard was alive until 8:32 at least."

Tracy nodded. Nick White's word could be trusted. He was a fine old Irishman, a veteran producer and a friend of both Tracy and Fitzgerald.

Tracy got shakily to his feet and went over to the tall cabinet in the corner. Mounting a chair, he fished carefully behind the books and papers atop the cabinet with a handkerchief-wrapped hand.

Fitz gave a quick yelp of excitement as he saw the gun.

"I managed to toss it up there just before Lord tackled me," Tracy said. "That's what he came back for."

Fitz took the gun with almost cringing care.

"English make, eh? A Webley. Two chambers fired. All right, Hanley, give it the works."

Hanley was the fingerprint man. He took the weapon over to Hilliard's desk.

While he was busy, Sergeant Killan came in. Killan was Fitz's right-hand man. He had a hoarse, friendly voice, a cobblestone head and a mouth like a mailbox slit.

"What did you find out upstairs?" Fitzgerald snapped.

"Not a thing," Killan said cheerfully. "Hilliard's wife flew the coop all right. So did the butler. Nothing upstairs to explain why."

Tracy gave Walter Furman a slow stare. "Were they both in the house when Hilliard sent you over to see Nick White?"

"Yes. Both of them came into the study to talk to Hilliard. Marcom—that's the butler—had some tradesmen's bills that had to be okayed. Mrs. Hilliard usually listened with her husband to the Tracy broadcast. But tonight she said she had a sick headache. She went up to her room, to lie down just before I left the house."

Over at the dead man's desk the fingerprint man suddenly ceased his monotonous whistling of a popular tune.

"Good news, Fitz," he said.

"What you got?"

"Two middle fingers of the right hand. Thumb blurred, but who cares? Maybe—"

He stopped talking as a woman's scream echoed with startling abruptness from the front hallway of the house.

Sergeant Killan, who was nearest to the door, bounced forward with a swiftly drawn gun in his beefy hand. He peered into the hall, gaped a moment, then holstered his weapon.

"All right, Halligan. Bring her in here."

Halligan was the cop who had been left on duty inside the front entry. He clumped stolidly into the room, his hand tightly gripping the arm of a dark-haired and exceedingly pretty woman.

"I caught her sneaking in the front door," Halligan said. "She had a key. She closed the door quietly and started to tiptoe down the hall toward the stairs. When I grabbed her she started to fight, till she saw my uniform, then she cooled down."

Tracy said dryly: "Better let go of her, officer. This is Mrs. Hilliard."

Betty Hilliard stood alone, very stiff and straight, seemingly aware of nothing except the murdered body of her husband. Her dark hair and eyes emphasized the pallor of her skin. She was like marble until she turned and saw Alice staring steadily at her. Then her face flooded with crimson.

"How did this happen, Alice?" she asked with an obvious effort at control.

"I wouldn't know, Betty."

"You could guess though, perhaps?"

There was pent-up hatred between these two women. Alice's jaw tightened at the sneer in Betty's voice. She turned swiftly toward Inspector Fitzgerald.

"You might as well know, Inspector, that it wasn't Bert Lord who tried to steal that gun. It was not his voice."

Fitzgerald didn't answer that. He walked across to Hilliard's desk and examined the two fingerprints that the headquarters expert had brought out on the butt of the Webley revolver.

"I'd like to get a quick check on these prints from London. Can you make a classification index for me right away?"

"Yeah." He took out of his bag a classification sheet printed in squared columns. Slowly he began to record with digits and letters the indices of the specimen print.

"How long were you away from home, Mrs. Hilliard?" Fitz asked the dead man's wife.

"Quite a while. I left shortly after Mr. Furman departed."

"Where did you go?"

Betty Hilliard took a long time replying. "I left to attend to some personal business which I have no intention of discussing with you or anyone else."

"Was your husband alive when you left?"

"Yes. He was in this room waiting to hear the Tracy program. I left with his permission."

Alice Hilliard's faint laughter had a sting in it, but the other woman ignored the implication.

"O.K. on that index synopsis," the fingerprint man said.

Fitzgerald went to the phone and called the exchange manager. He identified himself and explained what he wanted. It didn't take long to put through the trans-Atlantic call. Fitzgerald talked briefly to Scotland Yard and then handed the phone to the fingerprint man. It was not a very good connection. Hanley had to talk loudly and repeat his jargon of figures and letters over and over.

Fitz and Killan, who knew what it was all about, listened eagerly. But Tracy only pretended interest. His ear was cocked in an entirely different direction. Alice had drifted closer to Betty Hilliard. Her lips moved in a swift undertone.

"You're not kidding me. Who was the boy friend—Ken Dunlap?"

"It certainly wasn't Bert Lord! If you try to drag me into a scandal—"

"All I'm after is the truth. If those gun-prints belong to Bert, I want him to pay the penalty. But if he's innocent, I'll know who's guilty. And if you think I won't produce those letters of yours—"

Alice saw Tracy and her murmur stopped.

The fingerprint man was still yowling into the telephone. "Yeah. All right. 'By," He pronged the receiver with an oath of relief.

"If they've got a match in the London files, there ought to be an answer in about an hour. I told him I'd take it at the bureau in Headquarters. Drop in when you're finished. I'll check our own files while I'm waiting."

"I'd like to borrow your ink pad and a couple of specimen sheets," Fitz said.

He didn't explain what he wanted them for and the print man didn't ask. But Tracy knew. He was grimly glad he had sent Butch to keep a watchful eye on the penthouse of Bert Lord. The challenging talk between Alice and Betty Hilliard hadn't changed Tracy's mind about the identity of the man with whom he had battled in the dark for possession of the murder gun. He felt sure that was Lord.

The only thing that still puzzled him was the continued absence of the butler. Where in hell was the elusive Marcom?

Unexpectedly Marcom answered that question himself.

There was a timid knock at the rear door of the study and when Sergeant Killan sprang forward and threw open the door, Marcom was gaping with astonishment at the threshold.

His amazement changed to terror as Killan grabbed and yanked him into the room. He cringed at sight of Hilliard's sprawled body. Tracy, watching him narrowly, saw his eyes veer for a swift instant. They flicked toward Betty Hilliard and then went blank and expressionless.

"Where the hell did you come from?" Killan growled. "Sneak in the back door?"

"I didn't sneak through any door, sir. I came in the back way, using my regular household key. I heard voices here in the study and—"

"Was Hilliard alive when you went out? And how long ago was that?"

"About an hour, sir. I didn't speak to Mr. Hilliard about going out."

"Why not? Do you come and go as you please?"

"I had Mrs. Hilliard's permission. I was attending to an errand for her."

"Marcom is quite correct," Betty Hilliard said quickly. "As Mr. Furman has already told you, I retired to my bedroom with a headache. I found I had none of the special tablets I use, so I sent Marcom downtown to get some at the office of my physician."

"Why didn't you say so before?"

"You didn't ask me," Betty said calmly.

"Let's see those tablets," Killan told Marcom. He took the small package, unwrapped it, then smiled grimly. "I thought so. There's a half-filled box of these same tablets in the drawer of Mrs. Hilliard's night stand upstairs in her room. I know because I looked."

Betty's face paled. "I—I forgot I had them."

Inspector Fitzgerald waved his scowling assistant aside. His own voice was suave and friendly, "You're involving yourself in an unnecessary tangle, Mrs. Hilliard. If we don't know where you went—"

"You don't, and you won't!"

"The assumption, of course," Fitz explained patiently, "is that you got rid of the butler on a fake errand, so you could leave the house without the knowledge of your husband or Marcom. Probably by the rear door."

"Well?"

"I'm not accusing you of anything. I'm merely pointing out that a woman with a guilty knowledge of a well arranged murder might leave beforehand by the back door to avoid alarming her husband; and return by the front door in order to *discover* his murder, in case the butler was still away."

Betty's smile was ghastly. "You might do a lot better, Inspector, by waiting for London to report on the fingerprints of Mr. Bert Lord."

Jerry Tracy shot her a quick question. "Are you the woman who phoned me the scandal tip about him?"

"Sorry. I'm not the type."

"You are, you liar," Alice said harshly. "I should have guessed that the tipster was you! Why didn't you tell Tracy, while you were spilling your dirty hints, to investigate the love life of a sleek young lad named Ken Dunlap?"

"If you dare to soil my name—"

"You've already done that yourself, darling. Your husband

knew, too. If he hadn't died so suddenly tonight, there'd have been a divorce trial that would have sat you where you belong. In the gutter." Alice was shaking with rage. But Hilliard's wife remained frozenly composed. She said:

"As long as we're discussing charges, I think we had better stick to real facts. My husband's will, for instance."

"What about it?"

"It was about to be changed, cutting you and your precious British jailbird out of any share in your foster father's estate."

"That's a lie," Alice said.

"If it is, why did he give you a check this afternoon for fifty thousand dollars? Wasn't it your final quit-claim on the family—to get out and stay out?"

Tracy and Fitzgerald and Sergeant Killan were listening grimly. It was to them that Alice turned. Her effort to control herself made her voice almost inaudible.

"I've already told you that if Bert Lord is guilty of murder, I'll do everything in my power to help you convict him. I don't think he is, but the record of the fingerprints will settle that. The check to which my father's cheating little wife refers is actually a proof of Bert's innocence. It was given to me—and to him—here in this house this afternoon, as a wedding present."

"What?" Tracy gasped.

"It's true. Bert came here like a man and had a long talk with father. He denied those anonymous lies about his career in England and Father believed him. Father gave me a check for fifty thousand dollars and promised to stand back of Bert and me. All this talk about changing his will is pure spiteful invention on Betty's part."

She drew a deep sobbing breath.

"That's why Bert and I appealed to you, Jerry, at the broadcasting station tonight not to spill that lying gossip. It's why Father was angry enough to summon you to his home. He wanted the scandal covered up because he believed in Bert. He was trying to—to help us!"

"Then who killed him?" Tracy rasped.

"I don't know, I don't know."

She was weeping wildly. Betty, dark-eyed, somber, watched her with bold antagonism. For the first time in this whole cocksure evening, Tracy felt completely at sea.

Fitz rubbed his nose for a moment. "Remain here on duty until you're relieved," he told the gaping policeman at the study door. His glance moved toward Furman and the butler, toward the weeping Alice and the pale, scornful Betty. "Arrest anyone who attempts to leave this house. Come on, Sarge! Jerry, I'll need you, too."

The three of them piled into Fitz's shabby department car outside.

"Are you absolutely certain," Fitz asked Tracy sharply, "that it was Lord's voice you heard when you had that battle in the dark?"

"That's the one thing that's got me worried," Tracy admitted. "It sounded like him. I still think it was. But why did he forget the damned gun in the first place? And how did he know the house would be so conveniently empty when he killed Hilliard?"

"Where's this Lord live?" Fitz asked.

Tracy told him. The car began to hum downtown.

"I sent Butch to watch Lord's penthouse," Tracy said, "with orders to shadow him if he pulled a sneak."

Fitz nodded. "If he's innocent, he should have no objection to giving me a sample of his right hand."

"Suppose he refuses?"

"He can't," Fitz said grimly, "if he's arrested on suspicion of homicide."

BERT LORD'S ADDRESS was a swanky apartment house on the East River fringe of the midtown district. He occupied a penthouse eighteen stories up. The building had a canopy, two doormen and a string of empty taxis outside. But Lord's penthouse afforded his comings and goings a privacy not enjoyed by the other tenants.

The entrance to his self-service elevator was on the river side of the building. A short dead-end street extended between the building and the river wall. A few empty cars were parked there, cool and quiet in the darkness. Lord's entrance was a small, inconspicuous door, set flush in the ground floor.

Butch was nowhere in sight.

A quick twist of the bronze doorknob showed Tracy that the lock of the private entrance was broken. He stepped into a narrow hallway that was pitch dark. Before Fitzgerald could snap on a pocket torch, Tracy stepped on an extended hand that lay limply on the floor.

Fitz's torch clicked a bright beam of light as Tracy recoiled with a gasp. The light centered on the back of an unconscious man's head. It was Butch, and he was lying flat on his face with blood oozing from a lump on his scalp.

Tracy dropped to his knees and turned Butch over. The practical Sergeant Killan shoved Jerry aside. He had a flat half-pint flask in his hand, and he didn't seem to mind how much of it he spilt. Before it was half empty Butch was gurgling weakly. His eyelids fluttered open, then blinked dazedly.

A moment later Butch uttered a yell and bounced groggily to his feet. He aimed a wild swing at Killan which the sergeant hastily ducked. Fitzgerald grabbed Butch's arm and pinioned it. His torch flared into the dazed bodyguard's eyes, blinding him.

But it was Tracy's voice that cut through Butch's punch-drunk hangover from the blow on his skull.

"Snap out of it, champ! What happened? Where's Lord?"

Butch finished his own cure by draining Killan's flask.

It was Butch who had forced the lock on the street door, Tracy disclosed with a disgusted mumble. Butch had turned out the hall light himself, so he could watch the private penthouse elevator at the end of the corridor, without running the risk of being seen if someone looked in from the street.

"Just what the hell were you planning to do?" Sergeant Killan asked in a tone of blank wonder.

"Jerry told me to shadow the guy. I figured if he came down in the elevator, I'd rough the louse up, haul him back to his penthouse and phone Jerry. Ain't that what you wanted, Jerry—shadow him and then let you know how I made out?"

Killan snickered and Tracy said harshly, "Skip your detective methods and tell me what happened."

"Well, the bum wasn't upstairs at all. He musta sneaked in on gumshoes from the sidewalk while I was watchin' the elevator. I took somepin' on the skull....That's nice liquor you got, Sarge."

Fitzgerald said glumly, "Looks like a pick-up after all. Lord's probably hightailing it out of town, but a quick alarm ought to nail him before he can get far."

"He ain't outa town," Butch said patiently, "The guy's upstairs, unless he come down again."

"Huh?" Fitz stared at him with his mouth open.

"He went up. I heard him go stumblin' in the elevator before I passed out."

The shaft door at the end of the corridor wouldn't open. Fitz punched a button and a faint hum became audible from aloft.

"The car is still up above," Fitz muttered. "Did the sap actually waste time to pack a bag before he scrammed?"

They rode up in an uneasy silence to the penthouse. Lord's door was on the opposite side of a small foyer. Sergeant Killan tried the knob gently, then rang the bell.

Almost instantly a voice cried from within, "Who is it? What do you want?"

It was Lord's voice, shrill with fright. He was evidently standing tensely just inside the door. Tracy motioned quietly to Killan and stepped closer.

"This is Jerry Tracy. I want to talk to you."

"About what?"

"About my broadcast tonight. Mr. Hilliard sent me over to—"

"Hilliard sent you?"

"Yes."

"Is anybody with you?"

"No."

"You're a liar. Hilliard's dead! You've come racing over here with the cops. I didn't kill Hilliard. I'm not going to be framed for his murder. If you try to come in here you'll get more than I handed that stupid body-guard of yours!"

"All we want is a sample of your fingerprints." Tracy said quietly. "If you're really innocent, you can prove it in two minutes."

Lord's answer was a bullet that split the panel of the door an inch from Tracy's ear. Four more followed it in a crashing fusillade, but Killan's lightning grab at the first crash had yanked Tracy backward to the floor.

There was a hoarse cry from within, followed by the swift thud of retreating feet.

Inspector Fitzgerald's gun sent smashing thunder at the lock of the door. But it failed to blow out the jammed mechanism. Killan threw his shoulder against the door and so did Butch. Their combined assault did the trick. The door went flat with them and Tracy and Fitz sprang over their prone bodies.

They were in an empty living-room with wide French windows that faced on the darkness of a flat terrace. The scream that halted them in mid-stride didn't come from the terrace. It sounded from somewhere in the rear of the apartment. It was knifelike in its horror, and knifelike in the way it dwindled into silence.

Tracy had heard that kind of ebbing scream only once before in his life. His scalp crawled at the memory. He had a swift mental picture of a poor lunatic crouched tensely on a stone ledge at the peak of a Fifth Avenue skyscraper. The man had jumped with that same ebbing shriek as police had grabbed vainly to save him from suicide.

Tracy raced through the apartment toward a rear bedroom. There was a half-filled suitcase on the floor. Clothing was scattered all over the bed. The window was wide open.

Far below on the roof of a fourth story cutback was a small mass that didn't move. He must have taken a desperate chance to escape along a ledge that extended dizzily toward another window. A shred of his sleeve was hanging from the steel hook used for the belts of window cleaners.

"He must have grabbed for the hook when he lost his balance," Killan said.

"Guilty as hell," Fitz said quietly.

His face was as pale as Tracy's but there was not a tremor in his big, bony frame.

In silence they descended in the private elevator. They went around to the front entrance of the building. There was no alarm out front as yet. Chauffeurs in the taxi line stared curiously, sensing trouble but not saying anything.

The fat over-rouged woman at the fourth floor rear had left her door conveniently open when she had rushed out to the hallway to faint. Fitz and Killan climbed out to the roof of the cutback.

One look from the window was enough for Tracy. The man himself lay face down, mutilated unrecognizably by the fall. But the impact had torn loose a white carnation from Lord's lapel. It lay in a darkish stain alongside the body, shredded and no longer white. Tracy stayed inside, a little sorry he'd eaten so much for dinner.

When Fitz climbed in again his hands were smudged with recording ink and he had a fingerprint sample which he placed carefully in his wallet.

He grinned bleakly at Jerry's expression.

"A good cop has the soul of a louse, Jerry. Let's go over to Headquarters. These prints are about the only thing left of him."

A TYPEWRITTEN MEMO lay on Fitzgerald's desk. It was from the fingerprint expert who had phoned the indices of the gun-prints to London. The reply from London had come across ten minutes ago. Fitzgerald showed the memo to Tracy.

"Index of prints positively identify Hilliard's murderer as fugitive British criminal. Ronald Jordan, alias Harry Clifton, alias Richard Duke. Specialty rich women. Escaped custody after killing two constables. Believed to have reached America under forged passports. Photos follow. Extradition urgently desired.
Hanley."

Hanley was the fingerprint man. Fitz's ring brought him downstairs from the bureau. He came in with brisk cheeriness.

"Forget about extradition. We've got a copper-riveted case right here. Bert Lord is the phoney passport monicker. Two minutes with the guy will prove it. Have you picked him up?"

"You do it," Sergeant Killan said. "He dropped thirteen stories without a parachute."

"Suicide, eh?"

"He tried an outside get-away along a stone ledge while we were breaking down the door."

Fitzgerald opened his wallet and handed Hanley two sensitized sheets of paper with the record of the second and third fingers on Lord's right hand. He had taken two to make sure. Blood smears had ruined the first.

Hanley said, "Beautiful!" and meant it. He took the good sample and laid it alongside the print he had taken from the gun. With a metal-tipped stylus he pointed to the complicated pattern of loops and whorls.

"Lemme show you what a really pretty science this business of—"

He stopped suddenly, his face queerly puckered.

"Gawd!" he breathed. He laid down the stylus with a gentle slowness as though he were afraid it might break.

"What's the matter?" Fitzgerald asked.

"Our guy didn't do it."

"Huh?"

"The prints don't match. The guy who gunned Hilliard wasn't Bert Lord."

Stunned, Fitzgerald stared at the expert. "You just told us that the British police—"

"Sure. They said that the guy who used that Webley on Hilliard was Ronald Jordan, alias Harry Clifton, alias Richard Duke. But you can take my word he wasn't Bert Lord! I don't know why the hell the fool went out the window, but his prints show he didn't kill Hilliard. If you put me on the stand, I'll have to be a defense witness."

"Nice joke on Lord," Killan said tonelessly. "Looks like you'll have to dig us up another Englishman, Jerry."

Tracy was on his feet, clutching at the edge of Fitz's desk to steady himself.

"But Lord fired at us through the door; tried to kill me. Why'd he run? Why did he—"

"Take it easy, Jerry," Fitz said.

"Take it—hell!" His hand quivered from his pocket and dropped a flattened slug and a wilted carnation on the desk. "Lord tried to wipe me out on the way to the broadcast tonight. He came back to Hilliard's to get the gun. He slugged Butch over the head. Why? Why, if he didn't kill Hilliard, did he kill himself?"

"They're still not his prints," Hanley said. "Don't blame me."

Butch stirred massively in his chair, his big fists clenched. "If any of you suckers are trying to say that Jerry is responsible for—"

Nobody paid any attention to him. "Lord said he was being framed," Tracy faltered. "I heard him yell that much through the door before he lost his head and—"

"Skip it, Jerry," Fitz said. "He was running from the cops, not you. You were just along for the ride. You know that, Jerry."

"I know that my broadcast tonight doomed Hilliard. I know that Bert Lord fell thirteen stories—and turns out to be innocent." He took a deep, quivering breath. "If you boys don't mind, I think I'll go home."

"Yeah. Do that," Fitz said gruffly. Tracy wasn't aware of Butch's presence alongside him till they reached the street. Butch called a taxi and Tracy seemed suddenly to wake up.

"Beat it, Butch. I don't need you."

Butch took one look at his employer's tightly wrinkled face. There were times when argument was a waste of breath.

This was one of them.

"O.K. Jerry. Don't make it too late. I'll wait up for you."

Tracy didn't answer. Butch got in the cab and drove away. The *Daily Planet's* ace columnist flagged another taxi. He went up Fifth Avenue to 59th and made a slow circle through the park. He thought of a million things about Hilliard's murder, but the core of his thinking was always the same: the flattened, battered body of Bert Lord.

He snapped out of his mental haze when the taxi emerged again from the park at 59th. He drove to the nearest drug-store and thumbed swiftly through the D's in a telephone book.

Ken Dunlap was an Englishman. Ken Dunlap had once

been in love with the dark-eyed Mrs. Hilliard. When she had married the tobacco tycoon there had been no pretense of love on her part. Suppose that Dunlap and not Lord was the sleek Ronald Jordan alias everything else that the British police had let slip out of England. The scandal tip about Lord had come from a woman using a disguised voice on the wire. Betty had been a grade A radio actress when she signed off to marry Hilliard. If Betty Hilliard had planned for Dunlap to kill her husband and split a fortune between them, the affair between Lord and Hilliard's adopted daughter was a perfect smoke screen.

Betty's refusal to tell where she had been when she left the house might be a deliberate bit of cleverness. A belated infidelity alibi from Dunlap would smirch her and save her at the same time. The cynical columnist's section of Tracy's brain handed him a headline: *Dirt for Dough's Sake.*

KEN DUNLAP'S APARTMENT house was on Park Avenue. It was one of those expensive stone hives in the Fifties, the sort from which news trickled like a perennial spring into Tracy's notebooks. The night doorman was a stooge on the Tracy payroll.

In two minutes Jerry learned that Dunlap had gone out alone around 7:30 and hadn't come back yet. The doorman had whistled Pete Malloy's cab from the corner hackstand and Dunlap had been driven uptown.

"You sure he's still away?"

The doorman grinned. "I'm sure enough to slip you a master key if you want to convince yourself."

"I won't go up, but slip me the key anyway."

He walked onward to the corner and spent ten dollars on Pete Malloy. The cabbie had taken Dunlap on an aimless ten-minute drive, and had dropped him finally at a west side corner about a quarter to eight. He was positive about the time and positive about the street.

Tracy blinked. The spot where Dunlap had alighted was a short block from the Hilliard home.

Tracy ducked into a whitewashed alley that led to the basement of the apartment house. The service elevator, untended at night, stood open and empty at the foot of the shaft. Tracy rode the car to the floor below Dunlap's and climbed the last flight, leaving the car's door jammed open in case he needed it for a quick scram.

He rang Dunlap's service bell and ducked into the shadow of the dark stairs. No one answered his ring. After a while, he opened the door quietly with his master key.

The apartment was in total darkness. Tracy tiptoed through the kitchen and pantry, went through a dining-room. In the huge adjoining living-room, he snapped on the lights and began a quick, noiseless search. What he wanted was some small object which might reasonably contain a set of Dunlap's fingerprints.

He didn't see any personal object small enough that could be wrapped and slipped into his pocket.

He went into the bedroom and turned on a lamp. Almost the first thing he saw was a flat gold cigarette case lying on a night table alongside an extension telephone. He wrapped it carefully in his handkerchief and slid it into his pocket.

He was turning to put out the lamp when he heard the grate of a key in the apartment's front door.

Tracy never moved faster in his life. A click, and the bedroom went black. A swift dart across soundless rugs and the living-room lapsed into darkness.

Utterly unaware that the lights had been blazing a second earlier, Ken Dunlap walked quickly into his living-room and snapped on the wall switch.

The few seconds interval between the slam of the apartment door and the unwelcome arrival of Dunlap had enabled Tracy to melt noiselessly into the blackness of the bedroom. Trapped, he stood behind heavy velour curtains, watching his suspect.

Dunlap seemed to be as nervous as a cat and in a coldly vicious temper. He kept muttering a low-toned growl of profanity; but it was without emphasis, as if his mind was centered on something else. He had heavy shoulders and a broad, clean-shaven face.

Tracy heard him mutter: "Mustn't get the wind up, or we'll both be lost!"

The sudden ring of a telephone bell halted Dunlap in midstride. Tracy, aware of the phone set on the night table, stiffened behind his curtain. Then he realized that its bell was silent. It was merely an extension phone; the bell was ringing in the living-room.

Tracy tiptoed away from the curtain and lifted the duplicate phone with cringing care.

He heard the sharp bite of Dunlap's voice on the wire. "Who is it?"

"Betty."

"Right-o. What's up?"

"Ken, we've got to do something. Alice knows about the letters! And I don't trust Furman. That secretary has sharp eyes and big ears."

Dunlap swore. "Don't worry, sweet. I'll take care of them both if necessary."

"You'll have to risk coming here, Ken. I've got to see you. There was a nasty little columnist here from the *Daily Planet*. I think he overheard Alice telling me about the letters."

"I'll handle it. Now listen—"

Tracy didn't wait for the rest. His only chance to get away unseen was to risk a sneak while Dunlap was still hunched tensely over the phone outside. He lowered his own instrument gently into its cradle.

Before he could take two steps there was a sudden rush of heavy feet. The velvet curtain that screened the doorway of the dark bedroom was swished viciously aside. Light flooded the room. Tracy blinked but Dunlap didn't. He stood there with fists knotted tightly, his voice ominously quiet.

"Cheerio, Mr. Tracy. You seem to be awf'ly clever at over-hearing things. But not clever enough to hide a click on a busy wire."

"You didn't, by any chance, murder Bruce Hilliard tonight, did you, Mr. Dunlap?"

That stopped him. "You think I did?"

"You were there tonight after Betty Hilliard obligingly emptied the house for your arrival. I have two witnesses to prove you left here and went there."

"Right-o." Dunlap remained polite. "But unfortunately for your logic, I didn't go in. Hilliard was already dead on his study floor when I peered through the window."

"When was that?"

"A quarter of eight."

"It won't wash. Hilliard was still alive at eight-thirty. He phoned me right after my broadcast ended. Do you know Bert Lord?"

"We're fairly friendly," Dunlap said.

"Friendly enough to steal his gun?"

Dunlap exhaled faintly. "I begin to see your drift. Finger-prints, eh? Looking for samples in my apartment. That was bloody foolish of you."

Tracy's fist lashed out as Dunlap sprang. The blow didn't stop the headlong rush of the heavy-set Englishman. A heave jack-knifed Tracy backward. He tried to kick out with both feet but Dunlap was around him like an eel. Fingers closed on Tracy's windpipe. The pressure eased before Tracy lapsed into uncon-sciousness, but he lay utterly helpless with a red haze whirling before his bulging eyes.

Through the haze he could see Dunlap grimly examining the cigarette case he had found in Tracy's pocket. He also found the master key.

"So you sneaked in here with the connivance of the blasted doorman down-stairs! Well, it won't do you a particle of good."

He hauled Tracy upright with one hand, anchoring him on swaying legs.

"If I weren't in such a hurry to get somewhere else, I'd give you what-for, my friend. As it is—"

Tracy saw the fist shoot upward in a powerful uppercut, but he was too groggy to roll his head. The blow caught him squarely under the chin. He could feel the hammering impact of every tooth in his head. Then he didn't feel anything....

HE CAME RIDING out of nothingness on long waves of nausea. It seemed as if someone had launched Tracy on a surfboard that raced up and down the smooth chasms of endless waves. Flat on his face he held on desperately until he became confusedly aware that his fingers and his wide-open mouth were pressed against the soft texture of a rug.

He got up dizzily, clutched for a bedpost and fell over a chair. He felt weak and sick. He knelt with head hanging until the sickness reached its climax, then he felt better.

There was no sign of Dunlap in the apartment. Tracy glanced at his wrist watch. He had been unconscious over two hours.

He jumped to the telephone on the night table. He could get no answer from the operator. The line was dead. So was the phone in the living-room. Dunlap had done a neat job.

Tracy raced out the front door to the corridor and kept his finger jammed on the elevator button until the indicator began to move. To his relief the elevator was operated by his friend, the doorman.

The doorman gasped as he recognized the battered little columnist.

"Jerry! For Gawd's sake! Did Dunlap—!"

"Get this cage down quick! How come you're running it? Switchboard man off duty?"

"He went over to Madison Avenue for some coffee."

"Swell. I want to phone without any publicity."

"Jerry, you told me you weren't going up to his apartment. If I'd only known, I could have warned you when he came in."

"I know. It was a dumb stunt. I went in the back way after I spoke to the hackman at the corner. Did Dunlap hire the same cab this time?"

"No. He stopped a roller."

They had reached the street lobby. The doorman jumped to

the deserted switchboard and plugged an outside wire.

"Police headquarters," Jerry growled. "Hello? Jerry Tracy! I want to talk to Inspector Fitzgerald or Sergeant Killan. Either one."

"Sorry, Jerry. They're both out right now on that Hilliard thing."

"Did they go back to the Hilliard home?"

"I don't think so. It was some other angle."

"Try all of the mid-town precincts. If you get 'em, tell 'em I'll be over at Hilliard's. Wait! Better tell 'em to give me a quick buzz before they start." He gave them the number.

"Anything hot?"

"Hot enough. I've got a hunch two more people are due to get the works tonight."

"Wow! O.K."

Tracy hung up and called the Hilliard number. All he could raise was a busy signal. Sweating, he waited and tried again. Buzz-buzz-buzz.... Every minute he waited here he was giving Dunlap additional time. And yet if he quit and raced for a cab, he was giving him still more time. He got two more busy signals before he cursed and ran out into the street.

The doorman's whistle brought him the night hawk hack man from the corner. Tracy slammed in and went streaking uptown and across to the west side.

There were lights on in the Hilliard home, but Tracy's ring at the doorbell went unanswered. Racing across the dark grounds, Tracy found that the side window through which he had originally entered was still open. He squirmed over the sill and darted for Hilliard's study.

To his angry amazement Hilliard's butler was seated calmly

in an easy chair, smoking a cigarette. There was no sign of the cop who had been left on guard—or of anyone else.

"Why the hell don't you answer the doorbell?"

Marcom said placidly, "The policeman told me to remain in this room and see that nothing was disturbed. After he went I thought I'd better not leave the room."

Tracy felt a chill of anxiety. He had heard Fitz tell that cop to remain on duty until relieved!

"When did the cop leave?"

"I don't know. I stepped into the hall to speak to him a moment ago and he wasn't there."

"Has a guy named Dunlap been here? Did he and the cop go away together?"

"No, sir. Mr. Dunlap arrived before that. The four of them—"

"What four?"

"Mr. Dunlap and Hilliard's secretary, Mr. Furman, went away with Mrs. Hilliard and Miss Hilliard. They all seemed very friendly, particularly the two women, which puzzled me, sir."

"Me, too," Tracy growled. "What happened?"

"There was talk about going to Mr. Hilliard's Long Island estate in order to avoid newspaper reporters. The policeman vetoed that. Then the front doorbell rang and the policemen left me here."

The word "bell" reminded Tracy suddenly of the peculiar series of busy signals when he had tried to call Hilliard's home.

"Who's been using this phone?"

Marcom looked puzzled. "No one, sir. There haven't been any calls." Tracy noticed that a small screen had been shifted from its accustomed place and was standing in front of the telephone desk. He whisked it away and nodded with grim understanding. Someone had slyly disconnected the phone by lifting it from its cradle. He placed it back.

Tracy stood stiffly still, his brow wrinkled in thought. His preconceived suspicion of Bert Lord as Hilliard's murderer had long since vanished. There was the phone call which Tracy had received on his private line at the broadcasting studio from Bruce Hilliard. Remembering something that Ken Dunlap had told him sneeringly in his Park Avenue apartment, Tracy was coldly convinced that Hilliard had been dead when that alleged call of his had gone over the wire at 8:32. And if Hilliard was dead, only two people could possibly have made the phoney call.

One of them was a woman, one a man. The realization of the man's identity made the hair crawl on Tracy's scalp. He did a sudden, seemingly illogical thing. He darted toward the radio over which Hilliard had been listening when he was shot to death. He examined the dial swiftly.

"Has anyone been near this machine?"

"No, sir," Marcom said.

"Come on! I want to have a look at the front door."

The rug in the entry was badly disarranged. On the polished boards of the exposed floor was a tell-tale drip of blood. Tracy followed the trail a few feet to a hall closet. When he wrenched open the door, the unconscious body of the missing policeman tumbled head-first out. He had been knocked cold, probably by brass knuckles, judging from the multiple abrasions across his bleeding temple.

Marcom uttered a terrified cry. Tracy said, "Ah, shut up." The thing was too foolishly simple. The four of them had sneaked out the back door, while a dumb butler sat like a fool in

Hilliard's study and a cop stood jammed on unconscious feet in the hall closet.

The phone began to ring.

"Hello!"

A woman operator answered. She sounded angry. "Your instrument was off the hook. There's a call that's been blocked for five minutes. Are you Mr. Jerry Tracy?"

"Yes. Let's have it!"

Inspector Fitzgerald's crisp voice came on the wire. "I've been trying to get you, Jerry. What's wrong?"

"Plenty! Furman and Alice have gone to Hilliard's Long Island estate with Betty Hilliard and Dunlap. The trip was ostensibly taken to avoid reporters, but I suspect it concerns certain letters which Betty wrote to Dunlap after her marriage."

Tracy's words raced. "Fitz, we've got to get there fast, or there'll be another murder! A double one this time!"

"I'll pick you up with a police car that'll do eighty."

"Swell. Only phone the police air base first. Tell 'em to have an amphibian waiting. The car'll do as far as North Beach. We'll need the plane to make up the time we've lost."

"I'll handle it!" Fritz growled.

NORTH BEACH AIRPORT whisked away like a flat, black pancake in the uncertain light of dawn. The police pilot did not climb very high.

Banking, he gunned the amphibian into bullet-level flight. Fitzgerald and Sergeant Killan were packed uncomfortably together, with Jerry Tracy crouched between their knees.

The hills and coves of Long Island's north shore raced swiftly astern. Tracy stared ahead through the moonlit darkness, watching for the narrow entrance to the inlet where Hilliard's country home was located. Speed sang in his blood. The wild automobile race northward through Manhattan and across the Triborough Bridge—that was nothing compared to this!

Suddenly he pointed. A shaggy headland was shouldering the darkness straight ahead.

The plane curved outward from the shore, banking and slackening its speed in preparation for a water landing. The pilot was taking no chance with the cove entrance beyond the headland. He planned to taxi through on the surface of the water.

But a yell from Jerry Tracy changed the pilot's mind. Fitz, too, was pointing. A lengthening streak of foam showed on the surface of the water where the cove joined the sound. A dark speedboat was fleeing eastward toward Greenport and the open sea.

It was a fast streamlined craft with a knife bow, but it was no match for the police flying boat. The amphibian overhauled it with the ease of a dropping hawk. It roared less than twenty feet above the cruiser. Tracy, peering, saw the blurred faces of Betty Hilliard and Ken Dunlap.

Betty seemed to be tied hand and foot. Dunlap was free. He was springing to the engine controls, slowing the boat's mad speed. The amphibian curved into the wind and landed with a shower of spray. Its momentum carried it alongside the drifting boat.

Sergeant Killan risked a ducking with a wide, reckless leap. He was on his feet instantly in the rocking craft, his gun pointed at the tense figure of Dunlap. There was a fishing knife in Dunlap's hand.

"Drop it!" Killan rasped.

The knife clattered. Killan scooped it up. Fitzgerald and Tracy sprang aboard and the seaplane began to drift away from the rocking boat.

"Cuff him, Sarge," Fitz growled.

There was a quick scream from Betty Hilliard. "Let him alone, you fools! He's innocent. Ken, tell them what happened, quick! Untie me, someone!"

Tracy loosened her bonds. He didn't have much trouble with the rather hastily knotted cords that fettered her wrists and ankles. Fitz was listening to Dunlap, watching him like a hawk. His story sounded too fast and too phoney.

He accused Furman and Alice Hilliard of attempting murder. They had, he declared, lured him and Betty to the Long Island estate with a promise to return certain missing love letters that had passed between Dunlap and Hilliard's young wife. Furman and Alice had taken them to Hilliard's boat house at the edge of the cove. Before Dunlap was aware of treachery, he and Betty were bound hand and foot and tossed into Hilliard's speedboat. The rudder was lashed tightly, the engine started, and the boat was sent racing into the Sound to be blown up as soon as the delayed spark of a fuse reached the gas tank.

Killan said, incredulously, "A fuse? An explosion?"

"Where's the fuse?" Fitzgerald snapped.

"Overboard," Dunlap said slowly, his eyes watchful. "I rolled to the knife just in time. Guess they overlooked that fishing knife in the dark. It was under a seat. I cut my bonds, tossed the damned fuse over the side, a few seconds before your plane showed up."

Killan said dryly, "Funny you didn't draw any blood with those quick knife cuts."

"He's telling the truth," Betty Hilliard cried. "Furman and Alice wanted it to appear as if we blew up accidentally in a guilty attempt to flee. They must have been in cahoots with Lord."

Fitzgerald looked at the *Daily Planet's* little columnist. Tracy's dim smile was enigmatic.

"Lord didn't kill Hilliard," he said. "I've known that for some time. Hilliard was shot twice because *a man and a woman murdered him.* Each wanted a hold on the other, so each fired at him, using Lord's stolen gun. Then, you see, with them both witnessing the other's shot, neither could ever talk. We'd better get back to that boat house."

"You won't find them," Betty cried. "They're miles away by this time."

Dunlap didn't say anything. Tracy jumped to the speedboat's engine and started it. Fitz yelled an order across the black water to the drifting seaplane. As the boat raced back to the entrance of the cove, the seaplane began to taxi slowly in its wake, dipping along like an unwieldy gull.

The boathouse was a two-story wooden building on the left side of the cove. A light was burning on the lower floor. It was the only light visible in the darkness. Hilliard's country home, perched high on the cliff, was black and formless among the trees.

Tracy switched off his engine and allowed the speedboat to ground on a shelving beach. He and Fitz hurried noiselessly toward the partly opened door of the boathouse.

A cautious glance inside made them both stiffen. Walter Furman and Alice Hilliard were lying close together on the floor. There were handkerchiefs thrust into their mouths; their wrists and ankles were tied with lengths of fishing cord. Their faces were livid with terror.

Fitz started to spring forward, but Tracy caught him in a tight grip and yanked him soundlessly back out of sight. He had seen something that Fitz hadn't. The knob of a rear door was turning slowly! Someone behind the boathouse was about to make a stealthy entrance.

A small window allowed Tracy and Fitz a hidden view of the interior. The back door was wider now, although no one was visible in the blackness beyond, On the floor Walter Furman was threshing furiously.

A man bounded suddenly into the lighted room. There was a gun in his hand and it swung toward the pair on the floor.

Fitz's yell of amazement startled the murderer. He was a man alongside whose smashed body Fitzgerald had knelt only an hour or so earlier to take fruitless fingerprints.

Bert Lord! The man who had jumped or fallen thirteen stories.

Lord's gun muzzle jerked toward the window. His shot and Fitz's roared simultaneously. Glass showered Tracy as Lord's bullet grazed his scalp. Fitz's bullet missed the whirling killer's chest, but it drilled through the palm of Lord's outthrust left hand.

The stairs to the upper floor were closer to Lord than the rear door. He raced upward. That was a mistake. Fitz was inside the front door like a lean-limbed tornado, pumping lead.

He fired four thunderous shots and one of them drilled Lord's back below his shoulder blades. Lord clung with one hand to the wooden bannister, trying to aim his gun muzzle downward toward Fitz. To Tracy it seemed like a million years, but it was really not more than three or four seconds.

Lord toppled almost leisurely over the bannisters. He struck on his head and rolled over. His neck stayed twisted at an unnatural angle. He looked as if he were slyly peeping over his shoulder at the rigid figures of Tracy and the police inspector.

Fitz said huskily, "That's one for the book. He falls thirteen stories and doesn't get killed. Then he flops six feet over a bannister and breaks his neck."

"Only, of course," Tracy said, "he didn't fall thirteen stories. He pushed someone out. When you have time to get an autopsy done, you'll sure as hell find out it was his poor valet. "I've heard he had one the same height and size as he was."

Tracy breathed relievedly. "I'm glad I didn't scare him into suicide. He suspected we'd get a line on him from Scotland Yard where he's wanted for murder. So he undoubtedly bashed in his valet's head, dressed the body in his clothes—even to the flower—and tossed him out the window. He knew he'd have time to escape before the poor, smashed body could ever be identified and that, in the meantime, we'd think it was he."

DUNLAP AND BETTY Hilliard came in, herded by Killan. On the floor the bound figures of Alice and Furman had stopped writhing. Both couples were watching Tracy, who kept staring at the dead Lord with a bleak smile.

"Lord shot at me through the penthouse door, his scream at the window, was a bluff," Tracy said thoughtfully. "After Lord shoved out his valet, he jumped calmly into his bedroom closet. When we raced downstairs to view the mangled body of the valet he'd killed, Lord made a quick sneak.... Have you still got those prints from the murder gun?"

Fitz nodded. He smeared Lord's dead fingers lightly with fountain pen ink and pressed them gently against a sheet of paper. Then he compared the result with the prints he carried from the Webley revolver. "Check," he said. "A perfect match."

Tracy shook his head.

"It's not as simple as that, Fitz. Lord was framed."

"Then why did he fake his own death?"

"The prints answer that," Tracy said. "Bert Lord, if we'd caught him, would've been extradited to England and been hanged. Hence his desperate alibi at the penthouse window. But he didn't kill Hilliard! And he wasn't the man who ambushed me on my way to the broadcast studio tonight. Why should Lord, a clever crook, have been dumb enough to drop his well known white carnation where Butch and I would find it?"

Tracy turned suddenly toward Ken Dunlap. "You admit you went to Hilliard's house tonight. At a quarter of eight, you said. Three quarters of an hour before he was talking to me on the phone."

"Hilliard was dead when I saw him," Dunlap said calmly. "The back door was unlocked. Betty was gone. Her husband was dead. That's the truth."

"Why did you go there at all?"

"None of your damned business!"

"I'll tell you," Betty Hilliard said wearily. "Ken came because I love him. He wanted to ask my husband to permit a divorce so that we could marry. I phoned Ken and begged him not to come, afraid of my husband's violent temper. But Ken insisted. So I got rid of the butler and sneaked out to intercept Ken. I—I couldn't find him."

Fitz nodded grimly to Killan and the two cops moved closer to Dunlap. Tracy began to talk in a quiet, even voice.

"Hilliard was killed by a man and woman about 7:30 with Lord's gun. The gun was left to incriminate Lord. Alice even tried to make me think she was shielding Lord, by trying to keep the gun out of sight. The man who shot Hilliard then rushed downtown, bought a white carnation and took a shot at me, further involving Lord. Lord suspected the double-cross when he showed up at the studio and I accused him of the ambush. He raced to Hilliard's house, after a quick trip to his penthouse to find his revolver missing. He was the guy who tried to steal his own gun from me in the darkness—and failed.

"Lord knew, too late, what he was up against. So he faked his own death to make his fade-out easy. I should've suspected about his valet because I once wrote an item in my column about the town's best-dressed valet who could wear his master's old clothes. That was Lord's man. Anyway, Lord dared not tell the truth to the cops about the murderess and her boy friend, because to do so would be to hand himself over to British justice. The killers realized at once what Lord had done. But they, too, had to keep mum about his fake death or else disclose the fact that they had framed him.

"Lord was hanging around the Hilliard home when Ken Dunlap arrived in response to the call from Betty. I was in Dunlap's apartment when he got that call. Betty had already made a tearful appeal to Alice about the letters which Alice had found. The result was that a truce was patched between the two women. Lord knocked out the cop on duty, but he was too late for his real revenge. The two couples had already started for Hilliard's Long Island place. Lord followed—for revenge. He'd lost everything. The rest is obvious."

"But." Inspector Fitzgerald's voice sounded dazed, "it was Alice Hilliard and Furman whom Lord tried to kill."

"That's right," Tracy said.

"You mean that Furman and not Dunlap—"

"I mean," Tracy said quietly, "that you've got your killers already tied up on the floor here, in fake knots of their own making. Hilliard was killed by his adopted daughter and a crooked secretary who happens also to be Alice's lover."

Sergeant Killan said dully, "Then all that nutty stuff about the motorboat and the burning fuse was true?"

Tracy nodded. "Furman's a good psychologist. He figured that if the explosion didn't blow Betty and Dunlap to smithereens, their story would be too fishy to believe. That's why he played safe with the cords and gag. That's also probably why he didn't search the boat and find the fishing knife."

Walter Furman lay very still on the floor alongside Alice. He had spat out his gag. His voice was scornful.

"You've forgotten my alibi."

"You haven't any. You had enough time after you killed Hilliard to make your fake ambush of me, drop the carnation, and go to meet Nick White at his near-by hotel. Alice met me at the broadcast building with a fake tearful appeal to build her alibi. You thought you were both in the clear, because you intended to make it seem that Hilliard was still alive two minutes after my broadcast ended."

"How do you know he wasn't?" Furman said huskily.

"No one touched his radio set from the moment the body was discovered. Hilliard never missed one of my broadcasts. Yet his dial was tuned at another station. In other words, he was killed *before I came on the air.* He couldn't have heard my squib and, therefore, didn't summon me to his house. You did that!"

"Prove it, wise guy."

"Easily," Tracy said steadily. "My studio phone is unlisted. I use it to get last minute news flashes from my private secretary. Only two other people know that number. Hilliard, who was already dead—and his confidential secretary, Walter Furman."

"I really ought to have a motive."

"I can guess at one. That check Hilliard gave Alice this afternoon for $50,000. It might have been forged by—"

"No." Hilliard's wife spoke suddenly. "My husband signed it. He told me about it. It was a final gift to Alice in lieu of any share in his estate in the event she married Lord. He had already changed his will, cutting her off. Then Alice tried to blacken my character. My husband threatened to stop payment on the check. I heard him tell Furman to notify the bank in the morning. He wrote a notation on the stub. Make Furman tell you what he did with the book."

Furman's hand moved like a streak of lightning from beneath his prone body. He had slyly released his hidden right hand from the loosely twisted cords. As he heaved to his knees a pistol glittered.

"Quick!" Alice screamed harshly. "I can take it! Let's go this way!"

Fitz tried to clutch at Furman but he twisted like an eel. He leaned swiftly toward Alice. She had knelt to face him, and she took without a quiver the bullet that he sent crashing into her breast. A second later the smoking muzzle spat flame into Furman's temple.

He fell in a flat huddle. There was a ghastly smile on Alice's pale face. She had pitched forward across the body of her lover.

"She took it, all right," Fitz said.

"Some women can take anything—except decency," Tracy said.

His lips tightened and there was silence. What else was there to say?

Guide to Murder

Jerry Tracy spends a night at the World's Fair—with an Aquacade girl and murder.

IF THERE WAS one exhibition at the World's Fair in which Jerry Tracy's interest was nil, it was Babylonian archeology. To stare at the dull reproductions of an antique civilization made the back of Tracy's throat dusty. But it was a lot better than trying to make small talk with George Huston.

Huston seemed to resent Tracy's presence. Not once since their arrival at the Fair grounds had he spoken a direct remark to the *Daily Planet's* famous little columnist. He addressed his talk to Barbara Shipley and her father, including Tracy in the conversation with oblique nastiness: "As our journalistic guide will probably agree—" Small time stuff like that.

It amused Tracy for a while, then it began to get on his nerves.

He had given up an evening to pilot these three out-of-town-ers around the Fair grounds only because of a desire to do a favor for his boss. Shipley had wired that he was coming to New York with his daughter and her fiancé for a look at the Fair. He suggested that it might be more interesting if Jerry Tracy showed them around. Shipley published an important newspaper in Midport, Illinois. The paper was an essential link in a syndicate expansion scheme which the owner of the *Daily Planet* had been working on for months. Jerry grinned wryly and accepted the assignment.

He had expected to be bored, but he hadn't expected anything as terrible as George Huston. He had met a lot of small town wise guys in his day, but none worse than this man. Huston

never muffed a chance to be sneeringly sarcastic at Tracy's expense. He was so anxious to be smart he was nasty.

It was Huston who had insisted on going to the Babylonian Building. Tracy demurred. He pointed across Fountain Lake toward the brightly lit Loop, the amusement center of the Fair. The fire-work's display was due to start soon. They hadn't seen

the bathing beauties at the Aquacade. It was a gorgeous water spectacle, staged by a master showman—

Huston's laugh was like sandpaper.

Turning his back on Tracy, he made a sneering pretense of trying to convince Shipley with an ironic barker's spiel.

"You'll like it. You're bound to. Every girl a looker! They wiggle. They squirm. They wear postage-stamp tights. Our tired journalistic friend recommends them highly. You can't lose! All you need is your ticket of admission and a dirty mind."

Barbara Shipley protested indifferently.

"Really, George, that's not very nice."

Her indifference puzzled Tracy. Barbara had been pleasant enough on the trip from the hotel. Something had happened on the Fair grounds to change her. There was a repressed nervousness in her that had grown as the dusk faded into brilliantly lit darkness.

She said hurriedly, "I'm sure Mr. Tracy won't mind humoring us. It might be very nice to go where it's quiet."

"By all means," her father said.

Harold Shipley looked as if his nerves could stand a little rest. Ever since dinner at the French Pavilion he had developed a jerky habit of rubbing his chin. It gave him an excuse to twist his head and glance about him. Tracy wondered if this uneasy habit had anything to do with the man at the French Pavilion.

The man had sat at a nearby table. He had left a moment or two after they had been seated. Except for his eyes Tracy might not have noticed him at all. They were pale blue, almost whitish, the color of glacial ice. For an instant the eyes rested on the newspaper publisher from Midport. Shipley cringed and seemed to nod faintly. The man smiled without moving a muscle of his face. It was a trick of the eyes alone.

Tracy had a hunch that a wordless signal had passed between the two men. It took a couple of drinks to bring the color back into Shipley's strained face.

From that moment had come the chin-rubbing and the eye-roving of the Midport publisher. Coupled with Huston's sarcasm and Barbara's inattention, it made Jerry Tracy feel like a poor relation with a bad case of B.O.

But he swallowed his irritation until Huston made his crack about the Aquacade. Huston kept it up.

"It seems a shame to deprive our sensational little friend of the opportunity of seeing his flesh show. Perhaps he'd like to rejoin us later. Far be it from me to curb a Broadway columnist's natural—"

Tracy's angry clutch almost tore the buttons loose from Huston's coat. He whirled the young lawyer around. His voice was low, almost conversational.

"One more crack out of you and I'll hang one on your jaw!"

Huston tried to break loose and couldn't.

"Let go, damn you! People are watching us."

The crowd of sightseers on the way to the amusement area had begun to thicken. Tracy released his grip. Huston straightened with a forced smile. A Fair policeman, very natty in his broad Stetson and dark-blue tunic, gave Tracy and Huston a slow stare.

"Any trouble?"

"No trouble at all," Harold Shipley intervened huskily. "Just a small bit of horse play."

He took Huston's arm and pushed through the crowd. Tracy followed with Barbara. She murmured a vague word of apology for the conduct of her fiancé. But her mind was elsewhere. She and Huston were the damnedest engaged couple Tracy had ever met. If she was in love with the guy, Tracy was a six-foot Hottentott with a ring in his nose!

He trailed along to the Babylonian Museum, wondering more and more about the man with the pale blue eyes in the French Pavilion. As far as Tracy knew Barbara and her fiancé hadn't noticed the guy, but they acted a lot like Shipley. All three of them were obviously itching with the desire to get rid of Tracy.

Shipley made the first break. After glancing with ill concealed impatience at the faded Babylonian mosaics, Shipley excused himself with a muttered something about getting a drink of orangeade. He was off like a shot before anyone could comment.

A sudden crackle of aerial bombs sounded from the direction of the Lagoon of Nations. It gave Tracy an excuse to drift toward the door of the museum and crane his neck. He got there in time to see Shipley hurrying along the pathway outside—in the opposite direction from a refreshment booth! His goal seemed to be a cross path beyond the raspberry-colored concrete of a domed industrial building.

A man was lounging there. He ducked around the corner as Shipley approached, but not before Tracy got a glimpse of his lean face. It was the guy who had tipped Shipley the nod in the restaurant. The publisher from Midport vanished after the blue-eyed guy.

Tracy crossed the marble-floored museum to where Huston and Barbara were making a pretense of examining the exhibits. Barbara had the air of a girl elaborately trying to remember something.

"Good gracious!" she cried suddenly. "Souvenir cards! I completely forgot about them. Do you mind if I—"

Tracy didn't mind. Nor did Huston. He said, "Run along, dear," in a smooth tone. The muscles at the corners of his jaw were taut. He was holding on to a display case with both hands as if he were afraid the case might get away from him.

Tracy helped Huston look at the ancient jewelry display for a moment or two until she was gone.

"Pretty dull here."

"I don't think so."

"Perhaps you'd like to help Barbara pick out her souvenir cards."

"No."

"I think I'll drift over to the door and watch the fireworks."

"I don't give a damn what you do," Huston said in a strained voice, "so long as you leave me alone."

In the pillared portico, Tracy was able to keep an eye on Barbara Shipley without himself being seen. The girl went straight to a souvenir booth and for a moment Tracy thought he had been overly suspicious. Then he noticed the man who stood in front of a rack of postcards. Barbara stopped alongside him. His head turned and his lips moved in what looked like a quick appeal. His hand caught hers and held it in spite of her effort to draw away.

He had a small dark mustache and white teeth that gleamed when he smiled. He was smiling now. A sort of Rhett Butler guy, very sure of himself. They moved around the corner of the souvenir booth, out of sight of the employee inside. The man leaned quickly and kissed Barbara. She gave in to his embrace. Nothing polite about that love tableau! It was raw, physical, unashamed.

After a while Barbara whispered something to the dark guy. He faded down a side path toward the rear of the museum building, moving with an easy stride of his long legs and a cocky swing of his shoulders. Barbara picked up a half dozen souvenir cards, the first she could grab.

She found Tracy standing alone in front of one of the Babylonian showcases. Her eyes veered in search of her fiancé. Tracy saw quick suspicion pinch them when she saw no sign of Huston.

"Where's George? Did you see where he went?"

"I don't know," Tracy said truthfully, "I got interested in something else. When I looked around he was gone."

A moment later Harold Shipley came in. He was breathing

heavily. There was dull anger in his eyes. He, too, wanted to know what had become of Huston. He acted as though Tracy was responsible for the fiancé's sudden sneak.

"How did you like your orangeade?" Tracy asked him.

"Eh? Oh, excellent! Barbara, didn't George tell you where he was going? Weren't you with him?"

She flushed and showed her father the postcards she had bought. Shipley looked as if he were on the verge of pumping questions at her, but he managed to check himself. He turned and vented his anger on Tracy.

"Don't stand there like a fool! You must have seen where Huston went. Go find him! It's time to leave."

The distant popping of fireworks had ceased. An attendant behind a desk in the museum rotunda glanced at the clock and pressed a button. Chimes began to echo through all the corridors. Over at The Loop the closing hour was considerably later. But the final crash of aerial bombs from the Lagoon of Nations meant that the free educational exhibits at the north end of the Fair were ended for the night.

The few stolid sightseers in the Babylonian Building began to trickle toward the front portal.

"This is ridiculous," Barbara Shipley told Tracy. "Surely you must know where George went. We left him in your charge. Even an office boy would be competent to—"

"Yeah," Tracy said. "An office boy! That's me."

He was getting sicker and sicker of these screwy goings-on. His voice rasped.

"Stay here, and don't do any more wandering till I come back. In the meantime, talk about postcards and orangeades!"

A quick glance passed between father and daughter. Tracy

turned on his heel and left them.

Having seen no sign of Huston in the rear corridors, Tracy descended a marble staircase where a sign indicated the presence of a washroom. The room was empty. It added fuel to Tracy's mounting anger. The boy friend was like the father and daughter—up to something damned queer. But where in heck could Huston have sneaked?

Tracy descended another flight of marble steps. He opened a rear door whose presence he had not hitherto been aware of.

He gasped with instinctive pleasure as he stepped into the most beautiful formal garden he had ever seen. Dim blue lamps strung sparsely along the tops of hanging vines gave a shadowy effect of moonlight on snow. Snow-like, too, was the whiteness of cupped flowers in a formal garden that surrounded the pool.

The pool was rectangular and quite long. A flagged walk was paved with irregular chunks of flat stone, and between the edges of the stones was a carpet of cool green moss. Spaced at regular intervals were the nude figures of six stone goddesses. In the semi-darkness of the walled garden these kneeling statues seemed poised and alive. It took Tracy a dazed instant to realize that the peaked breasts and slenderly arched torsos were not creamy flesh but the cold perfection of marble.

He had never until tonight entered the portals of the Babylonian Museum. To Jerry Tracy the hanging gardens of Babylon were something you read about in dusty textbooks on a rainy day. He decided with a gulp that history had its points.

He stepped over a clipped hedge to have a closer look at the pool. The water looked cool enough to drink—and that's what the man behind the hedge was doing.

He was down on his knees, his face bent over the water. Both hands rested on the stone lip of the pool. He paid no attention to Tracy, not even when the columnist spoke. Tracy took a quick step forward.

The back of the man's bent head was a sticky blur of blood. The weapon that had smashed his skull lay alongside his elbow. It was one of the flat paving stones that had been ripped from its soft bed of moss. The dead man hadn't fallen into the pool because the raised edge supported the weight of his inclined body.

His ear and the side of his face looked as if it was just painted. Red drops dripped from his chin and dissolved into a smoky swirl in the water.

Tracy didn't touch him. He took one look at the dead face. It was George Huston.

JERRY TRACY BACKED up. Then he changed his mind. His glance, lifting beyond the corpse of Huston, flicked suddenly along the dim walk that bordered the length of the pool. He had an instinctive feeling of movement in one of those nude marble statues. The movement was not in the statue itself, but directly behind it.

Jerry sprang forward. A figure jerked into view with a barely audible gasp. The figure was white from head to foot. But not with the smooth nudity of marble. Tracy caught a blurred glimpse of a white rubber bathing cap, a woman's white silk swim suit, bathing shoes.

A cape fluttered upward like a milky sail in the darkness. It covered the head and body of the fleeing girl. She ran and Tracy sprinted after her. Not a sound came from either of them. It was like a queer nightmare pursuit in a magic garden.

On the fluttering cape ahead of him Tracy saw the outline of black letters across the fleeing girl's shoulders. The letters spelled the word: Aquacade.

For an instant Tracy thought the girl was going to dive into the pool and swim across to where a door in the vine-covered wall of the garden led to the fairgrounds. But the fugitive veered from the water at the last moment. She raced down the long side of the pool with Tracy pounding after her. Rounding it, she made for the wall gate, which Tracy could see was slightly ajar.

The girl vaulted a thick hedge and ducked out of sight. Tracy made the leap a moment later—too fast a leap, as he realized instantly. A foot from the blackness behind the hedge thrust itself between his legs. He sprawled. Before he could turn and grapple with the cloaked girl behind him, he felt the impact of a fist against his jaw.

It wasn't any female fist. It jolted him into a dazed huddle. He heard dimly the rasp of a masculine oath, then his wide-open eyes saw only blackness. The man who had waited behind the hedge to help the bathing girl escape yanked Tracy's soft hat downward over his ears and eyes, blinding him.

There was a quick echo of fleeing feet.

Tracy fought weakly to yank the jammed hat off his head. The more he jerked, the more his stumbling feet tangled. His muffled yells sounded like the bleat of a man in a barrel.

Then he heard another cry and the race of returning feet. Tracy managed to pull the jammed hat off his head. He backed up as a bulky man dove at him. He sent a wild punch bouncing off his foe's chest, then tried to grapple. He was afraid of a gun or the ripping slash of a knife.

He got neither. A powerful hand twisted in his collar and lifted him clear off his feet. Dangling helplessly a half foot above the ground, Tracy caught a blurred glimpse of a rock-like face and a broad-brimmed Stetson.

The sight brought Tracy to his senses. He didn't need to look at the dark-blue tunic or the swanky puttees to realize that the big guy who was shaking him like a monkey on a stick was a World's Fair cop.

He gulped helplessly. He was slowly choking to death in that inexorable grip and the cop noticed it. He lowered the gasping little columnist to the ground.

"What the hell's going on here? Who yelled?"

Tracy said thickly, "A guy's just been killed. Somebody—"

The cop's head veered suspiciously. He said, "Uh-huh!" as he saw the dead man at the other end of the pool. He dragged Tracy along the flagged walk like a sack of meal.

"What did you kill him for?"

"I didn't."

"Who did?"

"I don't know. A guy was hidden behind a hedge. He socked me and yanked my hat over my head. I didn't get a look at him."

"Nuts! What do you think I am, a dope?"

"You sound like one," Tracy snapped.

He fished out his press card and showed it to the rookie cop. He knew all these cops at the Fair were rookies, lads who had passed the police examination and were waiting for regular city appointments. The biggest and handsomest had been assigned to Fair patrols. This guy had been petted by the smiles of lady visitors into a tremendous sense of his own importance.

"So you're Jerry Tracy, eh?" the cop said. "So what? You're a liar by my time! Nobody ran out that wall gate or I'd have seen him when I came up the alley."

"Did you come up both ends of the alley?" Tracy snapped.

The cop's ears turned pink. He lost his temper and caught Tracy's arm in a hammerlock. But before he could twist it, there was a startled cry from the rear door of the museum building, Harold Shipley was standing there with his daughter.

He saw Tracy in the grip of the cop, and just beyond them the body of the dead man. He moved in front of Barbara and tried to block off her view. But she had seen George Huston. She gave a shrill scream and fainted.

Shipley paid no attention to her. He kept staring at Jerry Tracy and there was a queer edge to his voice.

"My Gawd, Mr. Tracy! Surely you didn't—you couldn't—"

"Couldn't what?" Tracy demanded sharply.

"Do you people know each other?" the cop asked.

"Of course. My name is Harold Shipley. I'm the owner and publisher of the Midport *Chronicle*. We came East yesterday to see the Fair. The dead man is—was—my daughter's fiancé. Mr. Tracy acted as guide for us. He and Mr. Huston got into an argument over something Mr. Tracy said about a girl show and—"

Tracy winced at the utter gall Shipley had! He was making it sound as if Tracy and Huston had quarreled over something nasty *Tracy* had said.

A new voice spoke up from the dimly lit garden. It was another cop whom Tracy remembered instantly.

"Shipley is right. I saw the little guy and Huston try to trade punches only a little while ago over in the amusement area. I broke it up and moved them on. Hold everyone here while I hop to a phone."

His tall, booted figure raced into the building.

"Why did you kill Huston?" the rookie cop kept asking.

He shook Tracy until his teeth rattled. Tracy clamped his lips and watched Shipley. There was a rigid expression on the publisher's face as though he were bracing himself against anything Tracy might say. Barbara Shipley had come out of her faint and was on her feet again, leaning on her father's arm. She, too, was tense.

Tracy knew that if he mentioned the handsome Rhett Butler guy whom Barbara had met secretly at the souvenir stand, the girl would deny it and call him both a murderer and a liar. So would Shipley if Tracy alluded to the guy with the ice-blue eyes who had tipped Shipley the nod in the French Pavilion.

"So you didn't really see the killer, eh?" the cop said grimly.

He didn't know a thing about the fleeing girl in the bathing suit and cape, and Tracy had no intention now of telling him. When the garden flooded with more cops Tracy refused to add a word to his skimpy story.

"I'll wait for the Homicide squad," he said flatly. "It won't do you a bit of good to bark. And if anyone lays another finger on me I'll crucify the whole lot of you in the *Daily Planet*."

He hated the thought of keeping quiet about the screwy behavior of Shipley and his daughter just prior to the murder. But he was loyal enough to the *Planet's* owner to want to keep quiet until he got the low-down on this fidgety newspaper publisher from the Middle-West. Besides, Tracy's truthful story of what actually had happened would sound too fantastic for belief. Even Inspector Fitzgerald wouldn't swallow that stuff about a bathing girl who had tried to double for a nude statue.

TRACY FELT BETTER when Fitzgerald arrived twenty minutes later. He and the Inspector were old friends. Fitz snorted at the idea of Jerry Tracy committing a murder because of a trivial quarrel. Under Fitz's cross-examination Harold Shipley toned down the quarrel story considerably. But he lied flatly to one of Fitz's routine questions—and so did Barbara.

They swore that they had been continuously with Tracy up to the moment he had left them to find out what had become of Huston.

By keeping quiet Tracy had them both over a barrel. They could kid Fitz but not him. But Tracy flushed as he met Fitz's honest gaze. He, too, was holding out. He wanted time for a quick trip to the Aquacade before he spilled anything about the figure in the white swim suit. He had a protégé of his spotted in the water show. She ought to be able to tell him if any of the swimmers had ducked away from the performance that had been scheduled at the time of George Huston's murder.

But it was tough not to be able to play fair with Fitz.

While the Homicide men bustled around the quiet confines of the garden with camera and fingerprint apparatus, Tracy retired out of earshot with Shipley and his daughter.

"You first!" he told the publisher softly. "Who was the man you met, and why?"

Shipley tried to squirm out of it. Tracy turned to Barbara. He described the blue-eyed man, and added curtly: "Talk about your father's little pal or I'll talk about you."

She caved. The man's name was Eric Lundy, she admitted slowly. He was a Midport politician. He and her father didn't get along very well. Her frightened whisper seemed to infuriate Shipley.

"Just what I thought," he muttered. "You'd say anything to hide the fact that you had a sneaking date with Allen Webb."

"Who's Allen Webb?" Tracy cut in.

"A rat," Shipley rejoined in a savage undertone. "A man who hates my guts. He's tried to ruin me. He's even made threats to kill Huston, if that was the only way he could marry Barbara—"

"That's not true," Barbara said huskily.

"I can prove it is. That's why Eric Lundy asked me to meet him tonight. He told me that Webb was here at the Fair. He warned me that you were meeting Webb on the sly. You're crazy in love with Webb. Don't deny it!"

"What if I am? The engagement to Huston was your idea, I never *wanted* to marry him."

A cop was glancing curiously toward the marble bench.

"Take it easy," Tracy said. "Where can I find this fellow Lundy if I promise you to keep my mouth shut for the present?"

"He said he'd meet me at the Three Ring Restaurant over in the amusement area," Shipley said slowly.

"And Webb?" Tracy asked Barbara. "Did you have a date to meet him later?"

She denied it. She might be lying, but Tracy had no time to waste. Inspector Fitzgerald was coming toward the bench. The preliminary investigation of Huston's murder was over.

Tracy had no trouble convincing Inspector Fitzgerald that Shipley and his daughter could be safely released until their presence was needed. Barbara's pale face was proof that she had suffered a terrific shock. The owner of the *Daily Planet* would vouch for them, Tracy said. Neither had any direct knowledge of the murder and were not in any sense of the word material witnesses. They could easily be reached at the Waldorf where they had an expensive suite.

Fitz agreed with a troubled sigh. He was worried by the lack of clues or motive. The wealthy Midport publisher and his daughter hurried to the gate near the Administration Building, where they could hire a taxicab.

Tracy faded toward the garden exit.

"Where are you going?" Fitz asked. "I want to talk to you about this thing as soon as I get a chance to."

"You'll find me over near the Aquacade show," Tracy said. "I've had all the murder I want."

He headed through the darkened exhibit area toward the bridge over World's Fair Boulevard. The free exhibit buildings had all been closed by this time and there were few people in sight along the quiet thoroughfares. But beyond the bridge there was still plenty of noise and excitement. The amusement area closed late. People were streaming along the shore of Fountain Lake where the final fireworks display would put a crashing period to the night's festivities.

Tracy followed the crowd. He hadn't forgotten the girl in the Aquacade show he wanted to question, but he was afraid that if he delayed hunting up the mysterious Eric Lundy, he might miss him altogether.

Lundy was standing outside the entrance of the enormous Three Ring Restaurant as cool as an iced radish.

He said, smilingly, "Hello, pal. I knew you'd look me up."

His eyes at close range were like narrow lumps of pale blue ice.

"Let's skip the preliminaries," he added. "George Huston was bumped a little while ago and you think maybe I did it. Well, I didn't."

"Who did?"

"I don't know, but I'm not crying. Huston was a louse. I wanted him dead and someone did me a big favor."

He was the most self-possessed guy Tracy had met in a long time. Well dressed, but nothing flashy about him. A mouth like a steel trap. Apparently quite willing to talk.

This last was the thing that puzzled Tracy. Lundy answered his unspoken question.

"I'm talking because my own nose is clean. I think I can tell you who did the kill, and why he did it. It means talking a little about myself but I'll take a chance. I figure you're smart enough to smell an undertaker a block away."

"You wouldn't threaten me, would you?"

Eric Lundy merely grinned.

"Here's where I fit in. Off the record, and underline that if you want to stay alive! I'm a political fixer in the thriving little town of Midport. How I work is none of your damned business, but I run things out there. Harold Shipley and his newspaper have a private tie-in with me. He also has a public tie-in with law and order. So he plays both ends and I help him play."

"What about—"

"Shut up! This George Huston is an up-and-coming young lawyer. He does the crime crusading for Shipley's lousy sheet. He's so dumb that he got to taking his job seriously. So Shipley and I decided to get him married to Shipley's daughter to pull the rein on him. Huston was so socially ambitious that a promotion seemed easier than a kill. In fact, to kill him would gum things up. I'm telling you this to show you that the job in the garden of the Babylonian Building wasn't good business for me or Shipley. We had our man sewed. Someone else spilled the sap's brains."

He stared at Tracy for a moment.

"Now it's your turn. Pick a card. Any one."

"Allen Webb," Tracy said quietly.

"I knew you'd do it. You're smart."

There was no change in his flat voice.

"I don't say that Webb bumped George Huston, but I'll tell you why I *think* he did."

It seemed to Tracy that there was a sudden undercurrent of eagerness in the man but he couldn't be sure. Behind Tracy's back was the noise and confusion of thousands of merrymakers winding up a boisterous evening amid the sights and noise of the amusement area. But Tracy had a shivery sensation that he was alone in an igloo, watching a pair of frozen eyes that blocked off the entrance to a smart frozen brain.

"Webb's in love with Shipley's daughter. Barbara's in love with him. The payoff is that Webb and her old man are enemies. Webb's father used to own the newspaper in Midport. Shipley was the managing editor. Shipley squeezed out Webb's father and did it so neatly that the old guy hadn't a chance to prove fraud. He died of a broken heart—if you like movies. The son tried to make things tough for Shipley and pretty well succeeded. So you can see how far he'd get as a preferred son-in-law. That brings us to Huston, the dead guy. Am I boring you, pal?"

"I'll tell you when you do," Tracy said.

"O.K. Huston's engaged to Barbara, but Webb is the only man on earth to make her give. He may have already. They're both full-blooded, if you know what I mean. Webb made threats to kill Huston if he couldn't marry Barbara any other way. Trite, but I'm telling you facts. Webb also hates Huston because Huston was the lawyer that figured the stunt to hornswoggle Webb's old man out of the newspaper. If he bumped Huston—and that's your worry, not mine—the kill has a tie-up with the water show at the Aquacade. That's where Webb went earlier this evening. That's where he went right after the cops began to arrive at the Babylonian Building. And don't waste any time hunting for him in the paid seats. He went in the performer's entrance."

"Is that all?"

"So long and it was nice to meet you."

"You got any personal reason why you'd like to see Webb do a wiggle in the electric chair?"

Lundy laughed aloud for the first time.

"If I had to, I'd frame Webb to his ears. But it just happens I don't have to. I really think he lost his head and made things nice for Shipley and me."

He started to move off with tigerish grace, then halted and came back. His slow grip on Tracy's wrist hurt to the bone.

"Remember, you little punk, keep Midport politics out of it!"

NEW YORK STATE Building, which housed the Aquacade, was a huge semi-circular structure that faced the shore of Fountain Lake. The stage was out on the water. Between the stage and the spectators was a brilliantly lit lagoon where the diving beauties and the swimming champs did their stuff in an eye-filling spectacle.

Tracy had no trouble getting in the performer's entrance. He had been there before to see how Marjorie Field was getting along.

Marjorie was Tracy's protégé. A lousy dancer but a nice kid with a streamlined figure. She could swim like a fish and that made it easy to help her into the Aquacade show after three nightclub managers had held their noses following her dance tryout in a floor chorus.

Tracy hoped to find out from Marjorie if any of the girls in the water ballet had skipped the previous show.

A lot of the girls were already leaving the stadium. The show that had ended a few minutes earlier was the final performance. Tracy stopped a girl in the exit corridor and asked for Marjorie Field.

"I saw her a minute ago. Look in the reception room. That's where the girls come through from the dressing room."

"Thanks."

There was no sign of Marjorie when Tracy got there, but he saw someone else that made him forget the girl temporarily. Pacing up and down and looking extremely nervous was the tall and very good looking Mr. Webb.

There was no mistaking him. He looked more like Rhett Butler than ever at close quarters. He scowled as Tracy approached him and asked for a match. His hand trembled as he put the match box back in his pocket.

"Waiting for someone?" Tracy asked mildly.

"Yes."

"Aren't you Allen Webb?"

He gave Tracy a hard, unpleasant look. "Who are you?"

"I'm Jerry Tracy of the *Planet*. I heard you were in town. You're a lawyer from Midport and your father used to own a newspaper. There are some mutual friends of ours at the Fair tonight—Harold Shipley and his daughter Barbara."

"Did Shipley tell you I was here?" Webb snapped.

"Yes."

"You're a liar! I don't know what you're snooping around me for. But I think I know who gave you the tip I was here. Was it Eric Lundy?"

"Right and wrong. Sit down."

"What do you mean, right and wrong?"

Webb was very pale. He sat down slowly in one of the padded reception chairs and Tracy dropped into a seat beside him.

"You're right about Eric Lundy, but wrong when you say you don't know why I'm bothering you. A man was murdered over in the exhibit area tonight. Are you interested?"

Webb took out a handkerchief and mopped his damp forehead.

"All right. I know that George Huston is dead. But I had nothing to do with killing him. I wasn't near the Babylonian Museum tonight until after the police arrived."

"We'll save time by sticking to the truth," Tracy said. "You met Barbara Shipley outside the building at least ten minutes before the murder was discovered. You made a quick sneak to the rear of the Museum and then I don't know where you went. Maybe you went into the garden."

"I didn't kill him," Webb said.

"Who are you waiting for here?"

"A girl I happen to know in the water show."

"What's her name?"

"None of your business."

"Okay. That makes it police business."

Tracy started to get to his feet. Webb wilted and grabbed him appealingly by the arm.

"Wait a minute. The girl I came to see used to know Huston. He gave her a dirty deal but she's still crazy about him. I wanted to see her alone and break the news of his death. I—"

A cheery voice sounded suddenly across the room.

"Hello, Jerry! What are you doing here tonight?

A very pretty blonde had entered the reception room through the swinging door that led to the dressing area. She wore a smart tailored suit and swung a glossy patent-leather bag from one of her grey-gloved hands. A perky little hat sat jauntily athwart her blonde curls.

Tracy smiled and beckoned her over. She was Marjorie Field, the girl for whom he had secured a job in the water ballet. He wished she had delayed her entrance a while.

But he got a surprise when Marjorie approached the chair where Webb sat partly screened by a potted palm. She stopped short. A strange look of wonder blanked her face.

"Allen Webb, of all people! This must be old home week at the fair!"

"You two know each other?" Tracy asked.

Then he realized the truth. Marjorie was the girl Allen Webb had come to see, the girl who was supposed to be crazy in love with the dead George Huston. He saw the truth of it in the pallor that spread over Webb's face and transferred itself to the staring girl. Marjorie either guessed that something was badly wrong, or knew it already. She was trying to hide sudden fright.

Before Webb could say anything Tracy cut in with a question.

"I knew when you came to me to get you a job that you were from out of town, but you didn't say where. Was it a town out in the middle west called Midport?"

"Yes. I thought you knew. Why?"

Marjorie had too much make-up around her eyes. The lids were pinkish and puffy under the cosmetics. She'd been crying.

But she didn't quiver when Tracy informed her curtly that George Huston was dead.

"I don't believe I know him," she managed to murmur.

"It's no use, Marjorie," Webb interposed with a resigned gesture. "I told Tracy you were nuts about Huston. He's been doing some questioning. He seems to think that I killed the guy."

"And you suggested that maybe I did?" Marjorie said harshly.

"Not at all," Webb protested. There was a sleek something in his voice that Tracy didn't quite like. "How could I make such an asinine suggestion? You have an alibi. You were swimming in the water show at the time the murder took place."

"That's quite correct," Marjorie said. The strained look in her eyes was suddenly deeper. "Do we have to talk about this here? Jerry, I thought you were my friend? Are you trying to trap me, or something? Am I supposed to be under suspicion of murder?"

"I don't quite know what you're supposed to be," Tracy said slowly. He felt discomfited and unhappy at the turn things had taken. He had come to the Aquacade to get a line from Marjorie on the identity of the mystery girl in the Babylonian garden. Now it looked as if Marjorie herself might be the fugitive in the swim suit! He wished grimly that he had made a clean breast of the whole murder set-up to Inspector Fitzgerald. By trying to hold back and solve it alone, he had gotten himself in over his head.

"Maybe we better eliminate you at once by proving you took part in the final water show," he told Marjorie. "Can you prove it?"

"I don't know what you mean."

"I'd like to look at your bathing suit."

"This is a damned outrage," Webb spluttered. "You'll do nothing of the kind. Who the hell do you think you are—the detective bureau?"

He sprang suddenly to his feet. He made an angry grab at Tracy and started to push him around. To Tracy, Webb's anger seemed phoney, an overdone act. Thoroughly sore, Tracy hauled off and clipped him in the stomach.

Before they could mix it up any further someone gasped a quick remonstrance from the doorway. A young man had entered from the exit corridor. He was a meek looking youngster about twenty-two with a thin, student face and timid eyes.

Marjorie recognized him with a cry of relief.

"Richard, make them stop. Please!"

Richard didn't look as if he could stop much of anything. He moved ineffectually between the two men, pushing awkwardly at them in an effort to avert further hostilities. Tracy ended the argument by turning his back on the fuming Webb and staring at the new arrival.

"Who's Richard?" he asked the girl. "Another of your boy friends from Midport?"

Marjorie was near tears but Tracy badgered her grimly. He hated to do it, but he wanted to shatter her poise.

He knew he had failed when Marjorie laughed. Her laughter was even and metallic.

"Richard is my brother. He studies at Columbia. He also owns a small car. Every night when the last show is over Richard drives out to the Fair to take me home. If you want proof of that, ask the doorman at the stage exit."

"I'd still like to have a look at your swim suit," Tracy said.

"All right. Why not?"

She turned abruptly toward the swinging door that shielded the dressing room. Tracy followed her. So did Webb and the girl's brother. Webb looked white around the lips. But Richard Field's face showed nothing more than dumb, uncomprehending wonder. Nobody had taken the trouble to explain a thing to him.

He kept saying shrilly: "Marjorie, what's the matter? For the love of Pete, what has happened?"

She didn't answer. With tight lips, she led the way toward her wardrobe locker. She flung the metal door open and handed Tracy her white silk swim suit. The suit was bone dry. So was the inside of the cape with Aquacade printed in bold black letters on its back.

"I thought you said you swam in the last show," Tracy said.

"Well?"

"This suit is dry."

"I didn't wear this suit."

"Where's the wet one that you did wear?"

Her voice was soft enough to melt butter.

"My regular suit got smudged in the show. After the last performance I turned it in to the wardrobe mistress for laundering."

"And where's the wardrobe mistress?"

"She's gone home," Marjorie said. "Would you like her telephone number? Or would you care to hunt for the wet suit in the laundry?"

Richard Field said plaintively, "What's all this about? What's my sister done?"

"She seems to be trying to get away with murder," Tracy snapped.

"*Murder?*"

"PAY NO ATTENTION to him, Dick," Marjorie said harshly. "He's talking through his hat."

"If I am, you ought to know," Tracy rejoined. "You were in the Babylonian Garden when my hat was yanked down over my ears. You were the one who lured George Huston there. Huston was playing around with you in Midport before he got ambitious and dumped you so he could get himself engaged to Barbara Shipley. What did you do? Send Huston a note? Warn him that if he didn't meet you tonight in the museum garden that you'd queer his wealthy marriage?"

"You don't have to talk," Allen Webb warned the girl quickly. "There's no legal reason why you have to pay the slightest attention to the ravings of a dirt columnist on the make for phoney news."

"I wasn't in the garden," Marjorie said.

Tracy stared at her set face.

"Then you better do a lot of quick explaining. The girl who saw Huston murdered was wearing a white silk swim suit and an Aquacade cape. When I chased her she was rattled enough to run around the garden pool instead of swimming across it. That was bad for her because a wet suit would have given her a perfect alibi. She wouldn't have to invent a phoney tale about a soiled suit and a missing wardrobe woman to explain how she could swim in the last Aquacade show and still have a dry swim suit in her dressing-room locker."

"Did you tell the police this nutty tale?" Webb asked.

Before Tracy could reply, the question was answered from an unexpected source.

"No, damn him! He didn't!"

The swinging door that led to the dressing room flew violently open. A man shoved into view. At sight of his tall, erect figure and the mane of snow-white hair, Jerry Tracy felt a twinge of dismay.

It was Inspector Fitzgerald and he was crimson with rage. He walked straight up to the *Daily Planet's* columnist and tapped him on the chest with a rigid forefinger. The tap rocked Tracy on his heels.

"What was the idea of lying to me?"

"Take it easy, Fitz. I didn't lie."

"You held back, didn't you? You never told me a damn word about a girl being at the scene of the murder. You kept your lying trap shut."

"I'm sorry. I had reasons."

"Reasons?" Fitz was mad clear through. "You're a double-crossing little louse! I've a good mind to toss you in the can as an accessory after the fact."

"Do as you please," Tracy said.

His own lips were white. He was in the wrong and he knew it. Fitz had always played fair with him and he with Fitz—up to tonight. It was a two-way gentleman's agreement, with mutual trust on both sides. The fact that Tracy had broken the agreement filled him with a bitter and illogical hatred of Fitz and his bull voice. All he could realize was that he had been pushed around from the moment he had arrived at the fair grounds. Now Fitz was doing the pushing!

Tracy could have broken the tension by a frank admission of

his mistake in judgment. He could have told Fitz how he had started the mess by trying to cover up the peculiar actions of Harold Shipley and his daughter Barbara. Fitz knew enough about the ramifications of newspaper business to understand, even if he didn't sympathize with, the efforts of a loyal columnist to protect from scandal an important business associate of the *Daily Planet's* owner.

But Tracy was as sore as Fitz.

"I held back because I didn't want you messing things up."

"That's fine." Fitz's tone dripped with sarcasm. "The little two-timer has a private clue! Do you mind telling a dumb old-line cop who killed Huston?"

"Solve your own cases!" Tracy flashed. "I'm through!"

Fitz blocked his lunge toward the door.

"Wait a minute! Where's your car parked?"

"In the west field at the Fountain Lake gate."

"Go over there and wait for me. Don't try to drive away if you've an ounce of sense left."

"Am I under arrest?"

"That's up to you."

Tracy hesitated. Fitz's heavy paw reached out leisurely and shoved Richard Field aside from his sister. Allen Webb moved protectingly in front of the girl.

"You can't do this," Webb said. "You've got no proof. I'll tie you up with a court order before morning. I'll have Marjorie out of custody and make you sorry that you ever—"

"Stand aside," Fitz grated, "or I'll hang one on your jaw."

Webb moved aside. Fitz's hand touched Marjorie's quivering arm.

"All right. Let's go."

He walked Marjorie down the corridor to the exit. A police runabout was parked outside. The arrest didn't attract very much attention. A few people stared as the car started, but the bulk of the late evening crowd were on the other side of Fountain Lake where the final firework's display was making the sky gay with an inferno of noise and color.

"Remember what I said about trying to leave the grounds!" Fitz yelled to Tracy.

The police car rolled swiftly away toward headquarters in the Administration Building's annex.

Richard Field looked like a man in a nightmare. He stumbled away in the wake of Fitz's dwindling tail light.

Webb didn't follow him. He turned to Tracy and there was mockery in his low tone.

"You're not kidding me with that stuff about Marjorie and her swimming suit. She had no more to do with Huston's death than I did."

"I didn't accuse you."

"No? You must have a damned short memory. I told you where to look if you want a solution of the murder."

"You mean Lundy?"

"Yes. Lundy's no ordinary two-bit politician. He has a big stake in controlling and profiting from the Midport underworld. He and Harold Shipley are hand in glove, in spite of the fake reform crusade that Shipley's newspaper had been bluffing about with George Huston as a special investigator. My guess is that Huston got out of hand and made himself a nuisance. So Huston's dead."

"And?"

"And Shipley and his daughter are back in the Waldorf,

protected by a sap who calls himself a newspaper man. Eric Lundy tosses you a fellow named Allen Webb and a poor little swimming girl—and you swallow the bait."

"Why didn't you tell Inspector Fitzgerald that?"

"I'm telling you."

"You're wasting a lot of time, aren't you?"

"What do you mean?"

"I thought you were in a hurry to get a legal writ to free Marjorie?"

"Maybe I've decided that it's better to let her remain in custody for the present."

He didn't explain the remark. With the air of a man with all the time in the world, Allen Webb struck a match and lit a cigarette. Tracy shrugged and left him. Webb was still standing outside the Aquacade Building the last Tracy saw of him, an erect figure jostled by the crowd that was beginning to drift toward the exits of the fair grounds. The last boom of the fireworks had finished. The amusement area was beginning to quiet down.

TRACY WENT TO the parking lot where he had left his sedan. There were still plenty of cars ranged in long dark rows under the sparse glitter of overhead lights. Tracy was glad of a quiet spot to sit down and think. His anger at Fitz had evaporated. He knew that he was in the wrong.

He located his car and tapped at the locked door to wake up Butch. Butch was Tracy's valet, handyman and bodyguard. A lop-eared ex-pug, he had the mind of a ten-year-old. Tracy had left him curled up in the rear seat of the sedan reading a comic magazine by the glow of the dome light. Butch preferred Popeye the Sailor to wandering around the Fair.

"I've seen this joint," he had told Tracy wearily, "and there's nothin' to it. Now if it was Coney Island, at least yuh could take in a real, honest-to-Gawd girl show where everythin' ain't so highbrow an' stuff. Me, I'll stick to Pop-eye."

He must have changed his mind. Tracy made sure the locked car was empty by lighting a match and peering into the dark interior. Butch was gone and with him were the keys of the car.

Tracy sat down on the running board and dropped his head in his hands. The more he thought about the mess into which he had dragged himself, the more he was convinced that he had the correct slant on Huston's murder. He was certain now that Marjorie was innocent! Not by reason of anything she had said or done, but because of a simple physical fact which Tracy had forgotten in the rush of circumstances that had followed the tragedy in the museum garden.

He felt suddenly weary. Raising his tired face, he lifted both arms and stretched.

"Don't move!" a voice warned. "Keep those hands up!"

The voice was a menacing whisper. It came from behind the shield of a white cape that shrouded the figure. All Tracy could see was the shadowy sheen of bare legs, a partial glimpse of a pale face under a rubber bathing cap. The dark red of rouged lips was the only spot of color in that frightened countenance.

Tracy didn't have to look at the back of the white cape to know what was spelled there.

"The Aquacade girl!" he breathed.

His eyes stayed on the gun. He remained very still. He was smart enough to realize from the gun's uneven wobble that this was no professional killer, but an amateur in crime. A wrong move on his part would snap the tension of his captor and send a bullet ripping into his belly.

"Take off your shoes and socks," the whisper warned.

The order puzzled Tracy but there was nothing to do but obey. Slowly he unlaced his shoes and removed his socks. The concrete felt cold and scratchy under his bare feet.

"I want your pants too!"

For an instant he hesitated. He tried to remember if he had picked up anything in that garden behind the Babylonian Building, something so trivial that it might have escaped his memory. He knew he hadn't. There was nothing in his trouser pockets except some small change and a handkerchief. What good would the theft of his pants do a murderer except to keep him from pursuing? He couldn't fathom the motive behind the holdup. The gun gestured fiercely. Reluctantly Tracy removed his pants and kicked them with a bare foot across the concrete toward his captor. In an instant the discarded trousers were snatched up. The figure turned and ran. The faint thud-thud of rubber-soled shoes vanished down a black aisle between the rows of darkened cars.

Tracy came out of his daze. He went racing after his foe with a yell that raised a wild echo in the darkness. He saw a vague blob of whiteness wiggle between two cars and cut sharply to the right. He pounded after the fugitive, wincing as his bare feet slapped against the hard pavement.

The crack of a pistol brought him to a quick halt. Almost before he saw the flash of the gun and heard the report, he was conscious of a buzzing past his hunched shoulder. Another bee whizzed over his ducking head as Jerry threw himself flat to the ground.

Rolling over, he saw the caped figure sprint out of sight on the side of the parking lot that faced the fair grounds. The gun was still in one of the fugitive's clenched hands, but the other hand was empty. She had hurled Tracy's pants away somewhere in the darkness.

By the time Tracy had regained his feet, footsteps were pounding toward him from an aisle in the rear. He thought he recognized the flat slap-slap of those soles. He yelled shrilly. "Butch! Is that you? Hurry up!"

It wasn't Butch. It was a tall, broad-shouldered guy with a voice like a file and a gun as big as a house.

"Don't move, punk, or I'll drop you!"

Tracy took one look at the Stetson hat and the bronzed, clean-shaven face under it. His heart quailed. It was the same rookie cop who had nabbed Tracy in the museum garden.

The cop didn't like Tracy. He had made what he had thought was a legitimate pinch in a big murder case. Tracy had made him look bad by having an in with Inspector Fitzgerald and talking himself out of trouble. Now this wise little Broadway sharpie was in a spot, the possibilities of which made the cop's eyes narrow with unpleasant satisfaction.

"So it's you again, eh? What's the latest alibi? Taking a little athletic run-around in your drawers because you're a fresh air fiend? Shooting off a gun to liven things up? Or are you just one of these eccentric guys?"

Tracy was mad enough to chew nails.

"Listen, dope! I haven't got a gun. I've been held up. A woman fired a couple of slugs at me. She—"

"A woman, eh?"

He twisted expert fingers in Tracy's collar and anchored him.

"What were you doing sitting around with a woman in your

underpants? Whose car were you in?"

"My own, blast you. And I wasn't in the car. I was on the running-board when she—"

"That's one for the book," the cop said with a nasty chuckle. "So you're the running-board type, eh? Okay, we'll find out about this."

He dragged his prisoner toward the lighted exit of the parking lot. Tracy hopped unevenly along beside him, caught in a grasp that felt like a steel vise. The uproar had attracted a lot of people. More were coming at every step.

Jerry Tracy looked like a fashion plate from the waist up and not so good from the waist down. In the privacy of his bedroom he had rather fancied the brilliantly striped silk shorts he had paid good money for in an exclusive Fifth Avenue shop. But in the cool darkness of a parking lot, gawked at by men, giggled at by women, those bright little panties were not exactly an asset to his dignity.

Tracy wasn't cold any longer. He was sweating with the realization that the most envied and successful scandal columnist in New York—the great Jerry Tracy of the *Daily Planet*—had been caught in public with his pants off! If anyone recognized him—

"Let go of me!" he whispered fiercely. "I tell you I was held up! I—"

The cop sounded smug. He raised his voice for the benefit of the crowd.

"Shut up and save it for the sergeant. Forget about the woman. In a sex case the man is all we want!"

There was an instant murmur from the crowd.

"A sex case!" someone whispered. It ran through the crowd

like a foaming rivulet. "Some guy got caught with his pants off in a parked car. A sex case!"

It was hard for the cop to shove a way toward the telephone he was heading for. A man ducked close to Tracy from the mob in front. He took one look at the cringing prisoner and then let out a wild yell.

"Hold him!" he told the cop. "I'll make the charge against him! The girl he lured here is my niece. Wait a minute, I've got the proof in my car!"

He dashed off like a maniac. The cop halted. Tracy tried to rip free. The cop clouted him. Tracy's face was the sickish green of overripe cheese. He had recognized the man who had darted away and was now racing back. It was Ed Mullhauser, an ace cameraman of the *Daily Star*. The editor of the Star had been gunning for Tracy for years.

It was no good yelling. In the uproar no one heard a word of what Tracy was shouting. They thought he was caught with the goods and making a desperate effort to break away from the law. When he tried to duck his face close to the cop's broad chest, Ed Mullhauser spoiled it with a warning bellow.

"Make him face me! He knows I can prove what he was up to!"

The cop obliged. Ed had a beautiful little candid job under the flap of his coat. He yanked it out and aimed with the skill of a man trained for spot news pictures. A bulb atop the camera made a brief blinding flash. The cop and every one else saw black for an instant. Then Ed took to his heels.

By the time the cop realized he had been foxed, Ed's car was out in Grand Central Parkway and heading at a nice clip toward the Triboro Bridge and Manhattan. Tracy didn't need a map to know that a swell photo of Tracy without pants, shoes or socks, held a fighting prisoner in the brawny grasp of a World's Fair cop, was on its arrow-swift way to the art department of the *Daily Star.*

He quit struggling. He was a frozen hunk of despair when Inspector Fitzgerald showed up a few minutes later and fixed him with a bleak, accusing eye.

"What the hell have you been doing?"

Tracy told him with shrill fury. For an instant Fitz looked thunderstruck. Then he frowned. A few curt words released Tracy from the grip of the disappointed cop. The crowd was shoved back. Fitz seemed to have forgotten his anger at Tracy's earlier behavior. He looked completely puzzled.

"What makes you think that this pants-stealing stunt gives Marjorie Field an alibi for the Huston kill?" Fitz said in answer to Tracy's excited cry.

"Because Marjorie is already in custody! She's under arrest."

"She isn't," Fitz said. "I released her almost at once. I got hold of the wardrobe mistress and the guy in charge of the Aquacade show. They proved the girl's story that she was in the last performance—the one that was going on while Huston was killed. So I released her."

Tracy stared at him, his mind grappling with this utterly unexpected development.

"Why should she steal your pants?" Fitz continued. "Were you holding back another clue from me?"

"No." Tracy's face was flushed, but his eyes were as steady as Fitz's. "I'm through holding back, Fitz. The only reason she took those pants was to keep me from chasing her."

"You know where she went?"

"No, I don't. But she didn't take my pants with her. She threw them away somewhere before she vanished. I think maybe I know how to find them."

"What do you mean?"

"We've got to find an unlocked car, or one with an open rumble." His eyes were a-gleam with sudden excitement. He forgot about his embarrassing lack of attire. With Fitz at his heels he darted in and out the rows of parked cars, hunting swiftly. The search didn't take long. There were not many cars with open rumbles. Tracy's search ended near the side of the lot that faced the fair grounds. Fitz watched him while he went methodically through the pockets of his trousers.

"Anything missing?"

"Not a thing."

"But why?" Fitz's face was blank.

"An alibi stunt that went wrong," Tracy said. "The hold-up was an attempt to give Marjorie Field an alibi. The killer thought she was in police custody. That's why the stunt was pulled. Marjorie's premature release spoiled a desperate trick to clear a gal who had nothing whatever to do with Huston's murder."

"I wonder if Barbara Shipley and her father went straight home to The Waldorf," Fitz said softly. "Did you see them leave the grounds?"

Tracy shook his head. "I told them they could get a taxicab at the gate."

Tracy was folding his pants up into a careful bundle.

"You're not figuring on fingerprints, are you?" Fitz asked doubtfully. "The chances of getting anything from cloth are remote."

Tracy smiled bleakly.

"I'm figuring on the *fear* of fingerprints," he said. "These trousers are light-weave mohair that might conceivably show a print. At any rate that's what the killer will think, I hope. I've got an idea."

His voice raced.

"Take the pants with you to the Administration Building. Have someone wrap 'em up carefully and make the bundle look damned official. Then get on the telephone and put a guard at every exit gate of the fair grounds."

"Who do you want picked up?"

"A bunch of damned visiting firemen from a Middle-West town called Midport. One of them is a slick, cold-as-ice politician named Eric Lundy. Be careful about him. He probably packs a gun. Another is a lawyer named Allen Webb. Then I'll want Marjorie Field and her brother Richard. They're probably hanging around here somewhere like a couple of scared rabbits."

"You know what you're doing?" Fitz asked briefly.

"Yes."

They stared at each other with steady eyes. Fitz was satisfied. He nodded.

"Okay. Gimme a description of Lundy and Webb. What about Shipley and his daughter?"

"They're probably back at the Waldorf by this time," Tracy said. "Send someone there with authority enough to yank 'em back here in a hurry. This time I'm on the level, Fitz. Give me a free hand—and I'll solve the case."

His grin and the taut pressure of his hand did something to the strained relations between these two old friends. Fitz swore, but he swore the right way, the smiling way. He seemed cheerful for the first time that evening. He was off like a shot.

BACK AT HIS parked car, Tracy was satisfied that Fitz would be able to gather in the Midport suspects before they could leave the grounds. It usually took considerable time for visitors to drift out after the last performance had been given in the amusement area. The industrial end of the fair was already wrapped in darkness and silence.

Tracy sat on the running-board of his locked car and waited for Butch. He wasn't sore any longer at the mess the big fellow had gotten him into by wandering off. Even Butch's wild burst of laughter when he'd seen the bare shanks of the natty little columnist didn't disturb Tracy's grim satisfaction.

He merely rose and asked Butch firmly for the loan of his pants.

Butch goggled, but didn't refuse. Nothing that Tracy ever did surprised Butch. He was loyal to the core. He'd have given Jerry his liver on a platter if the Little Guy had asked for it. And he was remorseful about wandering off just when Tracy had needed him.

Standing in cotton underpants, his big legs looking like mottled oak trees, Butch explained his absence. A nice-sized dame with a healthy bosom had given Butch the eye. They had gone to look over some of the amusement concessions and Butch had spent four dollars and a quarter on her.

"Then I took a chance and she slapped me in the snoot," Butch said without any particular emotion. "So I came back."

He grinned foolishly at his reclothed employer. Tracy had turned up the legs of his borrowed pants. He yanked the belt in to the last notch. It didn't help much. The *Daily Planet's* dapper little columnist looked like a pint-sized aviator who had bailed out of a plane and was fouled in his own parachute.

But there was no mirth in his frosty smile.

"Stay in the car and wait here for me," he told Butch. "Put the lap robe over those massive legs of yours. If your girl friend with the bosom saw you now, she'd probably give you back your four dollars and a quarter and make you a counter-proposition. It's a nice thought, but we've had enough girl trouble on one night!"

He crossed the bridge over the parkway and hurried through the silent darkness of the industrial area to the annex in the rear of the Administration Building.

Fitz was waiting grimly for him. Some of the guests for whom Tracy had asked had already been rounded up. There was a titter from the staring cops as Tracy waddled in, holding tightly to the bunched belt of Butch's oversize pants. A cold stare from Fitz cut the police merriment short.

Marjorie Field and her brother were there. They sat miserably together in a corner, holding frightened hands. Marjorie was crying. Her brother looked as if he'd like to. Eric Lundy was there, too, as sleek as butter, with a face as expressionless as a papered wall. He exhaled slow cigarette smoke and his eyes blinked briefly.

"I hope you know what you're doing, pal," he told Tracy pleasantly.

After a while a couple of cops brought in Allen Webb. Webb wasn't taking his detention so easily. He had put up a battle when his car was stopped at the north gate. His face was like a thundercloud. But he calmed down the minute he saw Lundy.

He seated himself without a word and glared at the politician. Lundy didn't seem to mind Webb's wordless scrutiny. He seemed half asleep, contemptuous of the whole proceedings.

LUNDY'S HEAD JERKED up when Tracy took the sealed package from Fitz and told his guests what was in the parcel. He did this after a very indignant Harold Shipley arrived, a half-hour later, from the Waldorf with his daughter Barbara. Shipley was fuming. He intended to go to the mayor in the morning and have the whole police force fired. He also intended to see to it that Jerry Tracy lost his job on the *Daily Planet.*

Barbara kept trying to shut up her father. She had little success until Tracy began talking about his mohair pants. He dwelt calmly on the fact that their closely woven texture made an excellent medium for the preservation of fingerprints.

There was sudden silence in the room. Marjorie Field stopped sniffling. Everybody stared at Tracy. He gave the package back to Inspector Fitzgerald and smiled faintly as the pants were locked up in a small safe.

"I don't think I'm going to need those trousers. I have two other methods of determining who killed George Huston tonight. But the prints will cinch it when those pants go to the crime laboratory in Brooklyn for chemical and fluorescent examination. In the meantime I've brought you people here because I'm in a hell of a hurry. I can't afford to wait for laboratory tests. I've got a personal itch of my own to scratch." There was a flush on his lean cheeks. "It so happens that I've got to find that killer damned fast. An afternoon picture tabloid that would like to see me crucified has a photo of me that's going to be splashed into front-page circulation in tomorrow's first edition. It's a nice flashlight pose of a famous little guy in his drawers, snapped just after he had an assignation with a woman in a parked car. I can't stop that picture from appearing with a neat libel proof caption that will blow me out of New York on a wave of dirty laughter. But I can top that picture with another! I can make the Star sorry they ever printed it, if I nail my killer *right now!*"

He nodded to Fitz.

"Let's go. I want every one of these people taken back to the amusement area. The boathouse, if you please, on the east shore of Fountain Lake. Directly opposite the place where the fireworks display took place this evening."

Fitz looked startled but he said nothing. He gave crisp orders. The six suspects were jammed into a waiting police car. Tracy stood on one running board. Fitz and a cop got on the other side.

Tracy smiled faintly as he noted that the cop was the rookie he didn't like. The car sped down Grand Central Parkway and reentered the fair grounds below the darkened magnificence of the Florida State Building. Everything was quiet now. The grounds were empty of spectators.

LEADING THE WAY to the boat house float on the shore of Fountain Lake, Tracy pointed to one of the rowboats moored there.

"Can you row?" he asked the cop.

"Yeah."

"Then take the oars. Get in, everybody."

Fitz was beginning to get restive. "Jerry, are you sure you know what you're—"

Obviously Tracy wasn't sure. He looked ill at ease and uncomfortable.

"It's got to be over on the other side," he muttered defensively. "It just has to! I'll admit that there's a link missing in the puzzle, an angle I can't figure out. It depends on something I'm trying like hell to remember."

Lundy laughed sardonically. The cop bent with a grunt to his oars. He was scornful of this alleged Broadway smart guy, sullen at the indignity of having to row a bunch of people across a lake on the screwy hunch of an amateur dick. The boat moved away from the float. Tracy sat with frowning brows watching the bubbles on the dark water. Suddenly he gave a quick cry.

"I've got it! By the lord, I remember it now!"

He sprang to his feet. The overloaded boat tilted. Tracy's inept movement had dipped one of the gunwales beneath the surface.

Water poured in on the startled passengers. Their quick backward lurch and Tracy's hasty attempt to regain his balance sent the boat careening in the opposite direction. It turned turtle, spilling everybody into the lake.

Luckily the float was not far away. Tracy swam to it and hauled himself out. He looked soaked and crestfallen.

Fitzgerald said thickly: "Of all the damfool stupidity—"

Shipley was livid with rage. He flopped onto the float like a fat, puffing turtle a moment after Webb and his daughter. Shipley didn't know many good oaths but he repeated all he knew, Lundy didn't waste words. He took a punch at Tracy's jaw that staggered the luckless columnist. He was hauled back on his heels by the dripping Fitz. In the confusion no one noticed that anyone was missing until Marjorie Field gave a shrill scream.

"Richard! My brother! Where is he?"

There was no sign of him or of the cop who had done the rowing. Suddenly the heads of both reappeared in a flurry of foam on the black water. The cop was struggling fiercely to free himself from the locked embrace of Field. Unable to swim, Field had clutched with both hands at the cop's neck and had dragged him down.

"They're drowning!" Marjorie screamed. "Help!"

But the cop helped himself. Before anyone could move to his aid, he managed to tear one of the drowning man's hands loose and to twist convulsively in the water. His fist caught Field in the jaw and snapped his head under the surface. Then with a lithe circling movement, the cop was safely behind his man. He caught him by the hair and towed him to the float with a half dozen powerful back strokes.

Field's eyes were closed. He looked nerveless and dead. Marjorie dropped to her knees beside her brother. But the cop pushed her gently away.

"I'll handle it," he said.

He gave Tracy a wet, angry look and then forgot him. He went to work on the half-drowned man, pressing rhythmically on chest and stomach, his soaked body astride the victim's stretched legs.

Tracy stepped back to where Fitz stood glowering. There was a tight smile on Tracy's lips. He leaned for an instant toward the inspector's ear. His whisper was barely audible. But it stiffened Fitz as if Tracy had just slugged him on the skull with a lead pipe.

Tracy didn't pause to note the inspector's reaction. With a quick whirl he was back at the spot where Richard Field lay.

"What this poor fellow needs is air," Tracy said in a clearly distinct voice. "Better let me remove his shirt—and his pants."

He leaned downward.

His clutch at Field's soaked shirt sent the buttons popping. It was a foolish thing to do, for it left Tracy's arched stomach vulnerable to attack from the man beneath him. Field's eyes flew open. He had only been shamming unconsciousness. His dripping legs hinged at the knees with a motion so quick that it was like a blur. The feet caught Tracy in the stomach. The impact sent him head over heels into a gasping huddle at the edge of the wooden float.

The next instant Field dived at the surprised cop who was still kneeling alongside him. A wet hand clutched at the police holster. The barrel of the captured gun sent the cop sprawling with blood dripping from a ragged gash on his forehead.

There was a hammering crash of gunfire as Field backed up. He was like a stiff carving of death behind the muzzle of the stolen gun. His sister was the only one who remained on her feet. The rest flung themselves flat at the roar of the bullets.

"Richard!" Marjorie screamed.

She was whimpering with horror. She began to run toward her slowly retreating brother, but Fitz kicked at her and sent her sprawling. He had drawn his gun only an instant after Tracy's warning whisper; but Field's attack had come so fast that Fitz was slow getting into action.

He fired from where he lay, one hand supporting his wrist and forearm. He missed. Field's answering bullet sent a long splinter tearing upward an inch from the prone inspector's cheek. The rip of the splinter and the roar of Fitz's second shot came along simultaneously.

Field dropped his gun and pivoted slowly, both hands clasped tightly over his belly. He sat down with a thud and went over backward. Fitz reached him in a couple of swift strides. He kicked the dropped gun into the lake.

"Looks like you were right, Jerry," he said pantingly.

Tracy didn't reply. A grim heave of his hand completed the ruin of Richard Field's torn shirt. It showed that he had been badly wounded. Blood poured from his abdomen from intestines ripped apart by a .38 slug.

But Fitz gave the bullet hole only a scant glance. On his limp body under his clothing, Richard Field was wearing a white silken bathing suit. From one of his coat pockets Tracy took out a rubber bathing cap. From the other he showed Fitz a metal-capped lipstick.

"I wasn't completely sure about him until the last moment," Tracy said harshly, "but you can see now how he could get away with his clever masquerade. His thin, youthful face and his hairless body made the trick an even gamble for him. Any smooth face under a tight rubber bathing cap is practically sexless.

"Field helped things along by using a lipstick. Rouged lips are the first thing you notice in a woman's face. A quick glimpse—and your mind works automatically. Your mind says 'woman,' and ninety-nine times out of a hundred you'd be right. Field counted on that and nearly got away with his deception. Remember, also, that the cape muffled his upper body and his head, and it was damned dark on the two occasions I saw him."

Field's eyes opened slowly. His eyes were like flickering coals in a face whiter than ash. He was dying and he knew it.

"All right and so what? I did it—and I'd do it again."

"Why did you kill Huston?"

"Because the skunk had it coming to him. There's a nameless kid in a baby farm out in Midport that belongs to my sister—and to George Huston. He told Marjorie he loved her and promised to marry her. She was foolish enough to believe him. Then Huston ducked when he made his tie-up with Shipley and got into big politics. He wanted to cap his political and social ambition by marrying Shipley's daughter. Well, he'll marry nobody now!"

Field's words trailed. Blood dribbled from his straining lips. His voice was fainter than the flutter of a feather.

"Marjorie—knew nothing of my—plan....I tried to save her the—Marjorie didn't know a single damned—"

That was all. He died with his glazed eyes trying to smile at his sister. With a moan Marjorie fainted.

BARBARA SHIPLEY STARED at the limp figure of the girl for an instant. Then she ran forward and pillowed Marjorie's head in her lap. Beside her, Allen Webb dropped to one knee, his arm around Barbara's shoulder. He kissed her. His eyes dared Shipley to utter a word.

Shipley kept quiet. So did Eric Lundy.

There was a strained look of relief in Lundy's pale blue eyes. Politics was all he was interested in. And politics, the inner circle brand of Midport, had nothing to do with Huston's death, after all. But Lundy's calm fingers were a bit tremulous as he fished out a soggy cigarette. He tried vainly to light it with a damp match. His foolishly persistent effort showed how nervous he really was under the mask of his relief. Tracy paid no attention to him.

"I thought first there were two people in the museum garden where Huston was killed," Tracy said. "A man and a woman. The sex guess of a woman was merely a deduction on my part. But the man's fist on my jaw was real! Afterwards I remembered something that made me think a man was the only foe I had to deal with. I never actually saw anything but the cloaked figure that jumped the hedge into obscurity before I was socked. When I went down with my hat jammed over my eyes, I heard only *one pair* of feet run away."

Tracy's voice continued grimly.

"I eliminated Shipley because of his girth and his age. It could have been Lundy, or Webb or Field. I figured on Field after the second attack in the parking area. There was no sense to that holdup unless it was done deliberately to give his suspected sister an alibi. Whoever attacked me and stole my pants to keep me from chasing him, thought that Marjorie was in police custody and wanted to clear her of suspicion by a second appearance.

"Who cared enough about Marjorie to take that desperate risk of capture? Lundy? He's a cold-gutted louse who loves no one but himself. Webb? His only thought was of Barbara. It could only be Marjorie's neurotic, soft-spoken, girlish-faced brother."

"Why the boat upset?" Fitz asked.

"Because the fleeing murderer I almost caught in the garden where Huston was killed—couldn't swim! Otherwise there'd have been no race around the long end of the garden pool.

Richard Field took that long way to the garden exit because he didn't dare risk a dive across the pool! Proving, if he had only thought about it, that it completely exonerated his sister who swims like a fish in the Aquacade show."

Tracy's voice sounded tired.

"The second clue that I was pretty certain of was the silken swim suit itself. It was a tough disguise to get away with in the lighted thoroughfares of the fair. Field had to make a quick change after he left me dazed in the garden back of the museum. He also had to change quickly both before and after he attacked me again in the parking area. There was only one way a man could do that so damned fast—by wearing the swim suit under his own clothes."

"I guess that's all," Fitz nodded.

"The hell it is," Tracy growled.

His eyes were suddenly bright. The baffled, unpleasant look that had characterized him all evening was gone. This was the old Jerry Tracy, the hard-shelled, quizzical, nasal-toned little Broadway columnist who had endeared himself to Fitz by a thousand past favors, He quivered as he clutched smilingly at Fitz's wet sleeve. He was like a lean, sawed-off hound eager to slip the leash and race away at top speed.

"Quick! Can you get me a motorcycle escort to help me break the speed record into Manhattan?"

"What's the idea?"

"It's about a picture," Tracy snapped, his face agleam with a smile as thin as a razor blade. "A photograph that a certain dirty-minded evening paper is going to print in tomorrow's first edition. I want the *Star* to print it! I want that artistic shot of me with my pants off to appear all over town. But I want a chance for the *Daily Planet* to print one, too! There's going to be a lot of laughter in New York tomorrow—and it's going to shrink the circulation of the *Star* to zero."

Fitz said, "Huh?"

"I've got a date to pose for the *Planet's* art department. Jerry Tracy with his pants off! I'll write the caption myself. When it comes to nailing a murderer, Jerry Tracy never misses, if he has to strip to his drawers! The *Star* will wish to God they had never tried to frame me with a fake scandal photo and some nasty innuendo. They'll be on the newsstands fifteen minutes before we release our first edition. Before they can recall the issue they'll be sold out—in more ways than one!"

Tracy raced shoreward across the boathouse float. His voice drifted back as crisp as the crack of a whip.

"Have your motorcycle cops pick up my car at the main gate of the grounds. I'll be travelling fast! And, Fitz, while you're at it, see if you can dig up some pants for Butch—stylish stout!"

Fitz smiled grimly as he turned toward the paunchy Harold Shipley. The Midport publisher squealed. He was a shade too slow backing away.

My Candle Burns

*The strange death pose of a fabulous glamour
girl sets Jerry Tracy on a Blue Book kill*

JERRY TRACY LOOKED toughest when he was at his weakest ebb of sales resistance. Tonight he looked meaner than the law allows. His eyebrows were cocked crookedly. His mouth had a sour, southeast twist. When he replied occasionally to Butch's eager babble, he sounded like a discontented frog. Actually, Jerry was enjoying Butch's excitement.

They were on their way to the Garden to watch a featherweight leather-pusher named Harry Bendetto. Bendetto was in the first prelim bout. He was five feet ten, thin as a shad and twice as bony. The length of his jaw made the experienced Tracy wince in advance. But Harry Bendetto had one supreme virtue.

He was Butch's latest ring discovery.

Butch was always uncovering lunks like that. As soon as one of them kissed the canvas, Butch popped up blithely with another. With Butch, hope always triumphed over experience. Tonight was no exception. Butch was wearing his niftiest Garden ensemble: a fawn-colored coat, with a peak cap to match; the toes of his ox-blood shoes looked as if they had mumps.

"Jerry, I'm tipping you! Bet your shoit on this lad! He can't miss, not with that brand-new one-two I loined him. Your right comes up fast, see? Then your left hoils itself into de opponent's mush—"

Tracy backed hastily as Butch halted on the sidewalk and went into an elephantine dance, with both fists stabbing ferociously.

"If Bendetto tries a stance like that, somebody is going to light a cannon cracker in his belly," Tracy said somberly.

"Aw, nuts. You ain't getting what I mean. You're already leaning in close, see? You—brrrp!"

The *Daily Planet's* dapper little columnist recoiled.

"It musta been the onions," Butch said. "With me, they should never soive onions with hamboigers. Anyway—"

"Any way you serve 'em, they're terrible! Come on!" Tracy grabbed Butch by the arm and hurried him along.

Because Tracy was walking on the outside, he missed the full brunt of the collision when the man in the velour hat

bounced headlong into Butch. As it was, the impact shoved Tracy violently to the curb where he teetered wrathfully with one foot up and one foot down.

The man had darted swiftly out of an alley. He was twice as startled as Butch. He made no apologies. His left hand grabbed Butch by the necktie and for an instant the two scuffled awkwardly together. The man in the velour hat tried to toss Butch out of his way. Butch was too heavy to be tossed. He misunderstood what was going on. He thought that the well dressed man was trying to pull a stick-up.

Butch tore loose and ruined a sixty-nine cent tie. If he'd

thrown a quick, blind punch he might have knocked his panting foe kicking. But Butch was too eager to try out Harry Bendetto's brand-new one-two. He went into a massive crouch. Both hands flew up and one of them cocked backward.

The stranger lit the cannon cracker Tracy had predicted. It exploded in the pit of Butch's belly. His mouth flew open. He went down in an aura of stale onions.

The whole thing happened while Jerry Tracy was still doing his balancing act on the curbstone. The instinct to avenge Butch started him into battle. But common sense put on the brakes. Tracy was a little guy. He wasn't exactly yellow, but he did his best fighting when he was backed in a corner. He realized instantly that the man in the velour hat knew how to box!

Tracy ducked prudently away and allowed the guy to scram. The fellow raced up to the corner and jumped into a parked car. It looked like a Lincoln Zypher. In a moment the car and Paul Voisin were gone with the wind.

That's who the guy was—no doubt about it! He had tried to shield his face during the brief brawl. But Tracy had seen the long, supercilious nose, the tiny mustache, the iron-gray Toscaninni hair at the edges of the velour hat. The hat came from France. So did Paul Voisin.

His lineage was proud. He could trace his ancestry to an illegitimate son of one of the early French kings. In New York he was quite a café celeb. Not the place where there was always a table reserved for Jerry Tracy; Voisin's hangouts were the ones where the *Daily Planet's* ace scandal columnist would be ejected deftly on sight.

Tracy wondered what this Paul Voisin was doing tearing out

of a dark apartment house alley in so desperate a hurry. He scented scandal. A glance at the ornate front of the apartment building increased Tracy's hunch. He forgot about Paul Voisin and began to think about Linda Payton. Tracy hadn't shoveled any ermine dirt for a long time. Little goose-pimple shivers of anticipation went up and down his spine.

Linda Payton lived in that swanky building. Daughter of Cass Payton of Greenwich, Connecticut. Heiress to copper tubing and brass pipe in peace time, shell casings and armor plate in war. Betrothed to the elegant Paul and all set to move to a château on the Loire. The marriage contract signed, the dowry all arranged.

And the elegant Paul pulling a desperate sneak from a service alley!

Nobody had seen the swift encounter. Tracy leaped to where Butch was staggering to his feet. It was dark at the head of the alley. Tracy began pushing Butch out of sight.

"The punk didn't hoit me none," Butch mumbled. "I musta tripped. Did he get your watch?"

"No. And keep your big mouth shut!"

"Hey, cut out the pushin'! Ain't we going to the Garden?"

"You're going into the nearest ash-can if you don't stop that yapping!" Tracy whispered.

The basement door of the apartment building was closed but not locked. Tracy tiptoed cautiously toward a corridor angle from which he could see the rear elevator. The service car was at the basement level. There was no sign of the operator.

Tracy was not surprised. He knew that even in expensive joints like this economy ruled the night shift. Deliveries were spasmodic after six P.M. The furnace man or the porter doubled in the service car whenever the night button was pushed. Tracy tiptoed back and got Butch.

They rode the empty car to the third floor and left it there. They climbed the rest of the way up the staircase that boxed in the shaft. Tracy didn't need a guide book to tell him on what floor Linda Payton lived. He had tried to interview her several times.

Tonight Tracy had a magic password. All he had to do was to announce that he intended to print a squib concerning Paul Voisin's peculiar sneak via the cellar and alley. Tracy was sure that Voisin had sneaked *in* as well as out. Had the French play boy arrived by the front door, he would have had to leave the same way. An unseen departure would have made it look embarrassingly as if the elegant Paul had spent a pre-nuptial night with his intended bride.

Tracy grinned as he climbed the stairs.

Linda Payton was Grade A copy, even without dirt. Six years ago she had been America's most publicized glamour deb. Her father had hired most of the Waldorf-Astoria for elbow room when he had presented Linda to society. Linda's mother was dead; and up to that time Cass Payton had been too busy lining up his second billion to bother much with his daughter. He made up for that after her debut. Linda did everything, went everywhere. Her travels and escapades kept the society pages dramatic during the Depression.

But six years had worn Linda's glamour pretty thin. According to rumor, she was bored, blasé and unhappy. It was no longer fun to throw a drunken party at Pierre's to help the unemployed. Linda hadn't got tight since the night she had quoted Nietzsche and made a half-hearted attempt at suicide.

Night spots never saw her any more. She began to fancy herself as a serious poetess and had one or two volumes printed at her own expense. Her betrothal to Paul Voisin was her father's doings. Linda didn't love Paul; but it was a socially correct alliance and a château in the Loire valley would please Papa.

All this made a peculiar background for Paul Voisin's sneak act—to say nothing of his attempt to knock Butch and Jerry cold before they could recognize him.

Linda's service door wasn't locked. It wasn't even closed! Jerry Tracy widened the crack a little and peered.

The kitchen was empty. There was Scotch and soda and a bottle of sherry on a side table. A silver tray of appetizers was ready to serve. From the warming compartment of an enormous gas range came the savory odor of a cooked dinner. But there was no sign of a servant.

Tracy hesitated, wondering where the maid was. Then he saw two objects that made him remember suddenly that tonight was Thursday. Folded neatly over the back of a chair was a frilly lace apron no bigger than a man's pocket handkerchief. On the table, near the pearl onions and the celery, lay an open cookbook.

The maid's night out, of course! A tête-à-tête dinner for Paul Voisin to celebrate the approaching marriage. But why had the sleek Frenchman lammed out so stealthily? And why was Linda so damned quiet in the dining-room?

She didn't look up when Tracy stared at her lovely back from the doorway. Her back was bare from her neck almost to the base of her spine in a superb evening gown. She was seated in a chair, leaning over the table. Her gaze was concentrated on a small wine stain that marred the snowy cloth.

She was stone dead.

"Jeez a'mighty!" Butch gasped.

Tracy whirled. His face was white, his eyes like hard pellets.

"Get back to the kitchen! Shut the door and lock it! Don't make any noise. And stay there!"

Linda's dead face was contorted. But her hands were the most horrible thing about her. They were clenched close together, fist against fist, clutching something that couldn't be seen. The outside of each joined fist had been seared by flame. Peering with infinite caution, Jerry Tracy could see the blackened ends of two candle wicks.

The lighted wicks had burned closer and closer to Linda's dead fists until the searing of her own flesh had quenched the twin flames.

Linda Payton had died, burning a candle at both ends!

She had swallowed poison. Tracy thought about cyanide. He had seen cyanide deaths before. There was no way to prove it from the contents of the glass which Linda had drained. The bouquet of the dry sherry almost covered the fainter odor of bitter almonds.

No wonder Paul Voisin had fled! Linda had played a ghastly trick on him. She had invited him over for a cute tête-à-tête dinner—so that Voisin's arrival would point up her final dramatic exit from a stale life and a loveless marriage. Linda always liked the dramatic touch, the spectacular fadeout. It was like her, too, to pick a famous tag line from a first-rate poet:

> "My candle burns at both ends,
> It will not last the night.... "

Voisin, a realistic Frenchman, had taken one look and fled to keep his civilized name out of a mess. It fitted perfectly except for an annoying oddity. Why had the elegant Paul taken the cellar route to attend a private dinner cooked by his promised bride? Certainly not because Linda had warned him she was committing suicide! Voisin would be unwilling to stick his patrician nose smack into the middle of a coroner's inquest just to oblige the theatrical desire of his late intended!

JERRY TRACY WALKED around the table. He sniffed at the other glass, the empty one. There was no cyanide odor. The glass was as clean as a whistle. But when Tracy tilted it, using a napkin, he discovered a faint discoloration on the fragile surface of the table. Somebody had washed the glass and put it back wet. The maid, who had set the table for two before she had departed? Hardly! Voisin? Less chance than that!

"Maybe the murderer?" Tracy whispered aloud.

Murder suddenly seemed a lot more logical than suicide. The candle act didn't match up with the cyanide swallowing. Tracy had once seen a desperate little chorine take the cyanide exit. The stuff was not instantaneous; nor easy, either. It tied you into agonized knots. Linda would never have been able to hold on to that double-lighted candle.

Someone might have arranged the suicide prop after she had died! The same someone who had poisoned the inside of two empty glasses and had hastily washed out the other later.

Tracy's reaction to this slant was prompt. He darted across the room to the phone and called the managing editor's desk at the *Daily Planet*. He was trembling with eagerness. The story was so big that Tracy temporized in order to regain control of his voice.

"Mike, what have you got on the front page that's good? I'll match you for it!"

"No use, Jerry. We're loaded and ready to roll. We're after a cop killer tonight! Somebody bumped a motorcycle cop up near the city line. Battered his head to bloody paste. The mayor's up there now. So's the commissioner, We're heading a city-wide crusade to nab a cop killer. Top that, Jerry, or don't bother me!"

"How would you like me to kill Linda Payton?"

"Swell. But you'd better hire yourself a good lawyer beforehand. Old Cass Payton would just about—" The chuckle faded from Mike's voice. He caught the nervousness in Tracy's tone on the wire. "Jerry, wait a minute! You're not—"

"She's dead, Mike! Linda Payton. Violently. You should see her hands. Clean out the front page and leave a hole for some nice horror pix."

"Cripes!"

Tracy could hear Mike yelling fiercely to somebody. Then the voice was a whiplash on the wire again.

"How did she get it? Where is she?"

"In her own apartment. Cyanide. I just found her."

"Suicide? By Gawd, she tried the Dutch act less than a year ago."

"The set-up suggests suicide, Mike. But my guess makes it murder."

"Don't guess, damn it! Make sure! What about the police?"

"Out of it so far. Better call Headquarters after I hang up. We'd never get away with a stall on *this* one. Try to contact Inspector Fitzgerald. Fitz is our boy. He'll give the *Planet* a break."

"O.K. Here's your rewrite!"

Tracy shot the stuff in a swift, nasal monotone. He didn't mention Paul Voisin. In a murder set-up Voison was the most logical suspect. Too logical! Tracy decided to hold back about the Frenchman. He was never a guy to crawl out on a limb until he knew how far down the ground was.

"Keep it the old 'found dead in her apartment from cyanide poisoning'," he snapped, "Play up the candle. Run Millay's poem in a big box. Don't mention suicide. Let the customers take that for granted from the layout. If it turns out to be murder, we can switch and be the only sheet in town to call it right. Hold on for some more in about three minutes!"

Tracy prowled around the dining-room, his sharp eyes missing no detail. He examined the sideboard and china closet. He looked at the rug and all the chairs. Dropping to sharply creased knees, he lifted the lacy banquet cloth and peered under the table. He found nothing that added to the picture.

Linda Payton remained frozenly indifferent. Tracy's gaze kept jerking back to her in spite of his absorbed hunt for some added trifle that might point toward murder. It was hard to think of Linda as dead, even with her face twisted and stony. She had ebony-black hair and skin like cream. Her slumped pose was the only awkward note. Murder or suicide, Linda had made a superb exit.

The apartment was not a large one. Tracy didn't waste much time discovering that the dining-room, bedroom, bath and maid's quarters weren't going to be any help.

In the pantry broom closet, however, Tracy found a peculiar bit of carelessness. Somebody had upset a bottle of cedar oil, the stuff used to polish furniture. It had a strong, pungent odor.

It smelled like fresh sawdust. That was why Tracy had halted on his way to the kitchen to jerk open the closet door. He wondered why the fallen bottle hadn't been replaced upright. Everything else was neatly arranged. Had somebody ducked in or out of the closet in a hell of a hurry? Out, probably! Otherwise the person who had kicked the bottle over wouldn't have left it lying that way.

Frowning, Tracy went into the kitchen and found Butch cheerful and relaxed. Butch had the top off a bottle of pearl onions and was spearing them rapidly with a silver fork. Butch had opened the Scotch, too. It made a perfect combination. The onions made Butch thirsty; the Scotch made him hungry again. He was doing all right.

"Wanna poil, Jerry? I shouldn't be eatin' them, though. Onions always retoin on me. They—*brrrp!*"

Tracy said, "——!" in a vicious undertone. He capped the jar, and hauled Butch away from the Scotch.

"Listen, you blasted manhole cover! I want you to—"

He stopped talking suddenly and froze into rigid silence. A click came from the front of the apartment. It sounded like a door closing—the front door! Silence followed. Then feet began to move stealthily, heading inward toward the dining-room.

Tracy's heart did a frightened somersault. The man—those footfalls certainly sounded masculine—had reached the dining-room. He must already be staring at the glamorous corpse of Linda Payton. Yet not a sound came from him. Either he had magnificent self-control, or he *expected* to find death!

Tracy could think of a million reasons why the smart thing was to wait in the kitchen and see what happened. But Butch ruined that.

"Hey!" he growled. "Lemme take him!"

He shoved Tracy aside and raced thumping through the pantry.

"Look out for a gun!" Tracy shrilled.

He was just a step behind Butch when they burst into the dining-room. The man was across the table from Linda. There was no gun in his hand and scarcely any expression in his cold eyes. He uttered no cry. But he moved like chain lightning.

"Git back, Jerry!" Butch panted.

Butch's big fists came up, the left fiddling, the right cocked. He started his invincible one-two.

A fist flashed under his upraised hands. The impact against his belly sounded like somebody whacking a carpet on a clothes line. Butch went down and Tracy backed up.

He took a glancing blow in the ribs. A right hook grazed his jaw and almost tore his ear off. Tracy ducked desperately away and managed to get both hands on a heavy flower vase at his elbow. He shoved it like a spear at his foe's face, pushing him back. Then the vase lifted and came down.

Tracy found himself suddenly a little sick at his stomach, clutching a hunk of broken vase in his bleeding fingers. It wasn't much of a cut. Neither was the gash on the fallen man's scalp. The fellow was still conscious, but badly dazed. He was a young man with pale blue eyes and tight, curly hair, the color of hemp. There was something vaguely familiar about his wide mouth and drum-tight cheek-bones. The bronzed skin made Tracy think about brown rotogravure.

Suddenly he remembered. "You're Richard Druse!"

The blue eyes cleared and focused. The young man got up slowly. Tracy's hand tightened on his jagged weapon, but he didn't have to use it. The smack on the skull had taken the fight out of Druse.

"Who are you?" he said thickly.

Tracy told him succinctly. Druse looked scared at the mention of the *Daily Planet*. He didn't say anything. On the floor behind them, Butch was swaying to his knees, making hiccupping noises. He got no attention from either man.

"How did you get in here so neatly, Druse? Your own key?"

"None of your damned business."

"You're not acting very smart." And Tracy explained why, in a nasty tone, with special reference to the newspaper business and his own nationally syndicated column. It did the trick. Druse swallowed with a click like a billiard ball.

"Did you expect to find Linda dead?"

"My Gawd, no!"

"Yet you didn't make any outcry. Do you usually take the death of a girl you're in love with so calmly?"

Druse didn't resent Tracy's deliberate baiting. His face was flushed, but he held his temper in check.

"I was stunned."

"So stunned that I had to bust you over the head with a vase to keep you from doing wholesale mayhem?"

"I didn't realize you were newspaper men. I thought—"

"You thought maybe we had killed Linda?"

"Nobody killed Linda. She committed suicide."

"You expected her suicide?"

"No, I didn't. But I should have guessed it from her note. I—I thought up till now that it referred to something else."

"Let's see the note."

"Why?"

"It seemed two different things to you. It might seem a third to me. Murder, for instance!"

Richard Druse didn't lash out with his fist. But the effort of self-control drained even his lips of blood. He spoke in a monotone.

"Listen, you cheap, stinking, little garbage vender! Linda is not to be dragged through the dirty pages of your rotten tabloid, do you hear? She quit life gallantly by her own hand, for a reason you wouldn't understand. If you try to twist Linda's life, or her death, into something vulgar and mean to build up your moron circulation, I'll kill you!"

It was raw hate, distilled to a barely audible murmur. Tracy gave no sign that it scared him. He continued to watch his man narrowly.

This Richard Druse had been Linda's last stab at romantic love before her formal betrothal to Paul Voisin. Druse didn't have a dime. He was younger than Linda, a fairly recent college graduate who had never quite caught on. He was a neighbor of Linda's father in Connecticut, on the wrong side of the ridge. He did odd jobs on trees and bushes and called himself a scientific horticulturist.

Linda had really had quite a case on him. It was enough to pull her away from the night-club set, but not enough to make her want to ditch her fabulous inheritance for an honest, cotton-underwear marriage. Cass Payton had read the riot act to Linda. After that Paul Voisin took over, and the lawyers and genealogists stitched up the deal.

Tracy was itching to get hold of Linda's note. Druse's involuntary gesture told him it was in Druse's pocket. But he changed the subject.

"Have you any idea whom Linda invited for dinner tonight?"

"Of course. She invited me."

"Then what was Paul Voisin doing here?"

It was a bull's-eye. It knocked Druse off his pins. He quivered as if Tracy had slapped him. But he said nothing.

Tracy gave Butch a barely perceptible nod. Butch had shaken off the effects of the belly punch and had moved close to Druse. He moved closer.

Tracy kept talking about Voisin. He told about the Frenchman's peculiar method of arrival and departure. Druse listened rigidly, his pale blue eyes like blank stones.

"Take him!" Tracy yelled suddenly.

Druse's fist swung an instant too late. Butch anchored him in a bear hug that yanked him off his feet. The two men pitched to the floor in a writhing tangle. It was primitive stuff—knees and elbows and teeth. Butch was too busy to remember his scientific one-two. Druse's heels drummed spasmodically on the floor under Butch's gutter treatment.

Tracy's lean fingers poked into the mêlée. He jerked a small envelope from Druse's pocket. He opened it and read the folded note:

"Dear Ricky:

I have burned the candle at both ends—and I find the game is not worth the candle. I've decided on a clean break. I want you to know it first. Will you come to dinner with me Thursday night? There'll be no servants present—for reasons you'll understand after you arrive.

Linda."

Dismay flooded Tracy as he read the note. It knocked the props out from under his murder theory. And yet....

He started to read it again.

POLICE PUT AN end to that. They came boiling in through the unlatched front door of the apartment. There were yells and some prompt thumping action. Butch was hauled off the struggling Druse. He was jammed into a chair so hard that one of its legs cracked. Druse was pinned against the wall by another cop. The note was snatched out of Tracy's hand.

It was a lot like a Grade B crook picture.

Tracy was sure the picture was Grade B when he recognized the face of the inspector in charge of the wrecking crew. He had expected Inspector Fitzgerald. His heart sank as he saw Dominick Carlson. Carlson was making more noise than anybody. His red, beefsteak face was less than two inches from Tracy's.

"What's the idea, punk? Trying to mess things for that comic rag of yours?"

"If I have police news, I'll tell it to Fitz."

"You tell it to me, damn you! What was the idea of phoning your paper before you called Headquarters?"

"It's a strange journalistic custom," Tracy snapped.

"Yeah? For two cents I'll play stick-ball with that skull of yours! You can tell *that* to Fitzgerald, too!"

Carlson was Fitz's assistant. City politics, the backroom kind, had moved him close to the top. According to rumor, Carlson was being groomed to replace Fitz. No fool, Fitz had tried to make things tough for Carlson. Tracy had helped the counter-attack along with his column. He couldn't prove that

Carlson was a crook. But he could—and did—show up the assistant inspector's consistent stupidity in every case he tackled. It made for a nice gut-hating set-up between them.

Carlson's own men quieted the noise. Butch gave up the struggle to go to Tracy's side to protect him. A sock on the jaw convinced Druse that he had no further chance to attack Tracy. Carlson quit roaring. His squad got to work.

Druse told a meek, plausible story to the police. He hadn't realized Linda's intention to kill herself when he had received her note. Druse knew Linda loved him; but he knew, too, that Linda had decided to obey her father's wishes and marry Voisin. To Druse the "clean break," the "want you to know it first" had meant only one thing: A dismally gallant last toast to the ashes of their love. He couldn't face it. He had walked around for hours before he could make up his mind at last to come. That was why he'd been late.

He said nothing whatever about Paul Voisin's strange behavior. It puzzled Tracy why Druse held that back after Tracy had gone to the trouble to tell him. Tracy decided to keep his mouth shut, too, until he could see Fitz.

The note to Druse and the girl's dramatic symbolism with the double-lighted candle tied in neatly with the single poisoned glass. Inspector Carlson grunted and waved a fat, bored hand.

"Plain and simple suicide!"

Jerry Tracy laughed curtly. Carlson's ears reddened at the jeering sound.

"What's so damn funny?"

"It's not plain," Tracy said, "and far from simple. You say it's suicide. The *Daily Planet* says it's murder."

"For instance?"

"For instance, the other glass. Why was it washed out? To remove poison? Druse says he misunderstood the note. Maybe a murderer counted on that. A suicide pact would have been twice as good from the murderer's point of view. But Druse was late and Linda poured herself a sherry while she was waiting. So the murderer had to change his plans. He washed out the extra glass to fit the altered picture."

"Nuts! The maid washed the glass before she left."

"And left it wet to discolor the table? Maids don't do tricks like that in this sort of society."

"Oh, so you're in society now! Tell that joke to your Broadway stooges over at Lindy's. I'm too busy to laugh."

Tracy kept his temper.

"All right, laugh these off, too! The service door wide open. A bottle of cedar oil upset in an otherwise neatly arranged pantry closet. The knobs of that closet door were wiped by somebody, or I'll eat that soup-stained tie of yours!"

"Any more deductions, Philo?"

"Sure. Linda could have lit that candle at both ends, but she never could have held on to it. Not with cyanide chewing at the inside of her belly! The murderer did that stunt to fit in with the note."

Carlson turned promptly toward Richard Druse. "Did anyone besides you ever see the note?"

"No. I can't prove it, but it's God's truth. I showed that note to no one."

He stared at Tracy, rather than the inspector. Druse was not lying, Tracy decided swiftly. Whatever else had happened, Druse was honestly convinced that no one but himself had ever laid eyes on Linda's message. How then could any murderer know enough to add that final convincing suicide touch? Jerry's dismay showed in his face. It was enough to spark Carlson into action.

"Out!" he roared. "You and that flat-footed floogie of yours! Toss the pair of them out of here!"

"Who's a floogie?" Butch growled.

He didn't get a chance to argue that point. He and Jerry were bum-rushed to the corridor. The front door slammed. Butch was all for breaking down the door to go back for a little rebuttal on the argument. But Tracy grabbed him by the arm with a grip that made Butch squeal. He hurried him to the elevator and down to the street.

Butch had seen the Little Guy hot under the collar many times, but never any hotter than this. Tracy headed straight for a drug-store and slammed himself into a phone booth. He called the *Daily Planet*. He was fit to be tied.

So was the *Planet's* managing editor!

"Why'd you hang up? What goes on, anyway? I called back the apartment and Carlson told me to fly a kite."

"Why the hell didn't you get Fitzgerald as I told you?"

"I tried to. Fitz wasn't at Headquarters. They've put him in charge of that blasted motorcycle cop murder. You'll have to soft-soap Carlson somehow. Don't let the dirty son throw you."

"He already did," Tracy howled wrathfully over the wire. "I'm out on the street with a toe-mark on my behind! Carlson doesn't want any *Daily Planet* advice. He says the thing is suicide."

"Is it?"

"Mike, that thing smells funny to me. It's murder!"

"What have you got?"

Tracy told him. Mike snorted.

"Too risky a guess. We'd only be sticking our necks out."

"My neck, not yours! Run it under my by-line, just as I've told you. You know how to copper bets like that. Let the main *Planet* story handle the facts and the color. Play up my murder theory as a feature Jerry Tracy article. Lay into Inspector Carlson with both feet. Remind the public how Carlson came up with a handful of nothing on the last three cases he tackled. If I'm right, we'll laugh that pot-bellied political hack off the force. We'll do Fitz and ourselves plenty good!"

"Are you sure about your slant, Jerry?"

"Have I ever missed a big one?"

"No, but...."

"Then roll those presses!"

Tracy hung up, feeling tight and triumphant. He didn't realize what a spot he had let himself in for until he began to cool down. He cooled fast. The *Planet* was in the clear no matter which way the cat jumped. But what about Jerry Tracy?

His white face and blazing eyes scared Butch.

"Is anything wrong, keed?"

"Yeah. I've just burned my britches behind me. If Carlson's dumb guess turns out correct after all, I'm due to have some bare skin burned."

A taxi was rolling aimlessly along the avenue. Tracy shoved two fingers in his mouth and stopped the cab with an ear-splitting whistle. He and Butch took a quick ride to Tracy's garage.

Ten minutes later they were in Tracy's car, heading for the city line.

THE TRIP TO Connecticut was based on trigger-quick

thinking. Carlson's first official move would be to phone Linda's old man and get him into town for a formal identification. Suicide is always an ugly fact in any family. Cass Payton would fight the idea. Tracy's hope was to nail the millionaire on the way into town and sell him a murder. If Tracy could plant a few seeds of doubt in Cass Payton's mind, it might stymie Inspector Carlson's easy suicide solution. No New York cop would dare to give a tycoon like Payton the run-around. Through Payton, Tracy could force Carlson to do his dirty work—in short, to get busy on Tracy's own murder angle.

Tracy headed for the Hutchinson River Parkway, speeding as fast as he dared. The parkway was Cass Payton's natural route to the city. It was pretty dark, and Payton would be driving into town at a terrific clip; but Tracy wasn't worried about the problem of identifying and halting the millionaire's big foreign-made car. He knew the parkway like a book. He had already decided on the exact stretch of road where he intended to pull off his nervy job of deception.

He avoided cops as if they were the plague; but he ran into quite a bunch of them near the city line. They were huddled at the side of the highway on the lonely stretch between the Boston Post Road and Eastchester Road. Tracy bit off an oath as he saw the white-thatched head of Inspector Fitzgerald in the bright glow of a police torch.

This was evidently the spot where somebody had clubbed in the skull of a motorcycle cop—an unlucky nuisance that had pulled Fitz away from Headquarters just in time to mess up Tracy's whole evening with the dumb and antagonistic Carlson.

Ordinarily Tracy would have halted and poured out his troubles to Fitz. But recognition was the last thing he wanted now. He hunched low over the wheel and eased quickly past. Fitz was too busy to swing his head around. Tracy sighed with relief as he hummed over the city line into alien territory.

He increased his speed. Butch was fascinated by the climb of the speedometer needle.

"Hey, some time kin I let the boat out like that?"

His eyes popped at Tracy's savage rejoinder.

"That's why I've got you here, dope! Your turn comes on the way back. I want you to trail me into town in case I need the car again. You'll probably have to do a hell of a lot better than I'm doing—just to keep Payton's chauffeur in sight."

"Jeez, Jerry, thanks! You're a pal!"

Presently the little columnist slowed down. He curved off the side of the Connecticut highway to keep out of the way of traffic. The road at this spot ran as straight at a die. It climbed gradually to a distant rise, fully two or three miles off. Tracy kept his engine throbbing. He watched distant headlights pop into view over the crest, estimated their speed as they grew larger in the darkness.

There weren't many to watch. Traffic was sparse. But every time twin lights glared, Tracy quivered. He was as nervous as a man on the verge of suicide—which wasn't too remote a possibility, at that!

When the car he was waiting for showed at last, Tracy knew it in a second and a half. It whizzed over the black crest of the distant hill with a violence that bounced its bright beams skyward. The lights were all that Tracy could see. They grew fast!

Tracy straddled his own car on the center line of the road. It was a narrow enough stretch to make that a damned dangerous thing to do. Tracy's bright lights glared into those onrushing eyes. He took his hands off the wheel and grabbed Butch's arm to keep himself from swerving his car away. They both sat tight—and terrified.

It was like facing a streamlined express on a cleared track.

But the guy driving that other car wasn't feeling happy, either! His hurricane speed slackened as the power went off. He swerved left, realized he couldn't pass without risking the ditch—and then his brakes went on.

They screamed for a nerve-racking century that was probably thirty seconds. Tracy's guts were tied in small, tight knots. But there was no collision. That chauffeur knew how to handle a boat! This one looked like an ocean liner. It skidded sideways to an abrupt stop a couple of feet away. Its tires smelled like a fire in a rubber factory. Tracy was out in the road before the chauffeur could swallow his tonsils and yell a frightened foreign oath. The car was foreign, too. Tracy recognized it. Cass Payton was in the back seat with a woman.

Tracy flung up his palm briefly and let the cupped badge do his talking. It was an honorary deputy sheriff's badge, one of the ornamental gee-gaws of official favor that Tracy always carried. The quick flash made it look like a plain-clothes detective's shield. Payton thought so, anyway. The *Planet's* granite-faced columnist didn't correct him.

He slammed into the back seat and made Payton and the woman move over.

"Sorry. Orders!" Tracy said vaguely. "I wanted you to hear the facts about Linda's death on the way in."

"You might have killed us all, officer!"

He didn't reply. He was a little sore that Payton hadn't recognized him. Jerry didn't want to be recognized—but after all, he *was* Jerry Tracy! His sour expression helped the deception along.

The car got swiftly under way. Butch trailed in Tracy's car. Tracy went into a careful song and dance, leading delicately to the subject of murder. Payton jumped at the word as if he had been shot.

"Murder? That's idiotic!"

The woman beside him looked startled, too. But she made no comment. She continued to soothe Payton with the quiet pressure of her hand on his arm. The millionaire's face was ghastly.

"Perhaps it might be better to let this detective explain the basis of his theory," the woman said gently.

"But, Martha, I've known too long—and you have, too—how unhappy and depressed Linda was. She made one unhappy attempt...."

"I know. Try not to think about it."

Tracy had been studying the woman's profile. She was probably five or six years younger than Cass Payton. Her voice was nice. No longer young, she was still handsome, with dark hazel eyes and a clear outdoor skin. She suggested beagle hunts and station wagons. When Payton called her Martha, the *Daily Planet's* omniscient columnist guessed who she was.

Martha Nixon. Payton's nearest Connecticut neighbor. Not in the Payton money bracket, but socially a notch or two above it. Tracy had heard rumors of Payton's growing interest in this somewhat aloof Miss Nixon. A crusty widower for years, Payton had shown signs of remarriage. Tracy had never been able to verify it for his column. Now, however, he was certain.

The shock of his daughter's death had battered down Payton's defenses. His eyes gave him away. Martha Nixon's, too.

Mentally, Tracy filed away a marriage notice for a later column.

He told them some of his suspicions concerning the suicide set-up in Linda's apartment. He didn't mention Paul Voisin. But he did speak of Richard Druse and the latter's late arrival for Linda's last and tragic tête-à-tête dinner.

Payton growled at the mention of Druse. But it was contempt rather than anger. To Payton, Druse was obviously a cardboard nonentity, a penniless, good-looking nuisance. He dismissed Tracy's murder suspicion as fantastic nonsense.

"I don't want any police sensation made out of this," he muttered thickly. "I'm satisfied that Linda took her own life. She was terribly neurotic. If she had—waited, had only trusted to my judgment!" His harsh voice broke.

Martha Nixon patted his clenched hand. "Try not to think about it, dear."

"No. Let me talk, please! I wanted Linda to marry Voisin. It would've been a perfect marriage, but I couldn't make Linda see it. She signed the marriage contract just to please me. I knew that. But I thought—well, what does it matter now what I thought? Linda is dead by her own hand! And Paul, who is a civilized gentleman, has been drawn into an unfortunate mess through no fault of mine or his."

Tracy clucked sympathetically. But he shot in a couple of innocent questions about the elegant Monsieur Voisin. He learned that Paul was sitting pretty financially, regardless of the tragedy. Voisin had stipulated in the contract that he should receive the full dowry, even if the marriage failed to take place.

The only bar was moral turpitude or misstatements about his family or social position.

It was something to think about. But Tracy had more immediate things to worry him. Having failed to shake Payton's certainty of suicide, Tracy was anxious to get away from the millionaire's car before his fake role of plainclothes cop was revealed.

He didn't get a chance for a discreet sneak. At the city line two motorcycle cops were waiting to provide a fast escort into town for the bereaved father. Both of them knew Tracy. So he huddled back in the darkness of the rear seat, cursing his luck.

HIS LUCK, HAVING changed, ran out fast. When Payton's limousine halted finally in front of Linda's apartment house, the first face Tracy saw was the red, ugly phiz of Inspector Carlson! Carlson had come downstairs to interview the doorman. He stepped respectfully to the curb and assisted Cass Payton and Martha Nixon to alight.

There was nothing for Tracy to do but to get out, too.

Carlson went speechless with fury as he saw the dapper little scandal columnist of the *Daily Planet*. He made up for the delay when the yell finally burst from his fat throat.

"Why, you damned little rat! I told you to get out of this case and stay out! What the hell are you doing in that car? Has he been bothering you. Mr. Payton?"

"Bothering me? Isn't he a police detective? Didn't you send him out to question me?"

"Now wait a minute," Tracy began.

Carlson grabbed him by the neck. "Detective, hell! This little sewer rat is Jerry Tracy! I threw him out when he tried to twist a suicide case into a sensational murder yarn for that gutter sheet of his. Too bad, Tracy! I've been waiting for a break like this. Impersonating a police officer is a criminal offense. I'm going to drop-kick your tail into a cell."

"Did I tell you that I was a police officer?" Tracy asked Cass Payton.

"No, but—" Payton choked wrathfully. "You showed me a police badge!"

"I showed you this."

Tracy twisted in Carlson's grasp and yanked out his special deputy's badge.

"I told Payton nothing. He did all the talking. I can't help it if he made a bum guess. But I can help it if you're stupid enough to toss me in a cell. You're as wide open as usual, Carlson. Pull up your zipper!"

Martha Nixon intervened with a worried murmur. News photographers were shoving through the crowd. Payton and Miss Nixon retreated hurriedly into the apartment house. With a gulp of rage Carlson flung Tracy spinning. He followed Payton.

Butch was parked discreetly half a block away in Tracy's car.

"You should've given Carlson the one-two," Butch growled.

"Shut up and get going!"

"Where to?"

Tracy told him. Butch grinned with cold anticipation as the big car hummed along at a fast clip.

"Swell! I gotta bone to pick with this Wahsang guy. Lemme handle him for yuh. The guy must be a crook, with that alias of his!"

"Alias? What are you talking about?"

"Mush Ear. Ain't that what you called him? Mush Ear Wahsang."

Tracy chuckled. He lost some of his tension.

"You stay in the car. I'll take care of Mush Ear."

Monsieur Voisin lived in an impressive building in a very impressive neighborhood. But Tracy had no trouble getting past the hired help. Quite the contrary. The mere mention of his name eased him up swiftly in an onyx and gold elevator. Mr. Tracy was expected. But definitely!

Voisin himself opened the door. He was all alone. He looked amiable and very continental in a Japanese house-robe, knotted neatly over dinner clothes. But there was nothing French about his talk. That was pure American.

"How much?"

"How much what?"

Voisin shrugged. The waxed mustache ends lifted sardonically.

"Apples. Marbles. Whatever you want to call it. I expected you, of course. I was awkward enough to cause you some annoyance when I bumped into you earlier this evening. For that minor annoyance I am prepared to pay."

His cool effrontery annoyed Tracy. "This isn't France, boy friend. Over here the newspaper racket is dirty, but honest."

"How about five thousand? Dollars, naturally. Not francs."

"Did Linda send for you tonight, or did you sneak in through the cellar on your own hook?"

"Let's not haggle on the price. Ten thousand!"

"Linda might have called off the marriage," Tracy rasped, "and you bumped her to get the dough in a hurry. Either that, or there was something you were afraid might queer the legal payoff of the marriage contract. Payton let drop the fact that you collect whether you do the altar walk or not. There's a rotten egg somewhere in the nest! I can smell it, even if I can't locate it."

Voisin lost his amused composure. He was a big man but very light on his feet. Tracy ducked backward, and they glowered warily at each other. The silence magnified the sound of a key in the front door. Tracy suspected a planned ruse and kept his eyes on Voisin. But one glance told him the Frenchman was as rattled as he was by the unexpected visitor. Voisin's face went white, then a fiery red.

"You know better than this, Julie! Get out!"

Julie came in. Her laughter was softly indulgent.

"No need for you to look so stern, Paul. I'ave need of a small amount of money." She consulted a soiled slip of paper in her gloved hand. "Feety-five dollars and twenty cent."

She was a lot Frenchier than Voisin. She had the overlarge eyes, the small chin, the dusky pallor of the Parisienne. Tracy guessed that Julie's bosom would match her eyes. He chalked up a win as she languidly divested herself of her furred wrap. Julie was amused by Tracy's frankly slanting gaze.

Voisin spat something in French.

"Silly!" Julie said. "The taxi is waiting downstairs. Please pay him or he will not go 'way. Who is this cute little man? Has he never seen a woman before?"

Tracy's heart began to beat fast. Fifty-five twenty was a hell of a big taxi bill! Voisin's rage had plenty of fear in it. Voisin tried to shut Julie up by fumbling fiercely under his dressing robe for his billfold. Julie wasn't entirely at ease either. She was breathing a little too fast. She was afraid of Voisin, but she was trying not to let on.

"You must like taxi riding," Tracy told her. "Where did you go—Connecticut?"

The abrupt question startled them both.

"You will say nothing Julie," Voisin snapped. "I command it! Go into my bedroom and close the door."

"Doe she have a key to that, too?" Tracy ask dryly.

Voisin cursed. He was obviously itching to get downstairs and get rid of the taxi driver. But he was afraid to leave Tracy alone with Julie. Tracy tried to upset the girl's cool composure by a bold question about her personal relationship with Voisin. All it got him was a puzzled smile.

"But, of course! We have mutual living, naturally. Why else would Paul maintain me?"

"Be quiet!" Paul hissed. "This man is of the newspapers!"

"Is he then shocked because I am your mistress? But how droll! You go pay my bill, no? I will discuss life with this amusing little man. He is funnee! I theenk I like him."

A quick look passed between the two. Voisin hurried from the apartment. Tracy started after him, but Julie stopped that.

She had an unexpectedly strong grip. Her hands, Tracy discovered, matched her large eyes, too. There was nothing soft about them. He was wrist-yanked over to the couch. Julie plumped down beside him, still holding.

He tried, not too fiercely, to free himself. The struggle toppled them over sideways on the couch. Julie giggled.

"Ah no, M'sieu! That ees not nice!"

But she didn't let go. She flung a leg across Tracy to help anchor him, a very nice leg. Tracy was amazed at her savage strength. He was also amazed at his growing reluctance to escape. It took will power to keep thinking about that taxicab downstairs.

Suddenly Tracy began to laugh. He ducked his head and kissed Julie. He made it convincing enough for her to let go of one of his hands. The moment he got the hand free, he violated one of the Marquis of Queensbury rules. Julie recoiled with a shocked squeal.

Tracy bounded off the couch and raced from the apartment, his face red.

He didn't bother waiting for the elevator. He went down the fire stairs with reckless, thumping leaps. When he reached the sidewalk there was no sign of Julie's taxicab. Or of Paul Voisin.

Or Butch, either!

BUTCH'S IDIOTIC DISAPPEARANCE with Tracy's car made the *Daily Planet's* angry columnist madder than a hornet. He tried to find out something about it from the doorman. But the lad in the admiral's uniform was vaguer than a fog. He had a smug, a ten-dollar grin on his face.

There was a parked taxi up the street. Tracy headed for it on the run. Here he had better luck. The hackman was a company driver from one of the big fleets. He had seen the other cab race away and he was pretty sore about it. It had almost sliced off his fender. What's more, it was a damn Independent! He began to orate profanely on the subject of owner-driven taxis.

Tracy calmed him with five bucks.

"Did you get the bum's number?"

"I sure did!"

He fished into the pocket of his sheepskin coat and pulled out a crumpled hunk of paper.

"I figured I'd prob'ly run into the louse later on somewhere, and I wanted to make sure I'd get the right guy. So I wrote down his license. Believe you me, mister, I'll show him a couple of traffic tricks that will scorch his tool chest. I'll hook his engine out from under his hood!"

"Did you see anything of a fat-headed lug with big ears, driving an expensive private job?" Tracy asked.

But the cabbie hadn't seen Butch.

"I jist got here a few minutes ago, see? I'm jist hardly parked when this Independent hacker scoots off like I told you. Somebody from the apartment handed him a big, juicy bunch of bills—and the guy whoops off like an Indian. Believe you me, mister, I—"

Tracy didn't wait to hear any more. He had copied down the license number of the cabby who had driven Julie somewhere to the tune of fifty-five twenty. To Tracy it sounded like Connecticut.

He walked down the avenue, his eyes peeled for some sign of the truant Butch. But his thoughts remained grimly on that sexy gal friend of Paul Voisin's. He remembered her strong, sinewy hands, the tigerish way she had pinioned him on the couch. Julie hadn't wanted Tracy to find out where she had been, any more than Voisin had.

For the second time during this frustrated evening Tracy felt himself stabbed with an electric shock of blind certainty. It was better than a clue or a deduction. It was a Grade A hunch!

He thought about another murder—one that couldn't possibly be a suicide! He considered anew the case of the mortorcycle cop who had been bumped on a lonely stretch of highway near the city line. When Tracy had first learned about the cop killing, it had been merely something to sweep off the front page to make room for the Linda Payton case. Now he was ablaze with the instinctive feeling that there was a definite connection between the two tragedies.

If Julie had made a swift journey to Connecticut, she must have traversed that lonely stretch where the cop's skull had been battered to bloody paste by a halted motorist. Tracy had hitherto taken it for granted that the killer was a man. But a woman desperate with fear could have done the job just as easily. More easily! A cop, leaning forward to write out a summons for speeding, would have no suspicion of peril. A wrench over the skull would drop him in a heap at the edge of the road. Then a flurry of silken legs, a woman bending over the inert victim, smashing, battering....

If Julie's Connecticut trip was linked somehow with the "suicide" of Linda Payton, she'd be afraid to let that cop stay alive! His testimony later on might place Julie in a spot where she dared not allow her identity to be established.

It sounded like feeble motivation for a savage murder, but Tracy was convinced he was on the right track. Julie had just about time enough to poison Linda and dash up to Connecticut and back. But would she kill a cop under the eyes of a hired cab driver? Even if the guy was paid off later, Julie was sticking her neck into some nasty blackmail. And why was Voisin so thunderstruck when she showed up at his apartment to borrow money for the cab bill? Hadn't Voisin known where she had gone?

Tracy was so grimly absorbed with his whys and wherefores that he didn't hear the whine of an automobile racing along the curb behind him. His only warning was the staccato crashing of bullets. He felt his hat jump from his head. A hot wind tugged at the cloth peak of his tailored shoulder. Then he was down on his face, scrabbling desperately to flatten himself closer to the sidewalk.

In Tracy's frightened brain was the confused blur of a fast-moving shadowy car out of which orange streaks had stabbed with hammer-like concussions. He rolled over as he heard the car race for the next corner. It took the turn in a dry skid, rubber shrieking. Tracy was too shaken up to identify the dark, faceless blob hunched over the wheel. But the car itself was easily distinguishable as it vanished down the side street. It was a Ford V8.

Tracy didn't remember picking up his lost hat. The thing was in his hand somehow, as he ran onward toward the corner. He could feel the bunched felt, and a small, warmish hole under his fingertip. He kept thinking perversely about the hat. He had paid a lot for it. The brim had just suited him....

He almost ran headlong into a man as he raced around the corner. The man was panting. He could hardly talk.

"What happened?" he gasped. "I heard shooting and—"

He was a young man, with pale blue eyes and tight, curly hair, the color of hemp. Tracy looked past him. He saw a car parked midway down the street, its engine quietly purring. It was a Ford V8. The sight of the car and the pale, breathless face of Richard Druse made Tracy want to grab him by the neck. But he didn't. He got as cold as ice inside. He uttered a brief, metallic laugh that hurt his throat.

"Next time aim lower! You might have better luck."

"You're crazy," Druse said faintly.

"That's your Ford, isn't it?"

"So what? I had just parked it there when the other guy zoomed past. He had a Ford, too. They're not exactly an exclusive make. Maybe the guy was in the low-price group, like me."

Druse was losing some of his tension. Tracy stayed tight.

"I don't suppose you saw the guy's face?"

"No. I was just stepping out of my car when I heard the shots. He went past my back like a whirlwind."

"What were you doing around here?"

"None of your damn business."

Tracy shoved abruptly past Druse. He walked to the parked car, leaned in, pawed through it quickly for a gun. He found none. Druse watched him alertly until Tracy turned.

"Mind if I do a little pocket patting?" Tracy rasped.

"You lay your dirty paws on me and I'll pat you to death!"

They glowered at each other. Then Druse suddenly changed his tactics. He made a small, apologetic sound and his face twisted into a grin.

"This is damn silly! We ought to be teaming up instead of scrapping. Aren't we both after the same thing?"

"What are *you* after?"

"I'm not sure—maybe Paul Voisin. What you told me about him back in Linda's apartment stuck in my mind, you see. If you noticed, I didn't tell Inspector Carlson about Voisin's presence in the apartment, or his peculiar method of getting in and out."

"Are you on the murder side now?"

"I don't know. I came over here to interview Voisin and see what I could find out. I'm willing to cooperate with you, so long as we keep one thing clear between us."

"What's that?"

"Linda. If you honestly believe that Linda was murdered, I'll back you to the limit. But if you're deliberately twisting a suicide into a fake murder for the sake of building up a *Daily Planet* sensation—" Druse's shaking voice steadied into a whisper that was more ominous than if he had yelled. "Then I'll most certainly kill you!"

"Your idea is that this bullet hole in my hat is a circulation build-up?"

Druse's creased lips exposed his teeth. "The hat is why I'm proposing an armistice."

Tracy didn't trust this curly-headed guy with the bleak eyes. But he conquered the impulse to get away from him and hunt up Butch. God only knew where Butch had driven the Tracy car! And there was a scrap of paper with a taxi license on it that was burning a hole in Tracy's pocket. Tracy shrugged and stepped into Druse's Ford.

"O.K. Drive me to the nearest phone booth. After that, I may have a little something on *Monsieur* Voisin and his girl friend."

"Girl friend?"

"Didn't you know he has a mistress?"

"Hell, no! Are you sure?"

Druse wanted to talk about it, but a horn, sounding like the muted baying of an ocean liner, made Tracy jerk his head out the Ford window. He cursed with exasperated relief. Butch was beckoning with a pleased and guilty smile from the Tracy chariot.

"Hi yuh, keed!"

"Where the hell have you been?"

"Now, look, Jerry. Don't git sore! What I done was a perfectly yooman thing. This here dame had red hair and—"

"And a size 42 bust," Tracy growled.

Well, she wasn't exactly an ironing-board, Butch admitted.

He had coughed and the dame had stopped to admire the boat. Butch took her for an easy two-mile swing around town. Just to show her how smooth the boat worked.

"I told her I was Rockefeller's head chauffeur. We got a date for tomorrow night. She slapped me on the puss, but I don't think she meant it. Anyhow, I'll find out about that tomorrow night. I mean, if you're not busy, and don't mind lettin' me borrow the boat."

Tracy made a helpless gesture of rage. He and Druse crossed over and got in the roomier car.

"Drive, lunkhead! Find me the nearest drug-store."

IT TOOK TRACY a deal of telephoning to run down the license number of the hacker who had carried Julie. The fact that the motor vehicle bureau was closed for the night made it harder. But after some urgent cross talk and a switch to another number, a duplicate record file was turned up and Tracy's hot eyes quieted down.

His man sounded like a Greek. George Metaxas. He owned his cab and lived in Ozone Park, over in Queens. Butch speeded things up after a covert glance at the strained faces of his two passengers. The car skimmed over the Queensboro Bridge and made nice time along Queens Boulevard.

Tracy told Druse a few of the things in his mind, but not all. When Tracy swayed sideways he could feel a gun lump in Druse's pocket. There wasn't any especial warmth to it, but there had been plenty of time for a hot weapon to cool.

The house of George Metaxas was like all its neighbors on a dark, tree-lined street. Square ugly eggs, laid by a cheap realty company. Complete, with weedy lawns, sagging porches and a twenty-year mortgage plan.

Butch remained at the corner with the car. Tracy and Druse headed through the Metaxas weeds. The house was as dark as the grounds. Tracy had taken it for granted that the hacker had headed straight home after his payoff by Voisin. Now he wondered if the swift trip to Queens had been a waste of time. The damned Greek might have decided to spend Voisin's dough in some Manhattan bar and grill.

Tracy went around the side and tried the garage door. It was locked. Druse climbed the porch and rang the bell.

The door was opened with savage suddenness by a man with a gun. Druse squealed and flung himself backwards. He collided with Tracy, and the two of them rolled headlong down the porch steps.

The man with the gun cleared the porch with a single leap. He crouched over his victims, almost invisible in the blackness.

"Don't move, you ——, or I'll blast your guts!"

He seemed to have his mob with him. They leaped from behind bushes and shrubs. One of them crawled from underneath the porch. Another raced around the house from the rear door.

An electric torch made a blinding white oval of light on the prisoners.

Somebody said, "Damn it!" in a bellow of rage. It was a foghorn voice that Tracy recognized with a cold spasm of wonder.

He whispered tremulously, "Fitz?"

More lights flashed. The front yard of the hack driver's home began to look like the aurora borealis. None of the cops was in uniform.

Inspector Fitzgerald was twice as stupefied as Tracy. He stood staring at the columnist, his face like a hunk of weathered granite. He had tousled white hair and narrow, stooped shoulders. Inspector Fitzgerald was close to the retirement age. But there was nothing feeble about him or his gun.

"What the hell are *you* doing here?"

Tracy told him very meekly. He identified Richard Druse. He explained the wild hunch that had led them innocently into a baited police trap. Fitz uttered an oath of disgust.

"I thought I had a pair of cop killers! Well, my scheme is all nicely shot now. Turn on some house lights, Kennedy! We're through for tonight, it looks like."

Fitz's exasperation faded. He and Tracy were old friends. Tracy had cooperated many times on criminal problems that had brought exclusive scoops to Tracy's column and official prestige to Fitz. It was an ideal arrangement. Tracy didn't mind Fitz taking the credit. All Jerry ever wanted was the inside news before anyone else.

"We're hunting two different animals," Fitzgerald said.

"I think you're wrong. I think it's the same animal!"

"Why?"

"The more I keep chasing this Linda Payton suicide, the more I run into that motorcycle cop's bump. Don't you think it's damn queer that you and I start on two different cases— then ram heads together like this?"

"Coincidence."

But the idea interested Fitz. He found out about the hackman from the summons book of the cop whose head had been bashed in. It was the last entry in the book. The charge was speeding.

"Metaxas is in the clear," Fitz said. "If he or his fare had killed the cop, they certainly wouldn't have left that summons stub intact. They'd have ripped it out of the book! No, Jerry, the guy that killed the cop did it before the summons was written out. Maybe right after Metaxas was waved on, and drove this French dame to Payton's home. That's why I used the Greek as bait. I publicized the fact over the radio that Metaxas had lingered and caught a glimpse of the killing; then got scared and stepped on the gas. I figured the killer might get jittery and try to rub out a possible eye-witness. And all I get is— nuts!"

"Don't you think it's queer that Paul Voisin's mistress should be in such a hurry to get to Cass Payton's home on the very night his daughter is supposed to do the Dutch act?"

"I didn't *know* that the woman in the cab was Voisin's mistress. How did *you* find out that Metaxas drove her to Payton's home?"

"You just told me," Tracy said. "Bring that Greek out here! I want to talk to him."

Metaxas was a hammered-down little man with dark, liquid eyes and a face like rice pudding. He was sweating profusely. He didn't look like a murder accessory, or even a blackmailer. He admitted that Paul Voisin had tipped him plenty to keep his mouth shut concerning the excursion with Julie. But he insisted that the motorcycle cop had been alive and healthy the last he had seen of him after the ticket episode.

"A woman couldn't have done the kill anyway," Fitz said sourly.

"This woman could! She's as strong as a tigress. When she took a grip on my wrists back at Voisin's apartment, she left them black and blue. If Julie happened to have a wrench in her hand—"

"Listen, mister—" the hackman began.

Tracy ignored him.

"All she had to do was to let the cop lean over to write the ticket. Before he got his pencil to the paper, she let him have one over the skull. He went down dazed. She sprang out and battered his head in. You know that stretch of road, Fitz; it's as lonely as hell."

The hackman finally interrupted.

"You guys are nuts! I keep telling you the dame didn't do nothing! She just sat there and I took the ticket. She told me she'd pay the speed fine later, and that's why this feller later on gave me the century extra. Hell, would I take a chance on the electric chair for a hundred bucks?"

"Skip the cop murder," Fitzgerald told Tracy irritably. "That's my job! Yours is the Payton suicide. Why should Julie kill Linda?"

"Easy. Julie has a nice arrangement with Voisin. His marriage would queer that."

"Why should it? The way you described Voisin, he'd just carry on with his left hand, anyway. Julie's game wouldn't be to kill Linda. If she went to Payton, it was to tell him that she was Voisin's mistress so she could block the marriage. But why should she kill the cop?"

"Maybe she was afraid Voisin might discover—"

"Hell! Julie asked him to pay her cab bill!"

Tracy flushed. It did sound fishy, even to him. Fitz's ire was rising. "Look, Jerry! You don't often go wrong, but when you do, you smell. You haven't got a thing except a lot crazy guesswork."

"Do you call Voisin's guilty sneak from the alley guesswork? And what about the open service door? What about the wine glass that somebody washed out and put back wet on the table?"

Tracy's own gorge was rising. Fitzgerald's mocking smile made him think of the fat-headed Carlson. He mentioned the bottle of cedar oil polish that had been upset in an otherwise spick and span pantry closet.

"Whoever killed Linda got there in time to poison the inner surface of both wine glasses, Fitz. But not in time to get away. Linda showed up unexpectedly—or something. Anyway the killer was trapped in the pantry closet. Couldn't get out until Linda got tired of waiting for Druse and took her fatal drink. The killer had planned to make it look like a suicide pact between Linda and Druse. Druse's late arrival ruined that. So the killer washed out the other glass and—"

"I told you once before," Fitz growled, "that when you're bad, you smell! There can't be a murder, if the murderer didn't read that 'burning candle' note from Linda to Druse. And Druse says he showed it to no one at all."

"That's one fact I can swear is true," Druse said quietly.

If he'd shouted, Tracy might have held on to a ray of hope for his tottering murder edifice. But there was complete sincerity in Druse's low tone.

"Go on home to bed," Fitzgerald said. "You're tired."

Tracy was silent for a moment, looking forlorn and beaten. Then his slumped shoulders lifted. The stubborn look came back into his bleak eyes. He spoke quietly to George Metaxas. "Got a phone in your house?"

"Yeah."

Tracy went inside. A fat woman in a flannel nightgown was

holding a swarthy little Metaxas on her hip. The child was crying and the woman was trying to placate it with a chunk of buttered rye bread. The cop on duty looked bored. He didn't interfere with Tracy's use of the telephone.

Tracy called the apartment of Paul Voisin. Nobody answered the ring. Tracy's stubborn eyes brightened a bit. He dialed again and got the Waldorf-Astoria. Cass Payton always stayed at the Waldorf whenever he came to town. But he wasn't there now. Mr. Payton had already left, the clerk declared. He had telephoned for a Miss Nixon and the two had hurriedly departed in Payton's car.

"Thanks," Tracy said.

He went outside and spoke briskly to Metaxas.

"I'd like you to take a little ride to Connecticut with me."

"Nix! Why should I do that?"

"For dough. Voisin gave you a hundred bucks to play with. I'll double that offer. Two hundred smackers."

"What am I supposed to do?"

"Just answer a couple of questions, maybe."

Metaxas began to grin like a capitalist.

"It's a deal, if it's all right with the cops here."

Fitz frowned. But Tracy cut in eagerly. "Don't be a dope, Fitz. You can't lose! If my hunch is correct, you'll clean up your cop killing and the Linda Payton case with one shot. It will blow Inspector Carlson and his suicide theory into the ashcan. It will call off the political wolves that are on your tail. Carlson can't stand another public failure. He'll be ripe for the sewer."

Fitz rubbed his long nose slowly. "O.K., Jerry."

BUTCH DROVE THE big car across to Flushing and over

the Whitestone Bridge. On the way up through Connecticut the car's hum increased to a steady roar. Butch's grin widened. Tracy spoke to Metaxas only once.

"You got that speed ticket on the way out here, didn't you?"

"Yeah."

"You drove pretty slowly coming back?"

"Sure. I wasn't taking no chances on another pinch."

"Did you notice any fast cars passing you?"

Metaxas nodded. He growled angrily at the recollection. "Yeah, one. It musta been doing ninety. It come at me like a bat outa hell. Almost wrecked me in a ditch."

"Which way? What did it look like?"

"From Noo York. I couldn't see the driver on account of the bright lights. The car was a sport coupé. An expensive one."

Tracy nodded and resumed his thoughtful reverie. He woke up when Butch turned into the driveway of Cass Payton's estate. His hand dipped into his pocket as he hurried to the front door and rang the bell. A wooden-faced servant opened the door.

"I'd like to talk to Mr. Payton," Tracy said with an official rasp.

"Sorry, sir. He isn't at home. He stopped here briefly and then drove over to Miss Nixon's house."

"Where does she live?"

The butler told him and started to close the door. Tracy stopped that with his foot and a brief flash of his cupped palm. He used the same old badge trick. It worked.

"Was Mr. Payton here when the police first phoned the news of his daughter's death?"

"No, sir. He had left to keep an eight o'clock engagement with Miss Nixon. I transferred the call over there."

"Payton was there up until then?"

"No, sir. He was away all the afternoon until early evening. He came in, changed quickly to dinner clothes and left at once. That is, almost at once. There was a brief delay."

"What do you mean?" Tracy's eyes glinted. "Did a woman come to see him?"

"Yes, sir. She was very insistent. Mr. Payton talked briefly with her in his private sitting-room. He was very angry about her visit. I—er, showed her the door."

At Tracy's curt demand he described the woman. It was Julie, the luscious mistress of Paul Voisin.

"Any idea where Mr. Payton spent his time today?"

"No, sir."

Tracy went back to his car, his mouth a tight line. He took the wheel himself and drove to Martha Nixon's home. It was smaller than Payton's layout, but pleasantly wooded and very nice. Tracy parked the car in leafy shadow and took a look at the house. A lamp was lit in the living-room. Tracy got his eye promptly at a lighted chink under the drawn shade.

Payton and Martha Nixon were talking together. That is, Payton was talking. He seemed excited and pale. Martha listened, occasionally making what looked like a shocked protest. Tracy couldn't hear a word through the tight glass.

He circled the house, looking for a way to get in. The ground floor windows and the cellar offered no hope. But a glance upward showed Tracy an open window on the second floor. A near-by oak dropped a thin, shaggy branch toward the sill of the opened window. The branch didn't look very substantial, but Tracy's tight smile widened.

He sneaked back to the parked car and whispered to Butch

and Metaxas. "I'm going inside. There may be some trouble. If anything nasty happens, I'll raise some kind of a rumpus. If I do, bust in fast through a window and start swinging!"

Butch said, "Swell!" But the Greek hack driver looked dubious. "The hell with that! What do I git out of it?"

"You get two hundred bucks in cash. If somebody bumps me, you get nothing! Think it over." Metaxas pondered a while, then grinned. "Gimme a tire iron! I can't afford to be nootral!"

"One apiece," Butch growled. They took up positions in the darkness outside the living-room. Tracy sneaked back to his oak. He was a small man, as active as a monkey; but the frail branch was a ticklish proposition. Tracy was cold with sweat by the time he clutched the sill of the upper window and bellied inside. He tiptoed toward the hallway. But before he could leave the room, the dull glint of metal at a chimney opening caught his roving eye. It was a metal shield to cover a flue opening that was no longer in use on account of spring. Its carelessly crooked position made Tracy think instantly of a pantry closet and a spilled bottle of cedar oil.

He halted on the threshold and closed the hall door softly. He was in the room less than five minutes. When he emerged his eyes were like bright coals.

He crept down the stairs without sound, heading toward the voices in the living-room. He was so eager to eavesdrop that the darkness betrayed him. He fell over a footstool with a thumping crash.

There was a yell from the front room. Before Tracy could spring to his feet, the door opened and Cass Payton raced in. The light from the doorway outlined Tracy on hands and knees.

Payton had whipped a gun out of his pocket. His voice was as steady as the weapon's muzzle.

"Hands up! Back into the other room!"

Martha Nixon screamed at sight of the *Daily Planet's* columnist. But Payton wasn't frightened. He was livid with rage.

"You damned little gutter snoop! I ought to kill you!"

"You're not that dumb," Tracy muttered huskily.

"No. Killing won't be necessary. This time you've cooked your own goose, Martha, get on the telephone and call the state police! Tell them I've just caught a housebreaker. I'm going to cage this smart little busybody for a while in a Connecticut jail!"

Martha protested. Tremulously she tried to point out to Payton the unpleasant publicity that would follow the arrest of a scandal columnist in her home. But Payton insisted, and she telephoned the police. They waited in awkward silence. Tracy didn't dare lower his aching arms. The stony look in Payton's eyes scared him. He was glad when the front doorbell finally rang.

Martha backed away and opened it. She uttered a surprised gasp. So did her two visitors. It wasn't the police. Paul Voisin walked slowly in, accompanied by Julie.

JULIE DIDN'T LOOK very happy. Her strong-fingered hands were clenched into taut fists. There was fright in her eyes, a fright that seemingly had nothing to do with Payton's gun or Tracy's elevated arms.

Payton explained curtly what had happened. Voisin didn't seem too interested. He had a problem of his own he was anxious to discuss.

"I found out purely by chance," he said quietly, "that this smart young lady paid you a call earlier this evening."

"Skip it!" Payton snapped. "Wait until we get rid of this dirty little journalist."

Voisin's contemptuous shrug dismissed the nuisance of Tracy. "I understand that Julie came to you with a nasty story that she was my mistress, and that you very properly threw her out." He turned menacingly toward his companion. "Tell him the real truth, my dear!"

Julie swallowed. She looked cowed. In a low voice she denied that she was Voisin's mistress. She had lied, hoping to avenge herself after she had tried in vain to extort money from Voisin.

"I thought I could bleed him by threatening to make trouble about his marriage," she declared faintly. "That I 'ave ever shared *M'sieu* Voisin's bed, that ees simply one beeg lie."

"Like hell, it is!" Tracy growled. "Voisin's got a dowry coming to him, according to the terms of the marriage contract. *Unless moral turpitude is proved!* That's the catch! What did he do, Julie—threaten to kill you, unless you gave him a clean bill of health?"

Julie's clenched fists opened. Her long-nailed fingers curled into claws. She started to spring at Tracy, but Voisin shoved her backward toward the wall. He and Cass Payton moved ominously closer to Tracy. Payton's finger was tense on the trigger of his gun.

Tracy dropped both hands. A quick clutch unhooked the watch chain from his vest. It swung like a golden slingshot as Tracy ducked and pivoted. He threw the watch crashing through the living-room window.

Payton had expected the missile to be flung at his head.

He jumped nimbly aside. It gave Tracy a chance to uncork a wild punch that staggered Payton. Then, with a wild Indian yell, Butch and Metaxas came crashing headlong through the window.

Butch's tire iron smacked against Payton's extended forearm. It looked like a light, hasty tap. But the arm dropped limply, and so did the gun. Tracy kicked it skidding toward the wall.

Metaxas took care of Voisin. He didn't have to hit him. There was no mistaking his grim intent if the Frenchman batted an eyelash.

The Greek uttered a capitalistic yell. "Anybody that hoits Mr. Tracy gets his noggin cracked! The guy owes me two hundred bucks. Right, Jerry?"

"Right," Tracy panted.

His eyes jerked toward the ruined window sash. For an instant he looked puzzled. Then his face twisted with savage delight.

A car had roared in from the road. A lieutenant of Connecticut police came vaulting into the room. He had a big gun in his gloved fist. He looked dazed as he tried vainly to cover everyone in the mad tableau. But Tracy's grin was for the tall, white-haired figure behind the lieutenant.

It was Inspector Fitzgerald. With him was Richard Druse. They were both petrified with astonishment.

Butch and the taxi driver lowered their tire irons. They became sheepishly peaceful. Payton was yelling fiercely for Tracy's immediate arrest as a common housebreaker. The Connecticut cop reached out to grab Tracy, but Fitz halted that with a quick cry.

"Wait a minute, Lieutenant! There must be some sense to all this."

Cass Payton didn't like Fitz's interruption.

"You've got no jurisdiction here. I demand the arrest of this dirty little snoop. And I don't want Druse in here, either! Throw him out! He's nothing but a sly, fortune-hunting—"

Tracy said sharply, "Druse stays here. Fitz, I don't know how you did it, but you've brought me the one guy I want!"

Fitz was still fuddled. "I got to thinking after you left," he told Tracy slowly. "I decided to come up here and see what the hell you were up to. Druse volunteered to come along, too. Naturally, I have no authority in Connecticut, so I went over to Headquarters first. I was there when Miss Nixon phoned that you were being held at her home for housebreaking."

Druse eyed the columnist queerly. "What do you mean you want me?"

"You can help me clear up Linda's death by answering a single question. Did you have a woman visitor at your home this morning?"

"Huh? Why, yes. I—"

Everyone was watching Druse. But before he could finish what he was saying, Druse and everything else in the room was blotted out by blackness!

A WOMAN SCREAMED. A man snarled an oath. Then a quick stab of scarlet split the darkness. Something hit the floor with a jarring thump as the echo of a pistol shot hammered.

The next instant a white oval of light appeared. The Connecticut cop moved the beam of his flashlight over every face in the room.

Payton hadn't moved an inch. Martha Nixon was between him and Voisin. Voisin was down on his hands and knees, close to the gun on the floor. The gun was Payton's weapon, the one that Tracy had kicked away when Payton had been disarmed earlier. Julie was crouched at the wall, a foot or two from where Voisin was kneeling.

Richard Druse lay in the center of the room. Blood smeared his coat sleeve just above the elbow.

No one moved as the bright oval of the flash jerked from face to face. Fitz had a gun in his hand as well as the lieutenant. He sprang forward and shoved the loose socket of the lamp cord back into the wall. The room lost its horrible ghostly glimmer.

"I—I think the bullet broke my arm," Druse gasped from the floor.

The Connecticut cop darted forward as Voisin rose to his feet.

"I didn't do it!" Voisin yelled. "I didn't kick the cord loose. I didn't fire that gun. Somebody shoved me in the darkness and knocked me down. Then the gun went off. It was dropped alongside me." His face was like chalk as he glared at Julie. "You did it, damn your soul!"

"She was standing right next to him," Cass Payton growled.

"Why not let Druse answer my original question?" Tracy said. "Who was the woman who came to see you this morning at your home?"

"Martha Nixon," Druse gasped. "I—I see what you mean now! I didn't show her or anyone else Linda's note. But Martha could easily have read it while I was out of the room. She said she had come to get some shrubs I had promised her. I had to go outdoors to get them. Is she—"

"Linda's murderess? Of course," Tracy said quietly.

An involuntary groan escaped Payton.

Martha Nixon's voice was low, but clearly modulated. "Is this a joke of some sort?" The skin on her cheekbones looked curiously tight.

"A triple-barreled joke," Tracy said. "Look out that rear window, Metaxas! There's a car out there. See if you can recognize it."

The Greek hackman obeyed. He gulped audibly. "It looks like the job that almost ran me off the road, doing ninety, by Gawd, if it was doin' a minute!"

Payton recoiled from Martha Nixon. She didn't seem to notice. She stood as erect and regal as a queen. Her haughty glance at Tracy seemed to say: "We are displeased!"

"I told you the joke was triple-barreled," Tracy said. "Here's the third shot."

It came from his pocket with grisly slowness—a pair of half-burned silk stockings. As Tracy held them up, the smears of dried blood made ugly brown splotches on the delicate threadwork. A strong smell of fresh sawdust was perceptible.

"The blood came from that motorcycle cop you killed on the way home. The odor is furniture oil, from the bottle you upset in a pantry closet when you hid there to wait for Linda to drink your poison."

Martha Nixon's mouth opened. But she didn't utter a sound.

"You have one bad fault," Tracy said. "You're good on planning, lousy on execution. You had to do things tonight in too much of a hurry. The metal shield in your bedroom fireplace was put back too hastily. It was a botch job, like the spilled cedar oil. And you ought to have been smart enough to realize that silk doesn't burn like cellophane. It requires patient—"

Fitzgerald and the Connecticut cop were watching her like

hawks. But Martha's sudden pantherish leap eluded their clutch. She didn't run toward the broken window. Her swerve carried her toward a heavy bronze candlestick on a side table.

She swung it murderously at Tracy's ducking skull. Had it landed squarely, it would have smashed his brains. As it was, the blow, skidding down his shoulder and arm, made a horrible click like a dry stick snapping.

Tracy pushed himself up from the floor with his good arm. The other hung grotesquely. He bit his lips into a twisted grin.

"Looks like we're even," he told Druse faintly.

Fitz and the lieutenant had steel cuffs on Martha. Her final attempt to kill Tracy had drained her of fury. She submitted almost docilely.

"Why did you poison Linda?" Tracy asked her.

There was silence in the room. Then, suddenly, she laughed. It sounded like the raw scrape of a file.

"What the hell? You'll find out the minute you search the house and locate my records. My graft was blackmail. Polite; no howls from carefully selected victims. I made plenty, but I wanted more. I had a chance to marry Payton. Linda didn't like me and took time enough to get the goods on me. She promised to keep quiet if I let her father alone. Last week Mr. Payton proposed. From that moment I was on the lookout for a chance at Linda."

Tracy amplified for the benefit of the Connecticut lieutenant. Having read the ambiguously worded note that morning at Druse's home, Martha saw an opportunity to involve Linda and young Druse in a fake suicide pact. She got in after Linda's maid left, probably with a key she'd swiped from Linda some time. Probably while Linda was bathing and changing to a dinner gown, she poisoned the glasses. Then she waited in the pantry closet to make sure that Linda would drink the stuff. But Druse was late, and Linda's presence cut off Martha's escape.

There she was, with the minutes flying—and her chance to have an alibi dinner with Cass Payton at her Connecticut home dwindling fast! By the time Linda finally took the fatal drink, Martha was so jittery she didn't notice she had kicked over the bottle of furniture oil. She washed out Druse's glass to fit the new situation. She jammed the lighted candle in the dead girl's fists. But she forget to shut the service door tight when she fled. That was how Voisin was able to get in.

"Just why did you go there at all?" Tracy asked the Frenchman curiously.

"Linda phoned me and told me our marriage was off. She said she wanted to make a clean break with the past and marry young Druse. I was afraid Linda might persuade Payton to contest the dowry legally. So I hurried over after I had calmed down, in order to try and reason with Linda. I don't know why I sneaked in so secretly. It—it was a sort of premonition of danger."

"And that's that," Tracy said in a tight, painful voice. "Except that I almost sealed my own doom when I was stupid enough to tell Martha I suspected murder on that ride into town with her and Payton. After she left Payton at the Waldorf, she managed to get hold of a Ford—maybe she stole it—and she trailed me to Voisin's. Only Martha's murderous eagerness, and probably the kick of the gun, lifted her hail of bullets a mite too high."

He kept his eyes steadily on the Connecticut officer.

"The whole case was solved by the detective skill of Inspector Fitzgerald. You understand that, don't you?"

"Oh, sure. Besides, it's extradition."

"How about my two hundred bucks?" the Greek taxi driver yelled.

Tracy reassured him.

"Looks as if everybody collects but you," the lieutenant said.

"That's what you think!"

Jerry Tracy reeled over to the telephone. He crackled, "Hello! Long distance… Gimme the *Daily Planet!*"

About the Author

THEODORE ADRIAN TINSLEY
(October 27, 1894–March 3, 1979) was a
native New Yorker and a 1916 graduate
of the City College of New York, where
he edited the college magazine. After
serving in Meuse-Argonne, France
with the 2nd Anti-aircraft Machine Gun
Battery during World War I, Tinsley briefly
taught and then worked in the insurance industry. Through his
brother, illustrator Frank Tinsley, Ted sold his first pulp story,
"Cross Words at the Circle K," a humorous Western with a
crossword puzzle theme which appeared in *Action Stories* in
1925. During the 1920s, he wrote in various genres, but started
specializing in crime and mystery stories in 1932, after he had
returned from an around-the-world ocean trip which included
a stop in Bali.

In February, 1935, Tinsley married author and *Breezy Stories*
editor Mary Ethel White at the Little Church Around the
Corner in New York City. They met at a meeting of the American Fiction Guild, for which Tinsley served as National Trea-
surer for two years.

After scripting *The Shadow* for CBS, Tinsley was assigned to
write four Shadow novels per year, which he did between 1936
and 1942 for a total of 27 stories published under the byline
of Maxwell Grant. His first Shadow, *Partners of Peril*, served
as the basis for the debut Batman story published in *Detective*

Comics. His second entry, *Foxhound,* was adapted for the 1938 Shadow film, *International Crime.*

His series characters include Major John Lacy in *Black Aces,* Jerry Tracy in *Black Mask,* Martin Breed in *Clues—Detective Stories* and Terry "Bulldog" Black in *Nick Carter, The Whisperer* and *Crime Busters.* Tinsley's most famous creation, Carrie Cashin, of the Cash and Carry Detective Agency, headlined *Crime Busters* and its successor *Mystery Magazine* from 1937 to 1942. His only known personal pseudonym was Reid Sleyton.

Tinsley broke into the slick magazines with a sale to *Liberty* in 1937 and continued selling to that magazine until the end of his fiction-writing days.

During World War II, Tinsley joined the Office of War Information, which led to a post-war position with the Veterans Administration, from which he retired in 1960. While at the VA, he wrote radio scripts for Bob Hope and Bing Crosby, as well as speeches for General Omar Bradley and other notables.

In retirement, Tinsley moved to his wife's hometown of Auburn, Alabama, where he died at the age of 84.